Numb

New Species - Book Fourteen

By Laurann Dohner

Numbers

by Laurann Dohner

140

Dana is visiting Homeland when she meets a New Species who tugs at her heartstrings. As a widow, she knows firsthand the pain he's suffering after losing his mate.

Mourn isn't so certain that talking to a human female will help him heal but he desires her. It's possible she could become his new reason for living.

927

Candi lost the male she loved, but never forgot him. New Species are her only hope to seek revenge for 927's death.

A human female claiming to have been reared at Mercile has demanded entry to Homeland. Hero rushes to Medical and comes face-to-face with his past. One look at Candi and the life he's built since gaining freedom comes crashing down around him.

New Species Series

Fury

Slade

Valiant

Justice

Brawn

Wrath

Tiger

Obsidian

Shadow

Moon

True

Darkness

Smiley

Numbers

Numbers

Copyright © September 2016

Cover Art: Dar Albert

ISBN: 978-1-944526-65-8

ALL RIGHTS RESERVED. The unauthorized reproduction or distribution of this copyrighted work is illegal, except for the case of brief quotations in reviews and articles.

Criminal copyright infringement is investigated by the FBI and is punishable by up to 5 years in federal prison and a fine of $250,000.

All characters and events in this book are fictitious. Any resemblance to actual persons living or dead is coincidental.

Dedication

As always, I'd like to thank my wonderful husband. I couldn't do what I do without him. He's my hero, my best friend and my inspiration.

I'd like to thank you—the ones who have been so supportive of all things New Species. I appreciate you waiting so patiently for the next book. A lot of people asked to see more interaction between Species and what life at Homeland is like. I listened.

Last but never least, a big thank you to Kele Moon. She's my best friend and my critique partner. She's the one who listens to my crazy book ideas and keeps me on task when my mind starts to wander. You're awesome!

140 7
   Chapter One 7
   Chapter Two 24
   Chapter Three 42
   Chapter Four 63
   Chapter Five 82
   Chapter Six 100
   Chapter Seven 124
   Chapter Eight 139
   Chapter Nine 155
   Chapter Ten 177
   Chapter Eleven 198
   Chapter Twelve 211

927 214
   Prologue 214
   Chapter One 218
   Chapter Two 233
   Chapter Three 250
   Chapter Four 272
   Chapter Five 297
   Chapter Six 313
   Chapter Seven 329
   Chapter Eight 348
   Chapter Nine 369
   Chapter Ten 385
   Chapter Eleven 404
   Chapter Twelve 426
   Chapter Thirteen 441
   Epilogue 453

140

Chapter One

"I can't believe you get to live here," Dana whispered, afraid of being overheard in Medical.

Her brother, Paul, grinned. "New Species are really cool. I'm glad you decided to take me up on the tour and visit us for a few days. I think my wife is a little homesick."

"Maybe you should come back for Christmas this year. That way Becky will get to hang out with all of us and it will be a reminder of why you guys moved to California."

Paul chuckled. "Is Mom still driving you nuts?"

Her humor fled. "She set me up with her chiropractor, her pharmacist, and wait for it...her gynecologist. Talk about awkward." She rolled her eyes. "As if I ever want to be married to a guy who stares at girl parts all day. I'd be afraid to ask him how his day went. I really don't want to hear any gross stories over dinner. Can you imagine?" She deepened her voice. "It was the worst case of crabs ever. There were so many I had to use a net to catch those suckers."

Paul doubled over in a fit of laughter. "You're horrible."

She forced a smile. "Don't even get me started about the wrongness of knowing he's seen our mother's knees spread apart while she's naked. Can you say *ewwww*?"

He sobered. "That's not funny. You had to go there?"

"That's almost exactly what I said to our mother when she told me who she'd set me up with."

He carefully studied her. She knew that look.

"I'm fine. Don't do that. You're a nurse, not a mind reader."

"Are you dating anyone Mom wouldn't approve of on the sly?"

"Nope." She turned away, ducking inside one of the open rooms. "This is much cozier than a hospital. I like the soft wall colors and the nice bedding. It's pretty fancy for a small clinic. It has a homey feel."

"Dana?"

She swung around, and returned to his side. They strolled down the hallway to reception. "It's been two years. I should move on with my life. It's like riding a bike. Just get back on the dating cycle and take a spin." She paused. "Did I miss any advice you were about to give? Maybe you could stoop low enough to say how Tommy would want me to be happy by finding someone else? I hate that one the most. It pissed him off when some guy would check me out."

"I wasn't going to say any of that. I just worry about you. It's my job."

"You're the best big brother ever but I'm really fine. It has been two years. Time heals everything." She wished that were true, but it always seemed to set other people at ease. She really didn't want Paul to worry. "I have a vibrator, a body pillow, and a heating blanket. I'm good."

He blanched. "You went there."

"I'll make a deal with you. I won't over share things like that if you stop digging into my personal life."

He held out his hand. "Only if you promise to call me more often."

She grasped it and gave it a firm shake. "Done."

"Do you want to see the surgical rooms? We have two."

"Pass. Totally not my thing. I quit nursing school for a reason. Some of the equipment should be featured in horror movies." She let him go.

His eyes narrowed and she regretted her words. They both knew why she'd really changed careers. All the time she'd spent in hospitals had made her hate them. It reminded her of Tommy's suffering. She decided to say something fast.

"Why do you need surgical rooms in a clinic?"

He schooled his features. "In case of emergencies. We're fifteen minutes from a trauma unit."

It was her turn to study him. "I see. This is one of those topics you're not allowed to talk about, right? To protect the New Species?"

"It's a beautiful day, today, isn't it?" He grinned.

"Message received. I have one question you do have to answer though."

"What?"

"Do you like them? Are they as nice and friendly as they seem to be on TV?"

"They are different, but in great ways. They have my respect and yes, I really like them. I wouldn't want to live anywhere else."

"Good enough. I'll stop being nosey. We'd better get back to your wife before she thinks we've gotten lost. I'm really looking forward to—"

A blaring car horn cut off her words. She turned, watching a Jeep come to a stop part way on the street and sidewalk. Two big New Species jumped out of the front and lifted a third one out of the back. Her brother grabbed the counter separating him from the front doors and vaulted over the top of it.

The man they carried inside bled from one leg, his arm, and his forehead. He seemed to be unconscious since his eyes were closed and he sagged between the two New Species as they rushed inside the clinic. Paul met them there.

"Down the hall, first room!" her brother yelled. He hit a button near the front doors and an alarm sounded. Paul ran after the injured patient and two doors along the back of the large room burst open.

Dana watched a human guy rush after them and seconds later the doors in the back burst open again. A tall New Species woman sped past her without giving her a glance. It left Dana alone. She was unsure what to do.

She debated for a few seconds before following them. The injured man looked bad off and there were only three people to tend him, besides the two men who'd brought him in. She strode down the hallway and entered the exam room.

Paul cut the guy's bloodied pants leg open. The dark-haired Species woman put in an IV line and the human guy she guessed was a doctor flashed his tiny pen light in the patient's eyes after opening each lid.

"What happened?" the doctor asked.

The two New Species who'd brought him stayed against a wall, keeping out of the way. "He picked another fight and ended up stumbling onto the balcony. He fell from the second floor but landed on the grass. It was the tree he hit during the descent that did most of the damage. He hasn't woken since," one of them muttered.

"Fuck," the New Species woman growled.

"The leg doesn't appear broken," Paul muttered. "Just a deep laceration."

"He might have struck his head on a branch or two on the way down," the other New Species added. "We found him under the tree."

Paul turned his head and spotted Dana. "Get your ass over here and apply pressure to this."

She hesitated. "Where are the gloves?"

"Second drawer to your right," he snapped. "But they don't carry any blood diseases and they easily fight infection."

After putting on gloves, she clamped her hand down over the cut. Paul tore open the patient's sleeve to examine his arm. Dana glanced up and found the doctor frowning at her.

"That's my sister," Paul informed him. "Dana, meet Doc Harris and Midnight. The two along the wall are Snow and Book."

"She can't be in here," Doc Harris protested.

"She's cool and she did a year of nursing school. She's also done a shitload of home healthcare. She won't faint over seeing some blood. The arm doesn't seem broken but he's going to need stitches."

Midnight turned toward the door. "I'll get the portable X-ray machine for his head."

The doctor examined the patient's skull, probing, probably checking for fractures or lacerations. "It's okay, Midnight. This son of a bitch is too hardheaded. He probably just has another concussion, but we'll run a CT scan just to be safe. Let's deal with the issues we see right now first."

Midnight yanked a bag of saline from a cupboard. She growled low, a scary sound. "Who did he fight this time?"

"Darkness. Suicidal bastard," Snow muttered.

"I won't ask if Darkness is okay then." Doc Harris sighed. "I'm surprised he's not the one who brought him in."

"He will be along."

"Great." Midnight spun away after hanging the IV bag and killed the blaring alarm. "That's just what we don't need. He'll be angry. Please tell him not to bother. You two can go."

Snow and Book shot curious glances at Dana. She forced a smile but they didn't speak directly to her before they quit the room.

Doc Harris changed positions with Paul. "Let me see his arm."

"I'll grab a suture kit." Paul opened a draw.

Midnight caught Dana's gaze. "You're Paul's sister?"

"Yes." She tried not to stare. The New Species woman was the first one she'd seen up close since she'd arrived. She was pretty, with long dark hair. "I'm visiting him and Becky this weekend. He wouldn't come home so I came to him."

"Welcome to Homeland." She stepped closer. "Let me take over. This is Mourn." She glanced at the patient and then back at Dana. "He's a troublemaker. He comes in here every few weeks. Don't be alarmed."

Dana released the cut on his calf and backed up, doing what she was told. She tossed away the used gloves and made sure blood hadn't gotten on her skin above them. She turned and kept out of the way while they worked on the patient. Mourn needed six stitches on his forearm but his leg just needed to be cleaned and bandaged.

"Should I put restraints on him before he wakes? You know he's going to just get up and walk out the same way he did last time." Paul stared at the doctor.

"Yeah. I hate to do it but Snow had a point. He is suicidal."

"Why?" Dana regretted asking as soon as three pairs of eyes swung her way. "Sorry," she added. "It's none of my business."

"His mate died." Midnight helped Paul use thick, padded restraints to secure the patient's arms and legs to the hospital bed. They even wrapped a few across his chest and thighs to hold him in place. "You helped work on him. I'd be curious as well. He picks fights with other males, hoping one of them will kill him. We won't end our own lives the way humans do. It's a matter of pride."

Dana stared at the patient, really taking a good look at his face. He was feline. The shape of his eyes was a dead giveaway. His black hair was cut short. He had the over-the-top manly features that all the New Species possessed. Their bone structure was denser than a normal human. He was handsome, despite the bandage on his forehead. Midnight cleaned off the blood and backed away from him.

It pulled at Dana's heartstrings, hearing that he'd lost the woman he loved. She knew what the term mate implied, thanks to some of the things Paul had felt free to tell her. Some of the New Species were married, but they called their wives mates. They didn't require a ceremony, but instead could just share a promise of commitment, sign legal documents and make it official.

"We've got this handled, Paul." Doc Harris glanced her way. "You should take your sister back to your house."

Her brother hesitated. "Are you sure? I could hang here for a few hours. I know the two of you wanted to go out to have lunch instead of eating in the office. I could have someone escort my sister home."

"We'll both stay," Dana quickly added.

Paul frowned, glanced at Mourn and then her. His eyes narrowed. "You want to talk to him when he comes around, don't you?"

There was no use denying the accusation so she just shrugged.

"I don't think that's a good idea," Doc Harris snapped. "He's not fit for strangers. Your sister could chat with other Species if she is curious about them."

"He'll be rude," Midnight predicted.

Paul dried his hands. "You told her that Mourn lost his mate, Midnight." He hesitated, holding Dana's gaze. She realized he'd stopped talking because he wasn't sure if she wanted anything about her life revealed.

She turned to Midnight. "My husband died of cancer two years ago. We were childhood sweethearts and it was devastating." She swallowed the lump that formed in her throat. "You said Mourn is suicidal. I can relate to that."

"Dana…"

"I used to feel that way," she corrected, daring to look at her brother. She hated seeing his pained expression. "It helps to talk with others who have shared the same loss. I might be able to help him."

"No." Doc Harris came around the bed. "I don't think that's a good idea."

"I agree," Paul stated.

Midnight seemed to stare right into Dana's soul for long seconds. "Have you taken a new male into your life?"

"No."

"You can stay."

"What?" Doc Harris grabbed Midnight's arm. "I think it's a bad idea. You know how Mourn gets. She's an outsider. What happens if she tells someone about him? She has already heard too much. Can you imagine what the press would do with this story?"

"I won't repeat anything," Dana promised. "I attended group grief counseling after Tommy's death. It's like Alcoholics Anonymous. What is said in that room, stays in that room. I've never told anyone where Paul really works either. Most of our family, and all of our friends, believe he's overseas with some nonprofit charity group that provides free medical assistance to the poor. It would put our family in danger if anyone who hates the NSO targets us to get back at Paul for working here. You can trust me."

Doc Harris didn't appear happy. "Mourn is unpleasant on his best days. He's dangerous."

"I'm willing to risk it." Dana didn't even have to think about it.

"Damn. I hate when you get that determined look, sis. You're not going to let this drop, are you?"

Dana shook her head. "You said he's done this before. What could it hurt to at least talk to him?"

Paul looked grimly at Doc Harris. "She is as stubborn as shit. We'd have to drag her out of here now. Mourn won't attack my sister." Paul didn't sound so sure though. "He's restrained and I'll be here."

"Let the female talk to Mourn." Midnight took the doctor's hand. "We haven't been able to do him much good. She's female and wants to spend time with him. They both share the loss of their mates. What harm could it do? I agree with Paul. He wouldn't pick a fight with her."

"I think we should run this by the NSO first." Doc Harris attempted to reach the phone on the bedside table but Midnight yanked him back.

"I'm Species and I say it's fine. We don't need to hold a meeting about this. Let's go have lunch the way we planned." Midnight grabbed his hand and pulled him toward the door.

"I know what you're doing, Midnight. It's a bad idea." Doc Harris dragged his feet but the woman just yanked him harder, forcing him to follow her.

As they left the room, Midnight laughed and said, "She's cute."

"Damn," Paul muttered after the couple was out of hearing range.

"What?" Dana looked at him for clarification.

"She's hoping you and Mourn will hit it off. Let me just call for one of the Species to take you back to my house. I'll stay until they return to Medical so someone is here with Mourn when he wakes."

Dana took a seat in the only chair. "Go do whatever you do. I'm fine right here."

"Did you hear me? Midnight thinks you're cute enough for Mourn to be interested in you as a woman."

"I heard. He lost his wife. Believe me when I say that isn't going to happen. He obviously loved her very much. The last thing he'll want is to date someone. Take it from someone who knows."

Paul glanced at the unconscious patient, then back at her. "New Species don't date. I wouldn't mind you hooking up with one since you'd get to live here, but not that one, sis. He's all kinds of screwed up."

"That's not why I want to talk to him. I'm not looking for someone either. It might help him in some way. That's all."

Paul leaned against a cabinet. "Is that why you're still single? Don't you ever get lonely?"

"I go on dates that Mom sets up."

"We both know those don't count. You only do it to get her off your ass so she won't badger you."

"True. I get to tell her that I tried but there were no sparks. She can't fault me for that."

"But don't you get lonely?" He pressed the issue.

She decided to be honest. "All the time, but then I think about Tommy and what we had. We grew up together. Who is going to love me the way he did? I hear all the dating horror stories from my single friends. No thanks. Men play games, cheat. Those I've met just wouldn't mesh with me."

"There are good guys out there. I'm proof of that." He grinned. "I didn't need to date Becky since the seventh grade to make a good husband. We met much later and I'm almost ten years her senior. I worship the ground she walks on."

"I know. One day I'll be ready, but not yet."

"Have you told our mother that?"

"She thinks I'm wasting my life by being single and you know she wants grandchildren. She's given up on you and Becky presenting her with one."

He laughed. "Sounds like Mom. She was so disappointed when I joined the military instead of working for Dad. She used to throw everyone's daughter at me right after I graduated high school. It was part of the reason I wanted out. She always wanted a third kid and I think she figured a grandchild would be just as good."

Dana shrugged. "She's pushy. No one can deny that. It's gotten worse since Dad died and she lives alone. She asked me to move in with her or to allow her to move in with me." She winced. "I'd strangle her. Part of it is my fault. I was really messed up after Tommy died so I didn't fight her as much as I should have when she took over parts of my life. I just didn't have the strength or the will. She's way worse than she was when we were kids."

"I know. I couldn't wait to get out on my own. She loves us. There's no denying that, but she micromanages us. It drove me nuts."

"At least you got away from her. I envied you that while you were traveling around the world. She threw a fit every time I even went on vacation. You should have heard her rant when I said I was planning to visit you. It's just a weekend but she started in with the guilt trips of what could happen to her if I left her alone for a few days." She snorted. "As if she's some delicate flower."

"It wasn't so great being enlisted. It's why I got out and work here now. Not to mention, once I met Becky, I didn't want her worrying about me being deployed, or to have to leave her for months at a time. I sure as hell didn't want to live close to Mom. She'd drive us crazy."

She studied him. "Ever regret not becoming a doctor?"

"No. I like being a nurse. Way less stress."

She nodded. "I understand that."

"Is anyone here?" The male voice came from somewhere down the hallway.

Paul pushed away from the cabinet. "Stay put and yell out if Mourn wakes."

"Will do," she agreed.

Paul rushed out of the room and she turned her attention to the still patient on the bed. Time passed as she watched his chest rise and fall. Her gaze traveled over him, taking note that his arms had changed position and the restraints were pulled tight. She sat up a little straighter.

"I'm Dana, Paul's sister. We're alone so you can stop pretending you're still out for the count."

His eyes snapped open and he turned his head on the pillow. She was amazed by their color—blue surrounded the black pupils, but the outer irises were a reddish-yellow, reminding her of autumn leaves on a bright, clear day. They were striking and surreal, but she was certain they weren't contact lenses.

She stood, but kept a few feet back. "Hi."

"Release me." He had a deep, gruff voice.

"You know I can't do that. Your doctor put you in restraints for a reason. I hear you started a fight with someone."

He looked away and pulled roughly against the straps. They held, but she heard little ripping sounds from the Velcro. His arm with the torn shirtsleeve revealed bunched, thick muscles. He was really fit, reminding her of some of the bodybuilders who frequented her local gym. She decided to distract him since he looked strong enough to break free if he kept at it.

"You're Mourn, right? That's your name?"

He growled. It was a disturbing sound. He tried to move his legs next, shifting them on the bed. One of the bedrails groaned.

She stepped forward and grabbed hold of the metal to pull in the opposite direction in case it snapped. "Stop it."

He glared at her and his full lips parted to reveal some sharp fangs. "I don't take orders from you, human."

If looks could kill... She pushed that thought back though. "No. You just pick fights with other New Species. My name is Dana. You can use it. I'm Paul's sister, if you didn't hear me the first time."

"Let me go and I won't hurt you."

She wasn't afraid. "You look terrifying, strapped down on a bed, covered in bruises and fresh bandages." She forced a smile. "You'd be disappointed if you think I could inflict more damage. You'd hit me, I'd fall down and stay there. What would be the point?"

Surprise widened his eyes and he grew still.

"Does it help when you get beaten on by some badass? That's the impression I got."

He said nothing, just watched her.

"It's a valid question, but I've never tried that. I'm not into pain. I have enough of it on the inside, so I don't need to nurse physical injuries."

"Are you a head shrink?" He curled his lip in disgust.

"No. We have something in common though. We both have experienced the loss of someone we deeply loved."

He turned his head away, staring at the door. "I don't want to talk to you. Get out."

She moved into his line of sight to peer into those amazing eyes of his. "How long has it been since you lost your mate?" She remembered the term New Species used.

He didn't answer.

"I lost mine two years ago. Do you know what I hate the most? It's when I sleep. I dream that he's still with me, but then I always wake up and have to face the reality of his empty side of the bed."

His lips compressed into a firm grimace. She waited to see if he'd say anything, but a good minute ticked by as they regarded each other.

"I'll be visiting with Paul and Becky for a few days if you change your mind about speaking to me. I won't push any harder, but it does help to talk to someone who understands the loss. I didn't believe it at first when people told me that. I was wrong. You've probably tried everything else so what do you have to lose?"

She turned away and took a few steps toward the door.

"You should avoid sleeping."

The raw pain in his voice tugged at her heartstrings. She faced him. "I tried that but eventually exhaustion sets in."

"I know."

She hesitated. "Do you ever allow anyone near you besides when you're starting a fist fight?"

"No."

She approached his bed. He was a big guy, a stranger, but the haunted, pained look in his eyes was one she knew well. They were kindred spirits. "I'm going to hold your hand."

Surprise widened his eyes. "Why?"

"Try it."

Dana leaned against the bedrail and reached out to him. He felt really warm, as if he had a fever. She laced her fingers with his. He didn't jerk away, or try to avoid the contact. He also didn't clasp hold of her, but instead just seemed to endure her touch.

"Physical contact is a part of healing. It reminds us we're alive. We are, you know. Alive. Our lives didn't end with theirs, even if we wish it at times. You need to allow yourself to feel more than just the pain, Mourn." She squeezed his hand. "Let people help you. You only have things to gain by doing that."

He closed his eyes. "Leave."

Chapter Two

Dana stepped out onto the back porch and dug into her robe pocket. She pulled out the case and eased into one of the patio chairs. Her brother would have a fit if he caught her, but she'd waited until he and his wife had retired for the evening. Sleep never came easily for her.

She flipped open the case and withdrew the electronic device, inhaled slowly on the tube, and blew out the vapor. The minty taste of a menthol cigarette wasn't exactly the same as the real thing, but was close enough. She really wished for a bottle of vodka, but a quick search of the kitchen cupboards had revealed no alcohol in the house. A nice stiff drink would have been welcome after spending hours watching the loving couple interact. It only made her ache for all she'd lost.

A memory surfaced of Tommy standing in their kitchen, making spaghetti. It was the only thing he'd really known how to cook unless a grill had been involved. He'd smiled at her and poured two glasses of wine, offering her one. "To us, my love."

She took another drag on the electronic cigarette, that memory causing her pain. It had been the last anniversary they'd shared, right before the new tumor had been found. His blond hair had just grown in again after rounds of chemo and they'd been sure he'd stay in remission. Two months later it had come back with a vengeance and he'd died within five months. She pushed away the image of him in his hospital bed, struggling to take his last breaths. It hurt too much.

The wind stirred and she glanced up at the tree branches next to the short wall that enclosed the small backyard. The moon hung high in the dark sky. She tucked her robe a little tighter over her lap, against the chilly air. Her bare feet rested on another chair. She lifted the e-cigarette to take another drag, but it never reached her lips. A large hand wrapped around hers, freezing it inches from her lips.

Dana glanced up, expecting to see her brother. It came as a shock when she stared into a pair of catlike blue eyes. Mourn still sported the bandage on his forehead, but he'd changed clothes. He wore a black, long-sleeved shirt and matching black cargo pants. Her heart rate slowed as she realized he'd come to talk to her after all.

"That's bad for you." His voice was as deep as she remembered.

"I know. I only picked up the habit after my husband died. He would have hated me smoking since he never did it, but I was kind of grief stricken. It's an addictive habit. I stopped, but sometimes if I have a bad day, I'll use one of these vapor things instead."

He frowned.

She decided to change the subject. "Were you released, or did you break free?"

He pried the e-cigarette from her fingers and placed it on the table. "They'd have had to use chains if they expected me to spend the night at Medical."

"Would you like to sit down?"

He glanced around. "No."

"Is security going to come looking for you? We could go inside." She stood. "My brother and his wife already went to bed. They won't hear us as long as we talk quietly."

"Not here." His gaze searched the darkness beyond the yard. "Will you come with me?"

He was a stranger. That wasn't why she hesitated though. He had lost the woman he loved, yet he'd sought her out. He needed a friend, someone to talk to, and she wanted to be there for him. "I need to change my clothes first. I'm in my pajamas under this robe."

He studied her then. "We aren't going far and no one will see us. They might look here since they knew you spent time with me."

Dana made a quick decision. "Let me at least grab shoes. I'm barefoot."

"There's no need."

She gasped when he moved suddenly, scooping her into his arms and right off her feet. It was the last thing she'd expected. He strode to the low wall and just jumped, clearing the three-foot high, brick yard enclosure. She automatically wrapped her arms around his neck when he landed, jarring her. The last thing she wanted was to be dumped onto the grass.

It was a little frightening to be carried off by someone she didn't know, but she managed to push down the panic. Paul always said good things about New Species. He had told her dozens of times that they were way better than regular people, that there was no crime amongst New Species, and that they were honorable. Her brother's words rang through her mind as she took slow, steady breaths. Mourn probably didn't realize it wasn't appropriate to carry her off into the night.

"Where are we going?" She turned her head and stared as the dim lights from Paul's back patio grew more distant. He lived right next to a park. She hadn't explored it so wasn't sure how large it was.

"You're safe with me," Mourn whispered. "I'm just taking you far enough away for privacy without the officers finding us."

Dana lowered her voice. "Okay. Are they searching for you?"

He uttered a low growl. She took the frustrated sound as a yes.

The wind blew harder in the open area without the house to block some of it. Her robe was silky and paper thin. It was also short, reaching just to mid-thigh. A lot of her bare legs were exposed, but she wasn't worried that Mourn would leer at them. He'd lost the woman he loved and grieved her loss. He wasn't some creep. He was in mourning.

He stopped and turned, carrying her toward the dark shape of a low-hanging tree. When they reached it, he bent and gently placed her on the lowest branch, just a few feet from the grass. She released his neck and adjusted her robe. He crouched in front of her so they were face level.

"Does it get better? I feel so much pain."

The anguished tone of his voice killed the last of her fears. "Yes. When did you lose her?"

"She was ill for a long time and lingered. She died months ago." He paused, keeping his face in the shadows so she couldn't see his expression. "The pain doesn't ease and I'm angry."

"At her," she guessed. "She left you. It's normal."

"No." He snarled. "The humans made her sick. They tested drugs on her that destroyed her internal organs. She couldn't recover, even on the healing drugs. They just kept her alive longer. She fought hard to live, or she would have died sooner. She was brave."

Dana guessed it had something to do with Mercile Industries. She'd read enough about the pharmaceutical company to know they'd done horrible things to New Species and had used them as test subjects for their experimental drugs. That's why they'd created them. "Were the ones who did that to her arrested?"

"They were caught." He lowered his tone. "It didn't help. I'm still enraged."

"I don't blame you. That's normal too." She wrapped her arms around her waist and hugged her middle. The chilly breeze seemed to blow right through her robe. "So is the guilt that I'm guessing you feel because she suffered. My husband clung to life, regardless of the pain he was in. He didn't want to leave me. I think he fought so hard to keep breathing every day just because he knew I'd be devastated when he died. He had cancer and it spread to his liver, kidneys and lungs."

Mourn kept silent.

"I feel guilty," she offered. "It would have been so much easier if he'd just accepted the pain medication near the end and stopped submitting to every treatment they wanted to try. We both knew it wouldn't work, but neither of us wanted to face that. It was too heartbreaking. How can you give up when you know you're about to lose the person you love most in the world? That's what we were both thinking."

"She asked me to end her suffering many times, but I couldn't do it," he rasped. "I kept hoping she'd get better. We were engineered to be stronger than humans and we heal fast. She wasn't weak, but they'd hurt her too much for her to recover."

"I'm so sorry, Mourn. Sometimes a body can only take so much. We are all mortal. You didn't want to give up hope. That's a part of loving someone. You just have to remember how much she loved you and that even the strongest will to survive can't always defy death. It sucks ass, I won't lie, but the pain will fade over time. It will always be there, but it won't be the stabbing sensation it is now, like someone is shoving a knife through your heart and twisting it. That's how I felt right after Tommy died."

"You're cold." He grasped the bottom of his shirt, pulled it over his head and handed it to her. "Wear this. It will fit over what you have on."

The moonlight revealed his upper body. He had a wide chest, massive biceps, and he didn't wear anything under it. The white bandage on his arm was stark against his tan. She hesitated. "You'll be cold."

"I'm fine. Wear it."

She only hesitated for a second because she wasn't as hardy. The material was thicker than her robe and warm still from his body when she pulled it over her head and tugged it down. He was right, it was large enough to go over her pajamas and the robe. "Thank you. Tell me if you get cold and I'll give it back."

"I feel that knife," he admitted.

"It does get better. You have to release some of the anger and guilt. I kept hold of it as though it were a shield against the world. I needed it. People never looked at me the same way after Tommy died. I hated the pity and the whispers. I went from being Dana to becoming that poor soul who lost her husband."

He accepted that with a nod. "The others pity me."

"It makes it worse. I know. I don't pity you. You survived her death. That makes you strong. Some people just call it quits. They hole up inside their homes and never leave. They stop living altogether. I don't agree with how you interact with other people though, if you're initiating fist fights with big guys who are mean enough that you think they could hurt you. It might be a good idea to rethink that plan and start talking instead."

He shrugged. "The fighting helps me with the anger."

"You came to see me. That's a step in the right direction. As I said earlier, I'd be the last person to pick a fight with, because I won't hit back."

"It would kill you."

She smiled, not afraid in the least. His race was made up of strong, big guys. "Probably. Have you tried to talk to other New Species who have lost their mates? It might help."

"They don't discuss it. Few had mates. Most of them who did lost them when we were still in captivity. It's too painful for them to speak about the past."

"There's grief counseling available. It helped me when I was ready to face my loss head on. I'm sure the NSO could bring someone in for private sessions."

"I don't want to speak to a head shrink. I hate them."

His tone revealed his anger. The experience must have been a bad one. She understood. "You could go to group sessions somewhere close by. There would be a therapist on hand if needed, but mostly it's just people talking to each other, sharing their pain and how they are dealing with everything."

"Humans," he rasped. "No."

"I'm not a pork chop," she gently reminded him. "You're talking to me. Those support groups are for all the people who have lost loved ones. Their race doesn't matter. We're all the same inside. We hurt."

"You're Paul's sister. He's Species to us."

She liked being included, in a roundabout way. It also touched her that her brother was considered family by the people he had decided to live with. "I could extend my visit if you want to keep talking to me." She might lose her job, but she didn't love it anyway. It was just something to get her out of the house every day so she didn't sink back into hiding from the world. Her mother would have a fit, but she didn't really care about that either. "I'd be happy to stay for as long as you want."

"You could do that?"

"Yes. I'm lucky enough to have some savings. My husband wanted to make sure I was taken care of. I'm not dependent on a paycheck to make my bills."

"I could see if the NSO will pay you for being here."

"It's not needed." She studied Mourn. He was a large, intimidating guy, but he had a good heart. "But thank you. I'll extend my stay if you will talk to me." A blast of wind hit her and she shivered. "Perhaps indoors next time though, when I'm not dressed for bed."

"You're tired?"

"No. I don't sleep so well. That brings the dreams."

"I don't like sleep either."

"What do you usually do at night?"

"I run or work out. It helps to push my body to the limit until I'm exhausted. I don't dream then."

That accounted for how muscular he was. "Why did you get into a fight today? I got the impression it's something you do on a regular basis."

"I'm hoping they will kill me."

She chewed on her bottom lip, trying to think of the best thing to say.

"I'll be deemed unstable and a danger to others. It's possible that the NSO will put me down."

It horrified her. "I'm sure they wouldn't."

"I have nothing to live for."

"I used to feel that way too, but I was wrong. You're just immersed in your grief right now."

"What do you live for?"

The question surprised her and she struggled to come up with an answer. "I guess for my family. They would be devastated if I just gave up. I couldn't hurt them that way."

"I have no family."

"You have other New Species."

"I am not close to any of them. I only had my mate."

"What about your friends?"

"I have none. I spent my freedom time caring for my mate."

He was breaking her heart. She made a decision. "Well, you have a friend now. You're important to me. Don't give up, Mourn. Let me help you. I know you probably feel as if there's nothing that will make things better, but take a chance. Just give it a shot. You can't allow things to remain the way they are."

"You don't know me."

"I want to." She leaned closer. "What's your favorite color?"

He was silent for a moment. "I love red. It is so bright."

"It is. What about your favorite food?"

"Is this important?"

"We're getting to know each other. I love the color yellow. Have you ever seen a sunflower? I love those. I know they aren't as beautiful as roses or tulips, but they remind me of summer days. They are cheerful. Plus, I like to eat sunflower seeds. They are pretty and a food source as well."

He rose to his full height. "I should take you back."

Dana had messed up somehow. Perhaps talking about favorites with a New Species wasn't her best idea. She slid off the branch and got to her feet. Mourn stepped forward and bent, scooping her into his arms. He lifted her easily, as if she didn't weigh much. She wrapped her arm around his neck and curled her other hand over his bare shoulder.

"I could walk."

"You're barefoot and I don't want you to step on something sharp."

"Thank you." She hesitated before relaxing in his arms and resting her cheek against his chest. He was really warm and smelled of something manly, perhaps a scented body wash. "I hope I'm not too heavy."

"You're not." He stopped at the short wall that marked Paul's backyard. "You shouldn't smoke. It's bad for you."

She turned her head and their faces were close enough that she could make out his striking eyes. "So is fighting. Besides, it's vapor—not the real stuff. I'm not looking to hurt myself anymore."

His lips twitched but he didn't smile. "You want to live."

"So should you."

He bent forward enough to clear the wall and gently placed her on her feet. She missed the warmth of his body when they parted. "Your shirt..." She started to remove it, intent on handing it back.

"Keep it. I'll come back tomorrow night. Expect me. We'll talk more."

"I'd like that."

"Don't tell anyone."

That statement surprised her. "Why?"

"They will attempt to talk you out of it, or prevent me from coming near you. They know I'm unstable." He stepped into the shadows and turned his head as if searching for something. "I'll come when the lights go out."

She watched him disappear into the night. She turned, strolled up to the table and bent over to pick up her case and replace the tube. She eased open the slider. Silence assured her that Paul and Becky hadn't noticed her absence. She stepped in and locked the door behind her.

Dana entered the guestroom and ran her fingers over Mourn's cotton shirt after she removed it. She walked to the closet and hung it up, hiding it among her own clothes. He wanted to keep their meeting a secret and she would respect that. Her brother would have a fit if he knew she'd willingly allowed a stranger to carry her off. A smile curved her lips. It had been a pretty brave venture on her part and it beat sitting on the patio feeling depressed. Mourn needed a friend and she appreciated feeling useful.

Mourn kept his back pressed tightly to the tree trunk as he watched the slim blonde hang his shirt in her closet. She didn't pick up the phone to call Security. He had feared she might. She also didn't wake Paul or his mate. Instead she removed the robe and tossed it over the chair by the bed.

He moved to leave, but the sight of her nightgown surprised him. It was a white T-shirt that fell almost to mid-thigh with narrow straps at her shoulders and a big yellow, round face over her belly. The two black eyes and the curved smile on the big dot indicated happiness. She rounded the bed and climbed on it.

The shirt hiked high, and he sucked in air. The human wore white panties that barely concealed her sex. They were narrow and were cut high on her hips, exposing a lot of skin on each side of her ass. She had a curved, generous one with very pale skin.

She got under the covers and shoved pillows behind her back. Her gaze darted around the room and he wondered if she sensed him watching her. She didn't look toward the window though, or at the gap in the parted curtains. She hugged the bedding to her waist and her head tipped down. Her hair fell forward, hiding her features. She used her thumb to push it back, hooking it behind her ear. When he could see her face again, the sorrowful expression did something odd to his stomach.

She was suffering too. It was tempting to approach the window and knock to let her know she wasn't alone. He held still though, keeping in the shadows. She'd lost her mate. She also didn't seem to be in a hurry to fall asleep. They had much in common.

He replayed their conversation inside his head. She'd been right about many things. He did live with guilt. He wished he'd talked to her longer, but he'd noticed her shivering despite the addition of his shirt.

Humans were fragile, but especially the females. He didn't want to risk her growing ill.

Motion at the edge of his vision drew his attention. He turned his head and watched an officer on patrol stroll down the sidewalk, heading toward the front of the house. He shifted positions and took off before the wind direction changed, revealing his presence. He kept to the shadows until he was far from the house and back in the park.

"What were you doing?"

He started and spun, a growl tearing from his throat as his hands curled into claws. "You make no sound," he accused Darkness.

"I don't. I'm good at that." The male wore all black and stood about eight feet away. "Why were you watching the human female?"

He clenched his teeth, refusing to acknowledge anything.

"She didn't kill your mate."

"I know that."

"You hate humans, but that's Paul's sister."

"I know who she is."

"Then you are aware that she's not the enemy."

"I didn't say she was."

"I came to seek you out to talk about today, but instead I found you under a tree watching a human through the window. I would have confronted you there, but I didn't want to alarm her. This is her first visit to Homeland. Paul is very excited about that. He will not want her to have a bad experience. He'll want her to visit again. Stay away from the human areas. Do you wish for Paul to attack you if he believes his sister's life is in danger? He won't be able to do you much damage, but it would piss off his friends enough that they might seek retaliation if you harm the male. Is that your plan?"

"I wouldn't hurt Dana."

Darkness's eyebrows shot up. "You know her name?"

"I don't attack females." It was an insult to be accused of wanting to do her harm. "She's defenseless. There's no honor in that."

"You were curious about human females? Is that why you were watching her?"

He said nothing.

Darkness changed the subject. "Don't force me to defend myself against you again."

"I understand."

"You're not going to deny that you attacked me today because you thought I'd kill you for striking me?"

"I lost my mate."

Darkness stepped closer. "I'm aware. Let me tell you something about me. I don't like the situation I found myself in today. I've had to kill before, but that doesn't mean I enjoy it. Pick someone else if you have a death wish, Mourn. That was all kinds of fucked up. You want to talk about honor? I would find none in ending your life."

Anger stirred. "I'm not defenseless."

"You're broken," Darkness snapped. "You lost your mate and you also lost your will to live. You think you're the only one to know loss? Think again. We're Species. We were created to suffer and we all dealt with a shitload of it. We survive and thrive. Stop feeling sorry for yourself and get your shit together."

Mourn snarled, wanting to attack the male for the cutting words.

"Exactly. Get angry. Use that to get past the loss. I didn't know your mate well, but she seemed courageous. I witnessed the death of two of my brothers and had to kill the third one with my bare hands because his mind snapped. I had to prevent him from becoming something he would have despised. They were my blood, yet I'm still here. They would have expected me to live life. They weren't given that opportunity. Wouldn't you have wanted your mate to embrace her freedom even if you had died? Wouldn't you have expected her to go on without you?"

"I wasn't the one to die."

"She fought hard to live. Don't dishonor her memory by throwing the rest of your life away. She would tell you this if she could."

"Don't speak for her." Mourn felt as if it all his blood rushed into his head, and he wanted to punch the male in the mouth.

"Someone needs to and you brought me into this when you threw the first punch. I don't know what you were doing near Paul's sister, but I'll have you sent to the Wild Zone if I catch you within a hundred yards of her. Am I clear?"

"I'm not going to hurt Dana."

"Why were you there?" Darkness stepped closer. "Shit. You're not thinking about grabbing her, are you?"

"No!"

"She couldn't put up a fight the way one of our females would. They'd kick your ass if you attempted that bullshit. Is that your new plan? Stealing Paul's sister to take as a mate and forcing us to kill you when we take her back?"

Mourn was horrified. "That's what you think I'm capable of?"

"I don't know what you'd do. I'd have sworn you'd never take a swing at me before today, yet you did exactly that. She's under our protection. Stay the hell away from her."

"We were talking. That's all."

"Bullshit. You were watching her through a window."

"I was making sure she didn't tell anyone I visited her."

Darkness frowned. "Explain fast and don't lie to me. Otherwise, I'll personally knock your ass out and you'll wake up inside a cage. I'll keep you there until she's gone."

"I met her today at Medical and she offered to talk to me. We both lost our mates." He resented having to share those details, but what the male had assumed was outrageous. He wasn't anything like Vengeance. That male would be the one to steal a female to take as mate. "I sought Dana out tonight, we talked and I took her home. I wasn't sure if she'd call Security or tell her brother about our conversation. I didn't want anyone to know."

"Why would you care that she told someone if you did nothing wrong?"

Mourn hesitated. "Some might object."

Darkness blinked a few times as long seconds passed. "She lost her mate too?"

"I said that."

"Did he die or just leave her? Humans sometimes abandon their mates for a new one."

"He's dead."

"How did your talk go? Did you frighten her?"

"No." He scowled. "You believe I'd enjoy scaring a female?"

"I'm not sure."

"I wouldn't hurt her, nor would I take pleasure in making her feel fear. She's a kind female."

The male studied him closely. "Do you plan to talk to her again?"

He gave a sharp nod. "Do you plan on stopping me?"

"It depends. Are you going to do anything stupid that would piss off her brother, or me?"

"No."

"I'll be watching you," Darkness warned. "Remember that. You harm a hair on her head and you'll end up at the Wild Zone. They won't allow you to leave. Valiant will make damn sure of that, even if he has to lock you inside one of the cages for the newly acquired animals that are dangerous. Understood?"

"Yes."

"Are you planning on spying on her again tonight?"

"No. I was going to go for a run."

"Good. Do that." Darkness waved his hand toward the park.

Mourn spun and sprinted away, needing to rid himself of the anger. He wouldn't hurt Dana. It was an insult to be accused of it.

Chapter Three

Dana glanced at the clock and faked a yawn. "Wow. It's getting late. Don't you have to work tomorrow, Paul?"

He and Becky were snuggled together on the couch, looking way too content. "Not until midday."

"Oh."

"Are you tired?"

She hated to lie, but nodded. "A bit."

Becky stood. "Okay. Well, it is almost eleven." She shot Paul a teasing smile. "I guess it's time for us to all go to bed."

He jumped up. "Sounds good to me."

Dana resisted rolling her eyes. The couple may have been married for years, but they acted like newlyweds. She was pretty sure what Becky's look meant and why her brother suddenly seemed so eager to retire to his room. She didn't care if they were planning to have sex as long as they stayed there all night. Mourn didn't want anyone to know they were talking. She respected that wish.

"I'll see you two tomorrow." Dana hugged them both and fled to the guestroom. The living space separated the bedrooms so she pressed her ear to the closed door and waited. A full minute passed before silence reigned. She flipped off her light, eased the door open and peered into the dark living room.

She went to the slider, opened it and entered the backyard. Dana glanced around, hoping Mourn had already arrived. She didn't see him, but it took a moment to adjust to the darkness. Movement near the tree closest to the patio table drew her attention and she smiled when Mourn stepped out of the shadows. She waved and approached him.

"Hi."

He didn't appear as happy to see her as she did him. He was a handsome man despite the facial differences that marked him as a feline New Species. The color and shape of his eyes never ceased to fascinate her.

"You're wearing shoes."

She glanced down at her outfit. Part of her had wanted to dress up a bit, but it might have made her brother or his wife suspicious. She wore comfy, cream-colored cotton pants and a baggy black sweater with matching slip-on canvas shoes. "I am. Do you want to stay here or go sit in the park again?"

He swung his head around, searching the area around them. "Why don't we go somewhere new?"

"Okay." She was aware that New Species never left Homeland so he couldn't take her anywhere far.

"Don't be startled."

The warning did nothing to prepare her for when he bent and scooped her into his arms. He straightened, spun and strode to the wall.

She wrapped her arms around his neck, expecting it when he jumped over the three-foot divider since he'd done it before.

"Why are you carrying me?"

"You have short legs and I want to move fast." He kept looking in all directions as he quickened the pace. He wasn't exactly running but it was close.

"What's going on?" Dana knew something was wrong.

"Darkness keeps patrolling the area. He's watching for me."

"The guy you fought with? The one who put you in the clinic?"

"Yes."

She felt a little fearful as she glanced around as well. It was too dark to see much and Mourn moved fast. "Are you going to get into another fight?" she asked, worried.

"Possibly."

"Put me down. I can run."

He ignored her request and began to jog. It was a little jarring, but his arms cushioned her for the most part. She clung tighter until they came to a small building. He paused, turned and studied the area.

"Do you see him?" She whispered.

"No. It's windy again and it will be difficult for him to pick up my scent. That's another reason I carried you. I rubbed my shoes in the grass to make tracking me more difficult. You would have left a trail for him to follow."

"Wow. New Species can do that?" She filed that information away. New Species had to have a highly advanced sense of smell.

"He's feline like me and we're not as good at tracking as the canines, but he could call one here to assist him." He shifted her weight and opened the door to the shed-sized building and carried her inside. She was placed on her feet and he closed them in.

It was pitch dark. Dana held very still, afraid she might run in to something or trip if items were on the floor. "Where are we?" She kept her voice low.

"It's a storage building for our sporting equipment. I'll turn on the light. Close your eyes so it doesn't cause you difficulty. It can take a second to adjust."

She lowered her head and did as he asked. She heard the soft click of a light switch and peeked, blinking a few times. It wasn't a bright overhead light, but it was enough to see by. Shelves had been built along one wall and a long bench ran opposite it. Under the wood seat were boxes filled with various balls.

"It's private and warmer than outside. You may sit if you wish."

The wood slats weren't the most comfortable seat but she sat. Mourn hesitated and then joined her, a few feet away. He didn't look at her, but instead stared forward at the cupboards. The silence grew a little awkward until Dana spoke.

"How was your day?"

"Fine. How was yours?"

"I got a tour of the offices, the Security building, and we had dinner at the bar."

He looked at her and his mouth curved downward in obvious distaste. "You danced with Species?" His nose flared as he sniffed. "I don't smell any of them on you."

"No. I watched a lot of them dance though. A few men asked me, but I'm not at ease with that."

"You don't dance, or you don't like males touching you?"

"I'm not social and I didn't want to draw that much attention to myself. I know how to dance, but I don't like to do it with strangers. Paul and Becky went out on the dance floor a few times. I just stayed at the table."

He relaxed, the straight line of his back easing somewhat. "I don't dance. I would be afraid others would laugh at me. We didn't have access to music before freedom. It's new."

"What about your wife? Did she dance?"

"My mate was ill when we were freed. She spent all her time in our home, hooked to machines. She didn't want to stay in Medical so they set her up inside a home to accommodate her needs."

Dana nodded. "I understand. We did that with Tommy too, near the end, but he wanted to try one more treatment that had a very slim chance of success. He was admitted to the hospital ten days before his death. We thought he'd last longer, or I would have insisted that he be taken home." Sadness rose but she tried to push it back. "I think he planned it that way so I wouldn't have the memory of his passing in our bedroom."

"I moved into the men's dorm after I lost my mate. I couldn't stand the constant reminders at the home we shared."

"It is tough," she admitted. "I probably should take that step too, but I love our house. There are so many good memories there that they outweigh the bad. We were fortunate enough to buy our dream home the first time."

Mourn's brow furled.

"Most people buy what they call a starter home and later upgrade to a house they wished they could have afforded the first time. Tommy inherited money from his family and he owned his own business. He sold it after he realized his health issues were serious, but we were always financially blessed. It wasn't a problem."

"I understand."

The silence stretched and Dana realized Mourn wasn't much of a talker. She'd have to gently prod him. "Do you want to talk about her?"

He looked away. "No."

That's going to make conversation tough, she decided. "What do you want to discuss? Do you want to ask me questions? You can."

"What is the one thing you miss most about your mate?"

It was a complicated question. She pondered it. "I can't really say it's just one thing, but if I were to list a few, first I'd have to say the laughter." She smiled at the memories that filtered through her thoughts. "Tommy was very funny. He could make me laugh no matter what." She sobered. "I miss him when I climb into bed too. I felt safe and right snuggled up to him before I fell asleep."

Mourn turned to face her directly. She looked up into his eyes, awestruck by the tears she saw in them. The blue and autumn hues seemed to brighten, and it took her breath away.

"My mate gave me purpose and now I have none."

Dana could understand that. "What was her name?"

A muscle along his jaw jumped and the tears cleared from his eyes. "I can't say her number. It hurts."

"Number?"

"She never chose a name. Mercile assigned us numbers. I refused to take a name until after she died since she wouldn't."

It was horrific to Dana and heartbreaking. The woman Mourn had loved had been ill when she'd finally gained her freedom and had probably never enjoyed any of it. A mental image formed in her head of a gravestone with just a number engraved on the face of it. It was beyond tragic. "I'm so sorry."

"It's not your fault. Not all humans are alike. I know this. You had no part in her death."

"I'm still sorry for what both of you endured. Call it a general apology for all the assholes in the world. Life isn't fair."

"It isn't." He reached toward her, but didn't make contact.

Dana clasped his hand and held on. "Things are going to get better. I thought about Tommy non-stop when he died. It was constant agony. Time passed and it eased. Some days can go by when I don't think of him at all." She allowed her thumb to caress the side of Mourn's fingers, hoping it would comfort him. It did her. "Then I feel guilty." She smiled. "You wish for those days, but when they come, go figure, but you feel crappy about it. I've been assured that it's part of the healing process."

"I try not to think of her."

"That's normal too."

"I have guilt."

She nodded. "Survivor's guilt. That's the term they call it."

"I hate being alone."

"You aren't. I'm here and you're surrounded by other New Species."

"You know what I mean. Sleeping alone. Eating alone. The utter silence is horrible."

Dana nodded. "It is." She inched closer to him. "You should try to make friends. They do help. I lost a lot of mine after Tommy's death. Some of them avoided me because they couldn't face his death, or maybe they just didn't know what to say. Some people I avoided because I couldn't take the way they looked at me. Pity sucks." She paused. "Or some people acted as if the loss of someone is like a contagious disease they can catch from you. It's a reminder to them that their own lives can come crashing down around them. I was exhibit A."

He turned his head and peered at her. "Exhibit A?"

"Proof that it could happen to them, that they could lose the person they love too."

"Some Species use me as an example of why they shouldn't take a mate or want one. It makes them vulnerable to pain."

"Exactly. You're exhibit A too, for them." She smiled. "I made new friends who didn't know Tommy. They weren't comparing the before-and-after me. It helped. I was just Dana to them."

"Everyone knows me here and at Wild Zone."

"You still made a new friend." She leaned over a little and bumped his arm with her shoulder. "Me."

He smiled and it was devastating. It transformed his features and she had to avoid gawking a little. He was good looking before but a happy-looking Mourn proved that he wouldn't remain single for long, if other women could help it.

"I'm glad you annoyed me."

"Me too."

"I looked forward to talking to you today. It gave me purpose."

"I thought Paul and Becky were never going to go to bed. I was looking forward to talking to you too."

"What is your life like outside the gates?"

"I went back to work about nine months ago. I took an office job that keeps me busy. It gets me out of the house five days a week. That's where I met new friends. I'll go to a movie with a few of them on the weekends from time to time. That gives me purpose and it beats sitting in my home staring at walls, feeling sorry for myself. The pity party was over. I did that routine far too long."

"Pity party?"

His confused look amused her. "It's a saying. It means I was feeling sorry for myself and that I didn't do much to change that for a while. I just wanted to immerse myself in my pain. Even I got sick of it eventually."

"I'm not assigned duties at Homeland like other Species are."

"Maybe you should be."

"I'm not sure they'd trust me. They know I'm unstable."

"So don't be. Tell them you need something to do. It helps you start keeping track of what day it is again."

"I know what you mean."

She figured he would. "It's Saturday. At least, at the end of it."

He chuckled. "Thanks. I didn't know that."

"I'm sure the NSO will do whatever you need. Paul can't say enough great things about them."

"They are good people." He looked away. "What about sex?"

That threw Dana. "What about it?"

He cleared his throat. "A few of the females have offered to share sex with me. Will it heal some of the pain if I touch one of the Species females? They have said it might help me get over her."

"You mean the best way to get over someone is to get under someone else?"

He jerked his attention to her and scowled.

"It's a saying I've heard often. It means to have sex with someone new. I don't know. I have gone on a few dates since Tommy died, but I haven't gone to bed with any of them. It would have been too weird and I wasn't sexually attracted to them. We discussed it in grief counseling. Some of them swore it helped, while others said it made them feel empty inside. I guess it depends on the person. What do you think?"

"It would be uncomfortable."

"I agree."

The silence stretched between them. He finally spoke. "She was the only female I knew."

They had something else in common. "Tommy and I were together since we were young. He's the only man I ever dated. He was my first kiss, my first everything. My last too." Depression threatened. She shook it off. "But I have hope. That's new. I think I'm reaching the point where I might want to find someone to date again. I'm lonely. At first I wouldn't even consider remarrying. It's progress. You'll get there too. Give yourself time."

He seemed interested in the floor, studying it. "Have you found a male who interests you? Will he be angry that you're staying here longer than planned?"

"There's no one. One guy at work keeps asking me out, but he's totally not my type."

Mourn lifted his gaze and stared at her. "What is wrong with the male?"

She smiled. "He's kind of an office player."

His eyebrows drew together and he frowned.

"Morgan hits on a lot of women. It's his thing. He's a flirt. I don't want that. He'll probably be the type who cheats." She winced. "That's a fear of mine."

"Your mate was loyal? I hear some humans aren't."

"Tommy was special. He was pretty intense and he loved me. He set a high mark that I fear no one else can reach. He also had germ phobias." She laughed. "It kind of made me feel safe that he wouldn't sleep with other women. I was the only one he would touch without fear. Do you understand?"

"You are worried no other male can treat you as well and be loyal?"

She nodded.

"I don't think any other female will wish to be my mate. Species females resist commitment. They share sex with other males and don't allow us to stay with them to sleep in their beds. I miss having her next to me."

"Tell me something about her."

He resisted for a long minute. "She was primate and tall." He paused. "She snorted when she laughed. It was cute."

Dana smiled and stroked his hand, urging him to tell her more.

"She didn't talk much, but she always said important things when she did."

"Intelligent."

He nodded. "We were young when they put us together. She was terrified of me."

"You're a big guy."

Mourn didn't look at her while he spoke. "I was the first male they'd taken her to and she was my first female. They said we were a mated pair and told us we'd share the cell forever. We had to learn to live together. She kept far away from me, but I was curious. I kept trying to approach her. She'd make these funny noises so I'd back away. I didn't want to frighten her."

Dana could believe that of Mourn. He was a nice guy.

"I gave her the sleeping mat and would sneak onto it after she fell asleep. I liked to hold her. She'd wake in the morning and move away from me at first. It took a while for her to learn that I wouldn't hurt her. We started to talk. Then she went into heat."

That tidbit surprised Dana. "Heat?"

"Sexual need. She smelled so good and I wanted her bad. I might not have shared sex before, but I hurt. My dick was constantly hard."

Startled, Dana stopped rubbing his hand, but then started again, encouraging him. It was a reminder of what he was. New Species did have animal DNA. "I take it you two worked it out?"

"She was suffering and didn't know what was wrong with her."

"I didn't think primates went into heat that way."

Anger deepened his voice. "Mercile probably put something in her food. She didn't eat the same things that I did. They wanted us to breed and we weren't doing it fast enough. I later learned how dangerous it would have been if they'd drugged me. Males grow very aggressive and the pain is so intense that they suffer memory loss. 139 and I figured it out. I learned fast that if she enjoyed my touch, she'd allow me to mount her often." He grew silent.

"Her number was 139?" It made Dana think. "What was your number?"

"140."

She pondered that. "A number one off from yours."

"I don't know why we were given numbers close together. Mercile never explained things to us. They might have planned to make us mates from the beginning and only waited until we were old enough to breed before they put us in the same cell."

"Do you know how long you were together?"

"No. There's no sense of time at Mercile. It's endless. A long time. Then we were taken from there to somewhere worse. They kept giving her injections. It made her weak and sick. The humans kept promising me they'd make her better if I did everything they ordered me to do. They were using her to control me. I did it. Her life was all that mattered. The NSO freed us but she didn't get better. They lied to me."

"The NSO?"

"Mercile." He snarled the name. "They couldn't make 139 better. They were overdosing her with experimental ovulation drugs, hoping they would make her get pregnant. Our females can't breed though." His voice remained deep, his pain and anger clear. "It caused massive harm to her internal organs. The damage couldn't be repaired. They wanted a Species infant bad enough to kill her in the attempt. I didn't know what they were doing to her until we were freed. Doc Trisha said it poisoned her system and parts of her organs had suffered too much damage by the time she arrived at Homeland. The healing drugs kept her going for a long time but they couldn't repair what was done. She just lingered longer."

"I'm so sorry."

"Me too." He took a deep breath and blew it out slowly. His voice softened. "I should have killed 139 when she begged me to. She suffered so much. I was a bad mate."

"You had hope she'd get better."

He turned his face and tears glistened in his eyes. "She said, if I cared about her, I would snap her neck and stop her from breathing. I just couldn't do it." He tugged out of Dana's hold and stared down at both his hands where they rested on his thighs. "I was weak."

"Mourn." Dana choked up, suffering his pain too. "Don't do this to yourself. You obviously loved her a lot and couldn't hurt her. That isn't weakness. There's nothing wrong with not giving up hope on someone you love. That's all you're guilty of."

He leaned in closer. "How do I live with it?"

"You take one day at a time and you allow yourself to heal. Stop holding on to the grief so tightly. Make friends. Find something to fill your time. Realize that life goes on, even when you think it shouldn't. You are alive. I'm alive. We're here. Embrace that."

He blinked back tears and straightened. "Ask for a job to do and find purpose?"

"That's a great start."

He nodded, looking away. "I should take you back."

Dana reached over and held his hand. He didn't pull away. "Why don't we just sit here for a bit? Do you want to be alone?"

"No."

She didn't either. She laced her fingers with his. "Next time we need to find a more comfortable place though." She adjusted her ass on the wood bench. "Or I'll bring pillows."

He glanced at her and arched an eyebrow. "A pillow?"

"To use as a cushion for these seats."

He smiled. "Humans are too used to comfort."

"That's not a bad thing."

* * * * *

Mourn leaned against the tree, watching Dana climb into bed. They'd spent a few hours together and he'd enjoyed just sitting with her. It had even been nice to speak of 139. The human hadn't judged him, or been horrified by his words. They came from different lives. He'd expected issues to arise.

A soft noise alerted him and he turned his head, watching Darkness step closer. "I didn't want to startle you," the male admitted.

"I'm not going to harm Dana."

"Just watch her?"

"Don't you have a mate to sleep with? Doesn't she wonder where you are?"

"She knows where I am and that I'm keeping my eye on you. Is Paul's sister fascinating?"

"She doesn't sleep much either."

Darkness turned his head, to follow Mourn's gaze. "She's reading a book. What is the title?"

"I don't know. I didn't want to get that close."

The male leaned on the other side of the tree and crossed his arms. "You took her away for a bit. Where did you go?"

"To talk." Mourn stiffened. "You had Security searching for us?"

"No. I watched you return her. She looked unharmed and I don't smell her fear coming off you."

"I'm not going to hurt her."

"She lost her mate too. Does talking help?"

Mourn debated answering. Darkness could make Dana leave Homeland or send him to the Wild Zone. "Yes. She understands."

"Good."

He relaxed, the answer was non-threatening. His calm evaporated when Darkness spoke again.

"Do you plan to stalk her every night?"

"I'm not stalking her. I'm watching over her."

"She's in no danger."

"I don't wish to go home yet."

"I hated staring at ceilings too."

Mourn snapped his head in the direction of the male, studying him.

Darkness held his gaze and nodded. "I've been there and done that. I will give you a warning though."

"I won't harm Dana." He growled low, offended.

"I believe that. Calm your ass down or she's going to hear you. Humans don't have our senses, but get any louder and she won't be able to miss it. Her television isn't on to mute outside noises. My warning is that the last time I became fascinated with a human, I ended up mated to her. I have no regrets because it was the best thing to happen to me, but it came as a shock. I'm giving you a heads-up."

"No one would mate with me. I'm damaged."

"I used to say that too. Then Kat came into my life. She healed me when I didn't think that was possible. Stop fighting with other males." He jerked his head toward Paul's home. "She might become a reason for you to want to live."

"A human?" Mourn shook his head. "We are too different."

"She lost her mate. You have a lot in common with her, more so than with any of our females." Darkness inched a little closer. "Have you considered sharing sex with her?"

"No."

"Perhaps you should."

Mourn pushed away from the tree and faced the male head on. "Why are you saying this to me?"

"You spent most of your life with a mate. I did my research on Paul's sister. She met her mate young, as you did yours. She is used to sleeping with a male, as you are used to having a female in your arms. You both have emptiness inside. Fill the spaces together. It makes sense."

"She's human."

"So is my mate. It works." Darkness smiled. "The differences between us makes it a challenge, but the kind to be enjoyed."

"She did say she was thinking about finding a male." Mourn considered it. He could talk to Dana. He liked her. A memory of her crawling onto the bed the night before flashed through his mind. He was attracted to her.

"We're better than human males." Darkness sounded certain.

"Dana had no complaints about her mate. She loved him. He was good to her."

"So be better." Darkness lowered his voice. "Humans don't have our advantages."

"We're stronger and loyal. We don't carry sexual diseases or get sick."

"That's not what I meant, but those are valid points. I'm talking about sex."

"We're larger and have more stamina."

Darkness chuckled. "Do you know what a vibrator is? A human sex toy?"

Mourn shook his head. "No."

"You haven't watched human porn?"

"No." He scowled. "I had no interest in human sex."

"Good. You're already ahead of a lot of our males who've seen that garbage. It's a bad representation of what human males fantasize about, rather than the females. A lot of females find it offensive. Go down on her and purr. Don't hold back. They love the vibrations from our tongues. Human men can't do that without toys. Just be aware that they try to slam their thighs closed. They aren't used to that much sensation. It's overpowering for them, but pin her thighs open and keep going until she climaxes. Her male couldn't do that."

"They like to be licked?"

"Licked, sucked, and then mounted. Have her face you." He paused. "Just enter her slowly at first. They are damn tight because most human males aren't our size."

Mourn's dick stirred, just thinking about it. It had been a long time since he'd shared sex. Dana had a nice backside. Her hands were soft. He could adjust to their differences. "How do I get her to agree to share sex with me?"

Darkness straightened and dropped his arms to his sides. "They appreciate our bodies. We're fit. Kat swears we have muscles that make females very aware of us." He reached down, gripped the hem of his shirt and yanked it up to just under his nipples. He tightened his stomach and pointed. "Those especially. Kat enjoys running her hands across my abs."

"I just flash her my stomach? That sounds easy."

"It's a little more complicated than that. Do you know how you approach our females for sharing sex?"

"Be blunt, tell them what we want and show our strength."

"Forget that. Don't tell her you'd like to bend her over in front of you. Humans don't usually respond well to that much honesty." Darkness paused, obviously thinking. "Are you meeting her tomorrow night?"

"Yes."

"I have a plan."

"What is it?"

Darkness smiled.

Chapter Four

Dana closed the slider and stepped out onto the patio, glancing around, looking for Mourn. He immediately advanced from the shadows beneath a tree. She smiled, walking right up to the wall that separated them. He reached for her waist and lifted, placing her down on the other side.

He smiled back, reminding her how handsome he was. His mood seemed cheerful too. "What did you do today?"

"I hung out with Becky. She wanted me to watch a bunch of girl movies with her."

"That sounds interesting."

"They were romances." Dana cringed. "Those aren't my favorite kind of films, but it made Becky happy. I liked a few of the storylines that were funny."

He bent and she expected it when he lifted her into his arms. She didn't protest or point out that she'd worn shoes and could walk on her own. When he entered the park, she asked, "Are we going back to the shed?"

"No. I thought we'd go back to the tree. I did put a cushion on the bench for next time."

"That was so thoughtful."

He stopped and bent, setting her on the lowest branch. He crouched. "We could go there if you wish. I just thought it was such a nice night. Did you notice the almost-full moon?" He pointed up at the sky.

"It is beautiful. I love how clearly you can see the sky here at Homeland. I live in a pretty well-lit area so I don't get to see as many stars."

He chuckled. "Homeland is great, but there aren't a lot of places we can go. I live in the men's dorm. You are staying at Paul's. It's hard for us to find privacy."

"That's okay. I'm just glad we can talk every night."

"Me too. It gives me something to look forward to."

She'd grown to look forward to it too and would have been disappointed if he hadn't shown up. A slight click sounded and she turned her head, looking for the source. The sprinklers suddenly came on. She gasped as cold water doused her. Mourn shot to his feet and bent, scooping her into his arms.

It didn't keep her from getting wet. He had to be getting soaked too. She tucked her head against his shoulder and hugged him around his neck as he carried her away.

"Hang on," he urged.

So much for our talk. He'd have to take her home so she could change clothes. He stopped and freed one arm and then tilted her in his hold. She lifted her head when she heard the sound of a door close, and the sprinkler noise died down. It was pitch dark until he shifted, probably using his elbow to hit the switch for the light. She peered around. They were in the shed.

"Are you okay?"

She laughed. "Yes. Did they change the timer? I hear them come on from my room, but it's usually right before dawn."

He put her down and stepped back. His jeans were plastered to his legs. "Someone must have changed the timer setting. You're wet."

"So are you." She noticed his forehead. "You do heal fast." He just had a slight bruise there and the cut was almost entirely gone.

He stepped around her and reached up onto a top shelf along a wall that held sports equipment. He faced her. "I'll close my eyes. Strip and put this around you."

Dana studied the silky material. It had a wolf head printed on it. Her gaze shifted to Mourn. "Is that a flag?"

"Yes. There are more. I'll wrap one around my waist. I want to talk to you."

"You could just take me back to Paul's. We could go inside and I could use the dryer for our clothes."

"Your brother won't welcome me inside his home."

"He's sleeping."

"I'd rather not risk it. You're safe here. I'd never hurt you."

The serious look in his eyes made her feel safe. Mourn wasn't like other men. Not only was he grieving the loss of the woman he loved, he'd never made her feel uncomfortable. "Turn around."

He spun. She bent and tugged off her canvas slip-ons and just tossed them into the corner. She removed her leggings and T-shirt. Her bra and panties were only slightly damp. She debated, but removed them too. The flag was larger than she'd suspected when she unfolded it and wrapped it, toga style, around her middle.

"I'm decent."

"My turn." He faced her. "Close your eyes."

She presented him with her back. It felt strange to be in a small building, mostly undressed. It wasn't something she'd normally do, but she did trust that Mourn wouldn't do anything untoward. He still remained a bit skittish of their budding friendship and she needed to keep that in mind. He might not return if he escorted her back to Paul's to change her clothes. She'd rather stay in the shed with him for a bit than face the guest bedroom alone until sleep came.

"I told Paul I wanted to hang out with him this week." It was a safe topic to discuss.

"Did you tell him we are talking?" Mourn dropped something wet on the floor, probably his shirt or pants.

"No. I respected your wishes. I know you don't want him to know we're spending time together. Our mother called today. I used that as a reason to extend my stay."

"How is she a reason?"

"She's forever trying to set me up with men. It happened again. She made a date for me on Thursday night. I told Paul I wanted to stay longer so I could tell her I'd still be out of town."

"Who is the male?" His voice deepened slightly.

"Some son of a friend of hers whom I've never met. He's thirty-five and lives with his mommy. No thanks. I didn't need to hear any more than that to know it wouldn't work out."

"He's an adult male. I thought humans left home after they finished their schooling."

"They are supposed to, but some men enjoy being pampered by their mothers a little too much. I'm betting that is the case with this one. He's probably looking for a woman who can do everything his mother does, plus have sex with him. That's not going to be me."

"That's strange."

"Some people are."

"I'm covered."

Dana turned and had to seal her lips. Mourn wore a flag wrapped around his waist, but the expanse of his muscled chest, stomach and arms was an onslaught she had not been prepared for. It had been dark enough in the park the night he'd lent her his shirt that she hadn't gotten a really good look. The light inside the shed revealed every inch of him in detail. He had the best body she'd ever seen. He looked even bigger and more impressive in the small, enclosed space. The only flaws were a few bruises from the fight he'd been in, and his bandaged arm. The one on his leg was gone, and the wound looked as if it had happened a week or so ago instead of just a matter of days. It impressed her.

He smiled. "We're dry."

He'd said something, and it took a second for his words to sink in. She lifted her gaze to stare at his face. "Yes, we are."

He inched closer and sat on the padded seat. "Are you cold? Species have a hotter body temperature than humans. You could sit on my lap and I'll keep you warm."

She swallowed hard, staring at his body again. "Um…" Just imagining that made her cheeks feel flushed. He made it worse when he opened his arms, indicating he actually meant it.

"I won't hurt you, Dana."

The way he softened his tone and peered at her with those beautiful eyes actually lured her an unconscious step closer. "Um…" She didn't even know how to respond. It wasn't proper. She'd never gotten that close to a half-naked guy before, except Tommy.

"It's okay," he urged. "Come here."

She wanted to. That was the confusing part. He leaned forward a little, keeping eye contact. She didn't perceive a threat there, but couldn't discount his size or strength. Any other guy would have had her fleeing from the shed.

"I miss holding someone. Let me put my arms around you."

Those whispered, hoarse words were the temptation she couldn't resist. Her heart raced but she inched closer, uncertain how to gracefully take a seat. Mourn didn't seem to have that problem. He just reached out and gently maneuvered her until she found her ass resting over one of his thighs and her legs bent over his other one. She sat sideways and he hugged her closer, his arms wrapped around her in a gentle embrace.

They were both tense, but he relaxed first. The hard muscles under her butt softened slightly and he snuggled her against his chest. She leaned her head to the side a little until her cheek rested near his heart. She could hear it beating almost as fast as her own. That made her feel better. She took a deep breath, blew it out, and forced the tension out of her body.

"This is nice." He shifted a little. "You're so small."

He was really big, but she didn't comment on that. "You are warm." He felt feverish again, a reminder of when she'd first held his hand in Medical.

"You smell good."

She had to clear her throat. "Thank you."

"Do I?"

It was probably the strangest interaction she'd had with a man, but he was New Species, and they were very straightforward. Dana inhaled, closing her eyes. "Yes." He carried a manly scent, not overpowering but pleasant. He sure was different from Morgan, her coworker, who loved to douse on cologne until she could almost taste it.

"See? You're safe with me."

"I trust you." It was true. They had a lot in common. He had told her his mate was the only woman he'd ever had sex with. It wasn't as if he were some guy putting the moves on her. He was probably as inept as she would be at making sexual advances.

He brushed his cheek against her head, a light caress. "Warmer?"

"Yes."

"Good."

She struggled to think of something to say. The first thing that popped into her head came bursting out. "What did you do today?"

"I asked for an assignment."

It distracted her from her awareness of him as a man, and that she was held in his arms. "What happened? Did they give you a job?"

"They refuse to allow me to work anywhere near humans, but said I could patrol the interior of Homeland. I took a shift."

"How did that go?"

"It wasn't bad. I made some Species nervous but they spoke to me."

"Why were they nervous?"

"They expected me to start fights but I didn't."

"What do you do on patrol?" She shifted on his lap and got a little more comfortable.

"I entered each building to see if everyone was all right. I was on duty for four hours to test how I'd work out. No one complained so Fury said I could do it again tomorrow. My shift starts at noon."

"That's great." She wasn't sure where to put her hands so she rested them on her lap. "How do you feel?"

"Really good." His arms tightened around her and he sat back on the bench, taking her with him so she leaned more closely against him.

She couldn't disagree. He did feel really good. Warm, soft in all the right places, but that's when something hard pressed against the back of her thighs. It took her a second to realize what it was and she gasped.

"Don't be alarmed. It's a physical response."

He had a hard-on. There was no missing that with it pressed against the underside of her legs between her ass and knees, where she sat across his lap. Her breathing speeded up and she tried to slow it down. Fear wasn't the cause. She didn't think he was going to do anything bad to her.

"Dana? Are you okay?"

She nodded mutely.

"Look at me." He leaned his head away from hers.

Dana hesitated, but worked up her courage. It was slightly embarrassing to know they were both aware of his physical state. She lifted her chin and stared into his eyes.

"I'd never harm you," he swore, and sincerity shone from those striking eyes. "Please don't fear me."

"I should probably get off your lap. I guess this was a bad idea, huh?" She blushed. "I, wow, this is awkward." She wasn't sure what else to say.

He didn't open his arms. "Is it? I like holding you. I enjoy the way you feel in my arms and how you smell." He seemed to have no difficulty finding words.

Dana swallowed hard, keeping eye contact. "Paul told me to ditch the perfume and cosmetics. He gave me bathing stuff so I won't make New Species sneeze while I'm here. It's probably the new shampoo and conditioner I'm using. This isn't appropriate." That was a good way to put it.

"Human laws don't apply to me."

"It's not a law. It's just that…" She faltered when he leaned in closer and sniffed at her. A low purring sound came from his chest and it caused small vibrations against her arm where she leaned into him.

"It's just that what?"

He expected an answer but all she could do was stare into his eyes. "I should get up," she finally blurted.

He still didn't open his arms. "Why? I like you here. Are you uncomfortable?"

He was actually cozy to sit on. He was big, warm, and he held her gently. It was just that the feel of his erection pressed against the back of her thighs beneath the thin material of the flags wasn't something she could ignore.

"I'm male. I react to you. It doesn't mean I'm going to strip you bare and expect you to share sex with me."

Her breathing picked up speed and her heart pounded. The image of him doing that left her reeling. She wasn't certain how to feel about it. Her gaze lowered to his chest and then to his broad shoulders. He was strong enough to do anything he wanted to her but she didn't fear him. She looked up and studied his eyes. They drew her in, so unique and gorgeous. She'd never seen anything like them before and the novelty wasn't wearing off. She could stare into them for an endless amount of time.

"We like to talk. Tell me what you are thinking."

"You feel really big." She regretted the blurted words, and heat flamed her cheeks. She ducked her head and lifted one hand, covering her eyes. "Sorry. I didn't mean to say that. It was the first thing that popped into my head."

He chuckled. "I am big. See? We're talking and being honest. I like this. Why are you blushing? It is appealing."

Dana peeked back at him. He watched her with a slight smile on his face. His amusement was easy to identify. "You're enjoying this."

"A little." He shrugged. "I will let you go if you really want me to, but I'd like to keep holding you. It feels nice."

It did. *If* she could just ignore that it wasn't his thigh pressed against the back of hers. "It does," she admitted.

"I wouldn't know how to convince you to share sex with me. You're not Species." He frowned and glanced down at the top of where the flag was tucked around her breasts. "The last thing I'd want is to make you fear me. Humans are vastly different."

"Are we?" She wanted to steer the subject away from sex. He was too good-looking and it had been a long time since she'd felt an honest attraction to a man. She was very aware of Mourn.

"Yes. Species females are aggressive. They would grab me and rub up against my body. They don't blush or shy away from me the way you do."

"Does that happen often? You know, women going after you?" She didn't like the little seed of jealousy it spawned.

"Sometimes. They pity me."

"But you haven't, um, gone through with it?"

"You're the first female who has made me hard. I haven't shared sex with anyone except my mate."

He'd told her that before, but she didn't know what he did while he was away from her. Things might have changed. "Oh."

"It confuses me," he confessed, his voice dropping to a mere whisper. "I like you."

"I like you too, Mourn."

He stared at her. "Do I affect you?" He leaned back a little and looked lower, between their bodies. His body tensed. "Do you like how I look?"

Dana couldn't help but gawk a little. Every muscle in his abs showed. He had the kind of washboard stomach that tempted her to reach out and explore it with her hands. She resisted. "You're very…in shape." That was a safe way to put it.

"Is that good? Does my size threaten you?"

It was difficult to tear her attention away from his abdomen but she managed, looking up at his face again. "You don't scare me, if that's what you mean."

"Good. That is the last thing I want. You didn't answer my question. Do I affect you?"

Dana stumbled for an answer.

"It's okay." He closed his eyes and turned his head away. " I didn't think you would be attracted to me, but I needed to ask. We're too different."

She hated the way he sounded hurt. She reached out and hesitantly placed her hand against his shoulder. "Mourn?"

"I don't know what I was thinking. Deception is for humans."

"What does that mean?" She felt a little alarmed by that word.

He opened his eyes and turned his head to look at her again. "I set the sprinklers to go off and get us wet. I hoped that if you saw me mostly undressed, you'd be attracted to me."

"Why would you do that?" It stunned her. She wasn't upset, just surprised and confused.

"You make me feel good things. I wanted to hold you and see if you'd want to share sex with me."

It wasn't the first time a man had hit on her, but she had to say it was the most unusual tactic anyone had ever deployed. "Oh."

"You aren't attracted to me. I understand." Pain flashed in his eyes. "No female will ever wish to be my mate again."

"Mate?" The word staggered her a little. He wasn't just looking for a one-night stand.

He gave a firm nod. "We have so much in common, Dana. I'm attracted to you. I enjoy talking to you."

She finally recovered. "Those aren't reasons to marry someone."

"I mated to 139 because I was told to when they left her with me. We were happy."

It broke her heart and she leaned in closer, hating the pain she saw. "You're still grieving her loss. You can't just replace one woman with another."

"Is that what you believe? You're nothing like her." He frowned. "You're human and I still want you."

She wasn't sure if she should feel insulted. She let it go, not believing it was meant that way. "It's just sexual attraction. We're talking and growing closer. It's normal."

"You aren't attracted to me."

Dana debated and then blew out a breath. "I am."

His eyes narrowed and his arms tightened around her. "You are?"

"You're a very handsome man, Mourn."

"What else do you like about me?"

"Your eyes are..." She paused.

"Frightening? Strangely inhuman?"

"Spectacular," she corrected. "I could stare into them all day."

"What about my size? Do you think I'll bruise or crush you? I worry about that. You look delicate. I know how to be gentle."

"I'm sure you could be."

"I would never force you. My mate was ill for a long time. I never touched her that way, no matter how much I hurt to share sex. Her needs came first."

She believed that about him. "That makes you thoughtful."

"But not sexually appealing enough to be interested in sharing sex with me?"

She glanced down at his chest, stomach and bulky biceps. "You're really hot."

"My temperature runs higher than a human."

She smiled. He was kind of naïve if that was how he had interpreted her remark. "I mean sexy." She blushed a little when she said that, but didn't back away from telling the truth.

"You like me too." He grinned.

"I do, but I don't want to ruin our friendship."

That wiped the joy right off his expression. "I want more than that with you."

"You're still grieving. I'm not a replacement for her, Mourn."

"You're nothing like her. You talk to me with ease."

Questions sprang to Dana's mind. She wanted to ask them aloud but refrained. It was an odd statement to make. She remembered him saying his wife wasn't very talkative but did that mean they barely spoke unless they needed to? It created a bleak image of the kind of relationship they'd had.

"You don't look like her either." He frowned again. "She was very tall. Your coloring is different. I don't want you to be like her."

It helped that he said that. "You're just looking for a bandage to temporarily cure this pain and I don't want to get hurt when you realize that."

"What does that mean?"

"I deserve to be with someone who really loves me and is offering me a future beyond a few days or maybe months. We do this and you'll eventually realize that I was just the person there to get you through the worst of your grief. You'll walk away and I can't take losing someone I let get that close to me. Not a second time."

"Species mate for life." He kept hold of her.

"And yours died." It was a gentle reminder.

He closed his eyes. She took it as a sign that her words were penetrating and reached out, caressing his chest. His skin was so warm and it felt nice. He suddenly opened his eyes and held her gaze.

"Wrong words. We commit to the females we mate with until one of us dies. I am willing to commit to you."

That stunned her. "You don't even know me."

"You're kind and sweet. We have both known loss. No one is ever going to understand me the way you do and I understand you. Don't you want someone to hold you at night? Someone to talk to and laugh with?"

"We don't have to sleep together to do that. We could be friends."

"I don't want to be friends. I want more. Come home and live with me."

Paul had told her once that New Species didn't date. That information suddenly made sense. Mourn just expected her to jump right into a serious relationship. It was insane. Nobody did that.

"I promise to never touch another female, or want to share sex with someone else. I won't ever leave you. You will be mine and I will be yours. I will never hurt you. I'll do everything in my power to make certain you're happy. I'll crave seeing your smile. I would hurt if I hurt you. It's how Species are. Do you understand? I can't replace your mate, but I'm far better than any human you'd have to worry about when you decide to mate again. They aren't as honest as Species, or as loyal."

"It's not that simple."

"It could be." He reached up and lightly ran his fingertip along her cheek. "I've never shared sex with a human, but I promise I'll learn how to please you. I'm determined. It will be enjoyable to figure out our differences."

The gruff tone affected her. His voice took on a slight growl. It had been two years since a man had even tempted her to want sex. Mourn did. She glanced at his chest. He was beautiful and everything manly. He had the kind of body women would want to worship and she was affected as well.

"I—"

"You said I must take chances," he reminded her. "So must you. You wanted to help change my life since I only existed in loneliness and pain. You think I want you to cure me of that, but I think we can do that for each other. I see yours when you talk about what you lost when your mate died. I wouldn't humble myself if I hadn't thought this through. We could fill the emptiness and make each other whole again. Together."

He dropped his finger away from her face and lowered his arm. He slid his big hand under her ass, cupping it, and squeezed just enough to make her very aware of the sexual significance of having a man touch her. His nostrils flared, and a low growl surprised her. His chest vibrated under her hand. She glanced at it and then back at his face.

"A reminder," he stated. "I'm Species. I keep my word. I don't want to just share sex. I want you to live with me and become my reason for living. I want to be yours."

It really sank in. "You're serious."

"Yes."

"This is insane." The words popped out before she could worry about insulting him.

He smiled instead. "Let's be insane together."

"We just met. We should get to know each other first."

"Okay."

When he agreed, Dana relaxed, but it was a short-lived reprieve.

"We can do that as mates."

"Mourn, we can't just jump into a relationship. It never works out."

"It might not work for humans, but it does with Species. You're not in your out world anymore. You're Paul's sister and he's happy here. You could be too."

"This is too fast."

"You said I should change my life and find a reason to want to live. I chose you."

She was speechless. She frantically tried to form reasonable arguments to point out to him that it was a bad idea that bordered on crazy. He massaged her ass. He had firm, yet gentle hands. It made it worse as she stared into his eyes, observing that passion made them even brighter and livelier.

"Let me touch you," he growled.

Dana still couldn't form words. He inched his hand a little closer to her pussy while he continued to knead her butt. Her heart pounded and she was tempted to say yes. Life was too short and could end before anyone expected it to. She knew that firsthand, but the fear that he was using her to replace the woman he'd lost was a real possibility. It was the grieving version of someone on the rebound. If they jumped into a relationship too fast, no good would come of it. Her attempt to help him heal could hurt both of them if she didn't get off his lap and stop him from making a mistake.

Chapter Five

Mourn ached to tear the flag from Dana's body and stretch her out on the cushioned bench. He'd taken the padding off an outdoor lounge chair from the backyard of guest housing and brought it to the shed. It was thickly padded and plush. He wanted to stretch her out on that cushion and explore every inch of Dana's skin, touch her. He saw no fear in her eyes, but there was plenty of hesitation.

Did she really believe he wanted a replacement for 139? He couldn't understand her logic. She wasn't anything similar to the mate he'd lost and he didn't wish her to be. It would be difficult to learn how to live with a human, but he was willing to do whatever it took to make it work. Dana was someone he could talk to and she was the first female to rekindle his desire to live.

He also felt a healthy dose of pure lust. His dick hurt like nothing he could remember. He longed to be inside her, despite his worry that he might cause her harm. He'd have to take things very slowly and use every ounce of self-control. Dana didn't seem as if she was eager to share sex with him and that meant coaxing her into allowing him to remove that flag from her body.

"Mourn." Her voice came out a little breathless.

"Let me touch you."

"You are." Her cheeks were pink, and she licked her lips.

She wasn't wiggling to move away from his exploration of her ass. She had a generous amount of flesh in that area. He liked holding it in the palm of his hand. He scooted down the bench, keeping her on his lap as he did so. He twisted his body just enough to turn her so, when he bent forward, he was able to lay her on the cushion. She grabbed at his upper arms. He withdrew his hand from under her ass and gripped the material at her thighs, sliding it up. His talk with Darkness about human sex replayed inside his head.

"I want to strip you bare and bury my face between your thighs. You'd like me licking your pussy. I purr. Do you know what that means?"

She shook her head and swallowed hard.

"I'm better than a vibrator. I was told what one of those do to your kind and how good it feels to females. Do you own one?"

Her cheeks turned pinker and her lips parted. She remained mute, looking stunned at the same time.

"Do you own one, Dana?" He said her name to make certain she knew she was the female he thought of.

She nodded. It was slight, but he saw the movement.

"I'd make you come hard." He shifted a little, adjusting until his elbows rested on the cushion on each side of her ribs. He leaned in closer, careful to keep his weight off her. He worried she'd panic, perhaps roll away and hit the floor. "I want to show you the advantages of having a Species mate. Let me do that."

She stared at him, appearing a little dazed. Darkness had said not to be too blunt, but he couldn't help it. Dana had accepted everything about him so far and she hadn't shown any revulsion when he'd told her how he'd become mated to 139. Humans didn't end up together that way, but she hadn't judged him. He wanted to be completely honest. Lies were a bad way to start their bond. He'd tried deceit when he'd gotten her wet from the sprinklers. It had made him feel guilt.

"I want to spread your legs apart and bare you to my mouth." He licked his lips, noticing how her gaze darted down to watch his tongue. "I'll be gentle and take it slow. It will feel good. I promise you this. Don't fear my fangs. I thought all day about what objections you might have and that has to be one of them. Though I am bigger than a human male, when I mount you I'll be extremely gentle. I won't crush you with my weight, or bruise you with my hands. I am very aware of my strength. As for the size of my dick, your body will stretch to take me and you'll be very wet after I make you come. I'll work my way inside you with care to make sure it feels good for you. I have control. Let me show you."

She lifted her gaze to lock with his. Dana remained mute, still looking stunned. It was a possibility that he had been too direct, but he saw no fear. That was the most important part.

"You can trust me, Dana. What will convince you?"

"I..." She swallowed. "This is a bad idea. You're not thinking straight." Once she began to speak, it was as if she couldn't stop as words poured out. "You'll hate me and come to believe I took advantage of you when you were vulnerable. I couldn't stand for you to think that I—"

He snarled in frustration. He regretted it when she jerked under him and her nails dug into his skin. She stopped speaking. He still didn't see any fear in her expression, but he knew it could turn that way fast if he didn't control his reactions. She wasn't used to Species, and didn't understand that she wasn't in any danger. That was something she'd learn by spending time with him.

He softened his voice to soothe her. "Don't tell me what I'd think. I'll tell you where my thoughts are. I want you, Dana. You're the only female who has stirred my body and my interest. It isn't because you remind me of 139. Listen to me well and hear my words. You are nothing like her. It is part of the reason I am intensely attracted to you. I have never spoken to anyone with the ease that I do with you. I didn't have a choice when I was given 139 as a mate, but I'm choosing you. You told me to let go of the pain and try to live. That's what I'm doing right now if you will allow it. Say yes. Bend up your knees and spread them apart." He sat up a little and gave her room to move. She had to release his arms when he did it.

"You're confused about what you want. I'm the first person you've spoken to."

He scowled.

"It's true. Remember when I told you about how some people in the group turned to sex to try to deal with their grief? I think this is a classic case right here. You can't just make a long-term commitment to someone who is virtually a stranger. We barely know each other. I can't be your mate."

Perhaps the term frightened her and made her leery. He really needed to learn more about her kind. She was nothing like a bad human. He'd been certain his biggest obstacle would be his fangs, or his size. Instead it seemed that she worried about long-term commitment and that he'd come to regret offering to spend the rest of his life with her.

"Take one day at a time. That's what you said. Today..." He glanced down at her body, mostly interested in shoving the material out of his way to bare her pussy. "We will focus on pleasure. You are attracted to me. We will start with that. I won't push you for more, but I'm not going to change my mind. I want you as my mate. I'll show you how much I mean that if you'll spread your thighs and let me lick you."

She seemed mute again, just lay there staring at him.

He carefully wrapped his fingers around her thighs. "You talk about living and encouraging me to do it." He used his thumbs to stroke her skin. "Let me. You also said those humans felt empty having sex. I won't allow that to happen to you. I'll stay inside you afterward and all you will feel is me."

Her features grew flushed and she bit down on her bottom lip. "Mourn...that's not exactly the kind of empty I was talking about."

"I know, but you can't feel alone if I'm inside you and holding you." He paused, watching her closely. "How long has it been since you've been touched?"

She hesitated. "Too long."

He gently applied pressure to her inner thighs. She didn't resist when he parted them. He bent her leg up and adjusted it behind his back. He scooted down the bench at the same time. "You'll like this. Trust me."

She didn't protest when he lowered his gaze, taking in the sight of her pussy. It fascinated him. She wasn't completely hairless there. A small strip of short hair covered her mound. He rested her bent leg against the wall and reached out, stroking his thumb over that strip.

Dana sucked in air, but didn't try to slam her legs closed. He inhaled her scent. She was slightly aroused and he wanted to find out if she tasted as sweet as she smelled. He lowered his face, released her other thigh, and parted her vaginal lips to get a better look at her. She was pink and small. He wanted to snarl. It was possible he would accidentally hurt her when he mounted her.

Females stretch. He'd never taken a class about sex with humans, but he'd heard some of the males talk about what they'd learned in the community rooms at the dorm. He knew it was possible since some males had taken humans as mates. He'd figure it out. He needed to prepare her to share sex first though.

"Relax," he coaxed, moving in closer, fixing his attention on her clit. Excitement coursed through him when she didn't try to twist away as he put his mouth right on that pink flesh and lightly ran the tip of his tongue over it. His chest tightened and he took his own advice, relaxing. The vibrations started, and he didn't hold back the desire to purr. He deepened them, knowing she'd enjoy the sensations.

"Oh god," Dana whispered.

She didn't pull away so he licked at her, pressing his tongue against her more firmly, keeping it there as he rubbed up and down. One leg moved, and she pressed her thigh against his cheek. He shifted his arm, hooking her thigh, pinning it up and to the side.

She started to move against him, her hips rocking. He had to pin her other leg and press down on her lower stomach to keep her from moving too far away from his mouth. Darkness had warned him that humans tried to pull away from pleasure. He was intent on giving her a lot of it.

The scent of her arousal increased as he continued to lick and purr against her clit. The bud hardened under his tongue and he knew she was close when her moans grew louder. She bucked her hips, almost unseating his mouth. He put more strength into holding her in place, careful not to hurt her, but wanting to keep her still. Her fingers suddenly dug into his hair at the back of his head, but she didn't pull it. Her fingernails lightly raked his scalp, an encouragement since it felt good.

He snarled, his dick so hard it hurt. He wanted to be inside her. She had become soaked from arousal. It was tempting to slide his mouth lower and use his tongue to see how tight she'd be and get a better taste of her but he resisted the urge. He needed her to come first. Then he could enjoy that experience.

Dana was going to die. Her back arched and she clawed at the top of the cushion above her head with one hand. Her other one held on to Mourn. His hair was silky, and she was tempted to fist the short strands and tear him away from her pussy. He was vibrating and licking her at the same time. Her bullet sex toy couldn't do that. Nothing could, except Mourn.

It felt a bit surreal that she had allowed him to do that to her, but he'd managed to talk her into it. He'd been too sexy to resist and she had to admit she'd been curious. Now she knew. He hadn't lied about how good it would feel.

Every muscle in her body seemed tense, and despite him telling her to relax, she couldn't. She tried to slam her legs closed, but he had a good grip on them, keeping them spread apart so he could torment her with his mouth. It was almost torture since nothing should ever feel that incredible. It almost hurt. She'd been worried it would be awkward to have someone touch her, but now even thinking was impossible. It was all about sensations and aching.

She forgot how to breathe when ecstasy slammed into her. She must have sucked in air though, because she realized she was crying out Mourn's name. The climax was sharp, nearly brutal, and all-consuming as it rolled through her. Her entire body quaked. She panted and her body went lax in the seconds following her release. Mourn pulled his mouth away and she could feel his hot breath fanning her oversensitive clit.

She kept her eyes closed, unwilling to look at him, not even sure she could work up the nerve. He'd just gone down on her. It was slightly embarrassing to be that exposed to someone, especially since the only person who had ever known her that intimately was Tommy. She shoved back thoughts of him. *No guilt.* She hadn't cheated. She was more concerned about what she'd say to Mourn and if things would be uncomfortable between them now.

She jerked in surprise when his tongue pressed against the opening of her pussy and he breached it. He had a thick tongue. He snarled, the sound a little menacing, but she wasn't afraid. He withdrew almost as fast as he'd entered her. His hold on her thighs and lower stomach eased and he adjusted her legs. It was easy to do since she felt boneless at that moment.

The bench she lay on creaked a little and the sound finally forced her to open her eyes. She lifted her head to stare at Mourn. He was focused on her lower half, his chin lowered, his gaze locked there as he sat up and scooted his hips closer. He released her thighs entirely and reached up, grabbing the edges of the bench on each side of her waist.

"I'll be gentle." His voice came out unusually deep. He almost didn't even sound human.

Dana knew what he planned to do. She shifted her legs, bending her knees more and lifting them up. Mourn looked at her then. His eyes were amazingly beautiful and she licked her dry lips. He paused and then surprised her by sliding off the bench. He moved to the end of it and knelt.

"This will work better. I don't want to crush you."

He surprised her when he leaned forward, shoved his hands under her ass, and gripped her. He pulled her and the cushion down the bench until her bottom was at the edge of it. Mourn released her ass and gripped her calves, lifting her legs until her feet were braced on the sides of his chest near his shoulders. He parted her thighs farther and inched closer.

Dana tried to relax. Mourn was going to fuck her. It was scary and exhilarating at the same time. It might be a huge mistake, but she wanted him. He rested one arm over her lower stomach, as if he wanted to pin her there, and reached between them with his other hand. It was tempting to lift her head and look at his cock, which he must have gripped with that hand. She didn't though. She stared into his eyes.

Mourn brushed the crown of his cock against her clit. He rubbed it lower, using the tip to slide through her wet folds. He didn't enter her right way, instead rubbed higher, teasing her clit. Dana grabbed hold of the sides of the bench, needing something to grasp. Her toes curled when he kept doing it. Her clit was still a little oversensitive but it felt amazing. She was really wet and so was he, from rubbing up against her.

He maneuvered his cock lower and she felt it at the opening of her pussy. He froze there, but then lightly pressed against her. She spread her thighs a little more, adjusting her feet on his solid chest. She'd never had sex before with her legs up in that manner, but she'd never been with a New Species either.

The sensation of him entering her had her closing her eyes again. He was big and thick. It didn't hurt though. The pressure was welcome and it actually felt good when he drove deeper. He purred again, a deep, rumbling sound.

"Am I hurting you?"

She shook her head, unable to find words.

"You're so tight." He growled. "You feel perfect."

He moved slowly inside her. He was rock hard. He increased the pace. She clawed at the bench. She'd missed sex, missed having a man inside her, bringing her pleasure. One of her feet slipped off his chest, but Mourn grabbed her ankle, held it in place.

"Fuck," he snarled.

He drove into her deep, completely filling her and bent forward, groaning. His body shook. Dana opened her eyes, watching his face as he came inside her. She could feel it. His semen was hot and his cock pulsed against her pussy walls, almost like a heartbeat. He shook again. His eyes were closed, lips parted to show off his fangs. His handsome features twisted into a harsh but sexy contortion that looked a little pained.

His expression quickly changed to a frown when he opened his eyes. They stared at each other.

"I'm sorry."

"For what?"

"You felt too good. I tried to hold back, but I came."

She lifted her foot off his chest and lowered it, hooking that leg around his hips. Her heel made contact with his bare ass cheek and she dug in, pulling him closer. She opened her arms to him. His apology made him even sweeter and more endearing. "It's okay. Come here."

He released her ankle and lowered over her. She wrapped her arms around his neck. "It's okay. I came first." The aftermath of them having sex wasn't uncomfortable, as she'd feared. She mostly wanted to assure him it was fine. She understood being over-excited and not lasting long. She'd been guilty of that too when he'd gone down on her. "You said you'd hold me."

He braced his elbows on the padding next to her ribs and lowered his chest until her breasts were smashed against him. His weight on her felt right. It put their faces inches apart. She liked having him against her, still inside her. They were linked. She hesitated but then reached up, brushing his hair with her fingers.

"How do you feel?"

He hesitated. "Disappointed."

It was a verbal slap, and it hurt. "I knew you'd regret this."

"No." He scowled. "Not about what we did, but that I couldn't hold back. I'll do better next time."

Next time. He wanted to see her again. Dana breathed easier, grateful he wasn't sorry that he'd talked her into having sex with him. She didn't regret it either, but admitted to herself that she was confused over how she felt about it.

"It's been a long time since I've shared sex. I grew too excited. I'll do better in a few minutes."

"A few minutes?"

"I have to recover. My balls ache a little, but it will stop fast."

She was confused. "You hurt yourself?"

"I came so hard it hurt. I think it's from spasms. My balls feel twitchy and ache a bit, but it's lessening."

"Is that a Species thing?"

"Possibly. I'm not certain. I'll have to ask other males. It doesn't happen when I masturbate, but you excite me much more than when I'm tending to my own needs."

His candor stunned her, but she appreciated it. "Do you do that often?"

"Yes. Don't you?"

His openness about the subject of masturbation helped her to be honest too. "Sometimes. Not when I'm visiting Paul though. I didn't bring my vibrator. I was too worried about my bags being checked at the airport."

"I don't understand."

"You know." She winced. "An employee there could search my bag and find it. It would be horrible to know someone might have seen it."

"Why are you so shy about sex?"

"I don't know. I just am."

"I'll teach you not to be. Am I better than your sex toy?"

She blushed, the memory of his mouth on her was something she'd never forget. "Yes."

"How often do you use it?"

She hesitated, not sure how to answer that, or if she even should.

"I need to know so I can meet your needs. I enjoy masturbating at least three to four times a day. You must have been tense if you didn't bring your vibrator to Homeland. I grow testy if I don't find sexual release.

Are you the same way? Do you do it every few hours or just in bed before sleep and when you wake?"

He wasn't going to let it drop. "It helps me sleep."

He smiled. "That wasn't difficult, was it? I'll make certain I lick you every night. You should allow me to do it in the morning too so you start your day off feeling relaxed."

It was becoming a habit that his words surprised her. "Every night?"

"Every night. Every morning." His cock hardened inside her. "I'm recovered."

"I feel."

He withdrew a little from her and then drove back in. "This time I won't come until you do. I'm more prepared for how extraordinary you feel."

Dana moaned, clutching at his shoulders. Mourn had pegged it. Extraordinary was a great way to describe how it felt when he moved inside her. He lifted his chest off her by straightening up and she had to release him, but she locked her legs around his waist. He hooked one arm under her lower back, holding her in place while he fucked her.

She watched as Mourn lifted his free hand to his mouth and licked the tip of his thumb. He reached down between them and pressed it firmly against her clit. He wiggled it.

"Oh god."

"You're very religious."

She let that go, making a mental note to explain it later. He yanked her ass closer with his arm hooked under her, holding her in place as he fucked her faster. She closed her eyes, bit her lip, and just enjoyed the feel of him inside her while he played with her clit at the same time until she cried out his name, the climax tearing through her.

Mourn didn't let up on her clit, and she bucked, squeezing his waist with her thighs. He snarled, and she felt it when he came. His motions became almost violent and jerky, and then there was the warmth spreading inside her.

She wanted to ask him about his warm semen, once she caught her breath and could form sentences again. He pulled his thumb off her clit and came down on top of her, pinning her with his body. She wrapped her arms around his neck and he kept his word, not pulling out of her, but instead kept them linked.

"I'm getting better at learning how to please you," he rasped.

She opened her eyes and was enthralled at the way Mourn looked at her, as if she were someone very special to him. It might have been wishful thinking. She could easily fall in love with him and suspected she had already started to. Realization came next. It was going to tear her apart when he figured out she was just an emotional crutch. He might not regret the sex, because it had been fantastic, but he'd realize he didn't want to spend the rest of his life with her. She would return home with her heart in tatters.

"What are you thinking?"

She wasn't going to share her worries. "I'm just enjoying being so close to you." That was the truth.

"I am too." He turned his head, glancing around the shed. "We need a home. I don't want you to have to live in the men's dorm. It can get loud sometimes when the males play games. I doubt Paul will want to share his home with another male. We're territorial. It's his space." He smiled when he looked at her again. "I'll request housing in the morning. They will assign us to a house like Paul's. We can sleep here tonight."

"We can't just move in together."

That wiped his good mood away. "We can. I know you aren't ready to mate with me. You want time. I understand that you need to learn more about me before you sign the mate papers. The best way to convince you that I'm your male will be sharing quarters."

New Species don't date. Paul's words sounded in her head again. Most men were afraid to commit. Mourn wanted to go full speed into a live-in relationship, to jump in with both feet.

"I'll hold you while we're sleeping. We'll share meals. It will be nice. At least try it."

It was tough to say no when he looked at her with those gorgeous eyes, and was holding her, their bodies entwined. His husky voice didn't help matters. She had a hard time resisting. It's also how he'd gotten her thighs spread open to him in the first place. No man had ever talked to her that way and it had been a turn-on she couldn't resist.

"Sleep with me and see how you like it."

He gently withdrew from her body and rose. "This bench is too narrow. I'll sleep on it and you lie on top of me." He stood and held out his hand to her.

She hesitated and then took it. "Paul will worry when he realizes I'm not there."

"I'm an early riser. I'll take you home to get your things before he wakes. We'll tell him you're safe with me."

She imagined her brother's face if she announced she was getting a place with a New Species. He'd probably lose his shit. He'd told her not to get involved with Mourn. She was pretty certain he wouldn't be overjoyed or accept it without a lot of yelling first.

"I'll stay with you tonight, but I have to think about living with you. That's a huge step, Mourn."

He growled softly at her, and his eyes narrowed. "I'll make you happy."

"It's not that. It's just that this is moving too fast for me and living together is a huge step." She didn't mention that having sex was too and she was having a difficult enough time coming to terms with what they'd just done. "Let me think about it."

His expression softened. "I understand. Thank you for staying with me tonight, Dana. I really want to hold you and have you sleep in my arms."

She took Mourn's hand and allowed him to pull her upright. He stretched out on his back on the bench and smiled. She had to admire how incredibly sexy he looked naked. The flag wasn't wrapped around his waist anymore.

"Lie on me."

She hesitated. "I might be too heavy."

He chuckled and sat up just enough to capture her hand in his, pulling her down. She ended up sprawled over him, her legs slightly parted so she didn't smash his cock. It hardened between her thighs. Mourn adjusted her so his chest pillowed her head near his shoulder. He yanked her flag down to cover her ass, and then wrapped his arms around her waist.

"You are safe. Are you warm enough?"

He put off a lot of body heat. "Yes."

He nuzzled his jaw against the top of her head. "Good. This is nice, isn't it?"

She relaxed and had to admit, it was. "Yes."

He was big and solid under her. Warm. His arms around her felt nice. She even liked hearing his heartbeat under her ear. He began to stroke her back. That felt really good and relaxed her further.

"You feel right here," he rasped. "Is the light bothering you? I forgot to turn it off."

"It's not bright."

"Try to sleep. I'm with you."

She closed her eyes, but sleep didn't come right away. Mourn kept stroking her back, his big hand lightly massaging the curve of her ass every few minutes. There was no desire to ask Mourn to take her home. She'd just have to sleep in the guestroom alone. It wasn't something she wanted to do when being held by him felt so good. She finally drifted off.

Chapter Six

"I apologize for sleeping longer than I believed I would." Mourn didn't look sorry when he smiled. "That's the best sleep I've had in a long time."

Dana had to agree. "Me too."

"I usually wake from nightmares. I even worried I might turn in my sleep and dump you on the floor."

She grinned, fighting to get her pants on. The still-wet material clung to her legs. She managed to get dressed and faced Mourn. He'd put his wet clothes on too. They were probably a sorry-looking pair with their worse-for-wear clothing and messy hair. It was obvious they'd just woken.

"I'm glad you didn't. That wouldn't have been the best way to wake up."

"You should just wear the flag. Your clothes are still too wet."

"My brother is going to have a conniption fit as it is. I'll wear my damp clothes. Trust me. He'll really freak out if I come home without them on."

He chuckled. "Tonight we'll sleep in a real bed together with plenty of room. I'll have housing arranged for us."

She was ready to panic when she jerked her head up to stare at him. "I'm not ready to move in with you yet."

All trace of his good mood faded. "Don't say no." He stepped closer and brushed her hair off her cheek. "Try it for seven days. I'll let you go if you don't want to stay. This is a compromise."

"That's putting a lot of pressure on both of us."

"No pressure. Be yourself, Dana. I care about you. Let us live together. I think we will be happy and I hope you will learn this can work between us."

She chewed on her bottom lip, pondering it. The damage was done. She wasn't going to forget about Mourn any time soon. They'd been intimate. To return to her old life without trying to see if a relationship between them could work would leave her with regrets. She had enough of those to last her a lifetime.

"Let's date."

He stepped closer. "I want to sleep with you every night."

"We're already moving too fast. I've been told that New Species don't date, but humans do. We already skipped right to the sex." She glanced around the shed. "You have a home, right? Tonight you can take me there and we can spend time together. I don't expect you to take me out to dinner, or to see a movie. I get that it's not really possible to do that at Homeland. The bar seems like the only social place to hang out and that's not exactly romantic. I haven't seen a movie theatre here."

"I don't want to take you to the men's dorm. I'm worried it will be uncomfortable."

"Why?"

"The males hang out in the living spaces on the first floor. They might be alarmed, seeing you with me, and try to prevent me from taking you to my apartment."

Sympathy for him came fast. "Because you picked fights with them?"

He nodded. "They'd wish to protect you, believing I'm unstable."

"You don't think they'd try to stop us from living together?"

"We'd be assigned to couples housing—the cottages where Species live with their mates. It's more private and we'd have less males to deal with. Darkness might help us get a home. He thinks you are good for me."

She remembered that name. "Isn't he the one you fought with when we met?"

"Yes."

"You talked to him about us?"

He nodded. "I didn't have a choice. He knows we've been meeting at night and wanted to know why. He threatened to send me to Reservation if my intentions weren't good."

"Why would he do that?"

"He worried I would do to you what Vengeance has attempted in the past."

"What's that?"

"He has tried to grab human females and take them."

She gawked at him. "Take them?"

"Ven's mate died at Mercile. He's considered unstable too. He just wants a female to love and care for. He needs purpose in his life. Darkness was concerned I'd steal you from your brother and take you home with me by force. I told him I'd never do that."

"Did this Vengeance do that to someone?"

"He has tried to grab a female a couple of times but the males stopped him. He's very lonely. He just wanted to take one home and keep her."

"Has he had counseling? It sounds like he needs it."

"We've all had to speak to head shrinks, but they don't understand us. They think the way humans do, not like a Species."

She let that sink in, pondering what it meant.

"The head shrink I spoke to grew angry with me when I told him about how 139 became my mate."

"Why was he angry?"

"Kregkor said it was akin to rape when we mated and asked Justice to keep me away from 139. Justice refused his request and banned him from going near us. He tried but the officer at the gates of Species housing refused to allow him to come to our home. Kregkor no longer works for the NSO. The US government assigned him to work at Homeland but Moon's mate got him fired. Joy is a head shrink too. She said he was an asshole. She spoke to me after someone told her what he'd said to me and the accusations he'd made about how letting me care for my mate would damage her more. Joy understands Species much better."

"He does sound like an asshole."

"Thank you for taking it well when I told you how 139 became my mate. I understand that's not how humans form bonds."

She closed the distance between them and took his hand. "You're an amazing man, Mourn. You're sweet and kind. I'm so sorry for what Kregkor said to you."

He smiled. "Why do you always apologize for other humans?"

She grinned. "I don't know."

"It's adorable, but not necessary. I didn't take it personal. He thinks human. Our history is vastly different. We didn't have choices, even once."

She had the urge to kiss him but wasn't that forward. "We should get to Paul's before he really freaks out."

"I want you to live with me."

"I know, but I need to think about that."

"May I ask Darkness to get us couples housing so we can go there at night? I'll move into the cottage and you can visit me so we have privacy." He glanced around the shed, then at her again. "I want to take you somewhere nicer than this."

She nodded. "Do you think he can do that?"

"I do. I get off at four today. May I pick you up at around four thirty? I'll get takeout food for us and we can eat at the cottage together. It will be like a date, but no one will try to intervene."

"I'd like that."

"What do you like to eat?"

"I had their fried chicken dinner when Paul took me to the bar. I liked that a lot."

"I'll order it for you."

Mourn stepped around her and opened the door. The bright light blinded her for a moment, but she followed him. Mourn spun and she wasn't surprised when he just scooped her up into his arms. He seemed to enjoy carrying her, or maybe he thought her walking on grass wasn't acceptable. She wrapped her arms around his neck as he closed the door.

"Let me do the talking when we get to the house." She felt better prepared to handle Paul. "I have no idea how to make my brother understand why I spent the night with you, but I'll do my best. Just promise me you won't deck Paul. No picking a fight with him. He's not going to react well when we show up there. He's probably already discovered that I'm not in the guestroom."

"I have no desire to fight with males anymore, especially one who matters so much to you. I'll restrain him if he attacks me."

She winced. "I don't want you two to fight."

"You're a fully grown female. It's your decision to sleep with me, not his."

"You don't understand big brothers."

"That is true. I have no family."

The park seemed abandoned. They approached the back of Paul's house. It was the first indication of what waited inside. Two uniformed

New Species officers were on the patio, one of them talking into a cell phone.

"Shit. Paul must have called Security."

"It will be fine," Mourn murmured.

The guard on his phone hung up and slid his cell into his front pocket. Mourn stepped over the divider wall and carried Dana to them. He lowered her gently to her feet. The guard shot a glare at him, but addressed Dana when he spoke.

"Are you harmed?"

"No."

The slider opened and a tall, black-haired New Species stepped out. The harsh expression on his face made him kind of scary. He wasn't wearing a uniform though. Instead he wore jeans and a black button-down shirt.

"Darkness," Mourn stepped closer to Dana and put his body between her and the other man.

"It's ten thirty. Paul woke and was very alarmed when he realized his sister wasn't in her room. He called for a full-scale search of Homeland to find her. I intervened and have kept him here. I did, however, have to inform him that you two have been spending your evenings together." He swept his gaze over Dana—a quick examination. "I promised him she'd be fine. She looks it."

"We slept too long. I apologize." Mourn reached back and took her hand. "I've asked Dana to live with me, but she needs more time before she feels at ease with that. I'd still like to request a place at couples housing so she can visit me there. Would you speak on my behalf and make it happen?"

Darkness hesitated, apparently thinking it over. "What's wrong with the men's dorm?"

"The other males might wish to protect her from me. I don't want issues to arise."

The black-haired guy seemed to ponder if for long seconds. "I could arrange that."

"I go on shift at noon, but I get off duty at four. Do you think it can be settled by then? I don't want to have to take her to the shed every time we meet."

Darkness nodded. "I think I can." He looked at Dana then. "Would you feel safe in a more private location with him?"

She squeezed Mourn's hand, grateful to be holding onto him. The big black-clad guy scared her. "Yes. We're trying to get to know each other better," she responded, feeling the need to explain. The situation kind of reminded her of the first time she'd met Tommy's father after they'd started dating. She'd been terrified he'd tell her to get lost and not to go near his son.

Darkness sighed. "All right. You might want to speak to your brother. He's been pacing his living room and refused to calm until you were found." He looked at Mourn. "You stay put. He wishes to punch you. I refuse to allow you to fight a human, especially that one."

"I gave my word I'd only restrain Paul if he attacks me."

Darkness growled. "Let her go inside alone. Her brother won't harm her. It is best if she talks to Paul without you within his sight. You are going on duty in a little over an hour. You smell like the female. You need a shower and it will give you some time to pack your belongings before shift."

"I should speak to Paul to reassure him that Dana is safe with me."

Darkness shook his head. "It's obvious, even to a human, what the two of you did. Trust me, he will attack you. You shared sex with his sister. This is a family issue that she needs to address without you. Say goodbye to her. You can pick her up after your shift ends. I'll contact you with your new address. I'll stay here to make certain all is well. I won't allow anything to happen to her, but you will just exacerbate the situation."

Dana tugged on Mourn's hand until he looked at her. "He's right. I'll handle Paul. You should shower before you go to work. I'll be okay."

He scowled.

She rushed on before he could protest. He looked as if he planned to. "Go pack your things if you plan to move today. You should eat something too. You said you get off work at four. I'll be ready when you show up for our date."

"I don't want you to face Paul alone if he's angry that I kept you out all night."

"Fuck," Darkness muttered. He glared at Mourn. "Trust me. Go home, shower, and do what your female said. Eat breakfast and pick her up after your shift. Do you want to make things easier on her? Don't make her watch her brother attack you. He will."

Mourn growled low. "Fine." He released Dana's hand. "I'll be here when my shift ends, right after I pick up food."

"I'll see you then."

He spun and stormed away. Dana watched him go, worried. He looked angry. Darkness cleared his throat, and she tore her gaze off Mourn to face him. She tensed, not liking his grim expression.

"Am I in trouble?"

"For sharing sex with Mourn?"

She nodded. "I tried to talk him out of it."

Darkness stepped closer. "Did he force the sex?"

"No. It wasn't like that."

"Why do you think you'd be in trouble then?"

"He's grieving the loss of his mate. I told him it was a bad idea to get involved so soon with someone else, but he didn't agree. I can understand if you think I took advantage of him, but I promise that hurting him is the last thing I want."

He surprised her by suddenly laughing.

"What's funny?"

"Humans are. No one at Homeland will think you took advantage of him. It's funny every time I hear those words. He pursued you. Our males can be very convincing, as I suspect you've learned firsthand since he kept you all night and most of the morning. Go inside to your brother." He stepped aside.

Dana hesitated. "Is Paul really angry?"

"He's worried."

She nodded, took a deep breath and blew it out. She advanced, passing the two guards without glancing at them, and entered the house. Paul was in the kitchen with Becky. They were talking, but stopped the second they spotted her. Paul rushed forward.

"Where the hell have you been?" He came to a halt a few feet away, taking her in from head to toe. "Are you all right? Did that crazy son of a bitch hurt you?"

"Mourn isn't crazy."

"So you were with him? Darkness said you've been meeting him every night after we went to bed."

"Calm down, Paul," Becky urged.

"Stay out of this."

Dana winced. "Don't talk to her that way."

"I'm the bad guy?" Paul threw up his arms. "I woke and you weren't here. Then I find out you've been lying to me and hanging out with Mourn. I told you to stay the hell away from him. He's not right in the head."

"He lost his mate and has been struggling with that. I've been there, remember?"

"Yes." Paul nodded. "You were nuts after you lost your husband. We all worried you'd take a self-inflicted bullet to the head."

"Paul!" Becky rounded the island and grabbed his arm. "Stop it."

Paul closed his eyes. "I'm sorry." He took a few breaths, then opened his eyes. "I was scared shitless that Mourn would hurt you. He's in Medical all the time after picking fights with men. They aren't like regular guys, Dana." He looked past her. "Tell her, Darkness. Mourn is a danger to his own kind and she's not one of your females. My kind killed his mate. He could take it out on my sister."

Dana glanced back, realizing Darkness stood directly behind her. He was so close, she could move her hand a few inches and touch him if she wanted. He glanced down at her, then frowned at Paul.

"She makes Mourn stable. He sees her as a reason to live. He wouldn't harm her, just the way I told you earlier, Paul. He does have a lot of rage directed at anyone associated with Mercile, but what Species doesn't? He's aware that your sister is nothing like them. He's interested in her as a female."

"Fucking wonderful," Paul muttered.

Dana stared at her brother. "Mourn isn't going to hurt me."

"How do you know? You only spent a few nights talking to him. I've known him far longer than you have. I'm the one who keeps seeing him brought in with injuries. He's got a death wish."

"I know him better than you do."

"Bullshit. You are being naïve, Dana. You know nothing about Species. I'd rather you hook up with one from the Wild Zone than Mourn. You don't even know what that means, but at least I'd know one of them would never turn on you. They call it the Wild Zone for a reason. Some of them are almost feral, but Mourn is crazy. He lost his mate and he snapped. He attacks people who try to befriend him. Hell, he attacked the man standing behind you. Take a look at Darkness. Only a crazy son of a bitch would pick a fight with him. He's scarier than shit." Paul glanced over her head. "No offense, man."

"None taken," Darkness murmured.

"You're upset. I know you were worried. I get that and I'm sorry." Dana wanted to defuse the situation. "We overslept or I would have been back before you woke up. Mour—"

"You slept with him?" Paul lowered his head to stare at her clothes. He paled, and then jerked his gaze up. "You just slept, right?" He jerked out of Becky's hold. "Did he fuck you? Tell me you didn't let him touch you."

"Calm," Darkness ordered, his tone harsh.

"Did you let him have sex with you?" Paul reached for Dana.

Darkness suddenly hooked her around her waist and jerked her back against his body, retreating a few steps in the process. He snarled, the sound scary and menacing. "Don't touch her in anger."

"I wasn't going to hurt her." Paul let his hand drop. "That's my baby sister."

Darkness released her waist and stepped to her side, staying close. "You're the one acting crazy, Paul. She's a fully grown female who shared sex with Mourn. It was consensual. They are bonding and Mourn is moving into one of the cottages so they have a place to spend private time together. She's attempting to tell you that, but you won't allow her to speak."

Paul backed up and bumped into the island. He gawked at Dana. "Is that true?"

"I wouldn't have worded it just like that but yes. Mourn asked me to move in with him, but I told him I wasn't ready for that. We're going to spend more time together and see how that goes."

"Have you lost your mind?"

She could see how upset Paul was. She hated being the cause of it. "You wouldn't understand."

"You're right. I don't. He's the last person you should get involved with. He's emotionally unstable. I know you feel sorry for him, but this is taking it way too far."

She'd just dropped a bomb on them so she was willing to forgive Paul for being a bit of an ass. She could even understand why he'd be upset, but she needed to rectify his last statement.

"Stop right there. I don't feel sorry for Mourn. I actually really care about him. I haven't felt anything for anyone since Tommy." She paused, shifting her gaze to include Becky as she glanced between them. "Mourn makes me *feel*. I know it's irrational and a few days ago I'd probably be thinking what you are. You don't know him the way I do. He talks to me. I can open up to him too. He also wouldn't hurt me. I trust him. He's sweet and really wonderful, Paul. I don't know how to explain this so you'll understand, but I want to give a relationship with Mourn a try."

The silence in the room was terrible. Dana could see Paul's anger.

"You don't know what it's like to watch someone you love die, or the kind of pain that comes with it. I put on a brave face and tell people that time heals all. That's bullshit, Paul. There's this gaping hole inside me. I exist every day with just the hope that I'm going to feel something besides the loss and loneliness that has become my life. For the first time, I wanted to be touched by someone. I slept without dreaming about Tommy or waking up to the realization that he's dead. It's like reliving that loss over and over, ripping off a scab and making it bleed again. I opened my eyes this morning to Mourn holding me. I wasn't alone. I didn't even think about Tommy until now. Do you know how wonderful that was? How great?"

Tears filled Paul's eyes. "Dana, I'm sorry. Why didn't you tell me what you were still going through?"

"I knew it would tear you up and there was nothing you could do to fix my problems. I realize I can get my heart broken if things don't work out with Mourn, but I'd rather try this than go home to the life I left behind. It sucked, Paul. Mom setting me up with every loser she could find made it worse. You think Mourn is nuts? At least he doesn't live in his mother's basement, or give our mother pelvic exams."

"What?"

She glanced back at Darkness's horrified expression. "It's a long story but trust me, you don't want to know." She faced Paul again. "I don't expect you to be overjoyed, or anything. I want to get to know Mourn better and see if we can be happy together. I need to do this, hell, I want to do this. I'm taking a big risk, but guess what? It's living instead of just existing. I'm scared and nervous that this could be a disaster, but I'm also excited to see where it leads. I'm pretty sure that I'm falling in love with him."

Becky walked over to Dana and hugged her. "We support you."

Paul still didn't look thrilled, but the anger had drained out of him. "I will kill him if he hurts you."

"Fair enough," Darkness stated. "I'm going to arrange for Mourn to get new living quarters and make phone calls to explain this situation. I take it that everything is fine here now?"

"Yeah. Thanks, Darkness." Paul nodded at him.

Becky released Dana and Paul hugged her next. He held her close and sighed.

"I worry. That's all. Couldn't you have picked anyone besides Mourn?"

"No." She held onto him. "We're a lot alike."

"Why are your clothes damp? Do I even want to know?"

Dana laughed at Paul's question. "This was Mourn's attempt to seduce me. You asked."

He groaned, eased his hold on her, and stepped back. "These guys aren't normal. I'll forget I'm your big brother for the moment, but I'm a nurse. Are you okay? Did he hurt you in any way? Bite?"

Becky gasped. "Shit. I forgot about that. Did he bite you? That means he wants to mate you. They mark their territory."

"Mourn wouldn't bite me. He didn't hurt me at all."

"It's not to mark territory. I think it's more like getting a taste of their mate's blood."

Dana gave him a dirty look. "You're just saying that to scare me."

He crossed his arms over his chest. "No. That's a New Species trait and it's classified. They aren't fully human. They get those urges. He might bite you at some point. The good news is, he'll be careful not to tear your skin with his fangs. Just don't fight him if it happens. Hold still. Promise me."

She nodded, hoping he was full of shit. She'd seen Mourn's fangs. They were big, like everything else on him.

Paul suddenly tensed. "Tell me he used condoms."

Dana shook her head.

"Son of bitch!" Paul shouted, and stomped across the room. He punched the wall. "I'm going to kill him."

"Calm down, honey." Becky left Dana's side to rush to her husband. She grabbed his fist and inspected it.

He jerked out of his wife's hold, glaring at Dana. "Don't let him touch you without a condom."

"I highly doubt Mourn gave me a sexual disease. He's only been with his mate. I know *I* don't have anything. I only had sex with Tommy. He didn't have any STDs."

"Species don't carry STDs. They are immune. Just use condoms from now on if you insist on letting that bastard touch you, okay?" He looked furious. "I need to get out of here. I can't talk." He marched to the front door, yanked it open, and slammed it behind him.

Dana winced. "He didn't take that well."

Becky came back to stand in front of her. "He likes to take walks when he's really upset, but he usually kisses me goodbye first." Becky looked at the door sadly and then back at Dana. "He just wants to protect you."

Dana sighed. "I knew he wouldn't be thrilled to find out about Mourn, but I didn't expect him to storm out."

"He'll be back once he cools down and has time to wrap his mind around this. Are you okay? You look upset too."

"I didn't come to Homeland expecting to meet someone. I'm having a tough enough time coming to grips with this sudden relationship with Mourn. I didn't need Paul to blow up like that."

"You wanted a little emotional support and understanding," Becky guessed. "I'm happy for you."

That helped. "Thank you."

"Paul is right about the condoms though. Apply that no glove, no love rule."

"Why?"

"Paul has a lot of secrets he has to keep from me about New Species. I never press because he gave his word to the NSO not to repeat anything he learns about them. I do however read and watch TV. There's a rumor that their genetics can be transferred to humans via sex," Becky whispered. She suddenly grinned. "You might grow fangs if that's true. They interviewed some doctor with a long list of credentials and he thinks that's possible."

Dana didn't buy it.

Becky shrugged. "I didn't tell Paul about that show, because he's asked me to avoid that kind of stuff. He gets really angry when they write about, or do shows concerning New Species. Some of it is total bullshit. One of those talk shows interviewed some of the local residents who live a few blocks from Homeland. They were worried that the NSO would kill them in their sleep so their homes would go on the market after what is happening at Reservation."

"Why would they think that?"

Becky pulled her over to the couch and they sat. "Reservation is expanding. They've bought up some properties next to their borders. Keep in mind that Reservation is in a little town up north and most of the properties they are buying are usually fifty-plus acres. The Wild Zone started taking in rescue animals. You know how some people get illegal animals like bears and lions as pets, but then they get too big to care for? Reservation takes them in. The zoos can only accept so many of them and there aren't a lot of rescue places that can handle those types of large animals. Anyway, some of the properties came on the market so the NSO bought them. They offered to buy anyone's land that adjoins Reservation and they pay well over market price. Idiots around here think the NSO might force them to sell by any means necessary, but it's stupid. They don't plan to expand Homeland and they wouldn't hurt anyone unless they had no choice. You know, like in self-defense."

"Those people sound paranoid."

"They are. The NSO would never intimidate or force people to sell their homes. That's bullshit." Becky faced her. "You do realize there could be some fallout if anyone finds out you're dating Mourn, don't you? That's probably part of the reason Paul is so upset."

"I know. I do see the news and am aware of the stories about women who were attacked because of their associations with the NSO."

"There's also the issue of your mom. Paul is probably thinking about that too. It's one thing for her to tell her friends that her son works for a nonprofit organization overseas, but what would she say about you? She's used to him not being around. You're her baby. She's not going to like it if you and Mourn get serious. It would mean you'd live here and she couldn't keep you close."

"I'll cross that bridge when I get there."

Becky grimaced. "I don't envy you."

Dana dreaded the thought. "Me neither."

"Are you okay?" Becky studied her. "How do you feel about spending the night with a man? This was your first time, right?"

"Since Tommy, you mean? Yes. I thought it would be a really uncomfortable situation, but it wasn't." She felt a little heat rise in her cheeks.

"You enjoyed it a lot." Becky grinned. "I've heard New Species have some serious bedroom skills. I'll take that as fact."

"I don't want to go into details. Should I not stay here? I don't want to make Paul uncomfortable. Mourn asked me to move in with him. I don't think I'm quite ready for that yet, but I'd hate to overstay my welcome."

"You're fine. Paul will calm down. Our home is yours for as long as you want to stay at Homeland."

Dana rose to her feet. "I should shower."

"Are you hungry?"

"Starving."

"I'll make you something."

"Thank you."

Becky stood. "I'm happy for you, Dana."

"Thanks." She returned to the guest bedroom.

* * * * *

Mourn wished that Dana had agreed to live with him, but they'd get to spend more time together. Darkness had texted him right after he'd gone on shift that he'd secured couples housing for him. Mourn planned to stop by the men's dorm after work to grab the two duffle bags he'd packed, pick up food from the bar, and go get Dana. It made him smile, thinking about seeing her soon.

He exited one of the buildings and came to a halt when he spotted Paul leaning up against his Jeep. The male didn't look pleased, but he'd obviously sought him out. Mourn stifled a snarl, but couldn't keep the anger out of his voice. "I promised Dana I wouldn't fight you. Don't attack me, Paul."

"I'm not the suicidal bastard. That's you."

"Did you come to threaten me to stay away from Dana?"

"I would if I thought it would do any good." Paul shook his head. "She made it clear that she is set on getting to know you better." Paul reached behind him and Mourn growled, prepared to defend himself if the male had a weapon.

Paul withdrew a package that he'd stashed under the back of his shirt, and held it out. "Take this." He tossed it.

Mourn caught it and looked at the large padded envelope. "What is it?"

"Condoms. I wasn't going to walk around searching for you with a clearly marked box. I put a few dozen of them inside. I can't stop you from seeing Dana, but I'll be damned if I'm going to allow you to get her pregnant. She has no idea that can happen, and I know you can't tell her because she's not your mate. Don't ever touch my sister again without wearing one. Am I clear?"

"I wasn't aware you knew about the children."

Paul snorted. "Of course I do. I work with Trisha. They tried to hide it from me at first, but I'm not a moron. She'd never cheat on Slade. I knew as soon as she got pregnant who that baby belonged to and I also could figure out why it's classified. I'm not going to let you trap my sister into mating to you because you knocked her up. It's not like she can leave here with your baby. The NSO wouldn't allow it, because of the danger to her and the baby."

Mourn glanced down at the package, then back at Paul. "Thank you."

"Do you know how to use them?"

Mourn shook his head.

Paul cursed, spun around and put his hands on the hood of the Jeep. "This is so messed up." He turned around. "Ask someone. I can't even go there. She's my sister. It was hard enough bringing you those, knowing you need them because of what you plan to do with her. You hurt her and I'll make you pay. You come into Medical often enough. Remember that. You lay a finger on her in anger and I'll get even. You'll wake up in a full body cast. That's way worse than restraints. Am I clear?"

"I would never hurt Dana."

"Don't break her heart either. Are you sure you are serious about her? She's not like your females, Mourn. They can have sex with a guy and be your friend. She takes that shit very *non* casually. Do you understand?"

"I would mate her if she would say yes."

"I don't want to hear that. She needs someone who has his shit together and that's not you. Dana has been through hell and back. The last thing she needs is to have to take care of another guy on his way out of life. Did she tell you she was going to be a nurse like me until Tommy was diagnosed with cancer?"

Mourn shook his head.

"Hospitals remind her of all he endured so now she works in an office. My mom told me Dana would be all smiles in front of Tommy, reassuring him it was all great and good. Our mother found her one day in the garage hiding behind some boxes. She couched there sobbing. That's the kind of person she is. She was ripped to shreds inside, but hid it from her husband because she always put his needs first. Don't do that to her, Mourn. Don't make her be strong for you and help you deal with your shit. She's got plenty of her own that she can barely withstand."

It tore at Mourn, hearing of Dana's suffering. "I won't. We're helping each other."

"Are you sure about that?" Paul stepped closer, studying his face. "She needs someone who is going to take care of her, not the other way around. Just think about that. If you can't be that man, get the hell away from her."

Mourn watched Paul walk down the sidewalk, grateful the male hadn't come to fight him. He glanced down at the package in his hand and sighed. He'd have to ask someone how to use condoms. He climbed into the Jeep and went to the next building on his rounds. He spotted Jinx talking to a female who was picking up mail. He walked up to them.

"May I speak to you?"

Jinx excused himself from the other Species. "Sure." He walked outside and turned.

Mourn closed the door and held his gaze. "What do you know about condoms?"

The male's eyebrows shot up. "What?"

"I need someone to tell me how to use them. Did you take the class, or have you used them before?"

Jinx nodded. "Yeah. I take it that the rumors going around about you and Paul's sister are true?"

"Yes. We are spending time together."

"Let's go to the bar. Christmas keeps some bananas on hand to make shakes. It is a good way to teach you how to put one on. We'll need to go to my place first so I can grab a few condoms."

"I have condoms in my Jeep."

"Okay. Let's go."

Chapter Seven

Dana was nervous. Paul hadn't returned all day so she figured he must be avoiding her. Becky kept glancing at the door too.

"Your date is late. It's almost five o'clock."

"Mourn was going to pick up food first. He'll be here."

Becky grinned. "You sound pretty certain."

"I am." She had no qualms that Mourn would show.

"How exciting."

Dana arched her eyebrows.

"The whole dating thing." Becky chuckled. "I kind of miss that. I wish Paul would take me out on dates, but the only real place to go is the bar. That gets kind of old after a while. We never leave Homeland anymore."

"Does that bother you?"

"Not really. We used to go out occasionally, but it wasn't worth the hassle. There's always some idiots hanging out around the exits, even at the back gates. They shout at us and try to take pictures. We were once followed. Paul turned right around and brought us back. He couldn't shake them, and didn't know what they wanted or who they were. He wasn't willing to risk me being in danger."

"I'm sorry that happened."

"It's part of living here. We disguise ourselves with wigs and dark glasses when we do leave in case someone does take photos. Employees have access to the NSO-registered vehicles. That way our identities are protected and our families are safe."

"Wow. I had no idea."

"It was fun at first. I felt like a super spy." Becky laughed. "We changed clothes and got out of costume after we made sure it was safe, and then we'd have dinner or whatever we had planned to do. Afterward we'd change back before we returned. Then they started following us so it wasn't fun anymore."

"It sounds like a pain."

Becky shrugged. "It was worth it. I don't really have much family that I'm close to, but Paul worries about you and your mom. No one has ever shown up at your door asking about Paul and the NSO, have they?"

"No."

The doorbell rang and Dana sprang off the couch, excited. She rushed to the door and jerked it open. Mourn stood there with flowers in hand and a big grin.

"Hi. Are these appropriate?"

She took the roses. "Thank you. Yes. They are beautiful."

Becky held out her hands. "I'll go find a vase and put them in your room. Go. Have fun. We'll leave the door unlocked for you." She smiled at Mourn. "She doesn't have a curfew so she's all yours until she's ready to come home. Don't do anything I wouldn't. It's a short list." She winked at Dana. "Why do you think your brother married me?"

Dana laughed and handed over the flowers. She stepped outside with Mourn and closed the door behind her. "How was your day?"

"Good. How was yours?" He led her to a Jeep parked at the curb.

"Okay. Paul kind of blew a fuse, but he'll come around. Becky and I spent the day watching TV and talking."

He helped her into the passenger seat and rounded the Jeep to climb into the driver's seat. She turned her head, spotting two large duffle bags in the back, and a box placed between them to keep it from moving around. The smell of food reached her nose so she guessed what was inside. She looked back at Mourn.

"Where are we going?"

"To my new home. I haven't toured it yet. We can do it together."

"It sounds fun."

"I made sure Darkness didn't put me back where I used to live."

She nodded. "I understand."

"I wanted a place for us without memories. He said it's a different layout. I'm not certain what that means." He checked for traffic and pulled away from the curb.

"The same builder probably constructed the homes, but they have different floor plans. It won't be a duplicate of the home you once had."

He nodded, paying attention to his driving. "Don't be nervous."

"I'm not. Are you?"

He glanced her way. "A little."

"Why?"

"I want to convince you to live with me. I'm afraid I'll do or say something that will scare you away."

He was so sweet and she appreciated his candor. "Relax. It's just me. No pressure, remember?"

He smiled. "I really want you to sleep with me tonight. Think about staying."

She smiled too, and watched as they left the cottages, traveled down a road, and eventually came to another gate. The guard manning the shack stepped outside to meet them. Mourn slowed to a stop next to the large New Species.

"Hello, Mourn." He looked at Dana. "Hello, Paul's sister. You both are expected. You want to take the first left and it's the second cottage on the right. It's painted light gray. Supply has already come by to stock it for you. Welcome back, Mourn." He turned and pressed a button inside the shack, opening the gate.

Mourn thanked him and drove up a hill. Dana couldn't help but appreciate the slightly bigger homes. "It's so clean and nice. The homes here are spaced farther apart than where Paul lives."

"We take pride in our homes and their appearances." Mourn turned and parked in a driveway. "This is Species housing. Paul lives in human housing. There are more homes there. Homeland was built originally to be a military base. It was still being constructed when we were freed so they were able to redesign some of it to meet our needs. I heard that these were built for officers and high-ranking military personnel. Paul lives in an area meant for enlisted families. The dorms were created to include multiple apartments meant for privacy instead of large rooms to house many of us together."

"I didn't know that. I can't believe the government handed this place over to the NSO."

"They had their reasons." He got out, rounded the Jeep, and helped her out.

"Are you allowed to say why? I'm curious."

He held her gaze. "It's confidential, but not classified. I'll tell you. I know you won't share our secrets. They funded Mercile without knowledge of us. It would have been bad if that had come out. Your people might have been upset that their tax dollars helped create us and keep us imprisoned. The president apologized and gave us Homeland."

She inwardly flinched. That information would have caused a blood bath in the press. "It was a bribe."

He shrugged. "We were grateful. We have a home and don't have to live in the human world. I was told that was a fear when Species were first released. It would have put us in great danger if we'd been separated. The humans took the original survivors to remote motel locations to protect them and divided them up. They were given counseling and knowledge of the world outside of Mercile. Justice represented us and negotiated with the president for Homeland. Let's go inside and look at our home. I'll come back for the bags and food in a minute."

She noticed his use of the word our, but didn't comment on it. "Is it okay to just leave this stuff here?" She glanced around, not seeing anyone on the sidewalks or street. "You left the keys in the ignition."

"Species don't steal from each other. We have no crime." Mourn took her hand and they walked to the front door. He opened it and allowed her to enter first.

Dana openly appreciated the new furnishings. It was tastefully done in desert colors of soft browns, creams, and light-red hues. The living room was large with vaulted ceilings. A dining room was tucked to the left side and she could spot the kitchen through a wide archway.

"Do you like it?"

"I do."

He seemed to relax finally. "Good. Let's view the rest of it."

She liked that he still held her hand as they entered the kitchen. He paused. She did too, taking it in. "Nice."

"There will be food in the pantry, fridge and freezer. Supply will have also stocked the bathrooms with everything we'll need. They also will have put fresh linens on the beds."

"They do that?"

He nodded. "Every home comes furnished and ready to live in. We can't shop the way you can. We text a list of things we need to Supply and they can either drop it off the next day, or we can go pick it up ourselves."

"No grocery shopping?"

He shook his head. "We have no grocery store. We have Supply. They get daily deliveries from the out world."

"It's nice that they set up homes for people to live in."

"It's more efficient. We like that."

"Who doesn't?" She grinned.

They strolled down a hallway and checked out both bedrooms. He took her into the large master bedroom and stopped, holding her gaze. "This will be our bedroom if you will consent to live with me."

"No pressure, remember?"

"Is it nice enough? I had a lot of time to think today. You said your male bought you your dream home. We'd have to live at Homeland if you move in with me."

The sad look on his face made her regret telling him that. "It's very nice. I could live here if we become that serious."

"I want to be able to care for you as well as your mate did."

He made her ache a little because he was so concerned about her. "I'll tell you a secret."

"Please do."

"We didn't really enjoy that house much. Tommy's dad had a massive heart attack and died right after we graduated high school. Tommy had planned to go to college. We both had. Instead we took over the company and had to learn everything really fast. He needed my help, and that's why I'm so good with office work. We had a quickie wedding and bought the house, but we weren't home much those first few years.

When he reached the point that he could handle it all on his own, I started nursing school. We led very busy lives until Tommy was diagnosed with cancer. He sold the business before he had surgery and the chemo started for the second time. He had a really rough time of it. It was an aggressive cancer so the treatments were too. It was tough," she admitted.

Mourn released her hand and put his arm around her, leading her to the bed. They sat. "I'm sorry."

"I'm just telling you this because not all of my memories there are great ones. Our dreams died with Tommy."

Mourn surprised her when he suddenly lifted her up and placed her on his lap. She only hesitated for a moment before she wrapped her arms around his neck. They gazed at each other.

"I don't catch colds. We have really good immune systems. Species don't have any hereditary diseases. Mercile was able to delete them when they created our DNA...us. No Species has ever had cancer."

Mourn regretted saying that as soon as he saw the tears in her eyes. "I'm sorry. I didn't mean to cause you pain. I don't want you to ever worry about that. I won't get sick the way your mate did."

"I'm glad you said that. I never want to go through something that horrible again."

He held her tighter. "You won't." He wanted to distract her. "I'm stronger than a human. I growl and purr. I can roar if I'm highly angry or upset." He considered their differences. "You've probably noticed my

134

fangs, and the tips of my fingers and my nails." He showed her his hand. "My feet are the same."

She lowered her arms and examined one of his hands. "I didn't notice. I just thought you had calluses when you were touching me." She ran her soft fingertip across one of the pads. He liked her exploring him.

"I'm faster and I can leap, unlike a human."

"Leap?"

"Felines are good jumpers. I could leap onto the roof if I needed to."

She appeared a little stunned by that. "That's kind of cool. You won't need a ladder to clean out the gutters and drains."

He was glad that she accepted it with humor. "There's something else I need to tell you. I don't want any lies between us, Dana. No secrets. You're not my mate, but I want you to be. It's classified information, but I trust you will keep the secret. I might be able to get you pregnant."

Her lips parted and her surprise was clear. She said nothing.

"Justice said your people wouldn't react well if they found out we have children. I think he's right. Species can't breed together, but some of the mated pairs with human females have had babies."

She seemed to recover. "Now it makes sense."

"What does?"

"Paul ordered me to use condoms if we have sex. He was really upset after he found out we hadn't used any last night. He asked. Why wouldn't Paul just tell me that?"

"He's loyal to the NSO and promised he wouldn't. I'm not even supposed to tell you this until we're mated, but I want you to know that we could have a family if we're mated. It's possible. I'm worried that you'll reject me because you think we can't have babies." He paused. "Are you angry? I should have mentioned that last night but it didn't cross my mind."

She released his hand and reached down, placing a hand over her stomach. He watched her face, wondering what she was thinking. He didn't have long to wait.

"I'm not on anything." She lifted her gaze, staring at him. "That means—"

"I know. I'm sorry if you're upset. I didn't mean to put you at risk. I didn't think about it until today when your brother accused me of trying to get you pregnant on purpose. That's not true."

"Paul what?"

"He sought me out today. I thought he wanted to start a fight, but he brought me condoms."

She frowned. "I'm sorry he did that."

"No. I'm glad he did. I didn't think about being able to get you pregnant. I was more worried that you'd be afraid of me, or that I'd do something wrong since you're human. I asked a male today how to use them. He took me to the bar to teach me."

Her eyes widened. "What?"

"He got a banana from behind the bar and used it to show me how to put them on."

She surprised him by laughing. "I wish I could have seen that. How did it go?"

"Good. I think I can do it, despite not being shaped that way. I understood the concept. Why did you look so strange when I first said Jinx took me to the bar?"

"I thought you might have gone there to pick up a woman and have sex with her."

He growled. "You're the only female I want. Why would you think that?"

"Guys go to bars to pick up women to have sex with them."

"I'm not a guy. The bar is for eating, dancing, and socializing. I would never share sex with another female, Dana. Species don't cheat."

"I'm sure some do."

He shook his head. "None have. You've never seen mates together, have you?"

"No."

"You'd understand if you did. A mate bond is very strong. There is talk that we become addicted to our females' scent and none other will do. No other females tempted me when I had a mate, despite the fact that she wasn't able to share sex with me."

"I'm not the cheating type either."

"I knew that."

She let go of her stomach. "I could be pregnant."

"I don't think you are. I've scented ovulating human females before and don't smell it on you. Does that disturb you?"

"Not really. That just falls into the category of things I never thought someone would say to me."

He chuckled. "We'll take precautions from now on if you wish. I have the condoms Paul gave me. I would be happy if you had my baby, but I know you aren't ready for that yet." He tensed. "The food. We haven't eaten." He lifted her off his lap and they stood. "Let me go get our dinner. We'll eat."

"I am hungry."

He took her hand and they walked to the living room. He released her. "I'll be right back."

"I'll find plates and things."

"Thank you."

He exited the house and strode to the Jeep. His mind was on Dana as he leaned over and hooked a strap of the duffle bag that was closest to him on his shoulder, and slung it over his back. He lifted the box and spun, returning to the house. He dropped the duffle bag inside and used his foot to close the door. He could get the other bag later. He joined Dana in the kitchen.

She had put plates on the island and found the silverware. He put the box down and removed the sealed containers with their dinners. He watched Dana move to the fridge and open it.

"Wow. They really packed this. What do you want to drink? It seems they gave us about everything. There's milk, sodas, iced tea, juice and bottled waters."

"I like soda."

She removed two cans and came to him. He studied her face to see if she was upset about the possibility of being pregnant. He wouldn't blame her if she was angry. She didn't look it though. She smiled and took a seat on one of the barstools. He passed her the fried chicken dinner and rounded the counter to take a seat next to her with his own container. They were silent as they transferred the food onto plates.

It was a comfortable silence as they ate. He'd never seen someone use a knife and fork to cut fried chicken. He'd have eaten it with his fingers. It made him consider their differences. Mourn had so many things he wanted to ask Dana and discuss with her but he waited until she stopped eating. She couldn't finish it all but she wasn't a large human.

"What is that odd look for?" She drew him from his thoughts.

He chuckled. "The way you eat is amusing."

"Why?"

He shook his head. "It's just cute."

She tucked her head, but smiled. Mourn longed to reach out and touch her. He held back, not wanting to do anything that might make her withdraw from him. He finished his dinner and stood, taking their plates to the sink. Dana came up behind him as he rinsed them.

"Do you need help?"

"I have a lot of experience at this. Why don't you take a seat on the couch? I'll be there in a moment."

She moved away and he finished cleaning up. He found her on the couch and sat down close. "We could watch a movie. There are some left on the shelf by the last couple who lived here." He'd noticed them earlier.

Dana surprised him by turning to face him. She grabbed his hand and peered up at him with a worried look. "Did my brother upset you? He was out of line."

"I wasn't upset. I'm just glad I didn't have to physically restrain him."

"He shouldn't have done that. I'm sorry."

"You're apologizing again for what others do." He leaned in and touched her, lightly caressing her arm. "I know you come with family, Dana. I considered that before I attempted to become more than your friend."

She hesitated. "I worried the NSO would be upset with me because we spent last night together. Darkness set me straight on that."

"Why would they be upset?"

"You know, like I took advantage by having sex with you."

He laughed.

"That's exactly how Darkness reacted."

"You're thinking like a human. You couldn't make me do anything I didn't want to do. They are more worried about what I might do to you."

"You're not like that Vengeance guy you told me about."

"No, I'm not. I am so glad you're here with me."

"I am too. I enjoy our time together."

He studied her features. "Are you willing to consider moving to Homeland and living with me if you learn that I'm your male?"

"I wish I had your confidence in us working out long-term."

"You will."

She broke eye contact and leaned back on the couch, out of his reach. "That's so not fair."

His shoulders sagged. "I know it's asking a lot for you to give up your world for mine but I'd do everything to make you happy, Dana."

"I understand why we'd have to live here. That's not what I was talking about." She twisted to face him, but kept back. "You make me want to do crazy things when you look at me like that and your voice gets husky."

"I don't understand."

"I want to say yes. I'm trying to stay rational and not make a mistake."

"We are not a mistake."

"You know what I mean."

He scooted closer until his hip pressed against her leg. "I'm not going to change my mind about us, Dana. I won't regret asking you to be mine. I want you to be my mate. I won't leave you. I'm the one who worries that you'll do that to me."

Her expression softened. "I don't want to hurt you in any way, Mourn."

"Then agree to be my mate, move to Homeland and stay with me."

"I…" She seemed to falter for words.

"You need assurances that we'll be good together. I plan to convince you." He stood and held out his hand. "Come with me."

"Where are we going?" She allowed him to pull her to her feet.

"To our bedroom."

Her eyebrows arched, but she didn't jerk away from him.

He smiled. "I'm going to show you how good we can be together, Dana. I've thought all day about the things I want to do to you once I strip you naked. I'll do much better than what we shared last night."

"Now you're really not playing fair."

"I'm Species. I go after what I want and that's you."

Chapter Eight

Dana waited in the bedroom while Mourn ran outside to retrieve the condoms. She wanted him, but their relationship was so new that she worried sex would be uncomfortable between them. The first time might have been a fluke. He returned quickly, an eager look on his face.

She couldn't help but laugh. He closed the door and paused to toss a large padded envelope on the bed. He bent and tore at his work boots. Dana hovered near the dresser, watching him. "In a hurry?"

He straightened. "I'll slow down."

"Now I'm nervous," she admitted.

"There's no reason to be." He walked right up to her and gently gripped her upper arms. "I'll be gentle." He caressed her skin with his thumbs. "Didn't you enjoy it when I put my mouth between your thighs?"

The memory flashed through her mind and she nodded. "Yes."

"Remove your clothes. No pressure. Just let me touch you, Dana. I'll stop if you don't enjoy it. I will never make you do anything you don't want."

"I guess I'm kind of worried that all we'll have is sex."

He cocked his head. "I don't understand."

"You know, like our relationship is solely going to be based on sex."

"We talk and enjoy spending time together. I'm hoping I can convince you, with sex, to be my mate. I'm determined to learn everything about you. Do you want to return to the living room? We don't have to share sex. We could talk, or watch one of the movies."

She felt torn. "I want you. I'm just trying to stall taking off my clothes. It's bright in here."

He frowned. "The lights bother you?"

"I look better in dimmer lighting."

"Is this a human thing?"

She laughed. "I guess so."

"I like you naked. You're beautiful, Dana."

She just decided to be blunt. "Your women are kind of muscular and I'm not. I saw a bunch of them at the bar when Paul and Becky took me there. They look like fitness models."

His expression softened. "I'm attracted to you. Not them."

His words helped a lot. He released her and backed away. "Do you want to go into the living room?"

She shook her head. She did want him.

He started to remove his uniform. "I'll strip first. Perhaps that will make you feel more comfortable."

He was really sweet. She couldn't look away as he pulled off his shirt and then peeled the undershirt he wore over his head. The bandage on his arm was gone and the stitches were out. It had just left a red mark. His ability to heal quickly still impressed her. She shifted her gaze and admired the sight of his broad shoulders and chest, and all the muscles revealed down his stomach. He unfastened his belt, slowly pulling it through the loops of his pants. He tossed it to the floor and reached for the front of his pants. He kept his gaze locked on her the entire time.

"I'm aroused," he warned.

She hadn't really gotten a good look at him the night before and had avoided glancing at him while they'd gotten dressed in the shed. He pulled down his pants first. The outline of his rigid cock stretched the fabric of the tight black boxer briefs he wore. He kicked the pants away and hooked his thumbs in the shorts, slowly easing them down.

He was absolutely breathtaking and amazing. Her gaze lingered on his erection. She swallowed hard. Mourn was big all over. Her gaze lifted when he kicked the shorts away and just stood still. He watched her with those remarkable eyes, but then turned and walked to the bed. She appreciated the view of his well-formed, muscular ass. He took a seat on the bed and leaned back to rest his upper body on his bent elbows.

"Do you want to join me?"

Her hands trembled a little as she began to strip. "Yes."

He smiled. "We'll take it very slow. I don't want to startle you."

She kept on her bra and panties, and climbed onto the bed next to him. He held still, just peering at her. She settled on her side, keeping some space between them. She lifted her hand, but paused over his chest.

"Please touch me," he rasped.

It was sexy when his voice deepened that way, and she saw passion in his eyes. When she glanced at his lap, the evidence of his desire for her was unmistakable. His cock was really hard. She lowered her hand and splayed it on his chest. He eased back until he lay flat and placed his hands beneath his head.

"That feels so good," he encouraged. "Am I less threatening on my back this way?"

She grew bolder, changed positions, sat cross-legged next to him, put both hands on him, and explored his chest and lower stomach. His cock jerked when her fingers slid closer. A low growl rumbled from him and she looked at his face. She froze because he almost looked angry with his fangs showing and his lips parted.

"What's wrong?"

"Nothing. I just want to touch you too, Dana. May I?"

"Yes."

He moved fast, sat up and turned. He slowed his motions then, reaching for her. He helped ease back to lie flat. He got off the bed and slid his hands under the back of her thighs. He tugged her toward the edge and just dropped to his knees, spreading her legs so he fit between them. Mourn leaned forward, half on top of her, and studied her bra. He growled.

"What?"

"How do you get this off?"

She laughed. It proved he wasn't a womanizer. She reached up with both hands and found the front clasp, popping it open. She spread the cups off her breasts and twisted a bit to remove the straps, easing the rest of it from under her back to throw it out of the way.

Her amusement died quickly when Mourn lunged forward and his hot, wet mouth latched onto her nipple. She gasped at the sudden strong tugs. It didn't hurt. It instantly sent sensations straight to her clit as if they were linked by nerves. She gripped his shoulders, kneading them just to have something to cling to and anchor her.

He nipped her beaded nipple with his teeth and she felt his fangs, but they didn't break the skin. *So much for taking it slow.* She didn't mind though. His arm slid under her lower back and he jerked her hips closer to his. It put his rock-hard cock against her panties. He ground it against her pussy, rubbing her clit through the thin material that separated them. She moaned and lifted her legs, hooking them around his hips.

He released her breast and went for the other.

"Oh god," she moaned.

He stopped sucking her nipple and lifted his head. She stared into his eyes.

"You're very religious. Do you want to get married? Would that make sharing sex more comfortable for you?"

She laughed. "I'm not. Very religious, that is."

"You keep saying that when I'm touching you."

"I'm enjoying it. It's just what I say."

"I wish you'd use my name."

"I'll try to remember that, but you make thinking impossible when you're touching me."

He grinned, revealing his fangs. "I understand." He lifted up a bit and put a few inches of space between their bodies. "Do you care if I remove the rest of your clothing?"

She shook her head and eased the grip of her legs, where she held him against her. She expected him to back off and help her wiggle out of her panties but he surprised her when he reached for the straps on each side of her hips and just tore them apart. He yanked the material away.

He reached back and gripped her ankles, parting them and shoving her knees up. He lowered farther down her body and buried his face between her thighs. Dana threw her head back and her lips parted as his mouth attacked her clit.

She squeezed her eyes shut. There was no description for the way he tongued and sucked on that bundle of nerves. He wasn't gentle or slow. He began to purr and snarl, adding very strong vibrations into the mix. Dana clawed at the bedding. Moans tore from her. It felt amazing and was too intense. She attempted to slam her knees closed, but Mourn held her down and open. He was merciless until the climax brutally tore through her. She cried out his name.

He backed off and released her legs. She panted, opening her eyes. Mourn reached out, snagged the large envelop, and ripped the top off with his teeth. He turned his head and spit out the paper, and then dumped the contents on the bed next to her. She almost laughed at the number of condom strips that came spilling out. She might have if she hadn't seen the look on his face. It alarmed her and she struggled to sit up.

"What's wrong?"

"I want you," he snarled. He picked up a strip, tore a condom off, and then tried to open it. His hands shook and he dropped it, cursing.

She reached into the pile and pulled out a strip. "Let me."

He was breathing hard, but she realized he wasn't angry. He was just really turned-on. Her body felt sluggish and sated after having her mind blown, but one glance at his cock assured that her that he still wanted her bad. The skin had reddened a bit and it pulsed as if it had a heartbeat. She figured it was a Species thing. She used her teeth to tear the wrapper open and scooted to the edge of the bed.

She touched the slippery, lubricated condom and studied it. "I've never put one of these on before. Talk me through it."

"I'll do it." He seemed to have regained some control. "I just have to remember what side to press against the tip so it rolls on." He took it and examined it, reached down and put it on. He grimaced.

"What's wrong?"

"I don't like the feel of it."

"I'm sorry."

"It is fine. You don't want to get pregnant."

She thought back over the things he'd told her. "You said you can scent a woman when she's ovulating?"

He nodded. "Usually. Not always, but it's rare not to."

She studied his stiff cock. It looked uncomfortable for him to have to wear something so tight. "Take it off."

His eyebrows shot up.

"Do I smell like I'm ovulating?"

His nostrils flared. "No."

"Take it off."

"I won't put you at risk."

"I don't want you to be uncomfortable."

"I'll deal with it, to have you. We'll try this."

She eased back on the bed. "Okay."

He drew closer and maneuvered his hips between her thighs. She spread them wider, and he gripped his shaft, rubbing the latex-covered crown against her pussy. She was really wet as he teased her clit and slid lower to her vaginal opening. Mourn pressed in. She tried to relax as he entered her, but he was so big and thick. A soft groan came from him and he came down on top of her, braced his arms near her sides and captured her mouth with his, kissing her.

Mourn attempted to rein in his desire to take Dana hard and fast. She turned him on so much that it was difficult to find restraint. She made it more difficult when her fingernails raked down his back to his ass, and she grabbed hold of him to squeeze each cheek in her hands. Not even the condom could mute the pleasure of being sheathed inside her tight, warm, wet pussy. Her muscles squeezed around his dick.

She broke the kiss by turning her head. "Mourn," she moaned. "Yes! Faster."

He reached down and grabbed her hip, using his arm to pin her thigh against him as he drove into her more rapidly and a little more forcefully. She arched her back under him and he loved the sight of her taut nipples and bouncing breasts. He snarled, no longer holding back as he drove in and out of her. She felt too good. He clenched his teeth as he started to come. A white haze of rapture tore through his body and left him unable to think. She cried out his name loudly and her pussy milked his cock as she found her own release.

He collapsed on top of her but quickly remembered she was much smaller than he was. He feared his weight would make it difficult for her to breathe so he lifted up a little, released her hip and braced his arms on the bed. They both panted.

He couldn't look away from her face. She was beautiful while in the throes of passion, but even more so in the aftermath of what they'd shared. It made his chest hurt when she smiled at him and opened her eyes to stare back at him.

She's mine. Why can't she see that? We belong together. He cleared his throat, so many words wanting to spill out, but he hesitated, trying to think of the least alarming thing to say. She wasn't ready to mate him, or hear how he never wanted to live another day without her. He didn't want to frighten her off. "Stay the night with me."

She laughed. "You really aren't playing fair, Mourn. How can I say no after that?"

He felt relief. It would be so much better if she had agreed to be his mate, but he'd take it one day at a time. She was his until morning. Tomorrow he'd have to think of another way to get her to stay with him.

"Good."

She ran her hands over his body, exploring. He enjoyed the softness of them against his flesh more than anything he'd ever experienced. It soothed him and gave him a peaceful feeling. She didn't even seem to mind that he stayed on top of her, his dick snugly nestled into her body to keep them intimately linked. He could happily remain that way forever. There was nowhere else he wanted to be, nothing else he wanted to do. Dana gave him purpose and happiness.

It made him think of 139. He tried to push those thoughts away, but they haunted him. She had never smiled at him after they'd shared sex. She'd never been content to allow him to hold her the way Dana did. 139 would have pushed him away by now to separate them. She'd never stroked her hands over his body as if she enjoyed touching him.

Dana's smile faltered and she stopped stroking him. "What's wrong?"

He broke eye contact and leaned down, burying his face in her neck. He inhaled, loving her scent. "You matter so much to me, Dana."

She resumed caressing him. She even turned her head, pressing her cheek against his. She shifted her legs, wrapping them tighter around his hips, as if she hugged him with them to keep him close.

"You matter to me too. What made you look so sad?"

He shifted his arms closer to her sides and pinned her under him more firmly. He just wanted to hold her. "I don't want to tell you."

She twisted under him and put space between their faces. She gripped his cheeks and turned his head. He allowed it, meeting her gaze.

"You can talk to me about anything, Mourn. Remember?"

He nodded. "I need to remove this condom. Jinx said it's important to throw it away right after we share sex. Let me go and I'll be right back."

She released him and he withdrew his cock from her body. Thinking of 139 had softened him. He walked into the bathroom to dispose of the condom in the trash and washed his hands. He found Dana sitting up on the bed when he returned. He took a seat next to her. Both of them remained naked. He couldn't look at her though, instead he studied his hands.

"What is it?" She inched closer and surprised him by curling her bent knees around his hip, leaning in and putting her face in front of his. He lifted his gaze.

"I don't want you to replace 139. I want with you what I never had with her." He hoped she didn't become upset or angry at his words.

Dana looked confused.

He rushed on before she could speak. "There were things that weren't right between 139 and me. I am sorry I thought about that just now. I hope you aren't angry. I realized that what we share is better than what I had with her."

Dana pulled away and his shoulders sagged. He'd upset her. She'd leave and go home. Possibly refuse to see him anymore. It tore him up inside. She surprised him when she straddled his lap. He straightened and wrapped his arms around her as she settled her ass on his thighs. Her hands rested on his shoulders and she leaned in closer.

"I'm not angry."

"Have I hurt you because I spoke of 139?"

"No. Tommy and 139 were important to us. I'm just trying to understand what you mean. You can talk to me about her, Mourn. She was your mate. You're still grieving. So am I. We're going to think about them and I'd rather we be open about it. Wouldn't you?"

He nodded, holding her a little tighter.

"Tell me what you were thinking. We'll start there."

"I tried to be a good mate to her, but I failed. She didn't like me holding her. I like it that you do."

Dana lifted one hand and brushed her fingers through his hair. "I like you holding me. I don't think you failed, Mourn. Maybe she wasn't into cuddling. Some people aren't. That's nothing bad on you."

"She asked Destiny to hold her near the end."

Dana looked confused again. "Who is that?"

"He's a primate male nurse. He helped teach me how to care for her. He would come almost every day to check on her. She talked to him more than she ever did to me and she asked him to hold her as she died. It hurt me deeply, but it was what she wanted so I allowed him to lift her onto his lap and cradle her against his chest as she took her last breaths."

Dana paled, appearing shocked and horrified. "Mourn, I'm so sorry."

"Destiny said not to take it personally. She was on pain medication and not thinking clearly. He said it might have been instinctual for her to want to be held by another primate as she died."

"I'm sure he was right."

Mourn wouldn't lie to Dana. "He was being kind. There were other primates there. Some of the females had come to be with her. She didn't ask them to hold her. It was Destiny she reached for. Halfpint touched me by taking my hand. She fears males, but she must have seen how it hurt me, having to watch my mate die in another's arms."

"Who is Halfpint?"

"She's one of the Gifts. They bonded to 139. My mate was the only primate female rescued who wasn't a Gift."

"What's a gift?"

"Species who were created with domesticated, smaller animals and DNA from small humans. They were designed to be small and weak. They were to be given to the humans who invested a lot of money with Mercile Industries. They were gifted to them. Some thought of them as pets, others knew they weren't strong enough to fight back if...when they were sexually attacked. They kept them locked up inside their homes."

She looked horrified again.

He nodded. "Halfpint fears all males. She was heavily abused by the human who owned her. She still held my hand. That was comforting."

"I'm glad she was there for you."

He took a deep breath and blew it out. "We have total honesty, Dana. My mate never looked at me or touched me the way you do. I know you worry that I want you to take her place in my life, but I want more than what I had. I am truly happy when I'm with you. For the first time in my life."

She stroked his hair and leaned closer. "Oh, baby. I'm so sorry." Tears shimmered in her eyes.

"I know you can never say the same to me since you had a very close bond with your mate, but I hope that one day you will look at me and not wish it was him holding you instead."

"You're breaking my heart," she whispered. "Stop. Never say that again. That's not true. I have never wished he was here instead of you. Not once. You're Mourn. You're sweet and kind. You're the sexiest man I've ever met. There's no comparison. You make me happy and you make me feel alive. That's your doing. Do you understand?"

Her words helped, but they were being honest. "He was a good mate and you had no lack of anything with him."

She shook her head. "I wouldn't say that. I mean, he was good to me, but we had problems too, Mourn. Everyone does in a relationship."

"You're saying that to make me feel better."

"No. I'm not." She released his hair and put her hand back on his shoulder, holding his gaze. "Do you want to hear some of my marital problems?"

"You had some?"

"Everyone does." She paused. "Tommy always had to have things his way. He wasn't pushy or mean about it, but don't think he wouldn't use humor and a lot of cajoling to get me to agree to whatever he wanted. He insisted I be at his side at the company he ran, despite knowing I didn't want to work there. I had to put my career on hold. I resented it some, because I was always the one to bend and give in to what he wanted. He also liked to impress people and was very social. I didn't care what everyone thought. I'm also not outgoing. We sometimes had arguments about that. He'd just smile and tell me how much he loved me, that I'd make him happy if I tried a little harder to fit into the lifestyle he wanted. Sometimes that hurt me. Why didn't my happiness matter? I was downright miserable at times, but I had to smile and bear it because it was important to him. He figured if it was important to him, it had to be important to me too. That never went both ways though. I was aware of it, but I wanted our marriage to work."

"Did he ever abuse you, Dana?"

"No. Tommy wasn't like that. He never would have hit me, or anything along those lines. He was just kind of selfish about certain things. He would actually make jokes about it and he could be very charming to get me to stop being upset with him. Sometimes I resented that too. All his snobby friends ditched him as soon as they realized he wasn't going to beat the cancer the second time. I felt bad for him, Mourn. In the end he finally realized what was really important. That was us spending time together. He tried hard to make it up to me."

He stroked her back, wanting to comfort her. "At least he was human. I'm not. Does that bother you? You'd have to give up the world you live in to be with me. I'm asking too much and being selfish, aren't I?"

"No." She shook her head and smiled. "That's not being selfish. That's a necessity and it's beyond your control, Mourn. You can't exactly move into my house. Not to mention, I really enjoyed what we just did. You being New Species made mind-blowing oral sex happen. Did I tell you that you have the best body I've ever seen? You're beautiful in every sense of the word."

He chuckled, his mood lightening. "You like the purring."

"I do."

"I love your taste." He glanced down at her thighs, which were spread over his lap, and reached to stroke her pussy with his finger. He looked up, watching her face. "I'm grateful you enjoy my touch."

She bit her lower lip and her eyes narrowed. A soft moan came from her and he suddenly flipped her over onto her back. He spread her thighs and slid down her. She liked his mouth and he planned to show her how being his mate had its advantages.

"I could do this to you for hours." He used his tongue to play with her clit.

"Mourn," she rasped.

She was his female. He purred deeply and gripped her thighs to hold them open when she started to rock her hips against his mouth. He had her for the night and he planned to make it a memorable one.

Chapter Nine

Dana entered Paul's house, hoping he'd already left for work. She wasn't that lucky. He sat at the island on a barstool with his laptop open in front of him and a cup of coffee in hand. He turned his head and looked at her, then at the clock on the wall. His mouth tightened into a grim line as he glared at her.

"I probably should have called last night to say I was spending the night at Mourn's, but you knew where I was so you shouldn't have worried." She closed the door. "Where is Becky?"

"At the women's dorm. They are watching movies this morning. She would have taken you with her to meet everyone, but someone didn't come home all night."

Dana entered the kitchen and poured herself a cup of coffee She took the time to add creamer before she faced him. "Mourn told me you had a talk with him. Really, Paul? I'm an adult."

"I don't want you anywhere near him."

"At least he's not like that base tramp you brought to my wedding and dated for six months. How many of your service buddies had she slept with before she sank her hooks into you? She was looking for a soldier to marry. Any soldier. Didn't they warn you about those kinds of women when you signed up?"

"I wasn't going to marry her. I made that clear. That has nothing to do with this."

"It does. I didn't ride your ass for dating her or threaten her about what I'd do to her if she hurt you. You were an adult and knew her history. I gave you enough credit to be too smart to fall into that honey trap. Mourn actually cares about me."

Paul cursed. "I knew he'd tell you that I threatened him."

That pissed her off. "Actually, he didn't. I was just using that as an example of what I wanted to do to that woman but I resisted. You threatened him? Paul!" She glared at him.

He shrugged. "I'm trying to protect you."

She sipped her coffee so she wouldn't round the island and punch him. It was tempting. She set the mug down on the counter and took a few calming breaths. "I don't need you to do that. I appreciate it, but stay out of this."

He slid off the barstool. "I'm worried about you."

"I get that. It's why I haven't smacked you. I can't believe you threatened him."

"I had to talk to him about something important. You don't understand."

"You mean about using condoms so I don't get pregnant?"

His jaw dropped.

"He told me the truth. I won't repeat it. I only brought it up because we're alone in the house. Mourn is a good guy, Paul. I know what I'm getting into with him. I'll say it again. I feel things for him and I want to see if our relationship can work. Cut me some slack. I get enough shit from our mother. I don't need you trying to run my life too."

Paul seemed to recover. "I can't believe he told you about the babies. It's classified."

"He trusts me. I wish you would."

"I couldn't tell you. I swore an oath of secrecy, Dana."

"I'm not talking about NSO classified information. I wish you'd trust my judgment. I'm falling in love with Mourn. I know more about his past than you do. He didn't have anyone he could talk to and open up with. Now he does. He was self-destructive, but not anymore. I understand exactly what he's going through and guess what? We're good for each other."

"You deserve someone who is going to love you first and foremost. He had a mate." Paul lifted his hand and scrubbed it over the back of his head. "They aren't like married people. I don't know how to get my point across, but I'm terrified you're going to be unhappy in the long run." He dropped his hand to his side. "I don't want him to break your heart because he expects you to fill a dead woman's shoes."

She sighed, all her anger gone. "I had the same fears, but guess what?"

Paul waited, watching her.

"We both discovered that our marriages weren't all that perfect, okay? He told me about his problems with his mate and I told him about my issues with Tommy. Neither of us wants to duplicate that. We both want better than what we had."

He frowned. "What? But they were mated. I've never seen an unhappy, mated pair."

"Were you around 139 and Mourn?"

"Not much. They were moved into couples housing after they were freed. We wanted 139 to be more comfortable in a home setting instead of having to live at Medical. Destiny was the nurse assigned to check in on her since she wasn't comfortable with me, because I'm human."

"They weren't that happy," she confessed. "I'm not going to give you details, but I'll say that much so you'll back off."

"What problems did you have with Tommy?"

She sipped her coffee. "It wasn't all roses, okay? We had rough patches."

"You never told me that. You always seemed so happy."

"Do you call me to bitch about something Becky has done to piss you off or hurt your feelings?"

"No."

"Exactly. I'm not looking to replace Tommy. Mourn and I are totally different together than we were with Tommy and 139. That's one of the things that attracts us to each other." She set down her cup and walked up to her brother. "Stop being such a butthead and back off on the big-brother routine, okay? I'd like for you to give Mourn a chance. No more threatening him or trying to break us up."

"I just wish you'd chosen someone else."

"Get over it."

Paul nodded. "I'm just worried."

"Don't be. Mourn would never hurt me. He's really sweet, Paul. I wish you could see him the way I do. He makes me happy. He makes me feel alive."

"I take it you're going to keep seeing him no matter what I say?"

"Yes. Do you want me to go stay with him instead of here? I don't want to put you out if you're uncomfortable with me seeing Mourn."

"I wish you wouldn't live with him. You can stay as long as you want."

"Thank you." She reached up and patted the side of his face. He flinched away when she did it a little too hard the second time.

"Ouch. What was that for?"

"Don't threaten him again."

He rubbed his cheek. "You're mean."

"It could have been worse. I was thinking about going for the shorthairs on the back of your neck." Dana turned around and returned to her coffee. She lifted the mug to take a sip, but Paul's next words froze her in place.

"Mom called this morning. You're not going to like what I'm about to say."

She lifted her gaze. "What did she want?"

He cleared his throat. "She informed me that she plans to fly out here today."

Dana gawked at him.

"I know. She's never visited here before. I got the impression she's pissed that you didn't come home when she expected you to."

"I'm not a kid." She thought about how her mother would react to her dating a New Species. "Shit. Tell me you talked her out of it."

"I tried."

"Did you tell her that you're only allowed one visitor at Homeland at a time? We came up with that lie together so she wouldn't be tempted come with me, remember?"

"I told her that."

She blew out a relieved breath. "Thanks."

"So she said she'd stay at the local motel a few blocks away."

"No!"

"I even pointed out that there are no fancy hotels around this area and it's a dive motel. She still insisted on coming. She must really be worried that you'll decide to move to California to be closer to us. Can you imagine our mother staying in a motel?"

Dana shook her head. "I'm calling her." She slammed down the mug, spilling coffee on the counter, and snatched up Paul's kitchen phone to dial. It rang four times before the answering machine picked up. She waited for the beep. "Mom? It's Dana. Pick up."

She waited but the machine finally cut her off by disconnecting the call. Dana cursed, staring at Paul. "She's not home, or she's ignoring the call."

"Or she already got on a plane and is headed here."

"Shit!" Dana put down the phone and paced. "I told her I needed space. She was driving me nuts."

"That probably didn't help alleviate her fears. She depends on you to be close to her."

Dana stopped striding back and forth. "I see why you left home right after high school. Do you know what she did last week? She rearranged the furniture in my living room because she didn't like the way I had it."

Paul chuckled.

Dana flipped him off. "It's not funny. I had to move all of it back and told her to never do it again. She acted hurt and complained about it to her friends, who called me to tell me she was upset. What about me? Who walks into someone's home and does that?"

"Our mom."

"Can you tell the NSO not to let her in? Will they stick with our story of saying you can only have one guest at a time?"

He grimaced. "Dana…"

"Paul! You know she's going to raise hell when she finds out about Mourn." Suspicion rose. "Did you tell her I was dating him? Did you ask her to come?"

"No."

She studied him, but didn't see any telling signs of guilt. He was a bad lair. "I believe you."

"That's a shitty thing to accuse me of."

"Sorry."

"You know how she treats Becky. Do you think I want to subject my wife to our mother? She tries to guilt Becky and me into having kids. Becky finally told her she didn't want to hear it anymore. Mom gave her the cold shoulder. It was the last time we flew to visit her. It was miserable."

Dana wasn't surprised. "Poor Becky."

"Yeah. I would love to keep Mom out of Homeland, but how do you explain our mother to New Species? They think mothers are sweet and kind. They don't know some of them are controlling and pushy."

"She's going to find out about Mourn and flip her lid. She'll do or say whatever it takes to get him to stop seeing me so I'll go home with her."

"I don't want to involve the NSO in our family issues. What are the chances that she'll show up at the gates and demand to see us?"

Dana regarded him with a frown.

Paul's shoulders sagged. "Shit. She'd totally do that."

"I have to warn Mourn."

"I have to warn Becky."

"I'm totally moving in with Mourn if Mom stays with you."

"Does he have a guestroom?"

"You're not shoving her on him."

"I meant for me and Becky. Mom can stay here on her own. I don't want to subject my wife to our mother on a rant. You know she's going to yell when she finds out you're getting it on with a New Species." He chuckled.

She flipped him off. "I wouldn't laugh too much, big bro. She'll turn on you and your wife about those grandbabies you've denied her when she's done with me."

His amusement died. "Shit."

"Exactly. You'd better talk to someone at the gates and ask them to go along with you having a one-visitor limit."

* * * * *

Dana tapped her thigh as she sat next to Mourn at the island. He'd brought pizza for dinner. She just decided to spit it out. "I have to leave after we have dinner."

His chin jerked up, the large boxes he'd reached to open forgotten. "Give me more time before you say you won't see me anymore. We're good together, Dana. I know you enjoyed last night and this morning."

"I did. It's not that. I want to keep spending time with you. It's just that my mother is on her way to California. She's going to check in to a motel that is not far from here at around seven o'clock tonight. She wants my brother and me to meet her there. I have to go."

"Your mother? Why is she staying in a human motel? Call the gates and tell them to expect her. We can arrange human housing for her if she doesn't want to stay with Paul too."

She inwardly cringed. "Um, that's not a good idea. We kind of told her that it's against the rules to have more than one family member visit at a time."

"That's not true."

"I know. I feel a bit guilty about that, but it's complicated."

"She hates Species?"

"No."

"What is the problem?"

Dana sighed, trying to think of a way to explain her mother to him. "I'm just going to be blunt, okay?"

He nodded.

"She's going to be very unhappy when she finds out I'm dating you. It's not because you're New Species. It's because it means I'll have to live here if we get serious. She likes me being close to her. She also has it set in her mind that she'll get to hand pick my next husband. Don't even try to make sense of it. It's just how she is. She can be extremely rude and she will be. I don't want to subject you to her. Trust me. I'm doing you a favor."

"She will have to accept me if we mate. She's your family and welcome to stay at Homeland with us. We could put her in the other bedroom if she needs to live with you."

"No. Don't ever say those words again. I could never live with my mother and you couldn't either. One of us would kill her within a week."

He looked stunned.

"Look, I had to elope when Tommy and I got married. Do you know why?" She hurried on before he could say anything. "She went behind our backs to invite an extra hundred guests, changed the food menu for our reception, and the last straw was when I found out she'd called the bridal shop too. She pretended to be me during all that and told them I no longer wanted the dress I had chosen because she didn't like it. She ordered a different one, a dress that she picked. I guess she figured by the time I found out it would be too late to do anything about it, but luckily for me, I called to check on all those things. I blew my stack. Tommy and I canceled the entire thing and flew to Vegas with some friends. I had Paul meet us there so he could walk me down the aisle. That's my mom, Mourn. She's sneaky, underhanded and controlling. She will do or say anything to make you reconsider being with me."

"I wouldn't do that, Dana."

"I'll go to the motel tonight with Paul and try to handle her. She's angry that I extended my stay. I'm sure she'll try to lay a guilt trip on me, but I'm not having any of it."

"Guilt trip?"

"She's a pro at doing that. She'll bitch about the money she wasted to fly here, how she had to check on me because she believes I must be having a breakdown or something. It's just a ploy to try to get me to go home faster. I'm not giving in to her."

"I'd like to meet your mother."

"Not yet. We'll tell her after the fact if we get serious. Trust me. I learned the first time not to give her a chance to mess things up for me. She'll try to come between us, Mourn."

He growled softly.

"Exactly."

"Let's eat." He snarled the words.

She watched him tear open the boxes and put slices of pizza on their plates. She reached out and wrapped her hand over his forearm. He peered at her.

"Please, don't be angry. I'm sorry about this. I know we planned to spend the evening together. Would you mind if I dropped by when I get back? It might be late. I'd like to sleep with you again. I really enjoyed cuddling and waking up with you this morning."

Some of his frustration seemed to fade. "I did too. I'll wait up for you."

Dana leaned in and boldly brushed her lips over his mouth. Mourn turned, pulling her into his arms, the food forgotten. He lifted her onto his lap and deepened the kiss. She finally pulled away to take her seat again.

"Not to mention, we can't ever let my mother stay with us. We got kind of loud last night. She'd hear us."

He grinned. "We share sex really well together."

"We do."

He grasped her hand and pulled it up to his lips to kiss her palm. He opened his mouth and lightly traced his tongue over it. Dana jerked it away, laughing.

"That tickles."

"I know where it doesn't." His gaze dropped to her lap. "Forget food. I want to taste you."

Her body instantly responded. The night before, he'd shown her exactly what he could do with his mouth more than a few times. He was insatiable, not that she had any complaints. It made her wet just thinking about his hands on her and the memory of him inside her.

"Don't tempt me."

"I want to." He leaned over to kiss her.

She put her hands on his chest to stop him. It made her want to groan because she could feel the muscles underneath her palms. She wanted to help him remove his shirt so she could touch him all over without anything between them.

"We can't. I want to know about your day and we need to eat. Hold that thought until I come back later. Paul said he'd pick me up in an hour. I guess we have to put on disguises and borrow one of your SUVs to leave Homeland. He said we have to leave early to drive around so we're not followed to the motel."

Mourn grumbled.

"I know. I feel the same way. I took a nap after Paul left." She grinned. "I didn't get a lot of sleep last night. Are you tired?"

"No."

"How was work?"

"I got to walk some of the walls today. They kept me away from the human-inhabited areas where protestors gather, but I'm learning the security protocols to keep our walls safe from breaches."

"I don't know how that is possible. Those walls are massive."

"I was assured that they try. Some have shown up with hooks attached to ropes to toss at the top of the wall in hopes of climbing up. Two weeks ago a human male came with a big ladder and tried to prop it against the wall. They had him arrested for trespassing. A human female was caught with a hammer yesterday. Her intention was to beat through part of the wall to create a hole large enough for her to squeeze through."

"Why would they do that?" She let her hands slide off his chest.

He straightened in his chair and picked up a piece of pizza. "Some males wish us harm. The female was a mate hunter."

"What's that?"

"It's what we call the many human females who come to Homeland hoping a Species will take them as mates."

"They do that?"

"Yes." He took a bite. "They will yell up at officers on the wall, asking them to bring them inside. Some flash their bared bodies in hopes of tempting a male to comply."

Dana fixed her attention on her plate. His words replayed in her head. He could easily find a woman to be with him if they were outside the walls trying to break in. She hadn't missed what else he'd said either. Women were flashing guys and probably making all kinds of indecent proposals.

"Are you going to be working the walls from now on?"

"I'm not certain. They are showing me all the jobs to see which one I would enjoy most."

She ate her pizza, lost in her thoughts. Mourn bumped her arm and she looked up at him to find him watching her.

"What is wrong?"

"I didn't know about mate hunters."

"We ignore them. You should too."

"Have any of your men brought one into Homeland and taken her as a mate?"

He shook his head. "Most are unstable in their minds, or they are criminals."

"Criminals?"

He nodded. "Their police can't arrest them inside our walls. They have no jurisdiction so they can't be prosecuted for what they might have done in the out world. No male wants to be used that way. We want females who are attracted to us and wish to form bonds of real emotion."

"What about that Vengeance guy? Is he aware of these mate hunters?"

"He's kept at Reservation. No mate hunters go there. There are no places for them to sleep while they stalk our walls. The Sheriff there makes them leave and tickets them if he finds them sleeping in vehicles. The town there likes to keep strangers out and they don't have any motels."

"That's nice of them."

"They don't want our protestors coming to their town to create trouble. It's mutually beneficial for them and us. Why are you so curious about mate hunters?"

"You could have picked one of them to give you purpose."

He stopped eating and leaned in, staring deeply into her eyes. "They are not you. I want you, despite you being human." He smiled. "You draw me. No one else does."

She felt a little silly at that point for even having those thoughts. "Sorry."

He reached up and caressed her cheek. "It's a human thing, isn't it?"

"I guess so. You're a very attractive man, Mourn."

"You're a very attractive female, Dana."

They grinned at each other.

"Eat or I'll take you to our bed. Paul will arrive to find us naked. I know you don't want that to happen so I'm trying to resist my urges. You're not helping. I'm saving my thoughts of shared sex until you return tonight. I would like to meet your mother. Are you certain it's for the reasons you stated and not that she dislikes Species? Will she hate me for not being human?"

"She'll hate you just because of where you live. Homeland is too far away from her."

"Is that a human thing too?"

"No. That's just my mother. She's very possessive of me and can't stand the thought of me living more than a few blocks from her. It's like she lives to annoy me some days."

"I can understand wanting to keep you close. I do. I can no longer imagine my life without you in it."

Dana dropped her pizza and slid off the chair. "Get up."

He arched his eyebrows but stood. She grabbed his shirt with both hands and backed up. He followed her around the island with a curious expression. She liked that he just did it without asking her what she was doing. She stopped with the counter at her back and released him. She yanked up her skirt and hooked her thumbs on the sides of her panties, shoving them down.

His gaze lingering on the floor for a second, but then he stared into her eyes.

"Smell me."

He leaned in and sniffed. "You smell good and slightly aroused."

"Am I ovulating?"

"I don't pick it up."

"Good enough. Ever heard of a quickie before?"

He shook his head. She reached for the front of his pants. "I want you. Right here. Right now. The counter is about the right height for you."

He growled but didn't protest as she frantically opened his pants, shoving them down his thighs. She loved the soft black boxer briefs he wore. She pushed them down and was happy to see he was on board when she saw that he was aroused. She freed his cock and reached up to grip his shoulders.

"Set me on the counter."

He grabbed her waist and did as she asked. She hooked her legs around his hips and released him with one hand to shove her skirt up. She spread her thighs and looked down. "I was right. This will work. I'm glad you're so tall."

She lifted her chin and Mourn captured her mouth with his, kissing her. She pulled him closer, the passion between them hot and fierce. Mourn's hands slid from the sides of her hips to encompass her ass, drawing her closer to rub his cock against her pussy. She moaned.

He pulled away, ending the kiss. Both of them were turned-on and breathing hard. "I need to get a condom."

"I like feeling you better without them. You said I smell fine. I'll talk to Paul about getting on something later. Just take me." She wiggled her pussy against him. "Now."

He groaned and kissed her again. He released her ass to reach between them. She figured it was to guide his cock into her, but instead he shifted it out of the way to play with her with his fingers. She moaned louder, clutching at him tighter. She hated the feel of his shirt, and wished she'd taken that off him first, but she wasn't willing to stop long enough to do it.

Mourn stopped teasing her clit with his finger and pressed the crown of his cock against her, entering her pussy with one thrust. She had to tear her mouth from his as pleasure hit. She feared biting his tongue otherwise.

He surprised her when he adjusted his hold on her and locked one arm behind her back as he lifted her off the counter a little, his other arm hooking under her ass. He turned them, taking a few hobbled steps to pin her against the cool refrigerator. He buried his face in her neck, snarling as he started to move, fucking her hard and deep.

Dana hooked her legs higher, not caring that her skirt was bunched up between their stomachs. Mourn adjusted his hold on her again now that her back was against something solid. He held her by her hips as he continued to rock her world. She moaned, loving how strong he was, and how good it felt to have him inside her. He was big, incredibly hard, and every drive of his hips against the cradle of her thighs rubbed him up against her clit.

The fridge made creaking noises and banged a little against the wall, but she didn't care. He didn't seem to either. Dana moaned even louder when Mourn's fangs nipped her skin at the base of her neck. He licked where he'd bitten. She didn't feel any fear since that little pinch hadn't hurt. It escalated her excitement.

Dana cried out his name as she climaxed and Mourn snarled against her throat. She loved feeling him come. She'd missed the heat of his semen as it spread inside her. The condom would also have muted the heartbeat sensation of his shaft as he emptied his seed.

He held her as they recovered, both panting. She loosened her hold around his shoulders and smiled. "That's a quickie."

"I like. Now I'm going to take you to bed and do it all over again slower."

She laughed. "We don't have time. Hold that thought."

"I like holding you more." He brushed a kiss just under her ear.

She hated to part from him, but Paul would show up soon. She'd rather he not find her and Mourn in the kitchen that way. "Later."

He lifted his head to peer at her. His eyes took her breath away. They were always beautiful, but especially so after sex. "Now."

She smiled when his cock flexed inside her. He was still hard. No one could ever say New Species were lazy lovers. He recovered from sex super fast and was always ready to go another round. "Do you take blue pills by any chance?"

"What is that?"

"Never mind." She stroked his face, his hair. "I need to clean up and put my underwear back on before Paul comes to get me. Don't tell him we didn't use a condom. He'll flip out."

"Why didn't you want me to go get one?"

"I really do like you not wearing them. It feels better."

"It does for me too. I didn't think you'd notice the difference."

"I do. Can I ask you something strange?"

"Anything."

"You um, are warm when you get off. Why is that?"

"You mean my semen is really warm?"

"Yes."

He shrugged. "It's a feline thing. Darkness is feline and would have warned me if my semen would harm you. It won't. He has sex with his mate without condoms. I heard they are trying to have a baby."

"I just like feeling all of you."

"There is a chance I won't pick up the change in your scent when you begin to ovulate."

"I'm willing to risk it. Are you?"

"You're mine, Dana. You just don't realize it yet, but I'm going to convince you to become my mate. I would like a baby with you. It would make me happy if my seed grew inside you."

"I'm not ready for that yet so always sniff me before we have sex. I trust you to tell me if you pick up that scent, okay?"

He nodded. "I give you my word."

"That's all I need to hear. Now let me down. I am hungry now."

He chuckled. "I'd rather eat you."

"Definitely hold that thought until later. I love your mouth on me."

He still hesitated and his expression grew somber. "I'd like to meet your mother."

She clamped her hand over his mouth. "Never talk about her while we're in this position. Please? If I had a cock I'd have just gone soft."

He chuckled and amusement sparked in his eyes.

She released his mouth. "It's not you. It's her. She's not going to be nice to you once she sees you as a threat. And she will. You'll ruin her plans for me, which is to marry me off to someone she approves of who won't ever ask me to move away from her."

"I think I could make her change her mind and be happy for us if I tell her how I feel about you. I'll explain what mates are. You're my everything, Dana. That's never going to change."

Her heart melted, because there was no denying the sincerity in his eyes. "I wish that would make her accept us being together but it won't. It matters to me. I want us to strengthen our relationship before she has a chance to scare you off."

"I don't frighten, Dana."

"You've never met my mother. I want to run away from her when she's being mean." She backed away. "We need to clean up and finish eating before Paul arrives." She bent and grabbed her panties off the floor. "I'll be right back. I'm going to use your bathroom."

"Our bathroom."

She wasn't falling in love with him anymore. She had already fallen. She fled down the hallway.

Chapter Ten

Dana gawked a bit at all the people outside the back gates when Paul drove them through. Cameras flashed, blinding her. Many people stood on the sidewalks as Paul slowly maneuvered the SUV into the street. A few idiots darted out in front of them to snap pictures. Paul had to hit the brakes and honk the horn to get them to move.

"Tuck your chin and keep your baseball cap low," Paul hissed.

She followed his directions, even lifting a hand to block the side of her face. "This is nuts. It kind of reminds me of what celebrities go through."

"Welcome to life at Homeland." Paul snorted. "This is what you have to deal with when you live here and want to leave or come back."

"It wasn't like this at the front gates."

"You came early in the morning, like I asked. This is why. Most of these jerks are sleeping then."

"Why does the NSO let so many people back here?"

"The street is public property and it doesn't belong to the NSO. The cops come around once in a while to ask them to leave because they are a nuisance, but they just return. Every time the NSO is in the news for something, this circus parks their asses outside of any entry or exit to Homeland."

"I see why you and Becky don't have date nights outside Homeland anymore."

"She mentioned that? Was she upset?"

"She loves you, bonehead. She didn't complain about it. It was more of a cautionary tale of what I'd have to deal with if Mourn and I mate."

He drove a few blocks and turned onto a freeway onramp. "We're going to go a few miles, then turn around and go to the motel." He kept darting glances at the rearview mirrors.

"Is anyone following?"

"I'm not sure yet. They can be pretty tricky. Some of them will use multiple cars and communicate by cell phone so one will back off and another one will take up the chase."

"That's crazy."

"We deal with crazies all the time."

She mulled that over. Paul took an exit a few miles down, drove around a couple of residential areas, and then started back. Dana glanced in the rearview mirrors too. She didn't see any headlights behind them.

"We're in the clear?"

"Looks like. I think I'll just take side streets to be sure."

"You just don't want to go to the motel so you're taking your sweet time."

He chuckled. "Probably. You know Mom is going to fake tears when you tell her you're not ready to go home."

"I know."

"Are you going to cave?"

"No."

"You've never been that great at standing up to her. That's why you're the one who lives so close to her."

"I've gotten better at it and I'm motivated. You completely ignored what I said when I mentioned Mourn and me becoming mates. Don't think I didn't notice that."

"Are you considering it?" Tension sounded in his voice.

"Yes. It's all I think about. I wish you would give him a chance. He's amazing."

"You love him, don't you?"

She didn't hesitate. "I do. I saw fear in his eyes when we were saying goodbye, as if he was afraid I wouldn't return. I want to go back and I don't think I want to stay at your place anymore. I'd like to live with him."

"You've only known him for a few days."

"How long did you spend with Becky before you knew she was the one?"

He didn't answer.

She turned her head to stare at his grim expression. "Answer me and be honest."

"I knew after our first date when I woke up with her in my arms."

"She slept with you on the first date? I'm shocked," Dana teased.

"We hit it off. What can I say? I woke up and my first impulse *was not* to get the hell out of there like all the other one-night stands I'd had. I wanted to stay and cook her breakfast. Hell, I wanted to go home and grab a bag so I could sleep with her every night."

"That must have been some out-of-this-world sex. I don't want details."

He chuckled "Actually, it wasn't all that great, but we had the best time. She made me laugh and I just fell hard. I wasn't even ready to settle down, but she changed everything for me."

"I feel that way about Mourn. Only the sex is out of this world."

"I didn't need to know that."

"Just saying." She glanced in the rearview mirrors again, still not seeing headlights. "I think we're good."

"Me too. I just worry about you, Dana. You and Tommy were real social butterflies. You can't go to parties or the theatre with Mourn."

"That was all Tommy. I never enjoyed that crap."

"Really?"

"Yeah. We fought about it often."

"I didn't know that."

"There was a lot you didn't know. I've never felt this way before. Ever. Not even with Tommy. This morning it was tough to leave Mourn's house. I thought about calling you and asking you to just bring my stuff to me. I wanted to stay."

"Why didn't you?"

She decided to be honest. "I knew you'd argue with me again and try to talk me out of it. He's not used to family drama. I guess I'm afraid he's going to decide I'm not worth the trouble."

"He wouldn't care about that shit if he loves you. Hell, Becky puts up with Mom because she loves me."

"Mom is across the country and you only lived near her for a few months. You work at Homeland so he can't avoid it if you decide to be an asshole. You bothered him while he was at work."

"I told you I did that because I'm worried about you."

"Get over it and start focusing on what's going to make me happy instead. Like it or not, that's Mourn."

"I'll try to cut him some slack, okay?"

"You will?"

He nodded. "Yes."

"Thank you." She saw the motel sign ahead. "Is that it?"

"Yes. Stick close to me. I wasn't joking about that place being a dive. Keep the cap and glasses on. Don't talk to anyone. I have a feeling a lot of the protestors stay here. It's cheap and close to Homeland. I registered Mom under a false name and made her promise to avoid talking to strangers."

"Won't they recognize the SUV as belonging to Homeland?"

"No. This isn't a task force vehicles. This one is the smaller type they rarely use. It doesn't have any NSO markings. It will take them time to run the plates, if someone does, and it's registered under a false company name. We'll be good for at least an hour. If shit hits the fan, get behind me. I'm armed."

Her mouth dropped open.

He parked far away from the other cars, turned off the engine and unfastened his belt. He sighed. "It's procedure. I have military training and target practice every few weeks. I'd rather be safe than sorry."

"Isn't that illegal?"

"No. The NSO lists me as a task force member and I have a badge in my wallet to flash if I need to shoot someone. It is better than a permit to carry a concealed weapon. My ass is covered."

"Have you ever had to shoot someone?"

"I served a few tours. Of course I have. Let's go." He climbed out of the driver's side.

Dana got out and closed the door. Paul activated the alarm and came to her side, hooking his arm with her. She kept her head low. A few guests hung out in the parking lot in several groups. Paul drew her closer and took the stairs up to the second level. It was clear there. He stopped in front of a door and lifted his hand.

"You ready for this?"

"Yes."

He knocked and there was movement at the peephole in the door. The light disappeared.

"Go away or I'll call 9-1-1!"

Paul sighed. "It's us, Mom."

Within seconds the door opened. Their mother stared at both of them. Paul pushed her gently out of the way, drew Dana inside, and locked the door behind them. He released her arm and removed his glasses, grinning.

"Hi, Mom." He hugged her.

"I thought you were both drug dealers. Why are you dressed like that?" She glared at them.

Dana removed the cap, allowing her tucked-up hair to fall free, and took off the sunglasses. "We wanted to fit in with your neighbors," she joked. Her gaze traveled around the room. "Wow. Hello, low-budget porn set."

"It's horrible." Her mother pointed at the mirror on the ceiling. "I'm terrified that's going to fall on me when I sleep."

"I warned you this place was bad. You should have stayed in a nice hotel a few more miles away. I said that too. Do you want us to move you?" Paul waited for an answer.

Their mother ignored him, fixating on Dana. "This is what I do for you. Do you see this shithole? I'll probably be mugged, raped and murdered by morning. My headstone will read that it's all your fault."

"Mom," Paul chastised. "That isn't funny."

Their mother threw up her hand to silence him. "You can't run away from your problems, Dana. This is just another way you're hiding from living. Do you think your poor brother and his wife want you hanging around their place? They don't."

"Mom," Paul raised his voice. "That's not—"

"Stay out of this!" Their mother stepped closer to Dana. "I brought Dirk Hass with me. He's going to drop by in about fifteen minutes and talk to you. I also bought us tickets to leave on the first flight home in the morning."

Dana's temper finally exploded. "You brought your gynecologist with you? To talk to me? What is wrong with you?"

"Dirk likes you. You really need to give him a chance, Dana. He makes good money, has his own practice, and took time away from work to fly out here because I told him you're having difficulties. What other man would do that? It shows how caring and concerned he is for you."

"You manipulated him, in other words." Dana was tempted to leave.

"Don't talk to me like that," their mother hissed. "How dare you."

Dana took a step back. "What? It's the truth. You probably told Dr. Hass I'm interested in him when you know damn well I'm not. He's seen you naked from the waist down. Don't you think that's a little fucked up? I do. Talk about a dysfunctional family. And stop setting me up with men. I've told you that. I'm done."

"Don't cuss. It's not the way I raised you."

Dana opened her mouth but Paul moved fast, stepping between them. "Mom, you need to calm down."

"Your sister is so rude."

"Pot, meet kettle." Dana stepped to the side so she could glare at her mom. "I came to see Paul. I told you I needed a some space. You drive me crazy. Thank you for taking care of me after Tommy's death, but I'm trying to get on with my life now. Why can't you just let me?"

"You said you'd be gone three days. I had to come out here to get you."

"I'm not some wayward runaway teen." Dana clenched her teeth.

"You're acting like one."

"Shit," Paul muttered. "Do you fight like this all the time?"

"No," their mother answered.

"Yes," Dana said at the same time.

Paul removed his cap and scratched his head. "This is going to be a long evening."

"No. It's not." Dana put her hands on her hips. "I'm not coming home yet, Mom. I won't until I'm ready. You bringing your gynecologist with you…" She shook her head. "I don't even know what to say except I feel bad that you talked him into it. I won't even mention that he's twenty years older than I am. You date him if he's such a great catch. Go home."

Someone knocked on the door and Dana gritted her teeth as her mother sailed toward it and opened it to let Dirk Hass inside. He held flowers and smiled when he spotted Dana.

"Hello." He offered them to her.

Dana felt guilty. She knew her mother must have lied to him to get him to take a flight across the country. She accepted the flowers. "Thank you."

Paul saved her by introducing himself and taking the attention off her. Dana shoved the flowers at her mother and backed away.

Her mother beamed, obviously pleased with the mess she'd created. Dana wanted to strangle her.

Dirk turned to Dana. "How are you feeling?"

"I'm fine." It wasn't his fault that he'd been pulled into this mess, but someone needed to be honest with him. "I am so sorry about this but the truth is, I'm not interested in dating you."

"Dana!"

She ignored her mother. "I'm seeing someone. My mother didn't know. I haven't told her yet. I'll pay you back for the money you spent coming all this way."

Dirk appeared taken aback.

"She's lying." Her mother rushed forward and gripped his arm. "I told you she's having issues. She is inventing a make-believe boyfriend."

Dana was about to scream. "I am not. I just didn't want to tell you because he lives in this area. I knew you'd blow your stack when I told you that I'm relocating here. It's serious."

"You're lying." Her mother's face turned an angry shade of red.

"She's actually not." Paul shot Dana a hooded look as he ripped off his sunglasses. "He works security. She met him when she arrived and they've been spending almost every moment together when he's not at work."

"You're not going to date a security guard." Their mother shook her head. "I won't allow it. Dirk is a doctor."

Dana threw up her hands. "I'm done. I'm not going to fight with you anymore. I'm moving here and that's something you're just going to have to deal with." She looked at Dirk Hass. "You should ask my mom out. She's about your age and she thinks you'd make someone a wonderful husband." She pushed her sunglasses back on and added the cap. "Paul, I'll wait for you outside. I'm stick-a-fork-in-me done."

Dana stormed to the door and yanked it open.

"Dana," Paul called. "Don't go out there alone."

She turned. "I'd rather face off against drug dealers and hookers than stay in here." She stormed out, slamming the door.

She almost bumped into a large body and backed up, her chin lifting. The guy wore a black hoodie with matching black sweatpants. He was a really large man and the dim lighting hid his face. "Sorry." She tried to step around him

"Dana." He gripped her arms.

She froze. "Mourn?"

He tilted his head slightly so she could barely make out his features. "I was going to knock but I could hear what was going on inside. I knew it wasn't a good time to make my presence known."

"What are you doing here?"

"I wanted to meet your mother. I asked a few of the task force team members to bring me here. I changed clothes so no one would recognize what I am."

She started pulling on him. "Let's go."

"I still want to meet her."

"You said you heard us fighting. Trust me. Let's just go home."

He let her lead him to the stairs. She spotted his security detail immediately. Two men dressed in military-style black uniforms stood in front of a big black SUV. They didn't have any NSO patches to identify who they were, but she knew. Mourn caught her hand and stayed at her side as they went down the stairs.

Some of the motel guests quickly made their way to their rooms, probably mistaking the two guards for cops. Dana planned to walk directly to the SUV Mourn had come in and ask the two men to drive them back to Homeland, but Mourn suddenly pulled her under the stairwell and against the building.

"You're upset."

"My mom does that to me. She brought Dr. Hass with her. Can you believe that? She is so manipulative."

"I heard you tell her that you plan to move here. Does that mea—"

"Dana!" Paul's voice came from above.

"Down here," she called out. "I'm fine. Mourn is with me."

"Shit." Paul came rushing down the stairs and spotted them. He looked relieved. "Don't take off without me. What are you doing here,

Mourn?" He twisted his head, spotting the two guards. "Oh. You had the task force drive you. Good."

"He wants to meet Mom." Dana stepped closer to Mourn. She was upset, but him being there helped. She leaned against him and he put an arm around her.

"That's not a good idea. Ask my wife." Paul put on his sunglasses. "We should go."

Someone else came down the stairs and Dana lifted her head off Mourn's solid chest to look up. Her mother came into view. Dana clenched her teeth. It seemed as if Mourn would get his wish after all.

"Don't let her see your face," Paul whispered. "Just be cool." He tore off his sunglasses and held them out to Mourn. "Put those on. You work security at Homeland."

Mourn ignored the glasses and turned further, forcing Dana to move with him. She gripped him tightly as her mother spotted them in the shadows, her heels clicking on the pavement when she approached the stairwell.

"I'm not done talking to you, young lady. How dare you walk away from me? I brought Dirk all this way because he's a good man. He's willing to forgive this nonsense and he offered to go to couples counseling with you. We're all aware that you are having trouble coping with Tommy's death." Her mother stopped next to Paul and scowled at Mourn. "Get your hands off my daughter."

Dana sighed. "Mom, meet Mourn. This is my nonexistent boyfriend, as you referred to him. As you can see, he's very real. And tall."

"Hello, Dana and Paul's mother," Mourn rasped.

"Her first name is Daisy," Dana supplied.

"It's nice to meet you, Daisy." Mourn released Dana and held out his hand.

Her mother ignored it. "You look like a homeless vagrant. I see right through you, mister. My daughter has some money and you're looking for a free meal ticket. Think again. She's dating a doctor. Go find some other sucker to upgrade your life."

"Oh. My. God." Dana wanted to strangle her mother. "Stop it." She grabbed Mourn's extended hand and clung to it in case he had the same urge.

"Mom," Paul hissed. "Don't."

"Stay out of this," their mother snapped at him. "You're supposed to look out for your sister, but you let this security person get close to her."

Dana wished a hole would open up under her as she pressed tighter against Mourn in case he wanted to kill their mother for insulting him. She wouldn't blame him.

"Knock it off," she gritted out. "Right now. Don't you dare insult Mourn. You don't know anything about him. You're trying to be controlling again and chase him off. It won't work. I warned him about how you can be."

"Good. You're my daughter. I only want what's best for you and this security guard isn't it." She pointed at Mourn. "What the hell do you think you could offer my daughter with your minimum-wage job? Nothing!"

"Mom!" Paul groaned. "Stop. Everyone who works for the NSO makes really good money."

Mourn forced Dana to release his hand and unwound his arm from her waist. "You are very unpleasant." His voice had deepened to almost a snarl.

"Listen to you." Their mother huffed. "You sound like a meat-headed Neanderthal."

"Enough," Dana almost begged. "We're leaving."

"Not with him. I'll scream for Dirk. He'll get rid of this riff-raff." Her mother stopped pointing and fisted both her hands at her sides.

Paul groaned. "The task force is coming over here."

"Go away," Mourn ordered them.

Dana watched the two guards spin around and return to the SUV, taking up the same position as before.

"Don't talk to me that way," their mother huffed, unaware that he hadn't been speaking to her since her back was to the parking lot. "Do you hear that, Dana? He's disrespectful to your mother on top of it. He's a loser."

"That's it," Mourn snarled. He gently pushed past Dana and got closer to their mother. He stopped when Dana grabbed his waist, clinging to it.

"Don't. She's not worth it and she is my mother," she pleaded. "I get it. Believe me. I do. I want to hit her sometimes too."

196

"Is this overgrown thug going to hit me? I dare you, young man. I'll have your ass thrown in jail where I'm sure you belong."

Mourn snarled again and lifted his head just enough to reveal some of his face to their mother. She gasped, jerking back. Paul caught her before she tripped and held onto her to keep her from running away. Dana winced, seeing her mother's fear.

"I'm Species," Mourn ground out. "I'm deeply in love with your daughter. I won't back down from being with her for you or anyone else, female. I don't care if you gave birth to Dana. She's mine now."

Their mother's mouth opened and Paul suddenly clamped his hand over her lower face, leaning in. "Don't scream. He's not going to hurt you."

Dana released Mourn and stepped to his side. "You can't tell anyone, Mom. It will put you in danger. Stop being rude to him." What Mourn had said registered and she turned her head. "You're in love with me?"

"Yes." His tone softened. "How could I not be? You make me happy."

"I'm in love with you too."

Daisy yanked Paul's hand off her mouth. "Stop it. Both of you. This isn't happening. I refuse to let it."

"Shut up, Mom." Dana smiled up at Mourn. "I was afraid it was too soon to tell you how I felt."

"It's not." Mourn reached up and removed her sunglasses. "We were meant to find each other."

"No, you weren't."

Dana tore her gaze from Mourn and glowered at her mother. "Stop already. You're ruining our moment." She looked back up at Mourn and smiled. "You make me happy too. I don't want to go back to the life I had. I want to stay with you."

"We'll be mates." He leaned in.

Dana rose on tiptoe and braced her hands on his chest to kiss him. Someone grabbed her arm though and yanked her back. She cursed and jerked away from her mother. "What is wrong with you?"

"You're making a huge mistake," her mother hissed. "There's a wealthy doctor up in my room. What can this New Species give you that Dirk can't?"

Mourn snarled. "How about this?" He gripped his hoodie and ripped it open, exposing his chest and abs. "He doesn't sexually attract her. I do. I love Dana. I would do anything for her. She's the reason I want to live."

Dana chuckled, openly admiring the skin he'd exposed. "You are so sexy," she told him. Then she shifted her gaze. Her mother's eyes were wide, her mouth hanging open. "Any more questions, Mom?"

Her mom kept staring at Mourn's exposed chest. It amused Dana when she realized he'd rendered the older woman speechless.

"He has that same affect on me." Dana reached out and slid her hand over his stomach. "And he purrs. Meet your future son-in-law. We're getting mated."

Her mother finally snapped out of it, gawking at Dana. She still didn't speak.

"Priceless." Dana removed her hand from Mourn and held it out to him. "Take me home, Mourn. Paul, do you mind staying with Mom until she recovers?"

"Not a problem. I'll explain things to her once I get her doctor out of the room so we have privacy." Her brother cleared his throat. "I could have lived without knowing about the purring." He addressed Mourn. "Welcome to the family. It's a crazy one, but it's all yours now too."

Mourn released his hoodie and grasped Dana's hand. "Dana is worth it." He lifted his upper lip and revealed his fangs to their mother. "We'll learn to get along."

He didn't look pleased about it, but Dana was just relieved that he wasn't rushing away from her after getting a dose of his future mother-in-law. She tugged on him and he followed her back to his security detail. One of them opened the back door of the SUV for them while the other one climbed into the front driver's seat.

Mourn let Dana get in first and then followed. He pulled her onto his lap as the driver started the engine. The second guard belted into the front passenger seat. Dana wrapped her arms around Mourn and shoved the hood down to see his face better. The windows were tinted so she felt it was safe to do it in public. He looked angry.

"I'm so sorry."

"Stop apologizing for other humans."

"I warned you that she'd be rude and unreasonable."

"You did, but she birthed you. We'll have to find a way to get along."

"Or we could tell the guards at the front gates to ban her from ever visiting us."

He finally smiled and the anger melted from his features. "She is your mother."

"She's a pain in the ass."

He laughed. "I meant everything I said to you. I love you, Dana. I want you to be my mate."

"I'd like that so much."

"You aren't afraid to mate me anymore?"

She shook her head. "No. I just want to go home with you."

"You'll move in with me?"

"Yes."

"I won't ever let you go." He held her tighter. "You're mine."

"Promise?"

"Yes."

She leaned in and brushed her lips over his. He growled softly and kissed her back. One of the men in the front seat cleared his throat. Dana had forgotten about them, or that they were even in a moving vehicle. She reluctantly pulled away.

"Sorry," the guard in the passenger seat murmured. "We're not that far from Homeland and she's still technically a guest until you sign papers so she'll need to be patted down. Two canines are manning the gates we're going through. You might want to hold off on celebrating that she agreed to mate you until you get her home, Mourn."

He growled.

"What does that mean?" Dana arched her eyebrows, curious.

"They'll smell arousal on you and possibly tease us. I don't want to subject you to that."

"Oh."

Mourn shrugged. "It would be goodhearted teasing but you blush easily. I don't want you to be uncomfortable because they'll know I was touching you."

"Thank you."

Mourn pulled Dana against his chest and smiled. She would sign papers. He was grateful he'd insisted on leaving Homeland to meet her mother. The experience hadn't gone as well as he'd hoped, but the end result was all that mattered. It had been worth arguing with Slade and getting him to assign two task force members to escort him to the motel.

He'd had to tell the male how much Dana meant to him and how he wanted her to be his mate. It was important that he impress her mother so he'd have one less barrier to overcome before securing her agreement. To meet a human's family was important. Slade had understood. He'd warned Mourn not to start any fights and he'd had to give his word.

Regret surfaced as he reevaluated his actions. He probably shouldn't have bared his chest to her mother, but Darkness was the one who'd given him the idea. He'd said human females were impressed by muscles.

He'd been desperate to show Daisy why he'd be a better mate for Dana than some doctor with a lot of money.

"Forget everything my mother said," Dana whispered, resting her head on his shoulder.

"She doesn't like me."

"I don't care. She'll come around, or it's her loss if she doesn't, Mourn. You're a wonderful person."

"Perhaps I can train to be a doctor."

She lifted her head to hold his gaze. "That's not what you want to be, is it?"

"No, but I would become one if that will help your mother to accept us being mates."

"You are so sweet, but stop thinking that way. Do you know what I want?"

"Tell me."

"Don't let my mom get to you. I fell in love with you just the way you are. I don't plan to live the way she wants me to. You shouldn't either. We'll both be happier that way. We're building a future together. She can deal with it, or not be a part of it. Period."

He nodded. "I understand."

"Good."

"We'll be home soon. I remember everything we're supposed to do."

She grinned. "You held that thought, huh?"

"As if I'd forget." He reached up and stroked her cheek. "I swear, I'll be a good mate."

"I swear that I will be too."

"We're motivated to be happy together."

She nodded. "Yes. We are."

Chapter Eleven

It wasn't just two guards posted at the side gate when they entered. A third canine New Species met their SUV as they cleared the first gate. He wore jeans and a T-shirt instead of a uniform. Mourn got out and Dana scooted across the seat. He helped her down.

"Hello, I'm Slade." He smiled at Dana, but then focused on Mourn. "I take it there were no problems?"

"I didn't break my word."

"It went really well," the driver of the SUV stated. "We had no trouble. No one realized who we were and we were on the lookout for camera phones. It was very uneventful."

"Good. I appreciate you taking Mourn outside. You're relieved." Slade nodded to each man.

"Not a problem, sir."

Both task force members walked away toward a building, just leaving the SUV there. Dana studied Slade, wondering who he was. He seemed to sense her watching him.

"How did your mother take meeting Mourn and learning that you are with a New Species?"

She grimaced. "My mom is kind of difficult. It could have gone a lot better, but that's all on her."

"It's not because I'm Species," Mourn added. "She wanted Dana to mate with a wealthy doctor."

Slade put his hands on his hips. "Where is Paul?"

"He's with our mom, explaining how she can't tell anyone I'm with Mourn, and he's also probably trying to calm her down. She likes getting things her way."

Slade's mouth twisted into a grim line. "Do you believe that she'll go to the press to complain about you being here in hopes of putting pressure on us to force you to leave? We wouldn't do that, but I'd like to warn our public relations team if it's possible."

"No. She's aware that she'd have to move out of her home and go into hiding if anyone ever links our family to New Species. She won't want to leave her friends and start her life over. She complained to me often about how Paul could mess up her life when he took a job here. She's angry, but she will seethe without involving the press. My poor brother is getting an earful of it right now since he's the only one she can bitch at."

Slade nodded and looked behind Dana. He shook his head. "She doesn't need to be patted down. She's Paul's sister and she's with Mourn."

Dana glanced back, realizing one of the gate guards had waited patiently behind her to do just that. He nodded and returned to his post. She looked back at Slade. He glanced between the two of them.

"Dana has agreed to be my mate. We need papers," Mourn informed him.

Slade's mouth curved upward. "Congratulations."

They shook hands and Slade pulled him into a quick hug. He turned to Dana and just smiled. "It's nice to have you added to our New Species family."

"Thank you." She was relieved.

Slade gazed at Mourn. "I'll let legal know to draw up the papers. Do you want them tonight or is the morning soon enough? The ones who do them have gone home already, but I can place a call."

"Tomorrow is fine." Dana didn't want to put anyone out.

"I will prove I'm stable now." Mourn hesitated. "Do you think anyone will protest me taking a mate?"

"No." Slade shook his head. "We're happy for you both. Take my Jeep and drive your mate home. I need to stay in this area for a while. We're expecting trouble."

"May I help?"

"No thank you, Mourn. It's more of an irritation than a serious problem. A few aggressive protestors pitched eggs at some of our males who were patrolling the wall so we turned on the water cannons." Slade smiled at Dana. "It doesn't harm them but it stings severely and we use very cold water. It tends to make them run away, but they always return to antagonizing us after dark. Last time they splashed paint on a few of the gates. I volunteered to stay at this one for a while, to man the water cannons." He chuckled. "I admit that it amuses me to soak them before they can cause damage."

She laughed. "I can totally understand that."

"I'm just doing my duty by chilling them out." Slade grinned. "Last week I nailed one right after he opened the can, planning on walking to the gates to splash them. He fell on his ass as soon as the water hit him and dumped red paint onto his lap. I made a copy of the surveillance feed to share at a meeting. We all got a good laugh over it."

Dana snickered. "You should start a website and show those morons over the internet. It would probably be pretty popular. I know I would enjoy seeing that."

"I'll bring that up at the next meeting." Slade winked. "Have a good evening, and again, congratulations."

Mourn led Dana to a Jeep and someone opened the second set of gates for them to drive thru. Dana relaxed and enjoyed the warm evening air blowing on her as they made their way home. The guard at the gated entrance to the New Species cottages opened it and waved them through as soon as he spotted them.

Mourn parked and Dana followed him to the front door. He just twisted the knob and opened it. It amazed her that they didn't seem to lock anything. The lights were still on, their dishes from dinner remained on the counter as if he'd rushed out right after she'd left with Paul. He probably had since he'd reached the motel so soon after her.

"I'll clean this up." Mourn crossed the room.

"Leave it. We'll deal with that tomorrow morning."

He turned, one eyebrow raised.

She gripped the bottom of her shirt, pulled it over her head and tossed it on the floor. "We have more fun things to do."

He growled in response, desire showing in his eyes. "I love the way you think."

"I've been turned-on since you tore open your shirt and stood up to my mother. That was so hot."

He took a few long steps to reach her and hooked an arm around her waist, hoisting her up. She wrapped her arms around his neck and bent her legs, parted them, and hugged his hips. He hurried through the house to the master bedroom and used his elbow to flip on the light. He didn't let her down until they reached the bed.

"You make me hurt to be inside you."

She smiled as she leaned back on the bed and reached down to rip off her shoes and throw them across the room. She didn't hesitate to remove all her clothes that time, more comfortable with being naked with him now. The way Mourn looked at her made her feel sexy and wanted.

"I will treasure you." His voice turned husky and a bit gruff.

He stripped and her heart raced when he showed her just how much she affected him. The beauty of Mourn's body took her breath away—all that tan skin and sculpted muscles. She scooted farther onto the bed and lay back again, opening her arms.

"Come here."

Mourn didn't waste any time. He stretched out at her side and braced his upper body above her so she could stroke his hair and stare into his eyes. He had the longest eyelashes and they beautifully enhanced the stunning colors of his irises. His body, pressed against hers, felt so warm and solid.

"Thank you," she told him.

"For what?"

She smiled. "For being so insistent that we should be more than friends. I used to wonder how I'd get through every day and face another one. Now I'm so excited about what is going to happen next. That's all you."

"I feel the same way, Dana. You give me more than purpose. This is the first time since I gained freedom that I can embrace it with gladness. You are that reason."

She trailed her fingertips down his cheek, to his mouth, lightly brushing her thumb over his bottom lip. "How did I get so lucky?"

"Someone told me about karma. We were due for good things to happen to us after all we've suffered."

She laughed. "That is so true."

He glanced down at her breasts and growled. "I want to do lots of good things to you."

She released his hair and splayed her hands on his chest. "I could think of a few dozen good things I'd like to do to you too. Roll onto your back."

He arched his eyebrows but did it. He appeared to be a little baffled by her request. She sat up and bit her lower lip, openly appreciative of his body. "What's that look for?"

"I want to share sex with you."

"And?"

"We can't if you have me lying down flat. I'm too excited to just stay still so you can look at me."

"I don't plan on just looking at you."

She opened her palm on his stomach, slowly caressing him and trailing her fingers lower. His cock stiffened even more when she wrapped her fingers around it, playing with the shaft. She leaned in and opened her mouth over the crown, licking him.

Mourn snarled and Dana turned her head. He seemed shocked.

"You're going to taste me?"

"That was the plan. Is that okay?"

He suddenly lunged, sitting up and grabbing her. He rolled, pinning her under him. "Later. I want you too much."

Dana couldn't complain when Mourn scooted down her body, trailing hot, wet kisses along her throat. She spread her thighs to give him room to fit his hips there. She wrapped them around his waist to hold him in place when he reached her breasts, lightly sucking on each one.

"I want you now."

He reached down and slid his hand between them, cupping her pussy. He growled. She knew she was wet and ready. He shifted his weight a little and Dana moaned when he replaced his hand with his cock. He entered her fast and hard.

"Yes!"

He rose and brushed his mouth over hers, their gazes locking. His hands wrapped around her shoulders as he moved, thrusting in and out of her. Dana loved staring into his eyes. It made making love to him even more intimate than their bodies moving together and the pleasure of having him inside her.

"You are so beautiful," he rasped.

"So are you."

He ground against her, rubbing her clit as he increased the pace. Dana moaned, arching her pelvis to move with him. Ecstasy surged and she threw her head back, crying out his name.

Mourn growled, burying his face against her neck as he came. Dana felt the warmth of his release spread deep inside her. She clung to him as they both tried to catch their breaths, their bodies tangled together.

"I love you, Dana."

"I love you too."

Mourn lowered his head, his tongue and lips teasing her throat with light kisses. Her skin was so soft that he groaned. He knew he would never tire of touching her and showing her they belonged together. He inhaled her scent, understanding how males believed they became addicted to their mates. She smelled better than a summer day to him. Even better than food and everything else pleasant he'd ever experienced.

He'd hoped for death after losing 139, but now all he wanted to do was spend every day and night with Dana. He had more than purpose. He was happy and enjoying freedom for the first time. Dana had changed everything for him. He'd show her how much she meant to him every day. He'd treasure her.

They could try to have children one day if Dana wanted to. Just the thought of having a son with Dana, possibly a few of them, had him smiling. Mercile couldn't steal his and Dana's offspring. His family with her would be safe behind NSO walls. He purred, content.

Dana giggled. "That tickles."

"Sorry." He raised his head and smiled. "I do that when I'm happy."

"So am I and I like it when you purr. I wasn't complaining."

He stroked her hair, playing with the strands. "I like everything about you."

"I wouldn't say everything. You met my mother. She usually scares men off."

"She is just one female. The NSO has many humans who dislike us. I'm proud to be Species and your mate. I believe your mother will learn to like me once she sees how much you mean to me."

"I don't need her approval and neither do you. You once told me that human rules don't apply to New Species. You do things your own way. I want to be more like you, Mourn. I don't want to overanalyze everything. I am following my heart."

"You *are* Species. You're my mate."

She smiled. "You're my mate," she repeated. "I like the way that sounds."

"We can have a human marriage."

She hesitated, seeming to ponder it. "You know what? We don't need that. You said it yourself. I'm Species. I did the marriage thing with Tommy, but I want something new and better with you."

He understood. "I never signed mate papers with 139. We will do that together for the first time."

"Really? Why didn't you do that?"

"It's a legal way to prove to your world that we are bonded for life. 139 wasn't human. You are."

"I understand. I like that."

"Do you want a ring? I know the males bought their human mates one."

She shook her head. "Do you know what I would like instead?"

"Tell me. I will get it for you."

She grinned. "It could be something crazy or silly."

"It won't matter. I will find a way to get you anything you want or need."

"I've been thinking about babies."

"So have I." His heart rate accelerated.

"I'd like to throw out those condoms. No pressure, but it will be nice if it does happen, won't it?"

"Yes."

He loved her. She was offering him everything he had never dared dream of.

"Are you sure, Mourn?"

"I want everything with you."

"There are some things I've always wanted to do, but haven't. I'm sure you have some fantasies too. We could write out lists and compare them."

"Is sharing sex involved?"

She blushed, but nodded. "I'd like to take a bath with you. I've never had sex in water."

"We can do that. Didn't you bathe with Tommy?"

"No. I told you that he had germ phobias. He'd shower with me, but he hated bathtubs and pools. He said it was like dipping in a vat of viruses. Have you ever had sex that way?"

"No, but I'd like to."

"Is there something you've always wanted to try, but haven't?"

He considered it. "I'd like for you to teach me how to dance."

Her eyebrows arched, but she seemed pleased. "Really?"

"Yes. I've seen Species do that and it looks fun. I want to be able to take you there for dates."

"You're a romantic."

"You inspire me."

"I'd love to teach you anything I know. Just name it. Any time. Anything."

"I don't want my being Species, and you being human, to ever come between us."

"It won't. We talk."

"Yes, we do. We have total honesty. I never want that to change."

"The great thing about us is that we are determined to make this work."

"Yes." He paused, something on his mind. "Dana, would you like me to change my name?"

Her eyebrows shot upward and she looked surprised. "What?"

"I took the name Mourn after losing my mate. I grieved her loss. I could change my name to something to reflect us if you want."

She stroked his hair. "Why do you think I'd want that?"

"I'm worried that my name will cause you pain or it will be a constant reminder that I was mated before."

"It doesn't. You're Mourn. I don't want you to change. I was Dana when I was married to Tommy. Should I change my name to something new?" She smiled.

He grinned. "No. You're Dana."

"You're Mourn. I don't associate it with your past. The only reason you should change your name is if you hate it. Do you?"

"I'm used to it now."

"I'm kind of fond of it myself. I love you, Mourn."

"I love you, Dana."

He slowly eased his semi-hard dick out of her and turned them over so she ended up sprawled across his body. She settled onto him, stroking his chest and arms.

"Dana?"

"Yes?"

"Thank you for talking to me and taking my hand that day."

"We're kindred spirits. How could I not?"

"I don't know what that means."

She smiled. "We're very much alike."

He chuckled. "Yes, we are."

Chapter Twelve

Three months later

"Dana? Open the bathroom door." Mourn gripped the locked handle and growled.

"Go away," she muttered. "I'm going to be sick."

"I know you dread your mother's visit but she's isn't staying with us. We feel bad for Paul, remember?"

"It's not that." She groaned.

Mourn snapped the lock as he viciously twisted the handle, opening the door. He rushed forward the moment he spotted Dana crouched on the floor. He just dropped to his knees next to her, wrapping an arm around her.

"I've got you."

"This is so embarrassing. It's why I locked the door. You're supposed to stay out there."

"You're my mate." He cradled her closer. "We hide nothing from each other."

"You don't need to see my lunch come up. Why do they call this morning sickness? It's afternoon."

He brushed a kiss on the top of her head. "You're carrying my son. I wish I could suffer this instead of you."

"Trisha said it should pass soon, because of the increased gestation thing while carrying a New Species baby. Morning sickness can hit fast and hard but it hopefully won't last more than a week or two."

"I hope that is fact. I worry so much about you."

"Don't. It's normal. I'm healthy. You know that since you have Trisha check on me every day."

"I can't let anything happen to you."

She clutched his hand and lifted her head, staring into his eyes. "I'm going to be fine. We're lucky. I mean, we got pregnant the first month. Some couples try for years."

He grinned. "My seed knows it belongs inside you."

"You did promise that you wouldn't let me feel empty after sex." Dana took a few deep breaths. "The nausea is passing. It helps, having you stroke my back like that."

"Good." He kept doing it, staying at her side. "I'm going to take a few weeks off to be with you."

"You don't need to do that."

"I want to. I already asked and they are assigning my duties to another male until you're feeling better."

"You're the best."

"I try to be."

"You are."

He rubbed her back for a good five minutes. "How are you feeling?"

"Better."

He took his hand off her back, lifted her in his arms, and carried her into their bedroom. He set her on the bed, removed her shoes, and started undressing her.

"We have to meet my mom."

"We will after you take a nap. You look tired."

"I am."

"I am going to hold you while you sleep."

"She'll be pissed if we don't show up for dinner on her first night here."

"She's already pissed because you moved here and mated me." He shrugged. "We will cheer her with news of our son."

"I hope you're right."

"She wanted a grandbaby. Species young are cute. He will capture her heart."

Dana curled onto her side and smiled as Mourn got naked and spooned behind her, molding their bodies together. "I know you captured mine."

He chuckled. "Felines are irresistible. We purr."

"You don't have to tell me that. I know."

Mourn slid his hand forward to tenderly cup her belly. "We made a baby with our love. Do you feel amazement over that? I do every day."

She nodded. "We're really blessed."

He held her a little tighter. "Yes, we are, and this is just the start of our life together. It is only going to keep getting better."

927

Prologue

Twenty-three years ago

Christopher had one of the techs open the door and he carried the unconscious girl into the room. He glanced down, guilt making his steps hesitant. She'd seen too much. It was either kill her too, or put her in a place where she could never tell the police what he'd done. His plan would put her in danger, but she had a chance of survival if he made her part of one of his experiments. None of his supervisors would complain or refute his decision. They'd welcome having a human child at their disposal.

The male pup backed up into a corner. It sniffed the air, looking unsure and its big, dark eyes narrowed. Christopher glared back. "Her name is Candace." It helped to say her formal name, not the one he'd called her since her birth. "She's your new roommate. You hurt her and I'll kill you myself. Am I clear?"

The pup growled as Christopher lowered the girl to a sleeping mat and left her there. He backed up quickly. The pups were strong and fast, despite their young age. He'd never turn his back on the little bastard. Many of the staff had already learned to be wary. No deaths had occurred yet, but the test subjects were growing more dangerous as they developed. He felt a little safer knowing Tad would shoot 927 with a tranquilizer dart if he lunged for his throat.

"I mean it," Christopher warned. "She dies, you die. Got it?"

The pup growled at him again.

Christopher was certain the pup understood a lot more English than it pretended to, despite its refusal to speak. He'd bet the little animal would actually speak to his daughter after they spent enough time together. Mercile would welcome the opportunity to monitor their interaction and they'd learn exactly how smart the little bastards really were. Candace would be key to that research. She was about the same age as the pup.

He backed out of the room and the door slammed with finality. There would be no taking her from that cell, from the life he'd brought her into. His Candi might as well have died with the bitch who'd birthed her. His pain and rage were equal. Just the memory of coming home to find the woman he'd married in bed with the neighbor almost sent him into a rage again.

"Are you okay, Dr. Chazel?"

"Yes." Christopher wasn't about to admit to Tad that he'd just killed his so-called loving wife and the man he'd considered a friend. His house had to have already been reduced to rubble and ash. He'd set the fire himself. It had been easy to dig out the bullets expelled from his gun and bring some candles into the bedroom. He'd taken booze from the bar and spilled it all over the bed, then knocked one of the candles over. The *whish* he heard as flames spread had felt appropriate. His marriage had ended just as destructively and fast.

He'd almost walked out of the bedroom, but movement caught his attention. Candi had stood there, cowering against the wall behind the door. The shots from his gun must have woken her. She wasn't supposed to be home. It was one of the reasons he'd left work early. She'd been invited to a sleepover. He'd wanted to surprise his wife with a romantic evening but she'd started without him, with another man.

Candi had trembled in her little pink nightgown, eyes wide and showing signs of shock. He wasn't sure how much she'd seen but obviously too much. The bullets he'd dug out with a steak knife were in his pocket. So was the knife. He moved fast, the fire spreading at an alarming rate. She'd stiffened in his arms when he'd lifted her and strode down the hallway. Then she'd whimpered. He'd glanced down and knew without a doubt that she understood he'd just killed her mother.

"Where did you get the girl?" Tad tapped the monitor by the door after they entered the hallway. "She's a cute little thing."

The black-and-white screen came to life and pulled Christopher from his memories of an hour before. He looked up at the feed. The pup moved cautiously toward his daughter. His spine stiffed. He would kill the little bastard if it tore into Candi's throat, but it just sniffed at her and then reached out, touching her cheek with a finger. It explored her honey-colored hair next, sniffed at it and began playing with the strands.

"What?" He hadn't paid attention to what Tad had said.

"The little girl. Where'd you get her?"

"Mind your own business. Keep watch. Stun the little bastard and chain it up if it attacks her. I want to see if it'll accept her as one of its own. She's important to our research. Make sure she gets medical attention if she needs it."

"You gave a pup a pet?" The guard laughed. "That's hilarious."

Christopher wasn't amused. He had things to do. The police would contact him soon. He'd swear he never left work. The company would back him after he talked to his supervisor. Mercile Industries needed to make sure they produced bogus proof to give him an airtight alibi. Evelyn would salivate once she realized the kind of research they could do with Candi. *Candace*, he corrected. He had to distance himself from her.

He spun away and stormed down the hallway. He wasn't going to prison. His own daughter would put him there if she ever told the police what he'd done. No way did he plan to go down because his wife had been a whore. It was unfortunate but he needed to save his own ass. Evelyn would agree. She'd hired him herself and believed in his research. He'd be protected.

Chapter One

Four days ago

Candi sat calmly in the chair, her fingers curled around the arms. It was never good when Penny wanted to have a conversation. *Did someone notice I faked taking my pills again?* She'd mastered the pretext of being still and emotionless. Patience had been learned since the last time she'd tried to escape.

The door opened and the woman who walked in took a seat at the empty desk. There were no pens, mementos, or even a paper clip on the surface. The room had been stripped of anything a patient could steal. Sunlight glinted off the bars through the clean windows of the office but Candi ignored it. It would not attract her attention if she was as drugged as she wanted them to believe.

"Look at me."

Candi lifted her gaze and stared into what most would consider to be kind amber eyes, framed by a pair of matronly glasses. She knew better. Penny had no heart and the morals of a brick. The two of them had a long history. She'd believed once that the truth would set her free. Instead it had gotten her more heavily medicated and they had locked her in solitary confinement.

"I have some sad news. Your father passed away a few days ago of a pulmonary embolism. I was just informed."

Christopher is dead. Candi had dreamed of hearing that news for too long. It didn't bring a sense of relief the way she had once believed it would. That had been back when she'd been naïve, thinking her prison sentence would end once his life did. She knew better now, being older and smarter. They were never going to let her out, not even after she'd seen those news stories on the television. Penny would have seen them too. Nothing had changed.

Movement by the door registered at the edge of Candi's vision, but she didn't turn her head to look. She could just make out two big shapes. Orderlies had just arrived. *Shit.* She kept her emotions hidden, aware that the director watched her closely.

Penny turned her head. "Give us a few minutes."

The door closed and Candi verified that the two figures had left—their footsteps were soft in the hallway. She remained still, just blinking a few times.

"Did you hear me, Candace? Your father died."

She nodded slightly after calculating how long ago she'd been given her pills. Twenty minutes had passed, tops. She'd be pretty out of it, but not entirely.

"How do you feel?"

"Sleepy." She purposely slurred the word.

"I knew the truth," the other woman admitted, keeping her voice low. "I did a little side work for Mercile Industries. The money was too good to resist. I counseled some of the staff who had issues dealing with the important work they did."

It pissed Candi off. She'd suspected something was fishy when she'd seen those news stories with Justice North but no one had released her. She'd thought at first that Penny might have been afraid to admit she'd helped keep Candi under wraps, but time had proven that she didn't have the balls to do the right thing. Now she knew she'd never stood a chance of that happening. Her grip tightened on the plastic padding of the chair, but she relaxed before it was noticed. She'd worked too hard to give herself away in a fit of anger.

"Christopher and I were close." Penny reached up and adjusted her glasses. "Lovers. It ended a few years ago when he had to leave the country after the facilities were raided, but no one could tie me to that mess. He paid well for me to keep you here. I've felt guilty about that more than a few times. You know I looked out for you though, don't you? I made sure none of the orderlies or staff messed with you."

Candi yawned, blinking a few more times.

"You're a pretty girl," the director went on. "You were never beaten or sexually abused. It happens in these places, but not to you. I only assigned the people I trusted and made damn sure they knew your father was a rich, powerful man who would see them in hell if anyone ever laid a finger on you."

Penny paused for a few seconds. "That wasn't true. I mean, he had money, but he pretty much went off the grid once your mother died in that fire. He became paranoid that he'd be arrested. The thing is, now he's dead, and he won't be able to make the payments for your care anymore."

And here it comes, Candi surmised. *The death sentence.* She had to give the other woman some credit for at least finally telling her the truth, even if her reasons were selfish. It was a guilt dump in some sorry attempt to make herself feel better.

"I can't let you walk out of here. You'd tell them what I did. I never documented the things you told me from the therapy sessions about your childhood and that would look suspicious. I never allowed anyone else to work with you. The authorities would pour over your medical records if anyone actually believed your story. I'd go to prison."

That would be nice since you've kept me in one. Candi wished she could say it aloud.

"I can't afford to foot the bill for your care. That leaves me in a bad position. Do you understand?"

Yeah. You're a coldblooded bitch, willing to do anything to save your sorry ass. Candi yawned again and lifted her hand to rub her eyes. The signs of exhaustion were easier to fake. She was getting tired of hearing the bullshit.

"We're going to go on a little trip. We'll visit the woods." Penny paused. "I told the staff that your father wants you transferred. Because of a few lawsuits, we are legally bound to give your body to the coroner's office so they can perform an autopsy, or I'd just end things here. I can't risk that since I'd be held accountable if you overdosed or had an accident. They'd do an inquiry and then I'd have to explain too much. I told the staff your father is retiring and wants you closer." Penny stood and rounded the desk, stopping behind Candi's chair.

By sheer will, she didn't flinch away when the woman put a hand on her shoulder and bent, placing a kiss on the top of her head. Penny wouldn't dare kill her at that moment, but she would soon. Candi's carefully laid plans to escape the building and grounds were smashed. She'd have to think of something else, and fast.

"You just sleep. You'll wake in a much better place. I'm sorry, honey. Close your eyes."

Candi fumed inside but she let her eyes close, making her body go lax. Her chin dipped and she concentrated on slowing her heart rate. She had a lot of practice at it. Time ticked by. It was probably only a few minutes, but it seemed to take forever before Penny moved away and opened the door.

"Jorg? Marco? Come in here. She's out. Can you please take her to my car?"

Candi knew it was Marco who slid his arms under her, lifting her from the chair. He wore a nice cologne that was her only reminder of what a summer day might have smelled like. It wasn't as if she could really remember that far back. He was one of the few she didn't hate. He never groped her or said mean things.

"Your car?" He sounded a little suspicious. "Why not an ambulance? That's how we usually transfer them."

"I told you about her father. The less paperwork, the better. He personally asked me to drive her to the private hospital and have her admitted. It's the least I can do."

"Do you want one of us to go with you? I mean, how far away is this place? She should be out for at least five hours, but there's a slim chance she might wake." Jorg sounded close.

"She's a doll now," Marco argued. "She won't give the director any problems. Hell, it's been about ten months since she had an episode."

"That's what you want to call that?" Jorg snorted. "She grabbed a nurse and threatened to break her neck if someone didn't give her a phone. She wanted to call that NSO place because she thinks she's one of them. She sure was acting like an animal."

"The private-care hospital her father found is less than an hour's drive away." Penny's voice came from behind them. "It will be fine."

Yeah, she doesn't want any witnesses when she kills me. Keep lying, Penny.

"I don't know," Jorg argued. "She's a tricky one. My first week here, she tried to tell me she was being kept prisoner and to please call the police." He laughed. "Like that was a new one. Most of the patients say that, but she was making up some crazy shit."

"We don't use that word," Penny snapped.

"Right." Jorg moved ahead, probably opening doors for them. "Just make sure you warn the poor bastards who are going to care for her next. She's a fighter when the drugs wear off. She broke Sal's nose and two of

Emily's fingers. Do you want me to sedate her a little more just to be sure, Dr. Pess?"

That terrified Candi. One jab of the needle and she wouldn't stand a chance. She was tempted to snap her eyes open and fight but held off. There wasn't any way she could get through the locked doors while they were still inside the building. Jorg and Marco were too strong. They'd take her down fast and subdue her.

"No." Penny sounded irritated. "She'll be fine."

Realizing she might actually survive, Candi's fear faded. She kept her muscles relaxed, even when Marco bumped her arm against one of the walls. It would probably leave a bruise, but that was the least of her troubles. She still needed to figure out what to do once she was alone with Penny, if something didn't go wrong before then.

Cool, fresh air caressed Candi's skin. It felt glorious. She was outside. The temptation to open her eyes made her ache. It had been what seemed like forever since she'd seen it without dirty glass and bars marring the view. She'd lost track of time, the only hint of its passing was the decorations the staff put up at holidays, but there were large gaps when they'd kept her so heavily sedated that she wasn't sure what year it was anymore.

A small dinging sounded and Marco maneuvered her body, putting her on something soft but firm in a sitting position. He slid his arms free and arranged her hands on her lap. Something crossed over her chest and lap. *A belt.* He gripped her chin and the back of her head last, turning it so it rested on something solid.

"There you go. I wouldn't take turns too fast. She'll slump." Marco let her go.

"She'll be fine." Penny kept close. "Thank you. I've got it from here."

"Are you sure you don't want one of us to tag along?"

Damn Jorg. Paranoid asshole. He'd thwarted her many times in her attempts to escape.

"I'm sure." Penny's tone took on a hint of irritation. "She's not going to give me any problems and the hospital staff will meet me outside with a wheelchair."

Something clicked next to her—the car door being closed. Another one opened and the car moved a little when Penny settled in somewhere ahead of her and a little to the left. Candi had learned to use her hearing as well, if not better, than her eyesight to keep tabs on everything around her. The second door closed and an engine started. It made slight vibrations under her ass and along her back. The vehicle pulled forward, soft music coming from four directions. They were moving.

Candi remained still, knowing they needed to pass the guard shack. Ten-foot walls surrounded the property. They were almost impossible to climb. She'd found that out once right after she'd been brought to her new hell. They also had barbed wire along the top. She had the scars on one palm to prove that, acquired when she'd climbed a tree to get that high. The car stopped and the music lowered. A soft whine came next and fresh air poured into the interior from the left.

"Hello, Director Pess. What's going on?"

"I'm transferring a patient."

"By yourself?" The guard sounded surprised.

"She's one of our special guests. Her father is a politician. He's managed to keep it out of the press so far that his daughter needs help and he wants to keep it that way. She's sedated."

"Of course. Have a good day."

There was a slight whine again and then the fresh air was gone. The car edged forward seconds later and picked up speed. Candi barely opened her eyes to stare at the backseat of the car. She'd been belted into the back right passenger side. The first time the car made a turn, she let her head roll, allowing her to see more. They traveled along a country road. A few cars passed.

She was outside the gates, no longer behind the bars and glass. Her heart pounded and adrenaline surged, but she kept still. *Patience. It's not time yet*. Penny would have to take her somewhere remote to kill her. *Boy, is that bitch in for a surprise*. A smile threatened to curve her lips but she resisted the temptation. *I'm so close.*

Candi allowed her mind to drift to keep her occupied during the wait. One memory always surfaced first. It kept her sane when she wanted to just give in and die…

~ ~ ~ ~ ~

His eyes were dark brown, almost black. They scared everyone but her. A glint of humor sparked in them and he fluttered those long black eyelashes. It was his attempt to look innocent, but she never bought it. She knew him too well.

"Don't," she warned.

"What?" He leaned closer until their breath mingled.

"You know." She was certain he did. She turned her head, glancing at the camera in the corner, and then back at him. "They are watching."

"They always watch." He smiled.

He had the best lips. She stared at them, wanting to run her finger over the bottom one. It was slightly fuller than the top. It looked so soft and tempting.

"Now who is being bad?" His voice grew husky.

She peered into his eyes. "They'll make me go back to my room if you touch me."

"I want to."

She'd never lie to him. "I think about you all the time."

He closed his eyes, a pained expression on his face. His boyish features had transformed into maturity over the past few years. He took on a harsh expression when he was angry or upset, but at the moment he just looked vulnerable to her.

"I heard them talking."

His eyes snapped open. "About what?"

It was a little embarrassing, but she never kept secrets from him. "Evelyn wants to put us together and let us share a room again. She doesn't agree with Christopher keeping us apart. They were fighting about it."

"She does?" He sucked in a sharp breath.

Heat bloomed in her cheeks. "She wants us to, um, you know."

His gaze roamed down her body. His breathing increased the tiniest bit, but Candi noticed. She could relate. He looked at her. "Are you going to say yes if she asks?"

"I would."

He reached out, breaking the rules Christopher had implemented. His warm hand brushed her knee. It was just for a second though, as if adjusting how he sat was the reason. She hoped the guard assigned to watch the camera had missed it, or wouldn't bust them for such a minor infraction.

"They know how we feel about each other."

"It's why they took you away." His temper flared.

"I know. Christopher showed me a tape of two people having sex."

"Did it frighten you? I'd never hurt you."

"I know. And no, I wasn't afraid. That was his plan, though. It just made me understand why I suddenly noticed things about you."

"Like what?"

She glanced at his chest and arms, and then his mouth again. "You know."

He smiled. "You want me too."

Her chest ached. "More than anything. I hate that they only let us see each other once a week now." She glanced around the room they used to share. "I miss this being our space." She stared into his eyes. "I miss you holding me when we sleep." Tears filled her eyes. "I miss everything about you."

"Talk to Evelyn. Tell her yes."

"It's not that simple. Christopher said no. They got into an argument in the hallway that was loud enough for me to hear. He said I'm too young, and we have to wait a few years before he'll agree to allow that experiment." She'd felt resentment. "Like what we are to each other is nothing."

His nose flared, a sure sign he was about to go into a rage. She shook her head, silently pleading with him to keep it under control. They'd pull her out of the room if he got loud or did anything aggressive. The chains secured to his wrists and ankles could be used to yank him against the wall, and he would not be able to stop them.

"I know it's frustrating," she admitted. "But at least he didn't say no outright. He just said that I'm too young. That means we'll be back together at some point. Be good. Please? Don't make them hurt you. I can't stand that. It tears me apart when I see bruises on you."

"I'll do whatever they want if it means we can be together."

"Thank you." She fisted her hand in her lap, wanting to touch him instead. She missed running her fingers through his silky black hair. "Don't let them make you angry. We'll be together again soon, and they won't keep us apart."

He bent a little, drawing closer. "You be good too. Do whatever it takes. I need you with me."

~ ~ ~ ~ ~

The car slowed and left the road. The motion shook Candi out her reminiscences, right back into the present. The wheels seemed to be on something uneven and bumpy. She peeked, letting her head fall when a really severe jarring caused her entire body to lurch to one side.

She spotted a lot of trees and grass. The car slowed and the engine died. So did the music. Penny opened the driver's door and slammed it. It was no longer possible for Candi to track her by sound. She closed her eyes all the way, her hand near the metal buckle latch. She twisted her wrist a tiny bit until her thumb found the release. She waited, still and ready.

The door next to her opened and she stopped feigning sleep. Penny bent, her attention on getting something out of her purse. It was a knife with a long blade. Candi pushed the button and the buckle released with a soft click. The other woman must have heard it because her head snapped up, her eyes going wide.

Candi lunged and grasped the handle of the knife. Penny shrieked and tried to stab her, but Candi had primal survival instinct and loads of adrenaline on her side. She kicked out, knocking the other woman to the ground. She fell out of the car, landing on the woman's chest. They struggled but the older woman lost.

Time stopped as another memory surfaced. It had been the last time she'd seen *him*…

~ ~ ~ ~ ~

He snarled, fighting his chains. Rage had taken hold of him. He pulled back his lips, baring his sharp fangs.

"I'll kill you!" he roared.

It tore her apart from the inside out, hearing him make that threat and knowing it was directed at her. He didn't understand. She kept far back from him, knowing he probably would unless she got him to listen. He seemed to have known what she'd done as soon as she'd stepped inside the room. He'd gone insane.

"Please listen." She had two minutes to explain and tried to do so, her heart breaking.

He threw back his head, bellowing his rage loud enough to hurt her ears. His muscles strained as he fought and he managed to snap the links of the chain attached to one arm.

One of the technicians grabbed her around her waist and yanked her off her feet. She fought. "No! Put me down."

They weren't listening either. The man she loved freed one arm and grabbed hold of the other chain still holding him hostage to the wall. "I'll kill you," he snarled again.

"I did it for you!" she screamed, wildly fighting the guard. She actually kicked him hard enough in the shin to make him stumble. She threw back her head, pain exploding from the impact when she made contact with his chin. He dropped her.

She rushed forward, right at the man who was losing his mind. "Please," she begged, crying. "I—"

Another guard grabbed her around her waist, stopping her in her tracks.

The second restraint broke and the man she loved spun, trying to grab her. The broken, loose chain still attached to his wrist flew out when his grasping hand tried to reach her. She never it saw it coming but felt the metal links slam into the side of her head. Everything had gone black. She woke to see the face of Penny Pess. Her old life was gone and her new hell had begun…

~ ~ ~ ~ ~

Candi plunged the knife into the woman's chest. Penny didn't scream but her mouth opened as if she wanted to. Candi jerked the knife free, grabbed the handle with both hands and stabbed her again, putting all her rage behind it. It sank deep, until the knife became stuck.

"Roast in hell!"

She stared at Penny, watching the life leave her. There was no guilt or sense of regret. She sat there for a short time. When she finally looked up there was trees and grass all around her. A slight noise came from somewhere behind her. The source was the highway and the cars passing along it. She got to her feet and looked up at the blue sky. *I'm going to avenge you,* she swore.

Chapter Two

Present day

Candi ignored the panic that rose when she approached those thirty-foot walls. Guards with guns stood along the top. There was no barbed wire, but it didn't alleviate the apprehension that she was willingly about to enter another prison. She ignored the idiots on the sidewalks who tried to talk to her. They weren't worth her time. She marched forward until the barrels of large, menacing weapons were aimed at her and a deep voice shouted, "Freeze!"

She stopped and took care not to make any sudden movements. She lifted her arms out, palms open so they could see she wasn't armed. Her right hand had a small cut from the knife fight, but it had scabbed over a bit. Her gaze darted to those black-clad figures, and she tried to determine who was in charge and who belonged to that voice. It was impossible to tell since they wore helmets and dark glass covered their faces.

She waited as more guards rushed to the gate, adding more guns pointed in her direction. She'd already endured the hard part. She'd hitchhiked across five states to reach the NSO Homeland without being killed or arrested. It was lucky that people knew exactly where it was located since she'd had to ask. Her time watching any kind of news had been limited at best. She closed her eyes, focusing.

"Miss, you need to turn around and leave. You're not allowed to come this close to the gates. Move on."

She opened her eyes and turned her head left, locating the one who spoke. It was easier to pinpoint him by listening. "You sound human. I learned a few things yesterday from a trucker. He said the NSO employs a task force team that is human. I want to talk to a New Species. Get one."

"How the hell would you know what I sound like?"

"Because you don't sound like one of them. Get me a New Species." She held still, closing her eyes. *Patience*.

"Who are you? State your business."

She cocked her head, focused on the new voice. "Say something else."

A very low growl sounded from the same person and she smiled. It was enough, even if he hadn't said a word. She fixed her gaze on the guard in the middle, standing behind the gate. "I'll talk to you. You sound like a canine, but that can be deceptive since you're probably irritated with me."

"What the hell?" The man from the top of the wall sputtered. "Lady, take a walk. You're sounding crazy."

"It wouldn't be the first time someone has accused me of that." She took a step closer but stopped, not looking away from the one who'd growled under his breath. "As much as I hate to say this, because I really can't stand to be locked behind gates, you need to let me in."

"We're going to call the cops and have you taken away if you don't leave. I'm done playing with you, lady." It was the guard up on the wall again.

"Shut up, human. I'm talking to him." She kept her gaze locked on the male behind the gate.

"Human? What the hell do you think you are?"

The guard on the wall was starting to piss her off. She pulled back her upper lip and snarled low at the one behind the gate. "I was told you were freed. Humans still tell you what to do? Are they as bad as technicians? He seems like an asshole. Can you shut him up?"

"I'm an asshole? Look, lady," the guard on the wall leaned over a bit, speaking louder, "I'll have your ass hauled away faster than you can say you're fucked. Now leave."

She took a deep breath and blew it out. It was obvious that the male behind the gate wasn't going to talk to her again so she'd have to deal with the annoying jerk up on the wall. She turned her head slightly to glare at him.

"You think you can frighten me?" She shook her head, then looked at the male behind the gates. "Four days ago I escaped captivity and killed a woman who worked for Mercile. You remember them, don't you? I'm tired, hungry, dirty, and I don't like what I've seen of this world so far. I don't belong out here, but I do belong in there, even with your walls."

Absolute silence reigned. She had their attention. She cleared her throat. "I'm going to slowly reach behind me and withdraw a knife. I'll toss it to you. Your nose will tell you I speak the truth."

They didn't shoot her when she did exactly that, tossing the knife a few feet from the gates and in the direction of the male behind it. The metal blade clattered on the pavement. She waited, watching him. He motioned with his hand and the gates opened a few feet.

"Stay still," he demanded in a harsh tone.

She didn't move a muscle. He stepped out and bent. She could hear him sniff, and his helmeted head snapped up. A deeper growl emanated from him.

"You're not a canine. You're feline. My apologies."

"You can tell that by the sound I make?" He picked up the knife and stood but didn't retreat.

"No. They can sound the same, but you had to get closer to that blade. A canine wouldn't have had to. His sense of smell is better than yours."

"Who the hell are you?"

"Candace Chazel, formally experiment H dash 01. Some of the asshole technicians shortened it HOL but said the word hole as I got older, because they knew what my purpose would be. I would appreciate not being called that. It was an insult and brings back a lot of bad memories."

The male passed the knife back to another guard, then his gun. He approached and tears filled her eyes. She blinked them back, but watching him strut forward—there was no other way to describe how a feline moved—was finally something familiar and welcome. He stopped close. She wished she could see his face, but that black, glass shield was too dark, too murky.

"Explain."

"That's going to take some time, but I was raised at Mercile too."

He sniffed at her. "I don't believe for a second that you're Species."

"I'm not, but I was raised there. One of the doctors decided they'd like to find out what would happen if they put a five-year-old human girl into one of the cells with a canine male." She peered up at him. "I was there until I was sixteen." She pushed back the painful memories. "After that I was taken to a human place where they kept me drugged and locked up. Do you know what an asylum is, for crazy humans? The doctor who made me an experiment paid them to keep me there so I couldn't tell anyone about Mercile, or what they did below ground. The woman in charge of that hellhole also worked for Mercile. That's her blood you just smelled. The doctor in charge of putting me inside Mercile is dead too. Two down, and so many more to go. I want your help finding the rest of the technicians and doctors. They need to pay for what they did."

He said nothing. It made her angry.

"I could have given up and just died. I refused. Do you know why? I spent every waking moment plotting revenge. They killed the male I loved. He was my everything. He's dead and they will pay for it." She growled low, furious. "I won't rest until every one of them is dead too. I am not asking for your help. I am demanding it. You owe him the same. We're here, but he's not."

The big feline reached up and pulled off his helmet. His long black hair reminded her of the male she'd lost, but his catlike, deep-blue eyes were drastically different from the dark-brown ones that haunted her. He frowned, seemingly unconvinced.

"Do you want me to describe our cell? One sink, a toilet, and a pad on the floor. No blankets. We had a hose to shower with. Every room I saw was the same. They had a medical supply closet in the far corner, past the kill-zone line. They had a mechanical rigging system of chains on the wall. Sound familiar? There were constant injections and they played stupid games while they tested their drugs. You were fed seared meat on platters they brought in while they restrained you against that wall." She lowered her voice. "Breeding experiments were performed, hoping to create more of you through natural births since they could no longer use surrogate births. I was there."

He paled a little.

"They used us against each other. You know how fucked-up they could be. They made me decide between doing something that would hurt my male, or watching my male be murdered in front of me as punishment. I would have done and endured anything to save him. I did." She inched closer and clutched his uniform sleeve. "I didn't understand the game that time and they used my decision to snap his mind. He died howling and enraged." Tears slipped down her cheeks. "He thought I betrayed him. That's the last memory I have of the male I loved. They killed him, but I have survived to see this day. Help me find every last bastard who was there and make them pay."

"Jinx?" It was the annoying guard up on the wall. "What the hell is she saying? Are you all right? Get back from her."

The male moved slowly and his big, gloved hand covered her own. He didn't force her to let him go, but instead just held on. "What do you like to be called?"

The tightness in her chest eased. "He called me Candi."

"Come with me, Candi. I believe you. You're safe."

She released his shirt, but he kept hold of her, laced their fingers together, and slowly turned. She kept pace with him as he walked her through the gates. All her fear and worry dropped away. For the first time she felt safe.

"It's okay." He glanced around at the males. "Someone get on the radio and tell Medical we're on our way there. Call Justice and tell him we have a situation. He needs to meet me there. Breeze too."

She jerked to a halt, instantly fearful. He stopped and turned his head.

"I'm not crazy. Don't drug me again." She yanked her hand out of his, backing up. "No more drugs. No more locked rooms and silence."

"Easy." He just dropped his helmet on the ground. "I just want a doctor to examine you. They work for us." He glanced down her body. "You don't look well. We do it to all incoming Species. No one is going to drug or hurt you."

Candi felt torn. "I'm telling you the truth. Don't send me back out there. I don't belong. I have to find the ones who killed my male and make them pay."

"We will." He eased forward.

She backed up. The slight sound of a footstep alerted her and she spun, snarling at the black-clad guard who'd sneaked up behind her. She reacted when he tried to grab her arm. Her reflexes were slow, but she threw up her forearm, batting his hand away. She frantically looked for a place to flee.

"Back off!" Jinx snarled. "Get away from her."

The guy threw up his arms, jumping back. "I was trying to help."

"Don't. Candi?" Jinx tried to regain her attention.

She turned sideways so she could see them both.

"It's okay." Jinx lowered his voice to a soothing tone. "I give you my word. I believe you. Did you learn that from him? The snarling? You're good at it."

She nodded.

"You said he was canine, right?"

She nodded again.

"Torrent?" He'd raised his voice. "Remove your helmet and come over here. Slowly."

She saw the motion at the edge of her vision and watched one of the other guards take off his helmet. He was canine, his silky black hair pulled into a ponytail. He approached cautiously, his blue gaze fixed on her.

"What's going on? I couldn't hear what was said out there. I was too far away and you forgot to turn on your helmet mic again."

He reminded her of 927, with that hair. Tears filled her eyes as she stared at him.

He stopped, his dark eyebrows arching. "No one will harm you, small female."

"Female," she couldn't help but laugh. "I actually miss being called that. How silly is that? Humans don't use those terms normally, unless they are describing the gender of a person. It's nice to meet you, male."

The dismay on his face was almost comical too. He glanced at Jinx, apparently confused. "What is going on?"

"What is protocol when we find one of ours from Mercile?"

Torrent gasped, staring at her.

"Answer," Jinx demanded. "Where is the first place we take one of ours?"

"Medical."

"Why?"

Torrent glanced at Jinx, then at her. "To check their health and see if they need medical care."

Jinx took another step closer. "I spoke the truth, Candi. He's not lying. Let's go there. Please don't fear us. We'd never hurt one of our own and that's what you are. Do you understand?"

She nodded.

He eased closer and held out his hand. "It's going to be okay. No one is going to hurt or trick you. No deceitful games. That's for humans. We don't play them."

"Okay." It was tough to trust anyone, but staring into his feline eyes, she was willing to try.

He pulled back his hand, tore off his gloves and dropped them on the ground. He reached out to her again and gently laced his fingers through hers. His skin felt warm to the touch. A tentative smile curved his lips. "Easy, female. It's okay."

"You don't need to baby me."

"Maybe I want to. You've been through a lot, but it's going to be okay. I promise you that."

* * * * *

Hero chose to take the stairs rather than the elevator down to the lobby. He was too impatient to wait for the slow-moving machinery. He had a night off his shift and planned to have fun. There would be dancing involved and he'd heard they were serving prime rib at the bar. He reached the first floor and came to a stop, staring at the group of males gathered by the couches. Some appeared downright angry. He changed direction.

"What's going on?"

Destiny was the first to speak. The primate male still wore his work uniform. It was obvious he'd just left there, judging by the smell of

Medical coming off him. "They brought in a female. I was just telling everyone about it. We're stunned."

"One of the females got hurt? Is it bad?" The news alarmed Hero.

Destiny leaned against the back of a couch, partially sitting on the edge. "I guess I'll start from the beginning. A human female showed up at the front gates. Jinx and Torrent brought her in about an hour ago. She's underweight, the palest human I've ever seen, but from her history, it's understandable. The humans kept her locked up in an asylum. That's a hospital for humans with mental illnesses."

"Tell him the important part," Snow urged.

Destiny nodded. "She is human but was raised like we were by Mercile. I didn't want to believe it, but you should have heard her snarl when we drew blood. She sounds just like one of our females when they feel pain. I was listening to her talk to Justice and Breeze while Doc Trisha examined her. This human female gave them precise details about her life at Mercile. A doctor took her there when she was just a young child and raised her inside a cell with one of our males. A canine."

Hero didn't hear any more as blood roared to his ears, obliterating sound. Reacting before he could think, he snarled, slamming into the door before he realized he exited the building. It gave from the force of his weight, and then he was outside, running toward Medical.

It can't be. He ignored the dull ache in his side when he pushed his body beyond its limits, not even bothering to check for traffic when he rushed into the street. Someone yelled at him but he ignored it. The building housing Medical came into sight and he jumped the curb. He only slowed since the automatic double doors couldn't open as quickly as he moved.

Paul, the nurse, stood up from the other side of the reception desk. "What's wrong? Is there an emergency?"

He inhaled the second he entered, ignoring the male. Familiar scents came to him, just not the one he sought.

"Hero? Are you okay? What's wrong?" Paul came forward. "Is someone hurt? Are you?"

"Where is the female?"

"Doc Trisha? She's talking to Justice and Breeze in her office."

Hero spun right, striding fast down the hallway toward the exam rooms. Paul called out to him, but he didn't bother to acknowledge him. He turned a corner and spotted Jinx and Torrent leaning against the wall across from a closed door. They both turned their heads to stare at him.

"Where is the human?"

Jinx pushed away from the wall. "Showering. I take it you heard? We're still processing the shock of it, but she is the real deal. We're certain."

He sniffed again. He could pick up an unfamiliar female scent but not the one he sought. A stabbing pain jabbed his chest.

"Are you all right?" Jinx studied him. "You're really flushed and panting. Should I get Doc Trisha?"

"No."

"Okay. Well, this area is off limits. We don't want anyone to frighten the female. She's been through a lot. Breeze is going to take her to the women's dorm as soon as the new female is done showering and is dressed. They are treating her as if she's a Gift."

It was a polite hint to leave. He turned around, a sense of loss making that pain in his chest worse. He might think he was having a heart attack if he was human. It was probably the stress of running that hard and then having his hope dashed.

"All done," a female voice called out. "I'm ready to go." The door opened.

He turned his head and stared at a slender female form framed in the doorway. She was a little thing, too skinny, and her waist-length hair dampened the baggy clothing she'd been given. His gaze lifted. She stared directly at Jinx, but the profile of her face was enough. She'd changed, but not enough to fool him. He'd know her anywhere, especially since she visited his nightmares often. A snarl tore from his throat and it jarred him to motion. He twisted toward her as she looked directly at him.

There was no mistaking those eyes that widened at the sight of him—light golden-brown with little splashes of green spread around the irises. Eyes he would recognize anywhere. They'd always made him dream of the parks she'd told him about, all those trees with leaves that changed colors with different seasons. He'd seen hope of a future that was never meant to be every time he'd gazed into them. Then that last time, the pure terror that he'd caused.

She took a stumbling step forward, hitting the side of her shoulder on the edge of the doorframe. Her mouth opened but no words came out. She looked as shocked and stunned as he felt. He got closer to her, inhaling her scent. It was foreign. He reached up and touched the side of her head. He wasn't gentle when he stabbed his fingers into the wet strands, tearing his gaze from hers to look where he parted it.

A faint scar marred her scalp just over her ear. He jerked back as if she'd burned him. He almost stepped on Jinx's boot.

"927?" Tears filled her eyes, giving them a sheen. "They told me you were dead." She reached out for him, but he avoided her touch by stumbling back. She froze.

"You died," he managed to get out. A roaring sounded in Hero's head and his vision blurred. He wasn't in Medical anymore, but back inside his cell at Mercile…

~ ~ ~ ~ ~

The chain slashed across the side of her head and she went down, blood spilling across the concrete floor of his cell. It was so red, wet and warm when he threw himself down, reaching for her. The chains still connected his ankles to the wall. The length barely allowed him to reach her, but he got a grip on her arm.

She was so still. The technicians shouted as they rushed out of his room. They didn't matter. Only she did. He hadn't meant to hurt her. *No*, he mentally corrected. He'd wanted to kill her, but seeing her fall, and all that blood, horrified him. He'd done that to her.

"Candi," he rasped, dragging her closer. Her body was limp as she lay in the blood that smeared the floor. "No. Open your eyes."

He pulled her close enough to put his face next to hers. She didn't open her eyes, but her chest rose and fell. She was breathing. He reached up, his hand shaking as he gently pressed his palm against the wound where the chain had struck. He needed to stop the bleeding. He applied pressure and looked toward the open door of his cell.

"Help!"

Where had the guards gone? They'd never left the door open before, but they had that time. There was shouting down the hallway and an alarm blared. He lowered his face, his vision blinded by tears. "Open your eyes," he pleaded.

Heavy boots thundered down the hall. Help would come. They'd take her to a doctor and fix her. He held her head until the first dart penetrated his back. He didn't fight when he could have. He didn't make a sound or move. He just wanted them to get into his cell and help her. Three more darts pierced his skin—tranquilizers.

"Help her!" His voice was ragged, panicked.

The drugs kicked in fast and he couldn't move anymore as they paralyzed him. His cheek hit the cold floor, but her head lay next to his. He felt her there. More boots pounded down the hall and the alarm stopped.

"What have you done?" It was Dr. C. "Oh my god. Get a gurney in here stat!"

He couldn't hear her breathing anymore over all the other noises in the room. She was taken away. The cell door slammed shut and all he could do was lie there, smelling the fresh scent of her coppery blood, fighting to remain conscious.

He woke chained to the wall. They'd replaced the ones he'd snapped. A stain remained on the floor inside his cell and his hand was crusty with her dried blood. Dr. C entered his cell minutes later.

"Is she well?" He was terrified, sick with worry. He didn't even care what they did to him. He just wanted to be told that Candi lived.

"You killed her." Dr. C looked at him with such hatred. He held something behind his back. "She died. You crushed her skull, you animal." His arm arched out as he swung the broken chain. It struck him in the stomach.

He closed his eyes and didn't feel it as the blows kept coming. His skin split in places, his own blood spilling. A few bones broke. It didn't matter. He didn't even try to twist away in an attempt to avoid the chain as it struck him over and over. He'd killed Candi. She was dead. He wished for death too…

~ ~ ~ ~ ~

"It's you," the voice of the dead female whispered.

The roaring faded, his vision cleared and he jerked back to the present to focus on Candi. She was real and alive. Another memory surfaced. The scent she had carried that day and the reason he'd fought those chains. He needed to get away from her. He'd mourned her loss a long time ago. She'd died that day, whether from his chain striking her head or not. She'd killed him inside too.

"Hero?" Jinx took a few steps toward him, but stopped. He looked at the female, his mouth open. Hero turned and fled.

Hero nearly knocked Paul over in his rush to leave Medical. He needed to get out of the building, away from her. He ran with no destination in mind, just kept going until his legs gave out. He landed on the grass. The park surrounded him.

A Species female came over and crouched next to him. "Hero? What's wrong?"

"Leave me alone." He didn't want to talk to Sunshine.

Her gentle hand stroked his hair. "Hero?"

He squeezed his eyes closed as he lay sprawled on the grass, panting. He would have gotten up but he had worn his body out in his flight for life. At least, that was how it felt. He had a new life now. The female in Medical would destroy the male he'd become. He couldn't allow it. She should be dead and buried. He'd left her in the past and she should have stayed there.

Sunshine sniffed at him and lay down to press against his side. She wrapped an arm around his back. They were friends. They'd even shared sex from time to time.

"I'm here. Whatever is wrong, you're not alone."

She continued to stroke his hair, keeping against his side. If other Species were nearby, they stayed away. He finally caught his breath, but refused to look at her. He wasn't certain how long he remained there, but it wasn't long. He needed to get up.

"Thank you." He rolled away, separating them. He glanced around, but didn't see anyone else.

Sunshine sat up, concern evident when he looked at her. "You can talk to me about anything."

"Not this." He stood. "Thank you." He headed in the direction of the men's dorm. He needed to leave Homeland and go to Reservation. He couldn't be in the same place as Candi.

Chapter Three

"He's alive." Candi still reeled from seeing him.

"That's who you were raised with?"

She almost collapsed but the canine male, Torrent, lunged forward and grabbed her around her waist, hauling her up into his arms. He carried her back into the exam room she'd just left and placed her on the bed. He slid his arms out from under her. "Jinx, get Doc Trisha. She's whiter than the sheets."

"Fuck," Jinx muttered and rushed down the hallway.

Torrent took her hand. "Look at me."

She did.

"Hero is the male you thought had died?"

"He's alive."

She realized she'd said that before. It was just too unbelievable. Christopher Chazel had visited her one time after sending her to Penny. He'd sat in a chair next to the bed where they kept her restrained, machines hooked up to her while she healed from a head injury. He'd told her in a cold voice that he'd personally terminated 927. It hadn't surprised her. She knew he could kill. She'd seen him do it before. But he'd lied.

927 was alive and the canine and feline males had called him Hero. She let that sink in, then jerked her hand out of Torrent's. She tried to sit

up. She needed to find 927. *Why did he leave me? Why did he take off like that?* It tore at her.

"No!" Torrent pushed her flat. "Stay down."

"I have to go after him. I have to find him."

"He took off like a bat out of hell. I don't think he wants to see you."

"I need to see him." She shoved at the male's hands and even resorted to kicking him hard in the thigh. He snarled and backed away.

She rolled off the other side of the bed and grabbed the first thing she could. It was a pitcher. "Move."

He gaped at her. "Or what? You'll beat me with water in a plastic container?"

"I need to find him!" A sense of desperation hit her.

Sympathy softened his features. "I understand. You both appeared deeply stunned. He probably just needs to pull his emotions together."

"I need to find him now!" She refused to back down. 927 was alive and she had to get to him. She lowered the pitcher back to the table and masked her emotions. "I don't feel so well. Can you wet a towel?" She leaned against the bed and lifted a hand to her face. "I think I'm going to faint."

He spun, striding into the bathroom to do as she'd asked. "Lie down."

She lunged once he was out of her way. The door remained open and she rushed through it. No one tried to stop her until she reached the area with desks and a long counter. Doc Trisha, Jinx, and the female canine, stepped out of an office on the other side of the room. They all appeared surprised and confused. Heavy boots hitting the floor sounded from the direction she'd just fled. Torrent appeared, having realized her ploy.

She spun and slammed into the double glass doors. They started to open and she tried again, twisting her body to squeeze between the parting doors. She darted out onto the sidewalk. There were buildings and a street. She made it to the road, frantically searching for 927. She sniffed but her sense of smell wasn't good enough to be of help. It was one flaw 927 had never been able to fix. He'd tried, but her senses weren't like his.

A feline male down the sidewalk turned. He seemed surprised when he spotted her. She twisted her head, looking the other way. Trees—a lot of them. *That's where he'd go*. She heard Torrent behind her.

"Easy, Candi. We'll find him. Don't make me grab you. I'm afraid I'll hurt you. Come back."

"Don't touch her," the female canine growled. "Candi, it's going to be okay. Hero, or 927 as you knew him, probably just freaked a little. I'll personally track his ass down and bring him here if you want to see him. Just come back inside."

There were no cars. She ran into the road. When her bare feet hit the pavement she didn't care about the slight pain. She was fixated on those trees. He'd always wanted to see them. The hours she'd spent describing them to him when they were children would mean something to him. They pursued her and she was more than aware they could easily catch her. All Species were faster than humans, but they allowed her to run, staying close behind.

She entered a park with a large body of water. There were too many trees and rolling hills to see all of it. She stopped, panting. No one grabbed her but she heard them come to a halt behind her. She twisted around. The doctor wasn't with them but she disregarded Jinx and Torrent, imploring the female canine, "Sniff him out. Track him for me. Please?" She would beg. "He's here. I know it." She remembered the female's name. "Please, Breeze?"

The female hesitated but nodded. "Okay. I don't have to track him though." She reached into her pocket and pulled out a cell phone. She touched the screen and held it up to her ear. Long seconds passed.

"This is Breeze. Locate Hero for me now. Track his cell." She paused. "Priority. Do it."

"Breeze," Jinx whispered. "This might not be a good idea. You didn't see his face."

"I see hers." Breeze stepped closer, keeping eye contact with Candi. "We all carry cell phones and we can track everyone in an emergency. I'd say this constitutes one of those. It takes about a minute. We're going to find him for you, okay?"

"Thank you."

"I take care of my females, and you're one of mine now."

"Damn it, Breeze." Torrent lowered his voice enough that he might have figured Candi couldn't hear him. "He bolted out of there. I saw rage and fear. We should speak to him before we take her near him."

"Shut up," Breeze snapped. "I'd tear this damn place apart if I were her." She glanced at him. "I'd tear through you if you tried to stop me from going after a male I was raised in the same cell with, then discovered he was alive after being told of his death. You were right there while she talked about him. She went through hell and was just hoping to find the ones who took him from her. She's killed for him. Do you want to be next?"

Torrent scowled. "As if I'd allow her to harm me. She's a little thing."

"Females are mean," Breeze growled. "If you aren't afraid of her, be afraid of me. She might be underweight and scrawny, but I'm not. Want to tangle?"

"This is irrational," Jinx rasped. "Hero probably needs time to process all this. The female needs to be fed and monitored. You heard Doc Trisha. The doctor who kept her didn't make sure she ate healthy and the years of drugs have left her in a weakened condition."

Breeze extended her middle finger. "Tell it to the hand. I'm finding Hero for my female. He can feed her and help her regain her strength. She'd eat for him more so than for one of us. She knows him. I don't care what is wrong with him, he's going to man up."

"Breeze, this isn't cut and dried. You're acting as if she's his ma—"

"Where is he?" Breeze snapped, turning her back on Jinx to talk on the phone. She paused, listening. "Okay. He is? Right now? Say hell no. Do you understand me? I'm pulling rank. That's a big-ass no way. Thanks." She hung up and faced Candi.

She'd caught her breath. "You found him?"

"He's heading toward the men's dorm to pack. He just called Security and said he wanted to go back to Reservation. Let's go. How afraid are you of seeing a lot of our males?"

"I'd face anything to see 927."

Breeze pocketed her phone. "I know you would. He likes to be called Hero now. Say it in your head over and over. We hate the numbers. Okay? It reminds us of being at Mercile and you know what fun times we had there." Breeze walked toward her. "Come on. We'll go find him together."

Candi was touched that the female was being so nice. "Thank you."

"I'm putting myself in your shoes." Breeze glanced down and cursed. "Your feet are bleeding. You need shoes. Mental reminder. Where the hell are the ones you came with?"

"They didn't fit. I stole them off Penny."

"The doctor you killed?"

"I knew I'd need them. I took her pants and found her jacket in the car. I needed to get out of the clothes they kept me in. I was afraid humans would call the police if I still looked like a patient. I didn't know how to drive so I left the car there. I did take her purse. I remembered cash. She had some of that."

"You poor thing. It must have been terrifying being out there alone, but you made it to us. We're going to find your male and make him talk to you, okay? Do you need one of the males to carry you? They will."

"It doesn't hurt."

"I bet not. I'd be feeling no pain either, if I were you. Lift them up though and let me make sure it isn't bad. I'll worry otherwise."

It was a small request. Breeze was concerned with her health. Candi did as asked, noting a small cut on one heel and another on the meaty area by her big toe. "Minor. I don't have the protective pads on my feet that you were born with."

"We'll clean and patch them up at Hero's place. We all keep medical kits in the bathrooms of our homes. Let's go. If you start to hurt, speak up. One of the males will be more than happy to carry you."

Candi glanced at Torrent and Jinx. They both appeared irritated at best, certainly not happy.

Breeze turned, waving an arm. "This way."

Candi didn't care if the males were upset. Breeze was taking her to 927. *Hero.* She needed to learn his name. Her gut instinct was to trust the female canine. They walked on the sidewalk. Others stared, but she knew they were entitled to. They probably didn't see many humans. She'd only encountered the guards at the gate and the two in Medical—the female doctor and the male nurse.

"Do many humans live here?"

Breeze shook her head. "Only mated ones and a few of the most trusted ones who work for us. You met Paul. He lives here with his wife. She's human too. Trisha is mated to one of our males."

"I liked them."

"They are good humans and nothing like the technicians and doctors at Mercile. Hell, Trisha would use her scalpel to cut our old captors up, and Paul would assist her by holding them down. They have no love for anyone who harms Species."

"Why the name New Species?"

Breeze shrugged. "What else were we supposed to be called?"

"What you are. Canine."

"We have canine, feline, and primates here. We wanted it to be fair. We were new since the world didn't know about us. New Species seemed appropriate and fitting. We took a vote."

"Did one of you finally make it to the top and go back to save the others? We used to dream of doing that."

Breeze stopped walking and Candi paused too, staring up at the other female. "You don't know?"

"They didn't allow me access to much. I was kept locked inside a room and drugged most of the time."

"A rumor that we existed started and the human authorities sent one of their females, named Ellie, to work at Mercile. She smuggled out enough evidence to convince them we were real. They came and rescued us. None of ours ever made it to the surface until the good humans brought us out." Breeze resumed walking. "How did you learn that we were freed and live at Homeland?"

"One of the cleaning staff had a little portable television. She brought it in sometimes when she was mopping the floor in my room. I saw Justice

North a few times and he mentioned Homeland was where his people lived in freedom. I knew I needed to reach here, but I didn't know where it was. I figured humans would know what I didn't. No one seemed concerned when I asked them where Homeland was and how to get here. A truck driver told me a little, but I didn't want to ask too many questions after he looked at me in a way that set off alarms. I hitchhiked since I was afraid to go to the police for help. I killed a human to escape and they are human too."

Candi stayed at Breeze's side until they reached a tall building. Breeze stopped. "This is the men's dorm. Are you ready to see him? I don't know how he'll react, but he won't run away again." Her voice deepened. "Bet on it." She turned her head. "Stick close, guys."

"This is going to be bad," Jinx rasped. "I can feel it."

"You should have seen his face. He was enraged for some reason," Torrent added. "I think we should go in and speak to him first."

Candi knew why 927 had reacted that way. She said nothing in case they changed their minds and wanted to keep her away from him. *Hero. Hero. Hero.* She kept replaying that name inside her head.

"Please," she whispered. "Take me to Hero." It felt odd saying the new name aloud.

There were at least a dozen males in a large community setting, seated on couches in a wide U shape. A television revealed humans in strange uniforms running on a field with lines painted on it. The males stopped talking, stood and stared when Jinx used a card swipe to open the front doors. Breeze lifted her hand, waving at them once they entered.

"Don't mind us. Sit and pretend we're not here. Has anyone seen Hero?"

A primate male jerked his head toward the stairs. "He came in about a minute ago, looking as if he wanted to tear off someone's head. He didn't speak, just pounded upstairs."

"Where are his quarters?" Breeze glanced around. "Anyone?"

"I know," Jinx admitted. "Let's go."

The elevator moved at a snail's pace to take them to the third floor. It opened and Jinx took the lead. He paused before a door halfway down a hallway. He turned, frowning at Breeze.

"Let me go in first to test his mood."

Breeze advanced and placed both hands on Jinx's chest, giving him a light shove to move him out of the way. She fisted her hand and pounded on the door. "Hero? It's Breeze. Open up or I'll kick it down."

"Go away." The familiar snarl came from inside.

"I'm not kidding. I know I usually do, but not right now," Breeze yelled back. "Do you want me to hurt my foot? I'm not wearing my work-issued boots. I might break a toe. Open up."

927 snarled as he jerked the door open, showing fangs. "I'm packing and have to catch a helicopter that is leaving in twenty minutes for Reservation. I don't have time to talk."

He tried to slam the door but Breeze moved faster, flattening her hands on the closing door and shoved. It surprised 927 as he backed up. Candi lunged forward into the room, her gaze locked on him.

He paled when he saw her and his lips pressed into a tight line. The color leached from them as if that much pressure pushed out the blood. A muscle in his jaw flexed. He was furious. She gazed into his eyes and understood how the technicians and doctors had once feared the chilling looks he could give.

She licked her lips and her body trembled. He was really alive. She noticed other things about him. He towered above her, having grown much taller since she'd last seen him. His youthful body had matured, adding a lot of muscle and bulk to his frame. He was larger than either of them had ever estimated and he looked as lethal as she knew he could be. She noticed when his hands clenched at his sides. She'd seen it before. He was fighting the urge to attack. She was the target of that rage.

"Can we be alone?" She didn't turn her head, not willing to look away from…Hero.

"No," Breeze stated firmly. "But ignore us. We'll be as quiet as mice."

It frustrated her, but she didn't have time to argue. The male she knew wasn't good at holding his temper for long. She might have only seconds to calm him. She took a step closer, but his lips pulled back and he snarled, flashing fangs. It was a warning.

"Hero!" Breeze growled.

"Stay out of this, no matter what. Please," Candi whispered. "This is between him and me." She held still, trying not to approach him again.

"It's always been just us." She directed that at him. "I did it to save you. They were going to kill you if I refused."

He tensed further, the muscles in his arms straining, indicating that he battled the urge to attack. Years might have passed, but she knew him. He'd learned more control. It hurt when she saw his rage did not lessen. It actually seemed to incense him more. She had to try though.

"It was agree or be forced to watch you die. You know I would have done anything to protect you. Anything." Tears blinded her. "Do you think I wanted to let that happen? You're all I wanted." She blinked, clearing her vision. The tears slipped down her cheeks, but she didn't wipe them away. "I did it to keep you alive so we could be together again."

"You should have let them kill me."

They were angry words, snarled at her. She understood. She thought he might have felt that way. "We survive. It's what we do." She paused. "I survived to be with you. Do you think I wanted that? I wanted to die first, but that would have left you alone. If you had died, it would have left me alone. I did what I had to so we could see each other again."

He said nothing, but that rage burned in his gaze, the brown seeming to have disappeared, making them actually look as black as she figured his heart had turned. It broke hers into pieces. The pain that ripped through her chest was almost as bad as the day she'd been told he was dead. She'd lost him all the same. He was never going to forgive her.

She turned to Breeze. The female looked worried, confused. "Will you please do me one favor? Can I trust you?"

"Of course."

"You seem to be in charge of the females and you said I'm one of yours. Don't let them punish him for this. I deserve it."

"What are you talking about?"

She turned toward 927. She didn't care what name he'd been given. The male in front of her was the one she'd known, just older. She took a step closer. "Hit me, 927. As many times as it takes. Find your payback. Be at peace by causing me pain the way I hurt you with the decision I once made."

"Shit," Torrent growled. "Don't you dare, Hero."

Breeze stepped farther into the room to stand beside Candi. She gripped her arm. "Stop. What is going on here?"

Candi jerked out of her hold and kept her gaze locked on 927. His eyes narrowed and he watched her. He didn't move but his entire body vibrated as he growled deep. He was about to snap, his control nearly gone. He just needed that last push and she was willing to give it to him.

"I survived all these years believing I did it to make the ones pay for taking you away from me." She swallowed. "Now I realize it was what I did that took you from me, regardless of the reasons. I wanted revenge for you, but you can take your own. I understand. Do it, my pup."

He opened his mouth and howled. The killing rage twisted his features. It was just as before, the last time she'd seen him, minus the chains to hold him back. She didn't tense, just watched him, waiting for him to lunge. The fear never came. 927 had always been her motivation to keep fighting to survive, but she was willing to allow him to strike her if it made him feel as if they were even.

Candi was offering, no, taunting him to cause her harm. Hero nearly lost his mind. He'd let the rage and pain explode in a violent outburst of sound. He kept his feet planted firmly on the carpet, forced himself to stay away from her. He didn't want her blood to spill. *Never again*. He realized he'd closed his eyes. He opened them.

Breeze, Jinx, and Torrent flanked Candi. They stood close, ready to defend her if he attacked. He was grateful for their interference. Torrent cocked his head, uttered a curse, and moved fast to the open doorway. The male stepped out, but stayed near enough to return quickly.

"Nothing to see here," the male called out. "Spread the word. Just leave the floor. It's fine. Breeze, Jinx, and I have it handled. Nobody call Security. It's just a little, um, argument."

Hero studied Candi. She remained in the same position, waiting for him to strike her. She showed no fear, no hesitation. A sheen of tears still glistened in her beautiful eyes. Her words had been heard. The adult in him understood, but the youth raged from the pain.

It took time to form words inside his mind and force them to exit his mouth. "Canine or feline male? Was it just the one?"

She took a breath and he glimpsed that fleeting, sad look she quickly erased from her features. "Feline." Her throat muscles worked to swallow. "One time." She paused. "To prove to Christopher that it was safe. He swore I was too fragile to survive being bred."

"Oh shit," Breeze whispered.

His heart felt as if it were being squeezed in a vise. "Did you suffer?"

Tears spilled down her face, but she remained still. "More than you'll ever know." Her voice broke. "But nothing beyond the expected parameters, physically. That's what Evelyn said, anyway."

"What about you being too young?" It was tough to breathe and he felt as if he was suffocating. The tightness in his chest worsened. He needed answers though.

"I guess they considered me old enough. Evelyn got permission from the board to use me in a breeding experiment, but Christopher said he'd kill you first. He was in charge of you. He swore he'd make me watch you die. It was no secret that all I wanted was to be returned to our space, to be with you. Evelyn came for me with her plan to allow another male to mount me. She said Christopher couldn't harm one of hers. I fought at first. She had the techs restrain me and told me it would save your life. She felt Christopher would put me with you once she proved I wouldn't be damaged by the experience. I had to make a choice and play their game. Evelyn said, either way, someone would mount me. I could get you killed or stop fighting, and be taken to the feline. I couldn't risk your life. Never you."

It hurt deeply. He tried to think, to be rational. What if they'd brought him a female and told him they'd hurt Candi if he didn't comply? What if they had threatened her life? Would he have mounted another? Would it have even been possible? She wasn't male though. She could be taken whether she was aroused or not. She said she'd suffered. It ripped his gut out to imagine a male touching her.

"Did he hurt you?" He had to know.

"Evelyn gave me a shot first." Candi straightened her head, her arms wrapping protectively around her middle in a hug. "It didn't knock me out, but it muted some of my emotions. I was crying and she was having a problem getting the male to comply. He was pacing and snarling, willing to take pain rather than force me. He knew I was a prisoner too, from when they were taking blood tests, and was aware I was being held with you. He treated me as if I were one of your females."

"He should have suffered a beating instead of touching you." He fisted his hands so tightly that the bones seemed to show through his skin when he glanced down.

"The drug they gave me took effect and I felt strange, lightheaded. They were beating him because he refused. I just wanted it to end, but we both know it wasn't going to until they got what they wanted. I asked the male to stop fighting. We needed to survive. Do you hate me for that? I didn't want him to touch me, but I didn't want him to be beaten to death either. The technicians were brutal and they could go too far, despite their orders. It's a horrible way to die."

He growled and spun away, stalking to the window. It didn't help, not to be looking at her anymore. He could feel her in the room, inside his space again.

"He was gentle and I don't remember much. He didn't want to hurt me. I felt as bad for him as I did myself." A sob broke from her lips, her pain evident. "No one forced me. I just wanted us all to survive. I closed my eyes and just thought of you until they took me back to my space. I washed to remove his scent and his touch. I scrubbed my skin until it was red, but it's not as if they gave us soap often. I wanted to be taken to you. I did what they asked. Evelyn said we could be together." Another sob came from her, and there was a pained hitch in her voice. "Only you still smelled him on me. You lost your sanity and snapped."

He spun. "You were mine!"

She nodded. "Always." She took a step closer. Breeze tried to hold her back by gripping her arm but she tugged free. "Stay out of this. Please. This is between him and me."

He glanced at Breeze. He saw sadness in her face and understanding at the tragedy of what had been their past. She held his gaze, seeming to judge his mood. She wanted reassurances that he wouldn't attack. He knew that, sensed it.

"I'd never," he swore.

Breeze backed up. "Torrent? Jinx? Hallway, now. We'll be right outside the cracked door but close enough to come in here if needed."

Jinx moved. "I have to make a call."

He was going to share his and Candi's history. It was procedure. Hero knew that. The NSO watched out for their own.

Torrent bristled. "I think one of us should stay closer."

Breeze growled. "They don't need us here at this moment. Get to the door."

Torrent stared at him, looking grim.

"I won't hurt her," Hero swore. He'd already done that once. The image of her lying in a pool of blood was still the thing of his nightmares.

Torrent hesitated a second more but then left with Breeze and Jinx. They didn't fully close the door. He finally allowed himself to look at Candi. She watched him with deep sorrow. He could relate.

"I understand." They were difficult words to speak, but the adult in him won out over the youthful, heartbroken male he'd once been. "I might have done the same to save you, if I'd been forced to decide."

"Can you forgive me?"

He answered truthfully. "I don't know. It's still a raw wound. I am sorry you suffered."

She reached up and wiped at her tears. "Can I hold you?"

"No." He couldn't allow her to get that close.

She reacted as if he'd struck her, actually flinching. He hated having that affect on her, but didn't think he could withstand her touch. There were too many painful memories attached to it. He was still digesting that she wasn't dead and the full knowledge of what had happened that day she'd stepped into his room with the stench of a male coming from her. It had totally masked her scent, strong enough that he'd known she'd been mounted. She had belonged to another instead of him. At least, that's what he'd believed she'd come to tell him.

"I need time."

"Time?" Her expression changed to one of raw anger. "How long has it been since we saw each other? Do you know? There was no sense of time where I've been, but I know years have passed. I see it in your face and on my own. We've aged so much." She took a ragged breath. "They stole our future together. I hate time. It passes so slowly. Every second seems like a minute. Every minute, a week. Every week, a month. Every year, an eternity. I'm right here. We're alive. You're in front of me. Don't do this."

"Do what?"

"We're alive," she repeated. "Nothing is stopping us from being together. It's all we ever wanted." She stepped closer. "I'm right here."

"Everything has changed," he whispered, almost wishing it wasn't true.

She staggered a little. He tensed, wanting to go to her, but held back when she stabilized her balance. An agonized whimper came from her, the hurt reflected on her face, in her eyes.

"You share your space with a female?"

She thought he was in a relationship. "No."

"Have you mounted females?"

He debated answering, not wanting to hurt her. He knew that kind of pain and had lived with the memory of betrayal. It was hellish to feel the burn of jealousy and that kind of rage, to know another had touched what belonged to him.

His silence seemed to tell her what words couldn't. She spun away and hugged her middle, bending a little as if it caused her physical pain.

He found himself halfway across the room before he brought his need to console her under wraps. He backed up, his hands clenching into fists.

"I thought you were dead. Dr. C told me I killed you."

"Of course." Her whisper came out so softly that he barely heard it.

Guilt and regret mingled, knowing of the suffering she must feel, but he couldn't handle it so he stuck to talking about the past. "The chain..." He shuddered at the memory of all that blood after she fell. "I just wanted to get to you. I didn't mean for it to strike your head."

She reached up and touched the old scar, and then quickly dropped that arm to hug her middle again. "I know you didn't mean to do that. You wanted my throat."

He flinched. "I did." He wouldn't deny it. "I wake up in a cold sweat often, wondering what I'd have done if I'd reached you. I just know for certain what I did when you fell and I saw your blood."

"Did it help you heal?"

He snarled.

She spun, looking at him.

"Is that what you think? That I watched you bleed with satisfaction?"

"It was your right."

"I lost the ability to think." It was an easy admission. "They took the only thing I cared about and my mind couldn't take it."

"You wanted to kill me. I understood. I still do."

"I threw myself on the floor to reach you since my leg chains wouldn't allow anything else, and dragged you closer, begging the technicians to get help. I've never been so afraid in my life. I put pressure on the wound, trying to stop the bleeding. I would have died to exchange places with you. I prayed to that god you told me about that they'd be able to fix you so you'd be well. The sight of you on that floor bleeding killed my rage. It gave me fear and loathing of what I'd done. Not one day has passed where I have found peace or forgiveness for believing I'd killed you."

"Until now. I'm alive."

"I'm glad."

"You would never harm a female."

He closed his eyes and clenched his teeth. "I've killed females."

He heard her sharp intake of breath. It was his burden of guilt to bear for the rest of his life. Candi being alive was just one less, but there were others.

"I don't believe you."

He met her beautiful gaze. "Some of the techs took me from Mercile to another place. It was a very dark time in my life. They brought me a human female for a breeding experiment. The doctor in charge knew of our past and figured I'd accept one since I was raised with you. They were hurting her. I could hear her screams from where I was kept. They injected her with drugs that would make her more fertile and then brought her to me. She was hysterical, hurting herself trying to get away from me by smashing her body against the bars. I felt the monster they claimed me to be." He paused. "I didn't do it because I hated humans or that female. I snapped her neck."

He braced, waiting to see her sickened expression. It would set her free of him though, learning the truth. She wouldn't want to be anywhere near him.

"You didn't want her to suffer." She offered sympathy instead.

"How do you know that?" It surprised him. Even other Species had been wary, asking him questions when they learned what had happened after he'd been rescued with Tammy. They'd understood and told him to forgive himself but Candi should have been appalled.

"I know you. You'd never take a life for no reason."

Her trust in him, her faith, humbled him. "They would have killed her anyway. I could hear them talking. Two of the males planned to rape her when her use was up. They didn't believe the drugs would work to make it possible for them to successfully breed us. One of them was sick in his mind, boasting about the pain and humiliation he'd cause her. I didn't want to add to her pain by making her endure me first. I was also afraid the drugs might work. No child should be created and have to face what they had in mind to do to it. I made it painless and fast." He fought nausea. "Then they brought me another. I did the same to her. The third was different. She smelled of a Species and I let her live because she asked me to. We spoke and I had hoped that we'd be freed. Her mate came hunting for her."

"You mounted a female who belonged to another male?"

That seemed to shock her more than him admitting to the lives he'd taken. He shook his head. "No. We were able to survive until Tammy's mate found us."

The silence between them became uncomfortable. He wanted to know about what had happened to her after she'd been taken away, but he wasn't sure he could handle the answers if they were too terrible. All he knew was that she'd been kept in an asylum. Those were places they kept humans with disabilities of the mind.

"Do you want me to leave?"

He was confused and lost. "I don't know what I want."

Chapter Four

Candi knew she should leave. She wasn't welcome but she couldn't find the desire to go. The male she loved stood eight feet away and all she wanted was to throw her arms around him. It was everything she'd fantasized about, if she could go back in time before his supposed death. It had kept her strong when she felt weak, courageous when she'd been terrified, and whole when she knew inside that her sanity seemed to be fracturing into a million pieces. To get revenge for his loss had been her motivation to live and keep fighting.

"I killed."

He didn't seem to believe her. His expression was half frown, half scowl.

"That's how I escaped. It was the doctor who kept me locked up. She was taking me out of the asylum to the woods to kill me after Christopher died. He couldn't pay her anymore to keep me prisoner so she had to get rid of me. I stabbed her in the chest. You might have killed to spare suffering, but I did it for payback."

"You killed?"

She paused, giving him time to absorb that information. "I also knew the chances of me being caught before I could find Homeland were higher if she lived. She would have had orderlies hunting for me. I won't lie though. It felt good to kill her. I hated her. It was mostly rage. I could have locked her in the trunk or tied her up after the first time I hurt her, but she deserved to die. I don't feel guilt."

He still didn't seem convinced, but said nothing more, just studied her, his gaze roaming up and down her body.

She glanced down, trying to see what he did. She had lost a lot of weight. "They kept me heavily medicated most of the time. I slept for so long, in and out of it. It's tough to eat when you can't even walk. They used to give me shots, but then switched to pills because my veins weren't accepting the needles as well. I'd try to hide the pills at first, not knowing it would make me sick."

"You're sick?" He didn't look happy about that news.

"My body became addicted to the drugs they'd been forcing into me. I didn't understand why I was sweating, throwing up and shaking. I felt so bad. That's how they'd catch on that I wasn't taking them. Withdrawal, they said. I learned to take one of their pills and skip the next until I could hide the sickness. I tried to escape a few times after my mind cleared somewhat, but I was always caught. I couldn't get past the walls. They'd put me back on the shots and I'd lose more time until they'd switch back to the pills. I'd have to start all over again to wean myself."

"You saw Doc Trisha?"

"Yes." She smiled. "She doesn't think there is damage to my internal organs. They ran tests. I'm sure I'm okay, but she wants to wait for more results. She is worried because she doesn't know which drugs they gave me and she is trying to determine what the drugs did to me since I was on them for so long."

He stepped closer. "Did they feed you in Medical?"

"Yes."

"Are you still hungry?" He glanced at his kitchen. "I have food here. I could make you something. I learned how to cook."

That was remarkable. "You did?"

He nodded, seeming to ponder something. "You were locked up this entire time?"

"Yes. It was a room about a fourth of this size. Just a bed and one tiny window with bars. The glass didn't open." She glanced at his couch. "May I sit?"

"Of course."

That was good because she was emotionally and physically drained, but she wouldn't admit that to him. She didn't want to remind him how much weaker she was compared to him at that moment. It was bad enough being human. She sat and looked at him. The genetically enhanced always respected strength.

"There was a tiny bathroom with a shower stall, a sink and toilet. They didn't let me out of that room unless the doctor keeping me there wanted to see me in her office. I think Penny was afraid I'd talk to people if she let me have access to other patients and staff. Anyone who started to ask questions about me was reassigned to somewhere else."

"You were all alone?" Some of the tension eased from his body.

"I only saw people when they came in to feed me or give me drugs. There was the cleaning female. She'd mop the floor once a week and change the bedding every other day. They told her not to speak to me though. She only came in after they'd drugged me. I'd pretend to be asleep, or they'd have her change my bedding while I showered. One of the orderlies would guard the bathroom door to make certain I couldn't talk to her while I was more with it."

"They watched you shower?"

She nodded. "Yes. I wish I could have slipped down the drain to escape, but they actually acted as if it were possible."

That muscle in his jaw clenched. "Male guards?"

"Yes."

He growled. "Did they abuse you?"

She knew what he really wanted to know. "I wasn't force mounted."

"Did you allow—" He sealed his lips.

"Did I willingly allow someone to mount me? No. I've only been..." It was her turn to go silent, struggling to find the right words. The situation hadn't been forced since she'd agreed to share sex with the feline, but she hadn't wanted to do it either. "Just that once at Mercile."

He took a seat in a chair that was far from her. "That's good."

"Yes." She knew what he meant. Her hell hadn't involved physical abuse. Just silence, sleeping, and fighting drug addiction. She looked at him longingly, where he sprawled in that chair. She wanted to go over and curl up on his lap and hold him close. Some of her fondest memories were of being in his arms. He wouldn't welcome her.

He noticed the way she looked at him. "We shouldn't discuss this if it makes you sad."

"Who replaced me?"

His body jerked upright and his eyes narrowed. "What?"

"Who is your female now? Is she kind? Does she make you laugh?"

"It's not like that."

"How is it?"

He looked away from her, glancing at everything else. He didn't answer. It hurt her heart. He didn't deny that he'd mounted a female, and she knew he had from before, from his silence then. This just confirmed it all over again. He finally met her gaze.

"You should allow Breeze to take you to the women's dorm. You probably need sleep."

"I have slept long enough. I try to stay awake as much as possible. I don't want to miss anything." She figured he might understand.

He stood. "I need to pack. I'm leaving for Reservation."

She didn't know where he was going, but it was away from her. "Please don't." She wanted to beg him to stay with her. She just needed to look at him, assure herself he was real, and not a figment of her imagination.

"I must go." He took a step back. "I didn't expect this and I'm having a difficult time thinking." His voice rose. "Breeze?"

The door opened and the female entered. "Yes?"

"Please take her to the women's dorm and make sure she eats and sleeps."

Breeze glanced at her, then walked over to him. She invaded his personal space, putting one hand on his shoulder, and tugged him down enough to put her face closer to his. The words she whispered into his ear were too soft to hear, but all Candi noticed was that he allowed that female to touch him. It tore at her. It wasn't jealousy but pain at his rejection of allowing her to do the same.

Whatever Breeze said angered him. He turned his body, pressing closer to the female, and whispered in her ear. She caught what he said.

"You can't keep me here."

They were almost hugging as Breeze hissed something back. The tone was there, but the words lost. He growled in response. Breeze whispered again. He jerked away and stormed into another room. The door slammed. Breeze sighed and came closer.

"Stubborn, stupid male." She took a seat on the coffee table. "He's scared and trying to run. That shower he just turned on isn't going to cool his temper either."

"He won't forgive me."

"For what?" Breeze reached out and patted her leg. "I got the gist of that. You had to let a feline mount you to save Hero's life when you were at Mercile. He went insane when he realized another male had claimed what was his and he somehow hurt you." She glanced at her head.

"He didn't mean to. The chain snapped from the wall so there was a few feet of it attached to his arm and it whipped out, hitting the side of my head while he fought to free himself. It just split the skin and gave me a concussion. I healed fine with just a scar. My hair covers it."

"He's a good male. He feels such guilt about everything."

She believed that. "I know."

"Does he frighten you?"

She shook her head. "I'm just terrified he's never going to forgive me. He's still everything to me."

"I can see that. I just told him it would be best if he remained here at Homeland to care for you. He's the male who was raised with you. You're very fragile right now, Candi. The years of drugs they forced you to take and lack of regular meals has left you underweight and weak."

She couldn't deny those facts. Her body wasn't in the best shape, but her mind was solid. "I'm strong inside. I'll eat lots, just the way Doc Trisha said."

Breeze's phone rang and she whipped it out, accepting the call. "Hold on." She pressed it to her ear. "What?" Silence. "Butt out of this. I have it handled. My female, my decision." She hung up and smiled. "Everyone is worried."

"I would never do anything to hurt 927." She paused. "Hero."

"He's too busy hurting himself right now by being a butthead." Breeze threw an annoyed look at the closed door and then smiled at Candi. "Most males would have snatched you up and hugged you if they were given a female they thought they'd lost. I'd probably be trying to wipe out mental images of things I didn't want to see right now because he'd have ripped off your clothes to reclaim you, oblivious of who was in the room."

She wished he had reacted that way.

"I've never shared sex with him," Breeze said, surprising her with that statement. "Just so you know. I thought about it when he and I met right after he was freed, but it just didn't happen. I'm glad for that now. That would be awkward between us."

Candi wasn't sure how to respond.

Breeze's features softened. "Sorry. I've been around too many humans. You look like one, but I forget looks can be deceiving. You're more Species than not, aren't you?"

"I'm more like you than a human. Does that mean I'm Species?"

"Yes. It does. Do you know what I'd tell another Species female?"

"What?"

"Fight for what you want. He's your male, isn't he? A stubborn, stupid one, but yours. You feel guilt for the feline at Mercile. We did what we had to, to survive. It's a fact of life. We're still here because we're strong. Stop feeling as if you owe him submission and groveling. He should be kissing your ass and thanking you for saving his life. Don't forget that and remind him." She paused. "Males have their physical strength as an advantage, but we have the cunning skills to match them in other ways."

Candi appreciated the advice. "I can't make him listen if he won't be near me."

"He's not going to Reservation."

"What is that?"

"It doesn't matter since he's not going. I clipped his wings. No pilot will fly him there." She grinned. "Hero isn't leaving Homeland."

"He wants you to take me away."

"I'm not going to pick you up and carry you kicking and screaming to the women's dorm. The males will get their asses kicked if they try it. Do you feel like leaving?"

"No. I want to stay close to him."

Breeze grinned. "Give him hell." She glanced down at Candi's body. "You need to put on a lot of weight, but I can't see him kicking you out of his bed. Do you understand?"

"No."

Breeze winced. "You only shared sex once. I forgot about that. I didn't mean to eavesdrop, but canine hearing is good. Okay, get naked. He's a male with strong feelings for you. Nature will take care of the rest."

"He won't even let me touch him." She wasn't opposed to the idea. She actually wished he would mount her.

"Get naked and he'll be the one doing the touching."

"He will probably leave again."

"Perhaps."

"He has a female." It tore her up, saying those words.

"No, he doesn't." Breeze leaned in and took her hand. "You were part of a breeding experiment once so you might know that Species females were taken from male to male in hopes we'd get pregnant. Sometimes they would drug the males first. It made them violent and unable to think. We worried if we'd survive being mounted when they were in that state and some of us were badly injured."

"I'm so sorry."

Breeze squeezed and released her hand. "It wasn't the male's fault. It was the drugs they were forced to take. They don't remember their actions when they were in that condition and that's a good thing for all of us. Some of our females avoid the ones they were bred with while on drugs. A female won't tell a male he once hurt her because they'd tear themselves up the way your Hero is doing because he harmed you with that chain, only they'd be much worse. They didn't just strike us. We don't want them to suffer. Some of our females will share sex with one of those males from her past to make good memories in hopes of canceling out the bad. We have had good and bad experiences with them, and that makes it difficult to find absolute trust with a Species male. We're trying though. We do that by sharing sex with different males and not growing too close to one. So far though, we avoid mating with our males. I'd know if one of my females was serious about a Species male. It would be impossible to hide."

"He might have feelings for a female."

"There's no one female he's been steadily seeing. There isn't a bond." Breeze stood. "He just got out of the shower. I heard the water turn off. He might be able to hear us now." She winked. "I'm leaving an officer in the hallway since a few Species are worried about your safety and his sanity. I told them he wouldn't hurt you and you sure aren't a spy." She laughed. "But welcome to the NSO. We're a nosey, well-meaning bunch." She lowered her voice. "Give him hell and don't give up. Hurry in there before he gets dressed. He just opened his closet."

Breeze left and Candi stood and hesitantly walked toward the closed door. *Can it be that simple?* She wished, but didn't hold out much hope. It took courage to open the door but she did, stepping inside his bedroom.

The sight of a mostly naked Hero left her mouth dry. He had a lot of muscles and had really filled out since their youth. His chest was broader, so were his shoulders, and he was much darker skinned. The sunshine had given him a golden hue that looked really good. The towel wrapped around his waist dipped low, revealing more muscles spread from his rib cage to the top of this towel.

"What are you doing?" He spun, dropping a pair of jeans on the carpet.

Speak, she ordered, but no words formed. He was beautiful. It did funny things to her body and she understood. She wanted to touch him all over, explore him. She ached from the need.

"Candi?" His voice came out gruff and harsh. "Get out."

She stepped farther into the room and closed the door, sealing them inside. He might run. She wouldn't allow it. He'd have to throw her out of his way to leave his bedroom. That would mean having to touch her. That was something he didn't want to do. She leaned against the cool wood.

Her gaze lifted to his face. He was furious. She accepted that. Breeze had made some really valid points and her own anger surfaced. Rage was one emotion she had learned worked to her advantage at times. She'd survived hell, just for the chance of going after the ones responsible for 927's death. He was alive and they were in the same room. He should want to hold her as much as she wanted to be in his arms.

"My pup isn't a pup anymore."

He growled. "Don't call me that."

"That's right. You're Hero, an adult male." She stared at his chest, at his arms. "So strong and tough." She met his glare. "At least you look that way, but you're a coward."

His mouth dropped open but he recovered, snarling. "What are you doing, Candi? Do you want me to attack you?"

"No. I want you to stop running as if this is a game of chase. We played that as children. It's not fun right now."

"I'm not playing games. You need to go to the women's dorm."

"I don't belong there. I belong with you."

"You don't know me anymore. I'm not the same."

"Let me get to know you again."

"The past is behind us."

"You lie now? That's a trait of a human."

"It's not a lie." He seemed insulted.

"We are our past. It shaped who we've become." She tapped her chest. "I lived to be with you and then I survived after that horrible day so I could make the ones responsible pay for your death. You were in every one of my thoughts. Did you forget about me? What we were? All the years we spent sharing our space? Deny it and I call liar."

He growled in the back of his throat.

"Tell me that you never think about the future we could have had if that day hadn't happened. Try to picture how it would feel to kiss and claim me. I think about it often." She openly studied every inch of his body that she could see. "I hurt to touch you."

"Fuck." He spun away, giving her his back.

"That's a crude way to put it, but that too."

He snarled, spinning to face her again. "I can't do this. It was too hard to lose you the first time. It took me years to put my life together and find peace over what happened after you died."

"I'm not dead."

Some of his anger faded. "I'm grateful."

"I'm more than grateful that you're here with me. It's a miracle and a gift. You're trying to throw it away. How can you do that? All we ever dreamed about was being allowed to be together without anyone stopping us." She glanced around, then pointedly regarded him. "No one is here. It's just us. This is our chance."

"I'm not the same. Too many things have happened. You're not the same."

She grew silent, catching the pain in his last words. "If I hadn't allowed that feline to mount me, would you still be across the room, or would you be holding me? Be truthful."

He looked away. "I don't know."

It injured her heart, hearing the broken tone of his voice when he rasped the words. She'd hurt him so deeply that it might be impossible to forgive. Greif wrenched at her so strongly that she was grateful to be leaning against the door.

"Talk to me. Please? Tell me what you're thinking and feeling." She'd already told him why it had happened and how she'd suffered. Now he needed to tell her.

He paced the small space between the bed and the closet, staying away from her. He finally stopped and snapped his head up. "You were mine. You knew it would kill me inside so why didn't you just let me die?"

She understood. "It would have torn me to pieces if they'd brought a female to you and if you'd mounted her, but after I thought about it for a while, do you know what I finally realized?"

"What?"

"You'd help me heal from that pain once they let us be together. We'd have each other to console. I knew I was the one you wanted, not someone else. I thought you knew the same about me." She fought tears. "I knew you'd hold me and make me forget everything but you. It's what we always did for each other. Our love was too strong for them to break, no matter how hard they tried."

Tears shone in his eyes, but he quickly blinked them away. "We were young."

"In years maybe, but we grew up fast there. They didn't treat us as children."

He took a deep, shaky breath. "I don't know how to get past this."

A memory flashed of when they'd been kids. He'd endured a beating when they'd taken her away for a medical checkup. He'd thought they were going to hurt her and had fought to protect her from the techs. She'd returned to their space, and it was the first time he'd been chained to the wall. He wouldn't even look at her, had just snarled.

He'd snapped at her with his fangs when she'd tried to hug him, snarling for her to go across the kill-zone line on the floor where humans belonged. Even after they'd let him go, he'd refused to go near her. He'd slept on the floor instead of sharing their mat. He wouldn't speak to her. She'd cried and pleaded, but nothing had worked. Then in desperation, she'd come up with a plan. A plan that might work as well today as it had then.

Hero just needed space. He couldn't think with Candi invading his home. She had refused to leave so he needed to. The only problem was that she blocked the door. He refused to touch her. It would be too much, and he couldn't handle it. Not right at that moment.

"Why don't you go in the bathroom and get dressed?" Her gaze lowered down his body. "It's too mean to stand there in front of me when I can't touch you."

He noticed the way she looked at him and fought his natural responses. Just thinking of sex reminded him that she'd given herself to another male. It was ingrained in his mind, burned there from the years of pain he'd endured from it. He would have taken a thousand beatings rather than have her step inside their cell with the stench of another male all over her. To know someone else had kissed her and stripped her bare, killed his sex drive. He growled, his rage rising fast. He could handle anger better than the pain.

He bent and snatched up his jeans. He even had the sense to remember to yank a shirt out of the closet. He stormed into the bathroom and locked the door, needing that barricade against her. He'd forgotten underwear but it didn't matter. He dressed, his actions stiff and jerky. He stood there when he was done, not willing to face her just yet. He stalled for a while by washing his face and brushing his teeth. He even picked up a brush to comb out all the tangles from his wet hair.

He unlocked the door, took a deep breath. He had to make her understand that he needed time to think. She had allowed the male to mount her, thinking she was saving his life. He just had to work that information into his mind longer so the pain could dull a little. It was just too fresh. He stepped out and glanced at the door where he figured she'd be. She was there all right and utter shock slammed into him.

Her borrowed clothing from Medical was in a pile at her feet. Her legs were bare all the way up to mid thigh where one of his discarded tank tops now covered her body. Her arms were above her head, stretched high. He barely noticed that since his shirt gaped open on her sides, the large armholes revealing a lot of skin from her hips upward. He noticed then why her arms were up. She'd used two of his belts to secure her wrists and the ends of them were closed in the top of the door.

"What—" He couldn't even comprehend why she'd do that.

"You didn't have chains, but I'm restrained here all the same. They are thick enough that I really had to push to get the door to close. They are really stuck." She bent her knees a little, hanging there when her feet left the floor. "I'm not going anywhere unless you free me."

"Why would you do this?" It agitated him. She'd effectively restrained herself.

"It worked before."

"What are you talking about?"

"I chained myself to the wall. Remember? I thought about tying myself to your bed this time but figured you'd leave me there. You can't get out of this room unless you touch me."

"Oh hell." He growled, took a few steps forward, but then stopped.

She grinned. "You had that same amazed, yet dismayed look on your face when you woke up on the floor and found that I'd chained myself up the way you'd been."

"I had to call the techs in to unlock the restraints." He remembered. "I should have left you there. Nobody wants to be chained to a wall."

"You stopped being angry with me."

A jolt of amusement shot through him, ruining his foul mood. He'd forgotten that she had a way of getting into predicaments that left him laughing. "What if I left you there?"

"We're on the third floor. It's not like you can just climb out a window. The door is the only way out."

"I could jump down to another balcony until I reach the ground," he teased.

She straightened her knees and flatted her bare feet on his carpet. "You could, but you won't."

"What makes you so sure of that?"

Her smile faded as she licked her lips. "You won't. It would bother you, thinking about how eventually my arms are going to start to hurt."

He closed his eyes. "Candi..."

"Look at me," she whispered. "They took your pride away that day and embarrassed you in front of me. You thought I'd see you as the animal they claimed. I showed you that we're the same. There was no reason for you to feel that way. You didn't think any less of me, seeing me chained to a wall."

He opened his eyes and the dark mood returned. He just wasn't sure what to say. She spoke before he could.

"I took something from you by the choice I made. I really did it to save your life. I know I hurt you. I'd do anything to take it back if I could." She paused. "I'm at your mercy. Leave me here or touch me. You have a choice now."

"Your mind doesn't work correctly."

"That's the politest way anyone has ever accused me of being nuts. I'm okay with that. I spent a long time in an asylum when I was sane. I'm due some bad choices now."

She could drive a male insane. He advanced. She needed to be set free. He kept back, avoiding touching her directly as he gripped one of the belts. He tugged, but the leather band was really wedged in between the door and the jamb. He frowned, pulling harder.

"That's not going to work."

He glanced down. She was too close. He could smell the shampoo she'd used in her hair, knew she'd brushed her teeth with something minty, and underneath that, her feminine scent called to him. It always had.

"Why not?"

Mischief made those beautiful eyes of hers sparkle. "I might have chosen the two belts with the thickest, strongest buckles that stops them from sliding through the door. You're actually going to have to move me and then open the door to slide them off the top. Why do you have so many belts? Isn't one enough?"

"I only left you alone for five minutes."

"I have a quick mind."

He remembered that about her too. She was always the mastermind when they played pranks. He'd been the one with the strength and height to put them into motion. There had been the time she'd used loose threads from her clothes to braid a thin string. She'd tied a piece of meat on it and then had him lift her up to hang it above the door from an old nail. Dr. C had come in on his daily check and she'd casually mentioned that a spider was over his head. The doctor had looked up and cried out like a female. He'd realized what it was and glared at both of them. It had been funny. She knew Dr. C feared the eight-legged creatures.

There were a lot of good memories. Warmth spread through him as he continued to stare down at her, flashes of their time together coming back. Some of the drugs Mercile had tested in his system had made him hurt so she'd had him lie with his head on her lap while she sang softly and played with his hair. She'd tell him stories that distracted him from his suffering.

He examined her features. She was his Candi. He could see some changes. A few lines marred her skin near her eyes and mouth. His attention lowered and his cock stiffened. She had filled out in her chest. The soft-looking mounds of her breasts were clearly defined through the thin material of his tank top.

"You're going to have to touch me."

Her voice came out a little husky and he growled. He wanted to feel her. He opened his hand without thinking, almost touching the skin that was revealed over her ribs. She was too pale and looked so soft. She arched her back, as if to encourage him. It unsettled him. He lifted his gaze to stare deeply into her eyes.

"You want my touch?"

"More than anything."

"I'm angry."

"I know."

"I could hurt you."

She relaxed, keeping her gaze locked with his. "I'd rather feel your temper than nothing at all."

He curled his hands into fists and flattened his knuckles on the door next to her chest and closed his eyes. It was easy to inch closer until he pressed lightly against her body. She pushed her face forward to rest her forehead against his chest. He just stood there, feeling her warm breath through the thin material of his shirt. She felt small, but that was nothing new. His Candi had always been tiny but fierce. It also made it real. She was alive.

"Do you remember what you did when you woke up after they first brought you into my cell?"

"I cried," she murmured. "I knew my mother was dead and Christopher had taken her from me. He abandoned me in a cold room and I knew he wouldn't ever let me out. I didn't even think I'd see him again."

He lowered his chin, resting it on top of her head. She fit there, as she always had. "You hurt my ears with all that sobbing." He pressed a little closer. "You looked up and saw me crouched in the corner." He smiled at the memory. "I believed you'd start screaming or make louder sounds but you didn't. You just crawled off my mat and right to me. I thought you might attack and I tensed, prepared to knock you away since I'd been told I couldn't hurt you. Instead you threw your arms around me. You held on so tight."

She turned her face a little, pressing her cheek against his chest, nuzzling him. "You let me. You even took me back to the mat and curled up with me. I was cold and you were warm."

"You needed me."

"I've always needed you and I always will."

He stopped pushing his fists against the door and eased them back, opening his hands. He hesitantly placed them on her waist. Her skin, where it was bare, felt cool to his touch.

"You were my one weakness," he admitted.

"I never meant to be. You were always my greatest strength."

He tightened his hold on her just above her hips and backed up a little so their bodies were no longer pressed together. He opened his eyes, looking down at her. "I'm going to lift you up to take the pressure off the belts. Slip them off. Don't do this again. Do you ever listen to me? No one wants to be restrained to a wall."

"I'll do it over and over again until you stop avoiding touching me."

"What am I going to do with you?" She made him feel so much at once. Frustration, irritation, pain, but also good things. Amusement, warmth, and the need to get close to her and keep her there.

"Anything you want." She blinked back tears. "I've always been yours and nothing can ever change that."

He lifted her and his anger surged. He snarled. She didn't flinch at his sudden outburst. She just kept looking at him as if she had nothing to fear.

"You should weigh more." It infuriated him. She felt so frail. He hoisted her higher and adjusted his hold, wrapping one arm entirely around her waist to anchor her in place. It freed his other hand to tear at the tight belt to loosen its grip. The red marks on her wrists where the leather had indented would probably leave bruises.

"Silly female," he growled. He got her loose and backed away, carrying her over to his bed. "You've hurt yourself."

She tugged her wrists out of his hold before he could set her down on top of the mattress. It startled him when her legs came up and wrapped around his waist as she threw her arms around his neck. She clung to him tightly.

He lowered his face, burying it against her throat. He breathed her in. The scent wasn't quite the same, but it was familiar enough that there was no denying she was his Candi. He just stood there, holding her and allowing her to hold him. He remembered the first time he'd claimed she was his...

~ ~ ~ ~ ~

The cell door opened and one of the technicians shoved Candi into their space. When she nearly tripped and went down, 927 shot to his feet and snarled at the human male. Tears streaked Candi's face and he could pick up the acidic odor of her pain. He also picked up the scent of fresh blood. Hers.

He snarled louder and glared at the technician with rage. The male snorted, pulling his weapon to keep him from attacking.

"I didn't hurt her. Dr. C is to blame if you want to kill someone." He slammed the door.

927 went to Candi and grabbed her around her waist. He lifted her off her feet and took her to their mat. He sat, putting her on his lap. He sniffed to find the source of her pain. It didn't take long. He grabbed the shirt she wore and pushed the material up her arm. A bandage had been placed just under her wrist and the white gauze was soaked with bright-red blood.

"What did Dr. C do to you?"

She lifted her tear-filled gaze. "He took blood because he thinks I might not be his daughter. He's going to test it against his own to see if I am. He said horrible things about my mommy."

He spotted bruises that were forming on her wrist and upper arm. "You fought?"

"He was so mean and the needle hurt." She sniffed. "He said I might be a bastard. That means I don't have parents since he killed my mommy."

She was so little and harmless. It infuriated him that Dr. C would be so cruel to her, but then again, he'd locked her in a cell with him. "It doesn't matter if you are from his blood or not. I don't have parents. They call me a bastard." He reached up and gently wiped away her tears. "It doesn't make me cry."

"You never cry." She turned her face into his chest and wrapped her arms around his middle, hugging him tightly. "What if I am a bastard? I don't belong to anyone."

He rested his chin on top of her head and held her more firmly against his body. "You belong to me. He put us together. I would cry if they took you away and never brought you back. It would hurt me."

She stopped crying and tipped her head, staring at him. "Really?"

He nodded. "Yes. No more tears, Candi. I care about you."

"He told me the date. It's my birthday today." Tears welled in her eyes again and spilled down her cheeks. "My mommy invited all my friends to my party. Do you think they are looking for me?"

"I don't know." He wiped her face again, hating to see her in so much pain. The concept of having friends or a party was foreign to him, but it mattered to her. "You're not alone. I'm here."

"We don't have cake and my mommy promised me she'd bought me the doll I want."

He didn't know what either of those things were. "They will feed us soon and you can eat it all."

"I can't eat that much. I'd get sick. I don't want you to be hungry later."

"I would let you if you could." He pushed the hair away from her face, studying her features. She had grown on him since they'd brought her into his cell. He did care and it would hurt him if they took her away. "We will have fun." He got an idea. "It's your birthday. Sing to me. You like to do that. I'll try to learn the words and do it with you. That will make you happy."

Her smile warmed him inside. "You'd do that for me?" She turned her head to peer at the camera, then back at him. "They are watching. You don't want them to see that."

"I don't care if they know I want you to be happy."

"You're not a bastard, 927. You belong to me."

He grinned. "That is right, Candi. It is just us. That makes it perfect. Don't let them hurt you or make you cry again."

"I won't."

Chapter Five

Candi clung to Hero and she wasn't letting go. Her wrists did throb, but it was worth it to be pressed against her male, his arm around her. The feel of his hot breath fanning her neck tickled a little, but she had no complaints. She blindly reached for his hair, needing to run her fingers through those silky strands. They were wet, but she didn't care. He groaned when she did, giving her better access when he leaned his head closer to her.

Time could never move fast enough in her experience, but she suddenly wished it would just stop. She wanted to enjoy that moment forever. 927 was alive and they were together. It seemed too good to be true. She panicked. What if she was still back in the asylum, experiencing some drug-induced delusion? It had happened before when they overmedicated her.

She dug her fingernails into his shirt and fisted his hair. He growled a warning and she eased her hold. 927 lifted his head, frowning with displeasure, his dark gaze also revealing his puzzlement.

"I'm making sure you're real," she admitted. "Life is so cruel. I half expect to wake up and find myself still locked inside that room."

His other arm suddenly pressed against her ass, holding her up. "What did they do to you?"

"It doesn't matter. Nothing does but this, being with you. Please just let me hold you. Please?" She'd beg if that's what he needed to soothe his pride. Pride didn't matter when it came to him.

He twisted his head, glanced back, and then sat on the bed. He shifted her a little so she was firmly planted on his lap. She adjusted her legs, keeping them wrapped around his waist, and buried her face against him. She breathed him in, enjoying just being close to him. He was solid, big, warm and alive.

One of his arms loosened from around her ass and she tensed, worried he'd try to untangle them. He didn't. Instead he reached up and stroked her hair down her back. She relaxed. He nuzzled her head with his cheek.

"You feel so delicate. I'm afraid I'm going to hurt you."

"I'll gain weight," she promised. "I know I'm bony, but I'm tough."

"What did Doc Trisha say?"

He was worried about her health. It meant he cared. "She didn't find anything alarming, but I'm underweight. She said to eat lots, get some sunshine and tell her if I have any problems."

"You said she ran tests."

"Everything so far is fine."

"When do all the test results come back?"

"A few days."

His silence stretched but she didn't mind. He held her and stroked her hair, his fingers playing with the strands. It felt heavenly. She was touch starved. He eventually began to explore other parts of her, running his palm over her sides, and then down to her hip, wrapping his hand there as if to test her bones.

"I'm fine," she assured him.

"I should feed you."

"I just ate. I'll get sick if I force food into my stomach while I adjust to regular meals. I'm not used to it."

He growled, his displeasure clear. He released her hip and wrapped his fingers around her upper arm, exploring her shoulder on that side. She really enjoyed it when he lowered his hand and slid it between the shirt and her skin, running his palm over her spine. She arched into him, pressing her breasts tighter against his chest. He froze and sucked in a sharp breath.

"Careful," he rasped.

"What am I doing wrong?"

"Nothing. Don't push against me that way."

She lifted her head and he jerked his back. They peered at each other. "Why not?"

He glanced down between them at her breasts and growled softly. "You've gotten bigger in one place."

"My breasts grew."

She felt no embarrassment. It was 927. He'd been there the first time she'd gotten her period. He'd actually known it before she had…

~ ~ ~ ~ ~

927 sniffed at her and flipped her onto her back on their mat. Candi thought he'd lost his mind when he suddenly bent forward. He grabbed her legs, parted them, and shoved his face right against her private area. He sniffed and then jerked back. He looked confused, but stood and turned to stare up at the camera.

"She's hurt. Send in someone. There's blood."

Evelyn took her out of the cell and explained a woman's cycle. She gave Candi pads and sent her back to 927. She repeated everything to him that she'd been told. 927 helped her figure out how they were to be worn since they had loops and a belt to go around her waist.

Christopher came in later that evening. He was angry and demanded that she be taken to another cell. The order traumatized Candi. She fought him. She just wanted to lie down with 927 on their mat. Her tummy hurt and 927 had been distracting her by playing with her hair.

Every month after that, she had to leave the cell while she bled. Christopher wouldn't allow 927 to be around her during that time. She hated being alone in the room next to him, but they learned to tap the walls, to reassure each other that they were okay.

In time 927 had started reacting strangely to her cycle. He'd tell her she was about to start, then stay far away from her.

"Come here. I'm cold. Hold me," she pleaded.

He shook his head, twisted his body against the corner and growled.

"What is wrong?"

"They need to take you away now."

"Shush. I don't want to go."

"You need to."

"Why?"

He looked infuriated and turned. "This is why."

She looked at the front of his pants, stunned. He sometimes got hard in that area in the morning, the bulge noticeable, but it usually went away after he peed. It was afternoon now and they hadn't just woken.

"It happens when you start to smell of blood. Your scent changes and I react. It hurts."

Evelyn had another discussion with her. She repeated it to 927. It changed everything. They wouldn't allow Candi to return to the cell she shared with 927 except during what they called visiting hours. She cried buckets at having to sleep without him. He was enraged. Christopher didn't want to risk having 927 and her sharing sex. He said they were too young and he wouldn't allow it. The technicians would watch them and they were rarely allowed to touch.

Three years passed that way until that fateful day when Evelyn approached her about the breeding experiment. Her body had changed during that time. She'd grown breasts and gotten body hair. She told 927 about it, but hadn't been able to show him since the technicians would have rushed in to take her away if she'd attempted to bare her body...

~ ~ ~ ~ ~

Candi pulled her mind away from the memories and stared into 927's eyes. They were alone finally and no one could stop them from doing whatever they wanted.

He was still looking at her breasts. She lowered her arms, letting him go, and gripped the top of the shirt, pulling it away from her body. She tugged it down, exposing her breasts to him. She leaned back just a bit on his lap so he could get a better view. She even arched her spine and pushed her shoulders back.

His eyes widened and a low growl rumbled from him. He looked up. "What are you doing?"

"You were staring. Now the shirt isn't hiding them. You can touch them. They are soft."

He clenched his teeth and closed his eyes, twisting his head to the side. "Cover them."

She felt something under her ass where it rested on his lap. "You're hard."

"Cover them," he snarled.

She eased the material up over her breasts and gripped his shoulders. "I didn't mean to anger you."

He breathed through his nose, his nostrils flaring.

"I shaved off the hair at Medical. I'd show you that too but Doc Trisha said was good grooming to remove the hair on my legs, under my arms, and on my private area. I didn't remove all of that though. She showed me a picture of how most humans keep that area trimmed. I kept a little bit of it on my mound. I didn't cut myself with the razor."

He opened his eyes and turned his head, holding her gaze. He still looked upset, but it wasn't quite anger. She couldn't identify the emotion.

"Why would she make you do that?"

"She didn't make me. She looked at me strangely when I stripped naked for her to examine me and I asked why. That's when she told me about feminine hygiene and good grooming. I didn't know. Nobody ever said anything at Mercile or at the asylum. They wouldn't have given me a razor anyway. Doc Trisha wanted me to fit in. Species females don't have any hair on their bodies. She showed me a picture and taught me how to shave. It was kind of fun. Have you played with shaving cream? It comes in a can and it sprays white foam out. It's soft and gooey. It smells nice too. I had to spread it all over my skin where I wanted to run the razor over it. You don't have to shave, do you?"

He shook his head. "How did you reach the back of your legs?"

"I bent down and kind of twisted."

He reached down and ran his fingers over the back of her thigh. He leaned to the side, studying it. "You missed a few spots. The hair is soft."

"I did?"

"Stand up."

She hesitated.

He straightened. "I want to see."

"I'm afraid you won't let me close to you again if I get off your lap."

A muscle jumped just over his jawline when he clenched his teeth but then his mouth relaxed. "I will let you hold me. Stand. I want to see."

She climbed off his lap regretfully, stood in front of him, and then she turned around. He lifted the shirt she wore a few inches and ran his other palm along the back of her upper thigh. He surprised her when he slid off the bed to his knees and bent a little to study her closer.

"It's just a few spots."

She turned her head, watching him. He stopped stroking her skin and released the shirt. He lifted his head, holding her gaze. "Turn to me."

She faced him. His gaze lowered to her stomach and he sat back on his heels. He gripped his thighs with both hands. She saw his knuckles whiten as if he were squeezing his legs tightly. He cleared his throat.

"I want to see the hair. Show me."

She fisted the shirt that fell to her mid thighs and slowly pulled it up. She'd stripped bare to put on his shirt so she didn't have to do anything but bring the hem up to her lower belly. She studied his face, curious what he'd do when he saw it. It was tempting to just pull the shirt entirely off, but the sight of her breasts made him angry. That wasn't her intention.

927's breathing increased as he visually inspected her. Every muscle in him seemed to tense from his face to his shoulders and he flexed his arms as if his hold on his legs had increased. He closed his eyes.

"You need to lower your shirt and back away from me," he ground out.

She released the shirt and retreated a few steps. "Why?"

"Go into the bathroom. Give me a few minutes."

"No. You're going to leave."

His eyes snapped open and she saw anger glistening in them. "Do it or I'll toss you on my bed and fuck you."

She lowered her gaze to his lap. The outline of his cock was clear. His jeans weren't much of a deterrent to the evidence of his state of arousal. He wanted her. He was trying to send her fleeing in fear, but it had the opposite effect. Hope surged. He wanted to mount her.

Candi grabbed the shirt and lifted it, tearing it off and tossing it down on the carpet. "Do it."

His eyes widened and he snarled. His gaze locked on her naked body though.

She took a step closer. "Take me. I'm yours. I've always been yours."

Raw pain flashed in his eyes as he tore his gaze off her lower body and looked up. "I'll hurt you."

She understood those snarled words. "I'd welcome it." She took another step closer and knelt in front of him. She inched closer, putting her hands on his chest. The muscles under her palms were hard and firm. "Touch me," she urged. "Please."

He trembled.

"I want you," she whispered. "I need you."

He moved fast, but she didn't flinch when his hands suddenly gripped her waist. He jerked her up off her knees. She did gasp when he threw her onto her back on the soft mattress. She bounced once and stilled, a bit stunned. A door slammed and she pushed up to her elbow. He was gone. One sweep of her gaze revealed that he really had just left her in his bedroom.

Tears filled her eyes a second later when another door slammed. He hadn't just left her in his bedroom, he'd left his apartment. She turned on her side, drew her knees up and curled into a tight ball.

927 had forgotten about the officer who was stationed in the hallway outside his door. He stepped around the male. "I'm going for a walk."

He took the stairs down to the first floor and burst out the back door of the men's dorm. He nearly collided with a female and had to twist to avoid making contact, slamming his shoulder into the wall. Kit frowned at him.

"Where's the emergency, Hero?"

"There isn't one." He shoved away from the wall and tried to step around her.

"Not so fast." She gripped his arm, shoved him up against the wall and stepped into him, pinning him there.

He scowled but didn't shove her away. "Let go and move."

She eased her grip and removed her hand. "You stood me up. I was coming to find you."

He had forgotten he was supposed to meet her at the bar. "Something came up."

She growled as she gave him a once over with her shrewd gaze. "I see your erection. Who is the female I smell on you?" She leaned in and sniffed. "Not familiar."

"I don't want to talk about this. I apologize, but I need to be alone."

"You asked me to have dinner with you. I expected we would share sex after we danced. I'm owed an explanation."

"I'm not your mate."

She jerked back a good foot. "You're in a mean mood."

He regretted his harsh words. "I'm not having a good day."

"What happened?"

"I don't want to talk."

"Do you wish to fight?" She cocked her head. "Tell me what is wrong or we will. You look angry. I know I am. I'd like to punch you in the face for making me sit at a table waiting for you when you never showed up. Now I smell some unknown female all over you and you're as hard as a brick. I thought we were going to try to date like humans do and not share sex with others." She grabbed his chest and shoved him against the wall again, his shirt ripping a little in her hands. "I agreed to that because the sex between us is good and you aren't one to demand too much of my time. We both enjoy our space."

He gently pushed her off. "Stop touching me. I need space now. Share sex with whomever you wish. I can't attempt dating anymore."

She leaned in, sniffing at him. "Who is she?"

He hated seeing the anger in Kit's eyes. She'd been a good friend to him. They'd even become more recently, sharing sex twice. He hadn't minded that she didn't want a male to spend time with her afterward. He didn't want to stay. He'd only held two females in his arms while sleeping. One had been Candi and the other had been his friend Tammy. She'd had a mate and he'd held her to keep her safe from their captors.

He had the urge to call Tammy, but he'd left his cell phone on his nightstand. She had remained his friend and he might be able to talk to her about what was going on. They'd shared a harsh ordeal together.

"I mean it." Kit drew him from his thoughts. "I will punch you if you don't explain why you stood me up and who you've been with."

"Go ahead." He leaned his head against the wall.

"Stubborn male," Kit hissed. She flashed fangs. "I should bite you."

"Do it if it makes you feel less angry. I am sorry."

Her expression softened. "Talk to me. What is going on? You look bad and you are almost begging me to hurt you."

He shook his head.

"You're being self destructive. I know this state of being well."

"You have no idea what I am."

"I know you accepted the name Species call you out of some sense of self-inflicted punishment."

He regretted telling her that.

"You're not a bad male, Hero. We all know why you killed those humans when you were in captivity. It doesn't put me off the way it does some of our females. Most of our kind have killed humans and it wasn't out of a sense of giving them mercy. It was to inflict suffering and gain revenge. Is this your way of making certain I don't get attached to you by standing me up and having another's scent all over you? I'm not looking for a mate. I just wanted to share sex with only one male for a while. I chose you because you're not clingy and you have pain in your heart. We're the same that way."

"This has nothing to do with you," he answered honestly. "Or us."

She narrowed her gaze. "Do you know why I chose my name?"

"No."

"One of the head shrinks likes to build small toy model cars. He said they are called kits. There's a picture of what it is supposed to look like after all the parts are put together, but inside the box, when it's first opened, it's a jumble of confusing little pieces." She hesitated. "That's how I felt. I was a bunch of jumbled pieces contained inside this body. I look whole, but inside I'm not."

He reached up to take her shoulder in a gesture of comfort.

She flinched away. "Don't pity me. I don't want it."

He let his hand drop away. "I don't. You're one of the strongest females I know, Kit."

"It's a picture I show on the outside. Inside I'm a mess." She held his gaze. "I just told you something I've never shared with another. We both suffer deep pain from our past. You can hurt me now if you wish to tell others what I said. I don't want them to see me as weak. Bare yourself to me. I wouldn't betray your trust. Tell me why you let them call you Hero and why it hurts you."

He felt compelled to answer. "The one person I wished to be a hero to and save was a female I believed I killed. I was enraged at the time and in such deep pain that I wanted to hurt her. I did." He held her gaze, not looking away. "Today she walked into Homeland. It's her scent you smell. Mercile lied to me. She survived and just escaped from where they'd kept her locked up." Pain wrenched through his chest. "I even failed her that way. I've been free for a while but she was still in captivity. I wasn't even searching for her."

Kit sighed. "You have feelings for her. Did she work for Mercile? I won't judge."

"She's human, but was brought there as a child by her father. He murdered her mother and she witnessed it. He wanted to make certain she couldn't tell on him to other humans. He knew Mercile wouldn't punish him for what he'd done. She was raised with me inside our cell as if she were one of us. I regarded her as my mate but her father took her away from me and only allowed us to spend monitored time together when we reached the age when our sexual attraction began." It hurt him to say the words, but he did. "She allowed another male to mount her before I was able to claim her as mine. That's why I attacked her."

"Why would she do that? Did she not want you for a mate?"

"I thought so. That's why I lost my mind. I found out today that they made her accept a feline or her father would have killed me if I'd claimed her first. She did it to save me."

"Why are you out here and not with her?"

"I hated her for accepting that male. I've hated myself for thinking I killed her. I died inside that day. Now I find out she survived, why it happened, and I don't know what to do. I just feel rage at everything. All of it has made me who I am and I finally had some peace. It's gone now. I want the numbness to return."

"I understand. Things have changed though." She cocked her head. "There's no place you can run from this. There's no hiding from the things you must feel."

His body grew rigid, but Kit seemed to ignore his reaction or take it as a warning.

"This female mattered to you and still does, or it wouldn't tear you up this much. You're broken, Hero. She might be able to fit the pieces together to make you whole." She stepped closer to the back door. "The male I loved is dead. There is no hope of him walking into Homeland to seek me out. I watched it happen and saw his broken body. Go to her, Hero. Where is she?"

"Inside my home. I left her on my bed."

Kit reached down, withdrew her key card from her pocket and swiped it. She punched in the code and yanked open the door. "Go to her, Hero. Make your name count for what it should mean instead of a way to torture yourself with the irony of it."

"Why are you saying this?"

Her features softened. "I want you to be happy. It will give me hope that one day I won't remain this way. We're a lot alike. Get your male ass inside the dorm and return to your apartment. Face this female and the past. Try to make a future. You said she's human. She could leave Homeland to live in the outside world, but we both know she won't be safe out there. They are crazy and some would target her for her association with us. Save her now."

He still hesitated. "I'm afraid I'll hurt her. I am a mess."

"She's a mess too if she was raised at Mercile." Her tone deepened. "You're a canine, not a pussy. Go male up. I think that's the term. You're no coward. You're a survivor. So is she. You belong together. Go."

He shoved off from the wall and stepped closer to Kit. "I just want to run."

"I've been to your home. It's three flights up. Use the stairs. That should help alleviate that urge. Don't make me drag your ass up there. I haven't had dinner and I missed lunch. You're a big male and outweigh me. It would irritate me to use that much energy to get you up those flights of stairs."

He stepped inside and turned. "I—"

"You're welcome. I know you don't feel thankful right now, but you can mean it later." She grinned. "Stop stalling. Females hate to be kept waiting." She shut the door in his face.

He turned, staring down the corridor that led to the back stairs. "Fuck."

Chapter Six

Candi washed her face in 927's bathroom sink and put on the tank top that she'd tossed on the floor after she'd attempted to seduce him into mounting her. She left the bedroom and stared at the door to the hallway. It was tempting to go out and search for him but he wouldn't want to be found. He'd proven that already.

She moved around the living space, touching his things. He didn't have many personal items, but there was a photo of him with a couple on a shelf. The male was a big feline with harsh features who held a human female close to his body in a possessive way. 927 stood a few feet away from them and they all were smiling. There were a lot of trees surrounding them.

The door at her back opened and she turned, expecting Breeze or one of the males who'd escorted her to 927's apartment. She was stunned when 927 stepped in and closed it, sealing himself inside with her. He leaned against the wood, staring at her with a grim expression. She glanced down his body, seeing a few tears in his shirt. It was possible he'd gotten into a fight, but he looked fine, just angry.

"That's Tammy and Valiant," he murmured. "They are mated."

She realized she still held the framed picture in her hands and glanced down before returning it to the shelf. "I guessed she was his."

"I'd just been freed when that photo was snapped. They insisted on taking one with me since I'd saved her life. They gave me a copy."

"She's the one you mentioned? The one you didn't kill?"

"Yes."

She wanted to get closer to him but held still in case he decided to leave again. "Thank you for coming back."

"It's my home."

She glanced at his shirt. "What happened?"

He looked down, touching one of the holes. He sighed and lifted his chin, meeting her gaze. "It doesn't matter."

"It does to me. Did Breeze make you come back?"

"It wasn't Breeze. I'd have more damage to my clothes if someone had tried to force me to return when I wasn't willing to. I'd have fought. This was just to hold me still so I could hear her words."

"Her?"

"A friend."

"Have you shared sex with her?"

He pushed away from the door and strode into the kitchen. "Are you hungry?"

She flinched and pain jabbed at her. He hadn't denied it. He'd changed the subject. He must have a reason. "No."

"You should try to eat." He opened the fridge, peering inside it. "I could fix you a sandwich."

"Is she important to you? Do you feel a bond with her?"

He slammed the fridge and glared at her. "Don't ask. You don't want to know."

"I do."

"Fine. Yes, Kit and I have shared sex. I've been to her home a few times. I was with a few females while still at Mercile. They used me in breeding experiments after I was told I killed you. Christopher nearly beat me to death as punishment and I became one of Evelyn's. She brought me a few Species females and I mounted them. I refused to watch someone else die until they moved me and brought in those humans they captured. I killed them, as I said. Then Tammy was brought to my cage and her mate tracked her there. I was freed in the process. There have been others at Homeland and Reservation after I was freed."

Candi needed to sit. She retreated to a chair and collapsed into it. Jealousy and pain struck her at knowing so many females had touched him, but she also had heard everything he'd said. He hadn't wanted to watch anyone die. She would never forget the feline male and the beating he'd taken before she'd agreed to let him mount her. He had refused to take her by force. She understood.

"Is that the answer you wanted?" 927 snarled. "I won't lie."

She saw rage in his eyes as she stared into them from across the room. "I don't want you to."

"No. You wish me to watch you suffer. I see your pain." He fisted his hands at his sides, advanced a few steps, and then stopped. His nostrils flared. "I can smell it."

"I don't want you to suffer. Why would you think that?"

He spun away, pacing the small confines of the kitchen space. He finally punched a cabinet, the wood splitting from the force of it. Part of it broke off and hit the counter, and then the floor. He snarled.

Candi rose and rushed forward. His hand bled. "You're hurt."

He turned his head, growling. "Get back."

She froze.

He turned on the faucet and shoved his torn skin under the running water. She backed up a little but then stepped sideways, putting her body between him and the front door in case he tried to leave again. She wasn't above throwing herself in front of him to keep him there. It was obvious he didn't want her to touch him so she doubted he'd be willing to put his hands on her to get her out of his way.

He turned off the water and used a dishtowel to wrap his hand. "I don't plan on storming out. You don't have to stand there."

She didn't deny that's exactly why she'd chosen that spot. "Breeze said there should be a medical kit in your bathroom. Do you want me to get it?"

He shook his head. "Why would she tell you that?"

"She saw my feet."

He frowned and stared at her feet. "What?"

"I cut them when I ran after you."

He snarled. "I didn't smell the blood. Let me see."

"It's fine."

He lunged out of the kitchen. She held her ground when he grabbed hold of her waist and just lifted her. He strode to the couch and dropped her on it, grasped one of her ankles and yanked it up to study the bottom of her foot.

"Damn it. It's not bleeding anymore, but it needs to be cleaned. You're not Species. You can easily get infections." He released it and reached for her other ankle, capturing it in his uninjured hand, and lifted it. "You have two cuts. Stay put. Don't move." He let her go but then he looked at her, his expression tightening.

She followed his line of sight and realized the shirt she wore had ridden up when he dropped her on the couch and lifted her legs. Part of her pussy was exposed. His mouth tightened into a grim line when she glanced up to see his reaction. He held still, his attention focused there.

"I don't want you to suffer, my pup. Never. Why did you say that?"

That got a reaction from him. He twisted away and stomped into the bedroom. She sat up a little and pulled the shirt down. He returned quickly with a white box that had first-aid and a red symbol stamped across the top. He dropped to his knees, shoved the coffee table to the side, and set the box on top of it. He opened it, removed a few items, and then grabbed one of her ankles, lifting her foot.

"This might burn. Prepare."

She nodded, watching him use his teeth to rip off a corner of a packet that he'd pressed to his mouth. He used the wet swab to rub against the cut. It wasn't pleasant and he wasn't gentle. She clenched her teeth but didn't make a sound. He really made sure it was clean before he stopped and applied a bandage. He set her foot down on one side of his thigh and went after her other foot. She lifted it for him.

He glanced down between her thighs and froze. She knew what he saw with her thighs parted and one leg lifted. She was exposed again, flashing him the view of her pussy. She contemplated reaching down to hold the shirt in place over it but decided against it.

He tore his gaze away, cleaned the second cut and slapped a bandage on it. He unwrapped the dishtowel from his hand, twisted his body to the side and tended to his own injury. She stayed put, liking that he was just a few feet away.

"Are we going to pretend you didn't accuse me of wanting to hurt you?" She kept her tone soft.

"Yes."

"Do you believe that?" It would hurt her if he did.

He closed the box and made a pile of the discarded items next to it on the table. He refused to look at her.

"I don't want to upset or anger you. I'm trying to get to know the male you've become. That's all. I'm afraid you don't want me anymore and that another female matters more to you than I do."

He sat back on his heels and regarded her. It was clear that he masked his features to hide his emotions. "I don't want to talk about this."

"We tell each other everything."

"We did once. Not anymore. Things have changed."

That hurt. "Do you want me to leave?"

"I don't know. You're alive. I don't know how to react or what to think. I'm trying to stay calm, but I feel highly unsettled."

He was at least talking to her. "I might not have fought so hard to survive if I'd known I would bring you this much pain, my pup."

He leaned in. "Don't say that. And don't call me your pup." The anger was back in his voice.

She dropped her gaze to his chest. The sight of his tan, bare skin through the rips of his shirt was a good thing to focus on instead. "I'll leave if I only bring you suffering." She lifted her legs, turned, and tried to scoot down the couch to avoid touching him.

He reached out and put his open palm over her stomach. She stopped moving. He didn't say anything as long seconds passed. She liked the warmth of his hand there, heating her skin though the thin material of the shirt.

"No female could ever take your place."

She dared look at him and he appeared sad to her. She felt the same way. "Do you know what hurts the most?"

"What?" He pulled his hand away.

"It's not that you mounted other females. You believed I'd chosen another male over you and that I died. It's learning that you don't want me anymore. I'm nothing now except bad memories that cause you to have terrible feelings. That tears me apart inside, Hero." The name would always be foreign, but she did it for him. "I'll tell Breeze to let you go to your Reservation place and I'll stay out of your sight. I love you with everything that I am, but I won't be selfish. I give you peace. Forget I am alive. I won't exist to you anymore."

She eased off the couch and walked toward the door. She would ask the guard outside the door to take her to Breeze. She turned the handle and opened the door but a bandaged hand suddenly slammed against the wood, and the knob was torn out of her grasp. The door slammed closed. She turned, peering up at Hero. His eyes were scary and his lips were parted, fangs showing.

"I want you. That's the problem." He snarled the words. "I lose control when it comes to you. You make me feel too much, Candi. You always have. I once wanted to kill you over another male. You were mine! Do you know why I ran from you in my bedroom?" He didn't give her time to ask. "I was terrified I'd damage you. You're weak and ill. I can't mount you. It makes me furious that I want to."

He wanted her. She reached up and gripped his shoulders. "You won't damage me. I'm not ill."

"Bullshit."

"I just need to gain weight. Doc Tri—"

"Fine. You're weak. You felt easily breakable in my arms. Captivity does that. You need time to become strong before I take you to my bed. What if I do hurt you? I have enough guilt. I can't take anymore."

"What guilt?"

He spun away, stalking across the room. He ran his fingers through his hair. He began to pace, shooting angry glances at her.

"What guilt? I know you didn't mean to hurt me with your chains. I don't believe you would have snapped my neck if you'd reached me. I don't want to believe that. You would have stopped yourself from taking my life if you'd broken free and reached me."

He stopped pacing. "We'll never know."

"Let it go. I have. I never blamed you for your rage or pain. Never."

"How do you feel, knowing I was free while you were still being held captive? We have a task force team that looks for our lost females. No one searched for you. I never told them about you, Candi. I didn't mention anything to the NSO about the human child who was raised with me inside that cell, because I didn't want them to know I'd caused your death."

Some of it started to make sense to her. "You thought I was dead and you had no reason to question it. I was taken away from Mercile. How could you know?"

"I let you down. It's what I do. You allowed another to mount you to save me and I hurt you in return. You were locked up but I never tried to rescue you. You made it here on your own after having to kill to gain your freedom. You wanted me to hold you when we saw each other, but I ran away. Now you offer to stay out of my sight so I don't feel guilt for all the times I've failed to be the kind of male who deserves you."

Her heart broke. "I was wrong. This hurts me the most. You've never let me down. Stop thinking that way." She went after him. "You have always been the male I live for. You're the reason I am here. You're my entire world, 927."

She reached up when she stopped in front of him and slid her hand along the back of his neck, grabbed a handful of his hair and yanked. He grimaced but allowed her to tug his face toward her. She fisted his shirt in the front with her other hand.

"Listen to me, my pup." She paused. "927. Hero. Whatever the hell you'll let me call you. You're making me angry now. Don't ever say that you don't deserve me. You want to see how weak I am? Say it again. I will knock you flat. You taught me how to fight. I haven't forgotten that even if you have."

His eyebrows shot up.

"The only way you can break me is if you continue to tear into yourself. I won't allow it. Don't you dare. I love you." She eased her hold on his hair and wrapped her fingers around the back of his neck instead, drawing him down closer. "I love you."

Tears swam in his eyes and he wrapped his arms around her.

"You were there to hold me after my mother died. You were the one who kept me warm and comforted me every night. You gave me a reason to live in that cell. You made me laugh and feel so many wonderful things. The only reason I'm alive today is because you were my reason to fight and keep trying to escape. Don't you dare undermine any of that."

"Candi, I..."

He didn't seem to know what to say but she did. "Forget that I said I'd leave. I refuse to let you go. I found you and you're mine. I will fight any females who try to touch you. I'll chase you if you run. I will find you again."

He lifted her off her feet and she wrapped her legs around his waist. He turned with her in his arms and walked toward the bedroom. "No more running, Candi."

She clung to him. "Good."

"I'm not mounting you until you're stronger. Help me do that by keeping covered."

She could live with that. "But you plan to?"

He growled. "Yes. When you're stronger and we're sure you're healthy after Doc Trisha gets all your test results back. I can't live with knowing I've hurt you in any way."

"May I stay here with you? Sleep with you?"

"Yes." He stopped by the bed and gently lowered her. "But you need to help me get you better. That means rest and sleep. I'm going to care for you."

She didn't want to let him go but he stepped back and straightened from the bed, forcing her to. "You want to take things slow. I'm okay with that as long as you're with me."

"I won't leave. I'm going to call my friend Tammy. She's human the way you are and always complains about how difficult it is to keep weight off after having her cub. She will know how to put weight on you."

"Cub?"

He crouched. "That's another reason I won't mount you right now. I could get you pregnant."

She was stunned. "Mercile found a way to do it?" Horror came next. *They made more Species to torment? To torture with their drugs?* "Oh no."

"Easy," he rasped, reaching out to stroke her hair. He seemed to understand her reaction and the thoughts that came with it. "Mercile never accomplished that. It was after we were freed. Species can't breed together, but some mated human females have had babies with Species males. It's possible." He glanced at her body. "You're so weak that I fear a pregnancy right now might harm you more. I won't take that risk."

Mated. She heard him say it. "You're going to claim me as your mate?"

His mouth compressed into a tight line.

"That's okay with me. I want that."

His lips twitched upward a little before he opened his mouth. "You're mine, Candi."

They were the sweetest words she'd heard him say since she realized he still lived. "You're mine too."

"I'm going to make that call. Rest. You can't gain weight if you're using up all your energy. I'll return to you soon and I'll keep you warm until you're hungry."

She smiled.

Hero stood, pulling his hand away from her hair. He snagged his cell phone off the table next to the bed and left. He did keep the bedroom door cracked open. She lay down and curled into a ball. She couldn't wait for him to return, to feel him wrapped around her the way he used to do all those years ago in their cell.

She'd missed him. Part of her still feared going to sleep, terrified she'd wake inside her room at the asylum. Some of the drugs they'd forced into her body had caused very realistic dreams and hallucinations. She pressed her nose against 927's pillow and found his scent. It helped her relax.

Tammy took the news of his secret really well, even understanding his reaction when he learned Candi was still alive, sympathizing with the guilt that came with it.

"The important part is that you got a second chance," she stated. "Any mistakes you made in the past don't matter. What does are the things you do from this moment forward. You have her back, Hero. This Candi is the woman you've always loved and wished you had a future with. Grab hold, my friend. This is your chance at happiness."

"I'm flawed," he admitted.

"Aren't we all?" Tammy snorted. "Nobody is perfect. You're Species. I might be biased because of how much I love Valiant, but you guys make amazing mates. You'll meet her needs and you'll do whatever you can to make certain she's happy. That's the best thing you can do for her, Hero.

She's survived pure hell so now you get to show her all the wonderful things about life."

"I'm worried about her. She's so frail."

"Chocolate is the answer. I look at it and gain five pounds. See if she likes bacon cheeseburgers too and French fries. Add in some ranch dressing for dipping and she'll have some cushion around those bones in no time. Pretty much go on the internet and find foods that they say not to eat while dieting and feed them to her."

"I can do that."

"I know you can. Get some of the human mates involved. They'll help you out on what to feed her and how to cook it."

"I was considering bringing her to Reservation. I trust you to help me care for her."

Tammy hesitated. "I think it would be better if you keep her at Homeland for now. After telling me how those assholes kept her on drugs for so many years, she needs to be near Medical. Trisha is an amazing doctor and she's there right now. Besides, there are some excellent hospitals near Homeland in case she needs a specialist. Trisha can have them consult with her and that's easier to do if they can actually check your Candi out themselves. That means taking her to them. Flying back and forth would be tough if she does end up having some health issues. I want your Candi to have the best medical care and I know you want that too."

"I do, but I'm concerned I won't be able to care for her the way she needs."

"You'll do fine. Old Doc Harris doesn't have the best bedside manner and he's on duty here. Do I need to say more to convince you?"

"No. I'd have to hit him if he upset her."

Tammy laughed. "He's a good doctor but yeah, he needs a lot of work on the things that come out of his mouth. He blurts out whatever comes to mind. I think she'll feel more secure having so many Species living in the dorm too, after what she's been through. Exposing her to the Wild Zone residents might be something you want to do at a later date. You know how some of them are less than social. It took them a while to warm up to me because I'm human. They might see her that way instead of as a Species."

"She's one of us. So are you."

"I know that. Some of the Wilds really hate humans though. They had it far worse than other Species. Valiant tells me stories about how he was treated while at Mercile that makes me want to kill people too. They kept him in a lion cage and the staff would stare at him like some circus attraction. Get her stronger before you bring her to Reservation. You want your scent stamped all over her. It helps them accept us if we smell just like our mates."

He hung up with Tammy and felt better about everything. That was what good friends could do. She'd seen him at his worst when she'd been kidnapped and locked up with him. Her faith that he could become a good mate to Candi helped with some of his insecurities.

Hero returned to his room. The sight of Candi sleeping in his bed felt right. He bent down and removed his shoes. He'd dreamed about holding her again. It had been hell when they'd taken her away from him. She had been as much a part of him as one of his limbs. He stripped out of his torn shirt and even removed his pants, but put on a pair of boxers.

He managed not to wake her as he curled up against her back and wrapped his arm around her waist. Her steady, slow breathing assured him she wasn't having bad dreams. There had been plenty of times as children when nightmares had plagued her. She'd witnessed her mother's death at the hands of her own father. She'd loved the woman who'd given birth to her, always sharing stories of love and laughter.

He loved Candi. His life had been lonely until she'd arrived inside his cell. He hadn't believed until then that he could learn to trust anyone fully human. She'd been nothing like the technicians. Even knowing Dr. C was her father hadn't dissuaded him from forming a deep bond with her. Now, here she was, alive and where she belonged.

He lowered his chin to rest against the top of Candi's head, her small body molded to his front. He no longer wishing to run from his feelings or her, and would make sure it worked out between them. This was their new beginning. She hadn't been freed when he had been, but unlike him, she wouldn't have to navigate that new life mostly on her own. Friends were great and he appreciated them, but a mate was someone to spend the rest of his life sharing every moment with. There was no question that Candi was his. She'd always been his.

His body responded to having her so close but he ignored his stiff dick. He was terrified he'd harm her or get her pregnant. She really was frail. He made a mental note to talk to someone about what was being done to the humans who'd kept her imprisoned. They needed to pay.

Chapter Seven

Candi watched 927 carefully. He'd changed his entire attitude toward her and while she appreciated it, she wondered why he'd become so enthusiastic to accept her into his life. She finished the breakfast he'd brought her.

"Well?"

"I liked it a lot. My stomach hurts a bit. That was a lot of food."

"Tammy suggested it. It's one of her favorite things to eat. She said bacon cheeseburgers and fries are good for adding weight. I asked one of the males to cook it for you. He offered to teach me, if you like hamburgers, so I can make them."

"That was nice of him."

"Some of our males have really enjoyed learning things, but especially cooking. We like food."

"It was really good. There were so many flavors."

"What did they feed you after you left Mercile?"

"Mostly oatmeal, eggs, and lots of soup. It wasn't that good. I barely got meat since I was only allowed to use plastic spoons."

"No wonder you are so thin."

She smiled. "I actually missed the meat strips from Mercile."

"I'll cook you a steak. I am good at that." He stood.

"Not right now. I'm full."

He grinned. "Sorry. I'm eager to get you better. The females at the women's dorm are baking for you. They are going to drop off a cake, a few pies, and some cookies today."

"That's really nice of them."

"Everyone is concerned about you, Candi. They want to help you gain weight. I went there while you showered this morning and told them Tammy said you need lots of chocolate."

It touched Candi to learn that so many people wanted to help her. It also made her wonder if any of those females were ones he'd shared sex with. She didn't ask, not wanting to ruin the morning because of her jealousy. It was something she needed to deal with. 927 was really trying to integrate her into his life and that's what she needed to focus on, not what had happened in the time they were apart.

"How would you like a tour of Homeland today? Everyone is excited to meet you."

She hesitated.

"Too soon?" Concern showed in his eyes.

"I just want to spend time with you," she admitted.

"I understand. I remember when I was freed. It was amazing to see all those Species, but it was a little overwhelming. I spent a lot of time in the room they assigned me, just touching things and trying to figure them out." He suddenly grinned. "Television! It's a wonderful thing. How would you like to watch a movie with me? I have some of my favorites on DVDs.

Those are round disks that store it and you can play it over and over, as much as you want."

"Okay."

"Do you know what is good for movie watching? Popcorn. I'm out, but I know a few males who also got hooked on that treat. I'll go knock on their doors and see if they have any. I'll be right back."

"Popcorn?"

"You'll like it and it has lots of butter. That's probably helpful to gain weight. I'll be right back." He moved fast, unlocked the door, and left.

She shook her head, amused. 927 seemed determined to feed her until her stomach burst. She stood and carried the plate to the sink. She paused, glancing at the dishwasher. She had no idea how to use it. He'd given her a tour of his home that morning and pointed out what things were. She decided to hand wash her plate, something she was confident she could do. Someone knocked on the door so she turned away and opened it.

Breeze smiled at her. "How did it go? I heard you spent the night with Hero."

"I did. He let me sleep with him."

"Good. I'll relieve the officer since he's no longer needed."

"Come in."

"I'm on my way to work so I just have a minute." Breeze lowered her voice. "Did it work? I smell him on you, but you showered. Did he mount you?"

"No, but he held me while I slept. He's afraid he'll cause me damage."

Breeze glanced down her. "Understandable."

"He's going to wait until I weigh more."

"Does he understand that could take a bit of time?"

"I don't think so. You should have seen the huge breakfast he fed me and now he went to get some kind of treat. Popcorn. He might hurt me with too much food instead of sharing sex with me."

Breeze chuckled. "A for effort."

"What does that mean?"

"Sorry. You look so human I forget. It means he's trying and going all out to do it."

"He has his friends cooking for me."

"Aw. That's so sweet."

"I know. I just wish he wouldn't worry so much about me. I'm strong."

"Did you tell him that?"

"Yes, but he's not listening. He told me I could have a baby and he's afraid, in my condition, it could be very bad."

Breeze entered and closed the door. She lowered her voice. "He's not here, right?"

Candi shook her head. "He went to find popcorn."

"Okay." Breeze lowered her voice. "I heard you yesterday. You have almost zero experience with males and sex since you only were mounted once when you were young and drugged up. Are you afraid of touching Hero?"

"No."

Breeze smiled. "Good. Our males have a high sex drive. It means they constantly get hard-ons. They all keep lotion in their nightstand drawers and use it. You could do that for him and he could use that lotion on you if he doesn't actually want to mount you."

"Lotion?"

Breeze groaned. "You're probably the only Species female not to know about masturbation. Have you ever seen a male completely nude?"

Candi shook her head. "927 never removed his pants at Mercile in front of me. He even had me close my eyes and turn away when he needed to use the toilet. Christopher ordered him to hide that from me. I never pushed because I didn't want him to be punished. He'd get hard sometimes and I could see the outline of what he looks like down there."

"What about the feline?"

"I closed my eyes. He took me from behind so I couldn't have looked even if I wanted to. I didn't."

"Did he prepare you? Go down and put his mouth on you?"

"No. I didn't want him to touch me in any way he didn't have to. I just wanted to get it over with and asked him to do it fast."

Breeze snarled and annoyance creased her features. "That had to have hurt."

"I try to forget everything that happened inside that cell."

"I don't blame you. It won't hurt with Hero."

"It wouldn't matter. He's my male."

Breeze reached out. "I'm going to hug you. Deal with it."

Candi didn't mind when the female put her arms around her and gave her a squeeze. "Thank you."

Breeze released her and lowered her head, peering into her eyes. "Okay, males like to put their mouths on your sex down there. It feels amazing. You'll like it. Don't be shocked when Hero wants to do that. There's nothing to fear. Our males really enjoy it if you put lotion on your hands and rub up and down on where he gets hard. Expect a mess when he gets off. That's normal. I can understand why he is leery to share sex with you, but you can do those things without fear of getting pregnant. He'd have to come inside you for that possibility. Is that clear enough?"

"Yes."

"Find his lotion and get him undressed. That should motivate him to want to touch you back. It's going to be at least a month or two before you're at a size that will make him feel secure with mounting you. I don't want him picking fights with other males out of sexual frustration and sleeping with you every night is going to make him snap at some point. I also don't want you to have to suffer his bad moods. Our males get testy when they are sexually frustrated. You'll both be happier."

The door opened and Hero entered. "Breeze."

"I was just checking on your female." She smiled. "My shift is starting. I have to go. Carry on." She left.

Hero closed the door and locked it. He showed her two flat bags wrapped in clear paper. "I got us popcorn. I'll throw them in the microwave. How long was Breeze here?"

"Not long."

"What did she say?" He entered the kitchen.

"She said it could be months before I gain lots of weight."

He spun, horrified. "Months? No. I'll feed you plenty." He turned away and yanked open a metal box thing that was built into the cabinets, and opened the packets. "Meat will help. Every meal will have some."

She didn't say anything. He was in denial that it would take time. It was their first day spending their new life together. She didn't want to argue with him. Everything Breeze had said replayed through her mind. It would be easier to change his plan to wait to mount her than to allow that much time to elapse.

"I'm deciding what movie to show you first."

"I remember them but it was before I was brought to you at Mercile."

"Did you have a favorite?"

She shook her head. "I can't remember that much about them. They were cartoons."

He smiled. "I have some movies that are cartoons. That helps. There's one about a superhero family. I think you'll like it." He grinned at her.

"Okay. I'm going to use your bathroom. I'll be right back."

"Our bathroom," he corrected. He faced the microwave and put one of the packets inside. "This will take a few minutes. I'll find the movie."

She liked that he was excited. "I'll hurry." She rushed out of the room and entered the bathroom. She even took the time to brush her hair and teeth. It didn't take long to search the drawers and find the bottle of lotion. She returned to the living room.

Hero didn't glance her way, too busy pouring something into a large bowl. She shoved the lotion behind one of the cushions on the side of the couch and took a seat. He'd turned on the television and a colorful menu showed on the screen. Two sodas were placed on the coffee table with napkins. He strode toward her with two bowls and a grin on his handsome face.

"This will be fun."

It brought her pleasure to see his joy. "I'm excited."

He took a seat a few feet away, placed the bowls on the table and reached for the remote. She studied his clothes. "Can you do something for me?"

He froze and turned his head. "What?"

"I want to curl up to you. Your jeans are rough. Can you put those soft shorts on?"

His eyebrows rose.

"The ones you wore to sleep with me."

He frowned. "They are called boxers and that's not a good idea."

"It is. I want us to be comfortable." She glanced at his chest. "No shirt either. I want to be able to touch your skin."

"It's best if I keep fully clothed. I'd prefer you wear more, but you seem to only like wearing my shirts."

"Please?"

He growled. "Fine."

"Don't get angry."

"I'm not. I enjoy torture." He stood fast and marched into the bedroom.

Candi grinned. Her male looked cute when he was annoyed. He might not admit it, but she knew why. He expected sexual frustration. She glanced at the cushion next to her. He wouldn't be if she had anything to say about it. She just needed him to relax before she attempted to get him completely naked.

He wore black silky boxers when he came out. Candi swallowed hard. She'd rather watch him than some movie. Her male was beautiful and she loved seeing so much of him. He sat down again and snatched the remote off the table. His body looked tense and so did his expression, but he started the movie. He dropped the remote, grabbed one of the bowls, and placed it on his lap.

"Thank you." She inched over and leaned against his side. He remained rigid but didn't complain when she snuggled closer. He actually lifted that arm and wrapped it around her back to hold her close. He used his other hand to eat his popcorn.

It smelled good, but she wasn't ready to eat more. Her gaze fixed on the big screen and she had to admit to a little excitement at the prospect of watching a movie. She just didn't plan to see it all. It was just a matter of time before Hero let his guard down. She'd strike then.

Hero loved the sound of Candi's laughter. He glanced at her face and saw sheer joy as she watched the movie. He leaned forward a little and shoved the empty popcorn bowl onto the table and turned his body a bit toward her. It felt right to have her against his side. She didn't take her attention off the television, but leaned more solidly against him, resting her cheek on his chest. Her hand stroked his skin. Her soft fingers were playing hell on him when they brushed over his nipple. His dick hurt. He'd been hard since she'd started running her hands over him, but managed to keep his dick trapped between his thighs. He didn't want her to become aware of how she affected him.

The shower beaconed to him. He would tend his needs once he locked a door between them. His gaze lowered to her curled legs. The shirt rode up too high, exposing her thighs. He longed to touch her there, but kept his hand loose on her hip. It had been hell sleeping with her, but he'd thought the days would be better when they were out of bed. He'd been wrong. He wanted Candi so bad it was all he could think of.

He stared at the movie but couldn't get into it. That was new. He'd watched it dozens of times and always enjoyed the story. He hadn't had Candi next to him then though. She laughed again and ran her hand from his chest to his stomach. He clenched his teeth when her fingertips stroked the skin just over the waistband of his boxers. His dick throbbed when he imagined her sliding that hand lower.

She kept her hand there, rubbing and exploring. He tensed, unable to take it anymore. His dick was getting too hard to keep it trapped. "I need to shower."

She lifted her head and peered up at him. He tried to mask his emotions. "What? Now?"

"Now."

She sniffed. "You smell good. Why do you need a shower? We're watching the movie."

"Candi..." He paused, deciding to be honest. "I need to put some space between us. Finish watching the movie. I've seen it many times. I'll be back in ten minutes."

She didn't pull away from him, but instead lowered her chin. "Oh."

He cringed when he followed her gaze. The boxers were long ones that nearly went to his knees but the outline of his engorged dick was clear, despite him trying to keep it between this thighs.

"Ten minutes. I'll be back." He pulled his hand off her hip.

She sat up, and when she was off him he stood fast, ready to flee. She snagged the back of the waistband of his boxers. "Wait."

He twisted his head to look back at her, frowning. "Let go."

She stretched across the couch and dug her fingers behind the cushion. She withdrew his lotion and smiled. "Sit down."

He was too stunned to do anything but glance between the bottle and the smile on her face.

"Sit down." She yanked on his boxers. They slid down his hips and legs. She let go of them and they landed around his ankles.

He still resisted. She'd never seen him without something covering his dick. That wouldn't be the case if he turned. Her hand stroked one of his ass cheeks and he growled.

"Do you know what you're doing, Candi?"

"No, but I think I can figure it out with your help. Turn toward me or sit down."

"I don't want to frighten you."

She smiled. "You're mine. Let me see all of you."

He lifted one foot and then the other, kicking the boxers away. A smart male would make a dash for the bathroom as he'd intended, but he was too aroused to think straight. Candi wanted to use lotion on him. He turned and tensed, watching her face to judge her reaction. He'd flee if he spotted fear.

Her eyes widened and her lips parted. She said nothing as she studied his dick. He glanced down at it. It wasn't trapped between his thighs or hidden now. Her hand lifted and she gently brushed her fingertips across the top of his shaft. His knees weakened at that hesitant touch, but he locked them. She didn't look afraid.

"You're so hard and big."

"Yes." He couldn't deny that.

"Sit," she urged, pulling her hand back. She uncapped the lotion and poured some into her hands. "How do you like to be touched?"

He sat, the leather couch still warm from his body. He was excited and afraid at the same time. He spread his thighs and leaned back, shoving his hips forward a little to give her access to him.

"What feels good?"

Candi expected an answer. "Anything," he growled. He looked up at her face and she smiled.

"You look angry."

"Hurting. Excited. Not angry."

She dropped the lotion bottle on the table and rubbed her hands together. He had a difficult time breathing as he watched her. She'd reduced him to the ability to say few words. He tensed when she reached for his dick and moaned when she wrapped both hands around his shaft. She explored him, rubbing her palms and fingers around the sensitive flesh. He growled when she stroked the tip.

"You make me hurt too," she whispered. "I like touching you. Am I being gentle enough?"

He nodded. He couldn't speak. Her hands felt amazing. He wanted to come just from knowing it was her and from seeing his Candi's hands bringing him pleasure. He clenched his teeth until his jaw hurt. She played with him, stroking up and down his shaft, rubbing circles over the crown of his dick, gripping him a little more firmly to give the shaft a squeeze.

"What feels best? Tell me."

He had to tear his gaze away from her hands to look into her eyes. "Up and down. A little more strength. I'll come fast. I'm almost there." He wouldn't lie to his Candi.

He groaned when she stacked one hand on top of the other on his shaft and gripped his dick harder. She slid them to the base and then up until she swirled her thumb across the crown, and then back down. He threw his head back and stretched his arms out along the back of the couch, gripping it so he wouldn't grab her instead.

"You're so perfect," she whispered. "So beautiful. Should I rub you slow or fast?"

He didn't care. It didn't matter. Candi brought him pleasure. He opened his mouth, breathing heavily. His ass left the couch a bit. He locked his body so he wouldn't start rocking his hips. He imagined what it would be like if he was inside her and that was it. He came hard, unable to warn her before he did. It was just blinding rapture and his semen exploding outward. She kept touching him, almost killing him, and he blindly grabbed at her wrists and pulled her hands off his dick.

He fought to regain his composure but it took a minute. He opened his eyes and realized he still had her wrists captured in his hands. He held her gaze, worried that she would be upset. She smiled at him instead, as if losing his composure and coming all over his thighs, stomach, her hands, and on part of the shirt she wore, was okay.

"I'm sorry."

"For what?"

He glanced down his body. He wasn't surprised to see his semen everywhere. He'd felt it hit his skin. He looked up into her eyes. "I was really excited."

"I don't understand why you're apologizing."

"I should have said something before that happened and covered the head of my dick with my hand so it didn't go everywhere. I also swell a bit if you noticed the lump that formed near the base of my shaft after I came. It's normal for a canine."

She twisted her hands and he released her wrists. She reached down, shocking him by running her fingertips through his semen, spreading it on his stomach. "This is a part of you." She looked up. "Never apologize for that."

He placed his hand on top of hers, trapping it on his lower belly. He sat up, holding her gaze. "You're not unsettled by what happened?"

"No. I want to do it again and again. I love touching you and watching your body react to my touch. Your muscles tighten and you move in ways that makes me ache. I like to see that expression on your face. It's almost like pain, but not. You're sexy, my pup."

He released her hand and twisted toward her. "You ache?"

She nodded. "Yes."

"Show me where."

"You don't like it when I take off my shirt, but you make me feel that way all over."

"Take it off." He didn't bother trying to soften his tone. Candi had heard him growl many times. She ached and he picked up the scent of arousal coming from her. He couldn't mount her, but he wanted to make her feel good. His dick hardened again just thinking about how it would be to make her come. "Show me."

She eagerly wiggled out of the shirt. She moved to toss it away, but he snagged it as she released it and used it to wipe off her hands first, and then his belly, thighs and dick. He dropped it then and slid off the couch. Predatory instincts awakened inside him as he watched her lean back the way he'd been, and spread her legs open in front of him. He wanted to pounce on her, eat her alive, in all the good ways.

Hero rose to his knees and grabbed her hips, putting her where he wanted her. He tugged her toward him and she complied. She scooted down until her ass was on the edge of the couch. It put her pussy close to his dick. She placed her toes against the coffee table, her calves at the sides of his hips. He let go of her and clutched one of the cushions from the couch. He slid his hand under her back and lifted, shoving the thick padding under her. It arched her back and she was spread out in front of him like some beautiful, sexy feast.

He still saw no fear in her. Candi held his gaze and looked at him with anticipation. It sank in then. She'd accept anything he wanted to do to her because she trusted him. His hands trembled as he opened them and lightly placed them on the top of her thighs. She didn't jerk away or tense. He pushed upward, gliding them over her skin and up to her stomach. He paused.

"Are the pads on my skin too rough? You have such soft ones."

"I love your hands. They feel good. It almost tickles, but don't stop."

Her nipples beaded when he slid his hands upward and massaged them. They were perfect, so soft, and he loved playing with them. Candi's breathing increased and so did the scent of her arousal. He had to shove his ass back a bit since he glanced down at her spread pussy and realized his dick was in danger of coming into contact with it. He was hard as a rock again, as if she hadn't just gotten him off.

"That feels so good." She arched her back and pushed her breasts against his hands. He gently squeezed, pinching her taut nipples between his forefingers and thumbs. Candi moaned and her legs parted further. Her toes slipped off the coffee table and she hooked the back of his thighs with her heels.

He wouldn't enter her. He couldn't risk hurting her by taking her too roughly in his excitement, or risk getting her pregnant. She looked too frail and it enraged him that humans had made her so skinny. Mercile had killed plenty of Species, but not by starvation. He released her breasts and skimmed his hands lower. Her stomach muscles clenched under his palms and he looked up at her face. She watched him, her features flushed.

He needed to go slowly so he resisted the urge to do what he wanted. It might shock her if he grabbed her ass, sat back on his heels and put his mouth against her pussy. He massaged her inner thighs instead, inching closer to her sex. He continued to look for any indication that he was frightening her. He'd stop if he was, but he saw nothing to discourage him.

Hero grew bolder and brushed his thumb over her pussy. Her breathing increased, but she didn't protest in any way. He was glad his nose hadn't been wrong when he dragged his thumb over the proof of her arousal and eased that wetness up to her clit. He paused for a split second when her body tensed, but she didn't try to jerk away. He tested how she withstood his touch by circling the little nub with the softest part of the tip of his thumb, which was just above the thicker layer of tough skin.

Candi sucked in a sharp breath and her hands dug into the couch, getting a good grip on it. He cleared his throat so he was able to speak around the lump that had formed there. She liked it when he talked to her, so he did.

"You'll like this, Candi. It almost feels like pain, but don't be afraid. Just try to relax and let me do this. It will be wonderful."

She nodded.

He started to rub her clit again, circling it with his fingertip. Her eyes closed and she bit her lip. A soft moan came from her and the scent of her arousal grew stronger. He turned his hand a little so the length of his thumb rested against the crease of her pussy. She grew wetter as he played with her.

Blood rushed to his already-stiff dick but he ignored his discomfort. It was about his Candi, not his desire to be inside her. He slid his thumb off her clit and ran it through the honey silkiness of her arousal. He loved how wet she was. He coated his thumb and returned to her clit, bending it to slide up and down instead of in circles. Candi moaned louder and her fingers clawed at the couch.

"I hurt," she whimpered. Her calves squeezed against his hips as she tried to close her legs. He sat on his ass and leaned forward so his chest kept them spread. He used his upper arms to pin them open too.

"It's not pain. It's strong pleasure. Trust me," he urged.

She arched her back and wiggled her hips, grinding her pussy against his hand. He stroked her faster and applied a little pressure. He didn't want to draw it out for her. Not the first time. Her nipples were stiff, beaded, and her body rigid. He knew she was close. He twisted his wrist upward just enough to fit one finger between her sex and his thumb. He pressed his fingertip against the opening of her pussy and eased it inside.

Fuck. He managed not to snarl that word, but it ripped through his mind. She was so wet and tight. Her pussy would be paradise to his dick. His balls felt like pins and needles were jabbing at them as he pushed that finger inside her deeper until he found the spot he wanted. He wiggled his thumb and finger in a rhythm that would bring her to climax as her vaginal muscles clamped tightly around him.

Hero watched as she tossed her head, her body writhing on the couch, and her lips parted. She cried out loudly as she came all over his hand. She was gorgeous and his. He refused to remove his finger, or move his thumb off her clit. He just held still, feeling her vaginal walls twitch in the aftermath as that fleshy bud softened. Her body turned slack as she panted. He suffered physically since he'd never felt so turned-on in his life, but he kept his urges in check. It was one of the toughest things he'd ever done, because he wanted to withdraw his finger and sink his dick into his Candi.

Chapter Eight

Candi had tried many times to imagine how it would feel if 927 touched her down there. He always knew how to make her feel good by stroking her hair or lightly scratching his nails on her back. That was nothing compared to what he'd just done to her. Her body felt wrung out, but amazing. She opened her eyes and smiled as she lifted her head to stare at him.

His expression reminded her of when he wanted to kill someone. His fangs dug into his bottom lip and his features were tense. He breathed hard, as he had when enraged. The look in his eyes almost scared her, but not because she feared him. It was one she'd seen only once before. Sheer, absolute pain.

"What's wrong?" She sat up, causing him to withdraw his hand from her. She missed the loss of his finger inside her, touching her intimately. She kept her gaze locked with his and clutched his shoulders. He didn't speak. "What's wrong?" She massaged the rigid muscles. "Did I do something wrong."

He closed his eyes and tersely shook his head.

She leaned closer and something jabbed at her. She looked down his body to find the source. His cock was harder than before and it looked painful. The was an angry red color. It moved as she watched, kind of jerked, twitching once, and then again. The tip was wet, as if he'd leaked a tiny bit.

"Oh." She looked up at his face, but he kept his eyes closed, just silently kneeling in front of her.

She frantically looked for the lotion, but didn't see it. She reached down and curled her fingers around his shaft. She rubbed, but quickly realized there was a big difference between having lotion on her hand and not. He made a low grunting noise and she stopped.

Another quick visual search didn't reveal where the lotion had gone. She looked down at where her legs were spread. Her entire sex felt warm and soaked. She wiggled closer to him and gripped his cock again. She dug her toes against the carpet and scooted until she almost slid off the couch. It put her right where she needed to be as she rubbed the thick tip of his cock against her pussy.

He snarled and opened his eyes. His hands gripped her upper arms, and Candi gasped when she was shoved back. 927 came with her, bending over her as she landed against the cushion he'd placed behind her. His chest smashed against her breasts, trapping her arm between them. She still had a firm hold on his cock.

"No."

"You're in pain."

"Give me a minute. I'll get it under control." He shifted his arms, bracing some of his upper body weight on his elbows, but he didn't release her shoulders, keeping her pinned.

"You're not going to hurt me. I want to know what it feels like to have you inside me."

He stared at her with that terrible, pained look. "That isn't helping."

"You're crushing my arm."

He arched his back to make a little room between their stomachs. It was enough for her to move it a little. Candi was tired of her pup being overprotective. He wanted her and she wanted him. She lifted her legs and hooked them around his hips, digging her heels against the back of his thighs to prevent him from jerking away without taking her with him. She gripped his cock tighter near the base of the shaft and wiggled her hips. Between her hold on him and her movement, it rubbed them together so the crown of his cock slid along her pussy.

He snarled at her, even opening his mouth as if he planned to bite her. She wasn't afraid.

"Go ahead. Do it, my pup. It wouldn't be the first time you snapped at me."

She rocked her hips and watched his face. His eyes closed as she used her pussy to rub against him instead of using lotion. It felt really good to her and she figured it was the same for him. He growled low and twisted his head.

"Stop," he rasped. "I'll break."

She knew he wasn't talking about the thick, hard body part that she kept hold of. She'd make him break his resolve not to mount her. It was something she could live with. She wanted him and he wanted her. Sometimes males were irrational and overprotective. She knew he wouldn't hurt her, even if he didn't.

She rolled her hips and wiggled them until she had him right where she wanted him. His body, bent over hers, was as rigid as a statue. He wouldn't move, but that didn't mean she couldn't. She aligned their bodies until the crown of his cock pressed against where his finger had been. She used her legs, locked around him, to pull her body closer to his since he left her with no choice.

He felt huge and too thick. Her body resisted, but she was determined. A little more wiggling and rolling her hips and he eased inside her. Her pup snarled and his body grew more rigid, as if acting like a statue wasn't enough. He was as hard as one. She bent her knees and lifted her legs higher on his waist. That worked. More of his cock entered her. She released his shaft, pulled her arm out from between them and wrapped it around his middle. She raked her fingernails over his spine.

"Candi!"

He sounded panicked and angry at the same time, and his grip on her upper arms was bruising. She ignored the slight pain and looked at his neck near her mouth. She licked her lips and lifted her head enough to reach him. She lightly bit him and his body jerked. She ran the tip of her tongue over the bite mark and a little lower to the curve of his shoulder. She bit him harder there, knowing it wouldn't break the skin, but it would cause him to react. She knew her pup.

He released her shoulder and reached down, grabbing her ass with one big palm. She moaned loudly when he came down heavily on top of her. He drove his hips forward and she loved the sensation as he filled her. He was inside her deep, his cock so hard and thick that it seemed as if they were actually one person. He eased his hold on her shoulder and slid his arm between her and the cushion, gripping her again, but from the back. He withdrew a little and thrust forward. She moaned louder. He stopped, just holding her tightly.

"Yes," she urged. "Don't stop." She dug her nails into his back and wrapped her other hand around the back of his neck. "Claim me."

He turned his head and buried his face in her hair, his cheek against hers. His hand on her ass found a better grasp, his upper arm pressing against her outer thigh to pin it against his side. He rocked his hips, moving inside her at a steady but unhurried pace. Candi closed her eyes and clung to him, letting him hear how good it was through her moans and soft cries.

Being mounted by her male brought her ecstasy that increased with the speed of his cock driving inside her, his body rubbing against her clit, adding to the sensations that threatened to overwhelm her. "Don't stop," she panted. She knew her pup. He'd worry about hurting her. "So good."

He snarled and she knew he stopped holding back. He fucked her harder, the couch making creaking noises as if it were going to break. She didn't care if it did. She clung to her male until the pleasure hurt and it exploded, shattering her. She cried out his name as her body seized.

She was barely aware of him shoving his hand hard against her ass, but she hated the loss of him as he pulled all the way out of her. He kept hold of her though, pinned under him on the couch. He'd just withdrawn his cock. At the same time, he made a sound she'd never heard from him. It was almost a whimpered snarl.

His hold on her shoulder eased until it was no longer a death grip and the hand on her ass lightly massaged. It took time for both of them to recover, and he lifted his head when he did. Candi opened her eyes and stared into his. She expected him to be angry. He liked to snarl and lecture her when she did something that made him angry.

"You are soooooooo bad." He looked amused.

She grinned, remembering the past. "I am."

"You know what I have to do when you're bad."

"No!"

He eased his arm from beneath, but kept hold of her ass. He straightened up a little, dug his fingers into her ribs and tickled her. Candi squealed, laughing as she tried to evade him. His mood sobered and he stopped.

"Did I hurt you at all? Are you sore?" He leaned back, staring at her lower half. "You're so small down there."

"You're just too big." She wanted to reassure him. "You didn't hurt me, my pup. I knew you wouldn't. I enjoyed you mounting me so much. I want to do it all the time."

His slid his hand between them and touched her pussy, but didn't play with her. He just rubbed one hand there while looking at it. He relaxed.

"What are you doing?"

"I don't smell blood, but I wanted to make certain."

"Look at me."

"What?" He held her gaze.

"Stop worrying so much about me. I'm not fragile."

He twisted his body and reached for something on the floor. He used her discarded shirt to clean them up. He dropped it and held out his hands. "Come with me."

She grasped his hands and he pulled her to her feet. He kept hold of one and led her into his bedroom, through it, and into his bathroom. She thought he intended to take that shower he'd mentioned, but he stopped in front of the mirror and turned her to face it so he stood behind her.

"See what I see," he rasped.

She really looked at them both. He was wider and taller than she was. Her pale skin seemed stark compared to his golden tan. It wasn't her fault since they hadn't allowed her out in the sunshine at the asylum. Her body was too thin, caused by all the drugs they'd forced her to take and the few meals she'd been given. She had to admit she looked weak and small compared to him. Her body looked like a shrunken version of the sixteen-year-old she'd been when they'd taken her from Mercile.

Hero released her hand and wrapped his arms around her, bending down a little to put their faces closer together. Their gazes met in the mirror. "I'm going to worry until you're healthier and stronger. I'll worry even then because you're so important to me. Your inner strength and will is amazing. It's just contained in a frail body right now. Can you see that?"

Tears filled her eyes. "Yes."

He turned her away from the mirror. "Don't cry, Candi. That wasn't my intention. You will get healthy and stronger, but be tolerant of my fears. Can you do that?"

She nodded.

He wiped her tears away. "Thank you. I'm going to baby you. Deal with it."

She smiled. He'd learned that last phrase from her as they'd been growing up. She'd said that to him often when he'd complain about something too human that she'd do. "Fine but this no-sharing-sex thing is stupid. I refuse to wait until you deem me at a good weight for that."

"I want to disagree with you, but you're sooooo bad." He smiled. "I can't resist you but we'll only share sex with great care, and not too much."

"What is too much?"

He hesitated. "I don't know. We'll have to figure it out."

She asked him the question that had bothered her since she'd studied herself in the mirror and put herself in his frame of mind. "Do I disgust you?"

"No," he snarled. "Why would you even think that?"

"I don't look good."

"You're my Candi." He suddenly grinned. "You could have been very ugly in your face and I would have still loved you. You're mine."

She laughed. "You don't think I'm ugly even with my funny features."

"I said it when we were small and I still mean it."

She lifted her arms and he bent forward so she could wrap them around his neck. "I love you."

He enclosed her in his arms and lifted her off the floor. "I love you too. You have my heart and always will."

She wrapped her legs around his waist. "I missed you so much."

"This is the first time I've felt completely alive, and not broken inside, since I lost you."

"Me too."

He eased her down to her feet and removed her arms from his neck. "I won't lose you again. That means you need to help me make you stronger without being difficult. Shower now, we will watch the movie so you can eat popcorn, and nap after that." He paused. "Do you need a nap now?"

"No. I'm not sleepy."

He stepped away and turned on the shower, adjusting the temperature for her. He backed up. "Go in. I am going to clean up the couch."

"Shower with me and I'll help you when we get out."

"No. That will lead to trouble. You'll touch me and I'll touch you."

She grinned. "I'd like that."

He shook his head. "Movie, popcorn and nap. I'll feed you a big meal when we wake and that is when we'll consider sharing sex. Not before."

"What if I were to slip and fall?" Her grin widened. "I could get hurt if you aren't in there with me."

A deep growl burst from him. "You're being bad. I know you, Candi. Don't manipulate me."

"I had to try."

A slow smile spread across his lips. "You are a trouble maker, but one who won't share sex with me before you get some sleep and eat another meal."

"All right. I can compromise."

"We both will."

"I would have rubbed you all over," she teased, stepping into the shower stall. "I want to learn how to touch you in all the ways that make you feel good. That's difficult to do if you won't let me."

He didn't respond and she glanced back. He wasn't in the bathroom with her. He'd fled. She laughed. He might run, but he wouldn't go far and he'd come back. He was her male. An overprotective one who would be difficult to deal with until she had padding on her bones, but he wasn't the only stubborn one.

Hero scrubbed the couch down, grateful it was leather. It had been hell pulling out of Candi but his fear of getting her pregnant had motivated him to find the willpower and determination to do it. It had left a mess though.

He needed to get condoms, unwilling to further test his ability to pull away from her during sex. The shower turned off as he entered the bedroom to put on a pair of sweatpants. He jerked them up his legs and paused by the bathroom door, though he avoided watching her dry off.

"I have to leave our home for a few minutes. Find one of my shirts to wear and I'll hurry back."

"You need more popcorn?"

"No."

He didn't expand on that. He rushed to the front door, unlocked it and stepped into the hallway. Not many Species who shared the floor with him were at Homeland. They were doing their rotations at Reservation. He realized no one who might be home would have any condoms. Only Species who wanted to attempt to share sex with humans obtained them. He passed the elevator and jogged down a floor. He knocked on Searcher's door. The male opened it quickly.

"Hi, Hero." He examined him with a quick sweep of his gaze and inhaled. The male grinned. "Congratulations."

The male couldn't miss the scents coming off him. "Do you have condoms?"

"Somewhere." The male stepped back. "Come in."

"Thank you."

"I just have to remember where I put them."

"You don't know?"

Searcher shook his head. "I haven't opened them. I like to be prepared." He snapped his fingers. "Bathroom. They are right next to my first-aid kit. I used word association to remember where I put things. I'll be right back."

Hero scowled, replaying what the male had said. He decided not to ask why the male believed he should keep condoms next to the first-aid kit. Searcher returned and held out a large, sealed box. "Here."

"Thank you. I appreciate it."

"How is your female doing? Everyone is worried about her."

"She's well."

A smile curved the male's lips upward. "I would assume so since you're sharing sex with her. I'm happy for you. Is there anything we can do?"

Hero held up the box. "This is it for now." He spun away and left his friend's home. He hurried upstairs, but the sight of two males and Breeze standing in the hallway slowed his steps. Breeze faced him with a grim look.

"We have trouble."

"Candi!" He tried to shove past Breeze.

The female flattened her palms on his chest and pushed him back. "We called your cell but you didn't answer. I was about to knock until I heard you coming. She's fine. We need to talk."

"What is it?"

Breeze let her hands drop and eyed the box he held. She smiled, staring at up him. "I'm glad you worked out sharing sex."

"Breeze." He scowled. "What is the problem?"

Her expression sobered. "We interviewed Candi when she first arrived, but we only got basic information because she didn't look well. Her health was the priority and we planned to do a more in-depth one once Trisha released her and she was deemed fit enough to answer all our questions. Then she found out you were alive and we knew it was important for you two to bond again."

"You want to interview her now?" He shook his head. "Give her more time."

"We did." Fury spoke from behind him. "That's the problem."

Hero spun, studying the grim male. "What are you doing here? I thought you weren't working this week."

"Your female's photo is being shown on every news station. They found the body of the doctor she killed and the homicide investigation led back to the hospital where she was held. The police are actively hunting for Candi. We need to deal with this now, or it's going to look bad later when we admit she's here."

"They were keeping her prisoner." Indignation flashed hotly through Hero. "She killed to save her own life."

"We're aware of this, but we didn't reach out to the human authorities because we didn't have enough details." Breeze slid between Hero and the wall to stand next to Fury. "We can't put it off any longer, Hero. That's why we're here. I wish we had a few more days but this has to be handled right now before some human is mistaken for Candi. They have a full manhunt out for what they believe is an unstable and dangerous female who has already killed once."

"That's bullshit." Hero snarled.

Fury nodded. "We know that, but the human authorities don't. They only have the information that was given to them, which came from where she was being held. We need to clear this up fast before someone innocent is injured."

"I'm not allowing humans near my Candi." Hero wouldn't let them upset his mate.

"They won't be allowed to interview her directly. The NSO is going to handle this, but we need more details from your Candi. It will help us give them all the correct facts." Fury softened his tone. "We're going to protect her. She's one of ours. We just need specific details the police will ask about. That's all. We're going to go out of our way not to upset her. It's the last thing we want."

Breeze nodded. "We'll make this as easy as possible."

"Mate papers are being drawn up right now and post dated to when she stepped through our gates." Fury paused. "Sign them and get her to. We need the paperwork in case this gets messy. It covers our asses. Breeze will question your female and I need to sit down with you. I need details about when you were held with her at Mercile in case the humans want to establish why we'd accept her as one of our own, and that she was yours long before she made it safely to Homeland. We don't want this to become a publicity nightmare with our enemies accusing us of shielding a murderer behind our gates."

"I won't let them take her."

Fury reached out and gripped his shoulder with one hand. "We wouldn't allow that to ever happen. Human authorities don't have the right to storm our gates to try to take her away. They'd be met with force if they did. We'd just like to avoid that. Our entire task force and legal department are on this. They are just waiting for us to fill in the blanks."

Hero nodded. "Let me go talk to her. Give me a few minutes."

Everyone moved out of his way and he entered his home. He located Candi in his bedroom. She wore one of his shirts and smiled at him. "You took a long time."

He placed the condoms on the nightstand, snagged her hand and pulled her onto his lap. "Species are waiting in the hallway. They need to ask you questions. You're not in any trouble or danger. It's just that the humans found the body of the female you killed."

He hated the fear he saw in her expression.

"No. Don't be afraid. There's no reason to be. Breeze just needs to ask you questions. The NSO is behind us, Candi. They aren't going to allow anyone to take you from me. Humans have no right to come here. The human police might want to question you, but I said no. You won't have to talk to anyone but Species."

She took a few breaths. "I'm not sorry I killed Penny. She planned to kill me."

"I know. I would leave out the part about it feeling good to do it."

A smile played at her lips. "Okay."

"I understand. Are you okay? I can stay at your side while Breeze talks to you."

"I feel safe with Breeze."

"I have to tell the NSO all about our history. Are you comfortable with that?"

"I don't mind. Do you? You said you'd never told them anything about me. Don't say anything if it's going to get you into some kind of trouble."

"It won't."

"Let's just get this over with." She scooted off his lap.

He snagged her hand and stared down at her bare legs. "Let's find you more clothes first."

"It's just Breeze."

"There are more males in the hallway. I don't want any of them to see so much of you."

She grinned. "I'm yours."

"You're mine."

While she dressed, he thought back to their childhood. She'd always been strong inside, but there had been some things he couldn't protect her from...

~ ~ ~ ~ ~

When they returned Candi to their cell, her expression was solemn as she took a seat next to him on the mat. "Teach me how to fight so I can be like you."

927 scowled. "No. You are too little."

"I'm growing."

He stood and yanked her to her feet. The top of her head only came to his shoulder. "I seem to be the one growing. You are getting shorter."

She laughed. "I am not!" She made fists of her hands and threw a punch, catching him in the stomach. "Did that hurt?"

He shook his head. "No."

Her good mood disappeared. "I'm ten years old now, not a baby. I need to learn to protect myself. The technicians don't go near you unless they drug you first. They just grab me and drag me down the hallway because they know I can't hurt them."

"You want them to drug you?" Sometimes she made no sense to him.

"Well, no. But I need to learn how to fight."

He pulled back his upper lip to show her his sharp fangs. "They fear these." He reached out and gripped her chin, forcing her mouth open. "You don't have them. You couldn't tear their skin with those smooth little things."

She jerked out of his hold and threw another punch. That one caught him in the ribs and he took a step back. "Don't do that."

"It hurt, didn't it?" She grinned. "Teach me."

He shook his head. "It would only get you drugged and hurt more when you fight."

She grew solemn again. "They had a female in the place where they take me for checkups."

He cocked his head, curious. "A human?"

She shook her head. "They beat her, 927. She is about your size and she was so hurt. The technicians did that to her." Tears filled her eyes. "Worse than I've ever seen them hurt you when you fight before they take you away for their tests. She probably didn't know how to fight when they attacked her. I don't want that to be me."

Fury filled him. "Scream for Dr. C if they start to hit you."

"I don't think he'll protect me."

"You are his daughter. The tests said so. He didn't kill you so he must want you alive. You wouldn't survive a beating, Candi. He must know that."

"I'm not supposed to tell anyone that I'm his daughter. He said only a few people know. Evelyn and a few of the ones who watch our cell."

"Tell them if they are going to beat on you. It might make them stop."

"I don't think so."

He stepped closer and gripped her hand. He curled her hand into a clawed position. "You fight like this. Use your nails. You don't have the strength to hurt them with a fist." He yanked her hand to his face. "Go for the eyes." He positioned her hand lower. "The throat next." He released her hand and leaned forward and gripped her leg behind the knee and bent it, bringing it up to his groin area. "Do that as hard as you can to males. It will take them down."

She nodded.

"I'll teach you." He wanted her to be able to defend herself if she had to. It frightened him, thinking of all the times she was taken from his cell—for tests or if they wanted to ask her questions—when Dr. C ordered it done.

"Thank you."

"It won't be easy," he warned, backing up to the mat they slept on. "Come over here. I don't want you to fall on the floor. Are you certain about this?"

She followed him and curved her hands into claws. "I need to know."

She was brave for one so small and weak. He respected her inner strength, but that was his Candi. She always amazed him. He crouched a little and swatted at her with one hand, making sure not to make contact. "Block me. Use the backs of your hands and wrists to knock my hands away and prevent me from touching you."

She threw up her arm and did it. He swiped at her again and she managed to knock his hand away, avoiding his grasp. He grinned. She was cute as she scrunched her nose to concentrate. He moved faster and actually grabbed her that time, fisting her shirt. He pulled, yanking her right off her feet and dropping her onto her back. She landed hard and he instantly regretted it when she gasped. He crouched, worried he might have hurt her.

"Are you well?"

She smiled. "I'll get better. Don't treat me like a baby."

He wanted to. He never wished for her to need to use anything he taught her. He straightened and pulled her to her feet. "Come at me."

She did and he knocked her flat back onto the mat. She landed but rolled, coming back up. He admired her for that. She launched herself at him and he had to twist to prevent her from slapping his face. She tripped on his leg and he grabbed her around her waist to keep her from falling to the floor. She twisted in his arms and grabbed hold of his jaw.

"*Pow!* I could have hurt you if I'd done that hard."

He chuckled and opened his mouth, licking her fingers near his lips. She yanked her hands away. "I could have bit a few of those fingers off."

"Technicians don't have sharp teeth."

"Good point." He grabbed her with his other arm and eased her to her feet. "Are you sure you want to learn? This won't be easy and you might get bruises when we work harder to teach you how to defend yourself. I don't ever want to hurt you, Candi."

She nodded. "I know that, but I need to learn. I'm tougher than you think, 927. You aren't always with me when they take me from our cell." She got that determined look he knew so well. "Don't baby me."

"You are my baby." He teased. "My short one."

She took a swing at him and caught him low on his abdomen. He grunted and rubbed it. It caused her to laugh.

"See? I'm getting better."

He nodded. "We will do this if you insist."

"I do." She clawed her hands and backed up.

He crouched a little and she mimicked his stance. He took swipes at her and she blocked them. He grew more aggressive once he felt her reflexes were improving. He touched her a few times, but she never flinched, even when he knew it hurt a little. She just kept coming at him.

She was tougher than he had believed. He finally tackled her and twisted in the air so she would land on top of him when they hit the mat. She was out of breath. He chuckled, holding her close. "That's enough for today."

She turned her head and kissed his cheek. "I'm wearing you out. Admit it."

He laughed. "You are the one panting."

She reached back and dug her fingers into his side, wiggling them. He laughed louder and rolled, pinning her under him. He tickled her instead. He finally stopped when he knew she'd had enough. He stared into her face and knew without a doubt that it would destroy him inside if anything ever happened to his Candi. He wanted to protect her at all times, but Mercile made that impossible. He'd just do everything he could to make certain she was strong and could fight when he wasn't with her.

Chapter Nine

Candi watched Breeze leave and felt a large burden lift from her shoulders. She'd told the female everything. The door opened a few minutes later and Hero entered. He looked furious.

"Why was she carrying a video camera?"

"She asked to film some of my answers and I agreed. They are going to play it for the humans."

"I don't like that."

She stood and approached him. "You're being overprotective."

"Humans could use your image in bad ways."

"There's an active manhunt underway for me right now and some photo the hospital took is being shown on the news. My image is already out there. I'd prefer they have the truth instead of thinking I killed Penny because I'm insane and dangerous."

His gaze traveled down her and he snorted. "Humans are idiots if they see you as a threat."

She grinned. "They aren't like you."

He grabbed her hand and tugged her toward the kitchen. "I'm feeding you."

"Okay." It had been a few hours since they'd seen each other and she was a little hungry. "I'm fine though."

He stopped and lifted her up on the counter, gazing into her eyes. "I hate that you had to go through that."

"I'm grateful. Do you know how many years I wished someone, anyone would listen to me? Now the NSO will get my story out there. Everyone will know that Dr. C killed my mother and that Penny kept me locked up so I couldn't expose Mercile after I was taken from there. The police will stop believing I'm a deranged murderer."

He leaned forward, resting his forehead against hers. "Did you have to agree to Breeze filming you?"

"I didn't want to wait for them to type out things and sign them. Breeze said humans are anal about paperwork and statements. The video can just be shown to them to prove they were my words. I don't mind. Plus, Breeze said humans would see how puny I am and know I was abused."

He growled. "She didn't have you strip naked, did she?"

"No. How did it go for you?" She reached up and ran her fingers through his hair, stroking him. "Was it difficult talking about the past?"

"Yes. We went down to the conference room and more males showed up to write down what I said. They'll only share what they feel the humans need to know to protect you. The legal team came too. They've been busy since you arrived with what information they had."

"What does that mean?"

He paused.

"Just tell me."

"They located the homicide file on your mother. It was unsolved. They feel the police are going to be happy to close it once they learn that you witnessed Dr. C kill her and that other male. They also discovered a missing-person report on you. Dr. C had to file one once the police notified him of the fire at your home and the deaths. Your body wasn't located. They said it was standard procedure for a male to file one and it would have made him seem innocent of stealing you."

She let that sink in.

"It also establishes that you were at the sight of a double homicide as a young child and disappeared at that time. Dr. C's alibi was Mercile Industries. They said he was working that night, but now everyone knows they lied. One of the humans working on our legal team seemed really happy about that. He feels it proves where you were taken."

"Good."

"No one is going to take you away from me." He straightened. "Did you sign the mate papers? They had me sign them first."

"I did."

He smiled. "Good. You already were my mate but now the humans know it as well." He backed away and opened the fridge. "I will make you a sandwich."

Someone knocked on the door and Hero slammed the fridge closed. He grumbled as he passed her. "Don't get down."

She turned her head and watched as he unlocked the door and yanked it open. Two females stood there. He opened the door wider and they entered, carrying large bags.

"We brought cakes, cookies and a fried chicken. We heard what was going on and figured you'd be hungry for dinner." The tall female grinned at Candi. "I'm Bluebird and this is Sunshine. Welcome to Homeland."

Hero took the food from them and set it on the coffee table. "Thank you."

"You're welcome." The one with blue streaks in her black hair peered at Candi. "You poor thing. We'll put weight on you really fast." She turned to Hero. "You should move into the women's dorm. We got permission from the Gifts. They see it's more reasonable to have a mated couple under our roof. It will be easier for us to feed your female if she's there and we'll keep her company while you're on shift. They think she must be terrified, surrounded by so many males."

Candi almost laughed at his stunned expression. She slid off the counter and walked up to the females. "Thank you. It's so nice to meet you. I'm not afraid to be here."

The one with the streaks in her hair arched her eyebrow. "Doesn't the smell bother you?"

"What smell?"

The feline grinned. "I'm Sunshine. You don't have the nose. I forgot. This building smells of a lot of males. It's not a bad thing but you are the only female living here. We checked and Hero hasn't asked to be moved to couples housing." She shot him a curious look. "Why haven't you done that?"

"Um. I hadn't thought of it. I should."

"No. We're fine here." Candi leaned against his side. "This is our home. I like being surrounded by males. I feel safe."

Bluebird smiled. "You'd be safe at the women's dorm too. Hero works shifts and he'll have to leave you alone while he's on duty. Wouldn't you like to hang out with us when he's gone? We can teach you how to cook and work everything inside your home." She lowered her voice. "Make him vacuum. It's this scary machine that cleans the floors and sucks everything up. It's loud and you have to watch it closely. It tries to take things you don't want it to and then you have to wrestle with it to get your shirts back."

Sunshine laughed. "I told you to pick up your clothes before you run the vacuum." She rolled her eyes and smiled at Candi. "We all had a difficult time when we were first freed, but we'll help you adjust. We're your family."

Candi was touched. "Thank you."

Bluebird looked at Hero. "Consider moving into the women's dorm. It's probably best if you don't request couples housing. Most of the males who transferred into single homes did so with humans. Your Candi doesn't know how to cook or how to use the appliances. She needs the assistance to learn, and no offense, but you males grumble too much when you teach...and learn. She'd have more fun being taught by females."

"I'll think about it. Thank you."

Sunshine hesitated, her gaze on Hero. "I'm glad you're doing better. I was worried, but now I understand why you were so upset. Be happy."

Both females left and Hero locked the door. He looked a bit grim when he stared at her. "Do you want us to move to be with the females?"

"You don't want to move into the women's dorm, do you?"

"I would if you wanted."

"I like your home."

"Our home."

"I could visit the females when you have to work." The relief on his face was almost comical, but she managed not to laugh. It helped her make a decision. "I don't want to move."

He smiled. "Let me feed you." He rushed into the kitchen to get plates.

She helped by sitting on the couch and removing containers from the bags. They'd brought her a cake, cookies and lots of fried chicken. There were also side dishes. Hero settled next to her and grinned.

"We never saw the rest of the movie. I'll find where we left off and replay it."

"I'd like that."

"Just be certain to eat lots."

"I will." She wanted him to stop viewing her as too thin and fragile.

* * * * *

Candi woke and smiled. She lay sprawled over Hero's chest. The blue screen from the television provided enough light for her to study his features while he slept. His peaceful expression matched her mood. His arms were loosely wrapped around her waist to keep her from falling off him.

They'd finished their movie and dinner, and he'd put the rest of the food away. They'd watched a second movie and been halfway through a third when she must have dozed off. He had stretched out and pulled her on top of him to get them into that position.

Tears filled her eyes and she didn't try to stop them. Her pup was with her, alive and well. It seemed too good to be true, but she no longer feared waking up inside her room at the asylum. It wasn't a drug-induced dream. He was really with her and they had a future together.

She laid her head against his chest and just listened to his heartbeat under her ear. They'd lost a lot of time but every day would be precious from that moment on. Part of her was tempted to wake him and lead him into the bedroom. He seemed too peaceful though. She just lay there and enjoyed being close.

A slight noise came from the hallway. The body under hers tensed and Hero locked his arms tightly around her as he tried to sit up. She lifted her head. "Easy."

"I heard something."

A door closed down the hallway. "It's just one of your neighbors."

He glanced around but seemed to accept that. "Security is changing shifts about now."

"Do you always get jumpy at every sound?"

He stared into her eyes. "No."

"You're worried about me. I'm not going to leave."

"I keep thinking about how the humans might want to take you from me."

"Breeze swore they can't come into Homeland to take me and the NSO will never hand me over. I'm not a criminal. I'm a survivor and I'm not really one of them. The humans will understand all that once they learn what was done to me and why I killed Penny."

"I just don't trust them to be reasonable."

"Breeze isn't worried. Were the males you spoke to?"

He sat up, shifting her onto his lap. "No. They assured me this would be resolved quickly."

"See?" She smiled. "I'm all yours and no one is going to take us away from each other ever again. You are stuck with me."

He slid one arm under the back of her knees, his other one hooking around her back. He stood. "My mind knows it, but I still feel uneasy."

"I understand." She did. Them being together again seemed almost too good to be true.

He carried her into the bedroom and flipped on the light, taking her to the bed. "I'll be right back."

She watched him enter the bathroom and close the door. It gave her enough time to strip out of the clothes she wore. She'd just climbed onto the bed when he returned. She smiled when he softly growled.

"What are you doing?"

"Aren't we going back to sleep?"

"You're naked."

"I don't want anything between us. Take off your clothes."

"This is a bad idea."

"I ate and I slept." She grinned. "Get the box."

She expected an argument, some kind of resistance, but he surprised her. He picked up the box off the nightstand, tore it open, and laid a strip of condoms on the corner of the bed. He removed his clothes and she bit her lip, enjoying every inch of his body as he revealed it.

"I wish we could stay naked. I love to look at you."

"We can inside our home." He put one knee on the bed, bent over and braced his arms near her. "Lie flat on your back and put your feet my way."

She followed his orders. He grinned and she loved seeing him happy.

"Put your heels against each side of my shoulders."

She wasn't sure why he wanted her to do that, but she didn't hesitate. It meant her legs were almost straight up in the air since he was so close to her. He surprised her when he unlocked his arms and lowered his upper body. Her heels ended up on his back instead of resting against his shoulders. He grabbed her inner thighs and shoved them apart. She stared at him, not concerned that he wanted to take a look at her sex. She loved to examine him.

"Do you know what I'm going to do to you?"

"Look at me. It's okay."

He licked his lips. "Remember what I did to you with my hand? I'm going to do that with my mouth. It will feel really good. Let me hear how you enjoy it, Candi. You're a little different than Species so I want to make certain I'm doing it right for you."

It seemed a little surprising, but she was willing to allow her pup to do anything to her. "Are you sure about this?"

He chuckled. "Yes." He spread her open, gripping her thighs tighter. "I want to taste you."

She nodded. "Anything."

"I appreciate you trusting me."

"I know I can."

"Ready?"

"Yes."

She tried to relax when he leaned his head lower and his hot breath fanned her intimately. When his tongue touched her she jerked, but she was just surprised. He hesitated and licked her again, his tongue hot and wet. Using just the tip to apply a little pressure, he focused on one part.

Her breath caught. It felt strange but good. He used his lips, and she clawed at the bed. That felt really good. It was sweet pleasure. He grew a little more aggressive and Candi moaned.

"Oh!"

Hero growled and had to pin Candi's thighs against the bed when she tried to wiggle her hips away from his mouth. Her moans encouraged him and assured that she enjoyed oral sex. He loved the taste of her and how the little bud he played with stiffened. His dick could relate. She was addictive to him.

He wanted to use his fingers to fuck her while he tongued her clit, but she kept trying to twist away. She was close to coming. He opened his eyes, staring up at her. The sight of her clutching her own breasts, kneading them, made him snarl. It sent her over the edge and she climaxed hard.

He pulled his mouth away as she panted, her body relaxing. It was difficult to rip open one of the packages and get a condom on. He hated the things, but her safety came first. He tore a little hole in it with his fingernail in his haste to fit it over the head of his dick. He tossed it aside and opened a new one. *Slow down*, he demanded.

The confining condom felt unnatural, but he couldn't risk Candi getting pregnant. He rose and crawled up her body, making certain he kept his weight off her. She smiled at him, looking sexy and sated.

"You're so beautiful."

"So are you." She reached up, wrapping her arms around his neck.

He glanced down, almost feeling guilt since he wanted to be inside her. He should just go into the bathroom and handle his own needs. Candi seemed to read his mind though when he looked at her again. She lifted her legs and wrapped them around his waist. She squeezed, trying to pull his lower half against hers.

"We don't have to. This was about pleasing you."

She bit her lip and adjusted her leg, digging her heel into his ass cheek. "I want you inside me. I like when we're one."

That was a perfect way to put it. He lowered and adjusted his hips until his cock brushed against the vee of her sex. He found the right spot and pushed, slowly entering her. He had to close his eyes, the sensation too intense to do anything but enjoy how good it was to mount his female.

Candi raked her fingernails over his skin, along his back, causing him to growl. He sank into her deeper, loving the way her body held him, fit him. Her lips brushed his throat and she moaned.

"My pup. I love you so much."

He forced his eyes open to stare down at her. He didn't care that she called him that. It had once been a source of pain, but now, once again, it was the endearment that it had always been. "My funny-faced human."

She chuckled. "You love my tiny nose and that I can't hurt you with my flat teeth."

He grinned back. "I do."

She moved her arms from his shoulders to hug him around his ribs. Her fingernails raked down his spine, all the way down to the curve of his ass. He growled, driving his dick into her deeper. Candi moaned in response. He moved slowly, gently, taking his time.

He kissed her throat, arched his back and lightly bit her shoulder. He used his lips, tongue, and fangs to bring her pleasure. She finally grabbed his face, pulling it toward hers. He kissed her lips, deepening it when she opened up to him.

He taught her how to kiss. She was a fast learner and he couldn't hold back anymore. He pounded in and out of her, pinning her in place. He realized he should remain gentle but she encouraged him with verbal moans and choppy words. Her pussy clamped tightly around his driving shaft and he broke the kiss to clench his teeth together, fighting not to come until she did. He pressed his lower belly against her sex, making sure to rub up against her clit.

"Yes!" she yelled, her body shaking.

Hero gave in to the desire and had enough presence of mind to roll them onto their sides as he let go of his control. He held his Candi close, his body trembling and shaking from the aftermath of spilling his semen into the condom. She nuzzled her face against his chest and he smiled when she chuckled.

"I love sex."

"I do too. Am I hurting you? I am locked inside you from the swelling that happens at the base of my shaft. I told you about that."

"You feel amazing and there's no pain. Sex is so good because it's us having it together, isn't it?"

He stroked her back. "Yes."

She grew silent in his arms and he adjusted enough to look down at her. She kept her chin down so he slid his hand under it, tilting it up. There was a look in her eyes that he didn't like.

"What is it?"

"Nothing." She glanced away.

"Don't do that. We don't lie to each other. Did I hurt you?"

"No. It isn't that. I was just thinking about something, but I don't want to upset you. I think it would."

"You can talk to me about anything."

"Not this."

He gently rolled her onto her back when the swelling receded, and lifted up. "I have to throw this away. I'll be right back." He hated to withdraw from her body but he had taken the class about condoms. They'd shown the males how to put one on, and that they needed to remove it and throw it away before their dicks softened or it could slip off, defeating the purpose of wearing one in the first place.

He tossed it into the bathroom trash and quickly washed his hands before returning to Candi. He sprawled out next to her on his side and stared into her eyes. "Something is on your mind. Talk to me. We shouldn't have secrets."

She bit her lip.

"Candi," he growled. "Speak. Something bothers you. Share it with me and we'll face it."

"I was just thinking about how good sex is between us. I wondered if it was that way between you and other females." She paused, studying his eyes. "I didn't enjoy sex the one time I had it with that feline. Are you angry that I was thinking about that?"

"No."

"You withhold so much from me, being protective. I don't have the experience other females have. Do you understand what I'm saying?"

"No."

"I only have one bad experience to compare against what we do together. You must have many good memories. I don't have experience with sex like the females you must have known. I liked your kiss, but it was my first one. Did I do it right? Do you wish I knew more?"

That frustrated him. It wasn't directed at her. He had to calm down before he looked at her again. He regretted that his emotions had surfaced as soon as he saw the tears in her eyes. He'd somehow hurt her.

"We share love and it makes everything we do special. I like that I get to be the first to show you how to kiss and what it feels like to put my tongue on you. It's the way it should have been."

"You're not just saying that to make me feel better?"

"I feel more for you than I have for anyone else, or ever will. That is the truth, Candi. There is no comparison, and I am not thinking about anyone but you when we touch. You please me the most. Never question that. I wish you could forget about that feline. I am trying very hard to."

"I can do that."

"There's no need for you to worry about other females, or if you please me." He stroked her cheek. "I wish I could change the past, but it's done. You are my everything, Candi. That's all you need to know and remember."

"It's foolish to be jealous, isn't it?"

"I understand. I want to kill the feline. I'm adjusting to it, or otherwise I'd ask you to look at photos of all the feline males who were freed from Mercile to see if that male is still alive."

"You thought about doing that?"

He nodded. "He had no choice, nor did you. The reasonable side of me knows this. You saved my life. I don't ever want to know if he is alive and surviving. I'd be too tempted to kill him anyway just because of my jealousy."

"You're all I've ever wanted."

"That's how I feel too, Candi."

"I'll stop worrying then."

"Good. You're my mate, my female, and you are my everything."

Chapter Ten

Hero leaned against the counter, his arms crossed over his chest, and grinned. Candi looked happy as the three females taught her how to cook a steak in a cast iron skillet. Sunshine, Bluebird and Midnight had arrived at the men's dorm and taken over their kitchen. He stayed out of their way, but kept close.

"The pan is very hot," Bluebird warned. "Use the glove when you touch the handle."

Sunshine nodded. "I burned myself at least half a dozen times because I kept forgetting that."

"And I treated her injures every time." Midnight chuckled.

Movement at the edge of his vision had him turn his head. Torrent smiled at him and leaned against the counter next to him. "Your female looks a lot healthier. She's got more color in her complexion."

"She does."

"The females are eager to help her. They have started a campaign to have us talk you into moving to the women's dorm so they have easier access to your Candi. They've sworn to take over our dorm if you don't."

That news made him frown.

Torrent laughed softly, keeping his voice low. "Don't worry. We like them invading our space. No one is going to ask you to move. You should have seen all the males who volunteered to clean early this morning once word spread that they planned to use our kitchen today. There were two dozen of us down here."

"You too?"

"Who doesn't want to impress our females? We're also competitive. We wanted our living spaces to be cleaner than theirs. They always tease us about all the male hormones they smell when they come here."

"I'm sorry for all the extra trouble everyone had to go to."

"Don't be. It was fun. The females plan to teach yours how to use household cleaning appliances too. Expect a bit of a crowd for that. Word has it that some of them are afraid of vacuums. We're placing household chore-trading bets on whether that's true or not, and who has that fear."

Hero chuckled. "I see. What chore do you wish to get out of?"

"It's my turn to clean the main-floor bathroom on Wednesday morning. I bet Jinx that they'd hide their fear, if it exists, from your female. He thinks they won't be able to. He'll have to clean the bathroom if I'm right and I'll get to take over his chore of pulling weeds around the building on Thursday."

"What if he's right?"

"I have to clean the bathroom again next week when it's his turn on Monday and he'll have to dust the library for me on Tuesday."

"I'm supposed to mop the kitchen floor tomorrow."

"It's a good thing we're only assigned one lower floor chore a week."

"There are a lot of us. The females probably have more chores."

"That's probably why they want you to move with your female into their dorm." Torrent grinned. "I can guess who would end up moving all the furniture and vacuuming under it." He pointed at Hero. "You."

"I'm not planning on transferring to the women's dorm. Candi wants to stay here."

"She's comfortable living with all males around her?"

"Yes."

"Good."

Hero had something on his mind and he shared it with his friend. "Is everyone accepting her?"

Torrent held his gaze. "Because she's human? Is that what you mean?"

"Yes."

"They think of her as Species. She was raised at Mercile. They respect her, Hero. Her story has been told to all." Torrent turned his head, watching Candi. "She's like a Gift in size, but has the courage of one of our strong females. She escaped from captivity on her own and killed to gain her freedom. Then she walked right up to the front gates without fear and demanded entry. She's an amazing female."

"She is. I'm just worried that there might be some problems with her living in the dorm. Some of our males don't trust humans. I'm supposed to return to duty tomorrow and am hesitant to leave her in our home. I plan to take her to the females."

"Stop worrying. She could run around the dorm without you at her side and not encounter any problems. The males would love it."

Hero growled low. "Why?"

"Relax. They know she's your mate. Everyone is curious about her and Jinx has a big mouth. He told them how brave she is and they'd like to talk to her. That's all. No one is used to a female who looks like a Gift going near them without being timid and fearful. They feel protective of her and want to help her become accustomed to freedom."

He relaxed. "I understand."

"Speaking of which, some of the males have wanted to approach you with a list they put together."

"What kind of list?"

"They want to take turns helping you feed your female. Everyone knows you didn't excel at cooking when we were learning and you admitted as much by having one of them cook for you both. A group of them would like to offer to bring you meals for a while. The females have offered too. I know last night they covered dinner." Torrent shook his head. "You lucky bastard. No one wants to deliver meals to me. Accept the help."

"I will, for Candi."

"Some of them have offered to teach you how to make whatever she likes."

"I'm aware."

"Good. Take them up on it. That female needs to gain weight. It makes me want to beat whoever nearly starved her to death where she was kept."

"I know. I feel the same."

Torrent lowered his voice further. "How are you handling having her back in your life now?"

"I'm grateful. I was shocked when I realized she had survived. I didn't know how to process it."

"I don't blame you. You're lucky, Hero. You got her back."

He studied Torrent. "Did you lose someone at Mercile?"

The male refused to meet his gaze, shifting his body instead. "I got attached to one of our females that they brought to me a few times for breeding experiments."

"One who survived?"

He shook his head. "No."

"I'm sorry."

Torrent shrugged. "Not all of us got out. She probably would have rejected us bonding long-term. She was a primate and afraid of me. I was working to gain her trust, but then we were freed. I looked for her but…" He shook his head. "I even checked the other locations we were taken to while the humans were trying to figure out what to do with us and giving us counseling. She didn't survive. They allowed me to view some of the bodies they recovered. She was among them."

Hero felt bad for the male. "I'm sorry for your loss."

"We weren't bonded like you are with your female. I just felt for her. I grieved her loss but that's how it is. Appreciate your Candi."

"I do."

Torrent looked at him and smiled. "I leave in a week to return to Reservation. I look forward to that. I enjoy working with the Wild Zone residents and the rescued animals."

"I thought about taking Candi there, but Tammy said I should keep her here for a while."

"She'll be safer here at Homeland. We held a phone conference yesterday about the issues we're facing at Reservation as we expand our walls. Security isn't as tight as it could be. We're leaving the original walls up until the new ones can be built, but we've had humans infiltrate some of the areas we've bought. A group of them have been harassing our human neighbors."

"Why?"

"To try to force them to sell their properties to them instead of us. We leave the owners alone if they don't wish to sell. The same can't be said about that group. The local sheriff and deputies are helping, but we're spread thin."

"Can you send some of our task force members there?"

"They are filling in here for gate and wall duty since so many of our males are needed at Reservation. I'll be grateful when all the walls are up and we're secure again. I'm going to get more of the Wild Zone residents involved with protecting our borders. I'll be in charge of them."

"Were they tired of taking orders from Valiant? He's not the friendliest male."

Torrent chuckled. "No, he's not. One Wild Zone resident already moved to the hotel to avoid him. They were clashing."

"Leo? He's a mellow male."

"No. The other lion male. Lash took an interest in Tammy and their cub."

It alarmed Hero. Tammy was his friend and so was Valiant. He would protect their cub too. Noble was his godson. Tammy said that meant that if anything ever happened to her and her mate, she expected him to rear the boy as his own child. He took that responsibility with great honor. "Instinctual interest?"

"Not according to Lash. He doesn't want to take out the cub and claim Valiant's female as his own. This isn't a lion-pride thing. He's just curious about them, but Valiant was having none of it. They fought a few times and it made Valiant territorial. He isn't allowing Tammy or his cub out of his sight. Moving Lash helped calm him a bit, but I was asked to take charge of the Wild Zone residents for a while."

"Do you need help?"

"Your priority is right there." Torrent glanced at Candi. "We'll be fine."

"Let me know if you need me. I spent quite a bit of time with the Wild Zone residents. Valiant doesn't see me as a threat, regardless of how stirred up he must be."

"I will, but I think I can handle it."

Hero focused on his mate. She laughed at something one of the females said. He smiled, enjoying watching her have fun. Torrent moved away and left the kitchen.

Candi glanced over at Hero. He stayed close, assuring that she was happy and safe. Midnight sliced up the steak and Sunshine fried taco shells. Bluebird sliced onions.

"I hate these." The female sniffed. "They bring tears to your eyes and make your nose twitch, but they taste good."

Candi leaned in and sniffed a few times. She jerked back when it burned her nose. "That's awful."

Bluebird laughed. "Your eyes are watering now."

She reached up and wiped away the wetness. She sensed her mate behind her immediately. His hands curved around her hips. "Are you upset?"

"I'm fine."

"It's the onions, Hero." Bluebird chuckled. "We're not making her cry. Grab a knife and dice avocados. You might as well help since you're hanging around."

"I don't want to interfere." He released Candi and backed off.

Midnight snorted. "Just like a male. He probably can't identify what an avocado is."

Candi peered up at him. "I don't know either. Is it that red, ball thing?"

"That's a tomato." He pointed to a green, oval thing. "I believe that's it."

"I'm impressed." Sunshine turned off the fire under the oil. "You get to eat with us for that. Grab plates. You know where those are, don't you?"

"Of course." Hero spun, walked to a cupboard, and yanked it open. "They are right here."

"That's where we keep ours too." Midnight brought a plate of sliced steak over to the island. "Both main kitchens at the dorms seem to be set up the same way."

"What can I do?" Candi glanced at the females.

"You're learning. You didn't get burned frying steaks." Midnight shot Sunshine a grin. "So you're way ahead of some of us."

"I forgot," Sunshine hissed. "Not all pans have hot handles. The blue ones in my apartment don't burn my hand."

"They aren't cast iron skillets and our private pans have protective handles." Midnight took the plates from Hero. "Sit. I'll chop up the rest of this."

He took a seat and Candi sat next to him. The females handed them each a plate with two tacos that were filled with vegetables and meat. She sniffed at it, not sure about those onion pieces she could see on top.

"Try it," Hero urged. He leaned in closer and showed her how to hold one as he took a bite. "Mmmmm."

She grinned and mimicked him, taking a bite. She closed her eyes, enjoying it. She swallowed and stared at her male. "Good." She faced the females, all of them watching her. "I think I can make tacos. I like them."

The females got their own plates of tacos and took seats on the other side of the island. Midnight suddenly turned around on her stool and snarled. It was a scary sound. It surprised Candi and she dropped her taco on her plate. Hero leaned in closer, putting his arm around her.

A feline male backed up, raising his hands, his gaze locked with Midnight. "What?"

"You touch our food and I'll kick your ass."

The feline stuck out his lower lip, pouting. "It smells so good. Come on, Midnight. Just one?"

"No."

"How come he gets to eat?" The male glared at Hero.

"He's her mate and she helped us cook. You should have pitched in if you wanted to eat, instead of stalking around the living room area watching us." Midnight turned, hunching over her food. "Try to sneak one and I will bite you."

The feline crept closer, but he didn't make a move for her food. Instead he leaned in and whispered near her ear. "I'd like it if you bit me."

She snarled again and twisted her head. "Back off. I'm not playing with you." She sighed and looked at Candi. "Males. All they think about is food and sex."

Sunshine lifted a taco off her plate and held it out toward the male. "Here."

The male backed away from Midnight and grinned, approaching Sunshine. "Thank you."

Sunshine shrugged. "I can't stand to see someone beg for food. It's pitiful."

He took the taco and pouted again. "Now I'll feel guilt if I eat this."

"You'll get over it." Sunshine laughed. "Take it before I change my mind."

He quickly ate it. "Now I owe you," he purred softly. "Want to go to my room so I can show my appreciation? I'm still hungry."

Sunshine nodded. "Give me two minutes to finish this." She held one more taco out to the male. "So you have your strength. You're going to need it. I'm full of energy today and you can help me work it off."

He eagerly took it.

Bluebird rolled her eyes and bumped Midnight's arm with her shoulder. "I see why you chose a human."

Midnight kept silent, eating.

Sunshine finished her food and stood. "I'll see you guys later." She ditched her dirty plate in the sink. "Bye, Candi."

Candi watched her and the male walk away together and looked at Hero, arching her eyebrows.

"They are going to share sex," he whispered.

"Oh. They are a couple?"

"No." Midnight put her food down. "Our females share sex with males. It's a casual thing. Do you understand?"

She didn't and shook her head.

"Most of us don't want to be with just one male. We like our freedom." Bluebird shrugged. "It's tough to choose just one, so why bother? Besides, they get kind of territorial." She jerked her chin toward Hero. "He's almost glued to your side. See? That would annoy me. Does it annoy you?"

"No."

"She loves him," Midnight announced. "It's probably comforting to her that he cares so deeply that he wants to be with her as much as possible." She finished eating. "I need to go. I'm supposed to work. It was good spending time with you, Candi." She glanced at Bluebird. "Do you want me to help you with dishes before I go?"

"No. I have this. It's my day off."

Midnight left and they finished lunch. Hero stood. "I'll do the dishes. It's the least I can do."

"Thanks." Bluebird grinned. "We're going to bring dinner tonight at six. I'll see you then."

"They are so nice to me." Candi really appreciated that. "Can you teach me how to load a dishwasher?"

"Later. You look a little tired. Why don't you go to our home and I'll be there in a few minutes? Can you find your way?"

"Yes, but I want to help you."

"Rest." He reached out and brushed his fingers over her cheek. "Food, sleep and then sex. Remember?"

She laughed. "Ah. Now I understand."

"Go lie down. I'll be there soon. This won't take long."

She left him and took the elevator to their floor. The door was unlocked. She entered and was halfway to the bedroom when someone knocked. She spun around, went back and opened it. Shock slammed through her at seeing the male who stood there.

"Hello, Candi."

She couldn't speak.

"I waited until you were alone to approach you. I heard about you making it to Homeland and came from Reservation, hoping you were the female they spoke of." His pretty dark-blue catlike eyes peered at her with compassion.

"You can't be here," she finally managed to whisper. "927 will kill you. He knows what happened between us."

"Evelyn told me he attacked you for what we did. I'm so sorry. I heard he killed you."

"That was a lie. Dr. C took me away and had me locked up elsewhere. You must go. I'm glad you survived, but he can't see you. It would upset him."

The male blinked back tears. "I wanted to apologize. I tried not to hurt you. I fought and would have let them kill me before touching you if you hadn't asked me to. I've regretted it ever since. I should have kept saying no."

"Stop." She stepped closer, glanced down the hallway, and then stared up at his face. "We did what we had to do to survive. That technician was killing you. Do you think I don't remember your blood spilling? I do. It's done. Don't apologize and let it go. Forgive yourself. I hold no pain or anger toward you. We both had no choice. You tried not to hurt me. I thank you for that. Now you must go and forget about the past. Please? It would just hurt him. He thought I chose you over him."

"I'll tell him the truth."

"No! He will kill you."

"I wouldn't blame him."

"Please? I don't want you to die, or for him to have to live with another death. Just go and never speak of it. Don't think of it again. Forget. I have."

He hesitated. "Anything you need, anything I can do, contact me. I took the name Dreamer."

"I will. Please, let this go, Dreamer. For me and for yourself. It's the past. Go in peace."

He nodded. "I'm glad you are alive."

"I'm glad you survived as well."

She backed up and closed the door, her heart pounding. Fear and dread consumed her. What if Hero ran into the feline leaving the floor? What if Dreamer decided to confess to him that he was the male who'd mounted her so many years before? If it opened up old wounds anew, would it make him so angry and upset that he would decide not to be her mate anymore? Would Hero kill him and be locked up?

She paced the living room and didn't know what to do. She was torn between telling Hero the truth and keeping silent. A few minutes later the door opened and Hero entered, a smile on his face.

"You seemed to enjoy your first cooking lesson."

"I did." She stilled and tried to slow her heart rate.

"You should take a nap."

"Will you lie down with me?"

He nodded. "Of course. You are to sleep though." He approached her. "Nothing else."

She loved him with all her heart. The last thing she wanted was to see him hurt or angry. The words to tell him who had visited refused to form. "I know. I would just like to be held by you."

His expression sobered. "Are you feeling well?"

"I'm fine. I just want to be close to you."

He pulled her into his arms, lifted her, and carried her to the bedroom. "I'm not going anywhere." He laid her on the bed and bent, removing his shoes and then hers. He stretched out alongside her and opened his arms. "Come here."

She curled into him and rested her cheek on his chest. "It feels perfect right now."

He kissed the top of her head. "It does. Sleep, Candi. Get some rest."

She closed her eyes and focused on him, instead of the unfairness of their pasts. They never should have been parted. She blamed Dr. C and Evelyn for being taken away from her male.

"Hero?" It was getting easier to say his name.

"Yes?" He stroked his hand down her back, his fingers playing with her hair.

"Do you know what happened to Evelyn? Was she caught?"

His body tensed.

"I'm sorry. Forget I asked."

"No. It's all right. I was taken from that facility before it was raided. Once I was freed from where they held me captive, I asked about her and Dr. C. They weren't able to find him, but I identified her from photos they showed me of known Mercile employees. She died after what they did to us was released to the public. She had to know the authorities would come after her and she had family who knew she worked there. Most humans were horrified to learn about us and what was done. She chose to take her own life rather than face the consequences."

Candi felt torn. She'd hated Evelyn, but a small part of her still grieved. The doctor had been a big part of her childhood, even if it had been mostly bad interactions. "I'm glad she isn't free, but it hurts a little," she admitted.

"We were given counseling when we were freed. Perhaps you should get some. It helped to talk to the shrink. Some of the techs and doctors were so bad that learning they died somehow, or are locked up, is comforting. Some weren't so awful and that leaves us feeling conflicted. They were wrong for what they did to us, but they were all we knew for so long."

She nodded. "I wanted them to pay for what they did to us."

"The shrink I spoke to compared us to children who had been raised by severely abusive parents. I didn't really agree with that since we were never treated as if we were human at all, but I was assured it's normal not to feel total relief over discovering they met with unhappy endings. It shows we have compassion, something they never had for us. Evelyn made her own choices, Candi. She could have saved us by calling the human police to tell them what was happening but she didn't. She helped keep us prisoners and viewed us as test subjects. I know she was nice to you occasionally, but there were many times she wasn't. She had to know that Dr. C killed your mother, but she protected him. She allowed him to bring you to that place and treat you as if you were a test subject too. Remember that. It helps alleviate any bad feelings we may feel over their fates."

"Thank you. I was so filled with rage all these years and all I thought about was revenge. Now I just want to be happy with you."

"I want that too. We're together again and that is what matters. They couldn't keep us apart forever."

"I love you."

"I love you too." He wrapped his arms around her. "Now try to rest. We need to get you stronger and healthier. That's our future."

She bit her lip, still unable to shut her mind down. "Can I ask you something else?"

"Anything."

"Do you want to try to have a baby with me?"

He tensed, but relaxed quickly. "We'll discuss it in a few months."

"I'm not saying now. I just want to know if you want to try at some point."

"I won't do anything that would put you at risk."

"I'm going to get better and stronger. I'd like to try to have a baby with you." She opened her eyes and lifted her chin to peer at him. "I was afraid when they explained about breeding experiments to me. I feared, if they allowed us to be together, we'd have a child and they'd steal it from us. I was terrified because I knew you'd attack them to keep us together and I'd lose you both." She paused. "They can't hurt us anymore. Will you think about it?"

Tears filled his eyes. "Only if Doc Trisha is certain you wouldn't be in danger. I can't lose you again. I won't."

She nodded. "Only if Doc Trisha thinks it's safe."

"Then I will agree."

She smiled. "Can you imagine having a baby?"

"It kind of frightens me."

"Why?"

"We know nothing about how to care for one and what kind of parents will we be when we didn't have any?"

"I had a mother for a while. I remember her kissing my injuries and singing to me. She read me stories before bed. You will make a wonderful dad, because you will love our baby and keep it safe. I know how good you are to me. We'll learn and be the best parents because we are motivated."

He smiled. "We'll try, if we're able, one day."

"Good." She lowered her chin, closing her eyes. "I'll try to dream about that."

"It will be a male and look just like me. Our altered genetics are strong and carry on into our children. All the babies born are almost mini-replicas of their fathers."

Warmth spread through her. "You were such a cute little pup."

He chuckled. "You were such a funny-faced little human with your tiny, squishy nose. I wish we could have a mini-replica of you."

"Genetically enhanced is better. Our baby will be strong and big like you. You're so handsome."

He kissed the top of her head again. "We'll both try to dream of one then."

Chapter Eleven

She'd feared she would hate being left at the women's dorm when Hero had to work. He'd kissed her goodbye and made her swear to call him if she wanted to leave. He'd said he could have someone cover his shift, but she didn't want to interfere with his duties.

Candi put her hand over her mouth, trying to smother her laughter. The females around her tried to hide their amusement as well. Some outright chuckled, a few were doubled over with laughter, and two of the Gifts had just turned around to spare Bluebird from seeing their reactions.

"Darn it!" Bluebird shut off the loud machine and dropped to her knees, yanking on the vacuum and the rug corner that had been sucked into the machine. "It hates me! I told someone else to show her the fast way to clean the wood floors."

Sunshine shook her head, still grinning. "I said it was a bad idea to be lazy by not sweeping. You're the one who insisted, so you got to demonstrate."

Halfpint turned back around, her features masked. "Let me help you." She went down on her knees next to the larger Species and pushed her hands away. "I have small fingers." She freed the rug. "See? You have to make the wheel thing turn that way."

"These machines are dangerous." Bluebird sat back and glanced at her toes. She sighed. "At least I didn't lose any. That's my fear."

"Come on," Rusty teased. "There are no blades on that thing. I'd be more worried about the garbage disposal. That's a dangerous appliance. You could lose a hand."

"That's why we stand way back and don't put our hands near it when we turn it on." Halfpint rose. "Humans invent crazy things."

Kat, the human mate of Darkness, sighed. "I told you what garbage disposals are for. You dump uneaten food off plates into it and it keeps the drains from plugging up. It's a smart invention."

"As if we don't eat all our food." Midnight snorted. "No Species allows it to go to waste." She looked over at Candi. "You're Species. Eat all your food and you won't have to use the blades of death in your sink."

"Come on!" Kat laughed. "Blades of death?"

"Metal teeth of finger destruction then. Is that better?" Midnight laughed. "We watch those human horror movies. We just saw one where a man shoved another's fist into the hole and turned it on to force him to talk. He removed a bloody stump. I'd tell someone anything to avoid that."

"I'm with Midnight," Rusty muttered. "Metal teeth of finger death. We should all start calling it that."

"Those movies don't help." Bluebird stood. "Show of hands on who fears shower curtains now after last week's horror movie we saw." Fourteen of the sixteen females present raised their hands. "The glass shower doors would stop some crazy male from stabbing at us. I'd push it outward, knock him on his ass, and use his weapon on him."

Kat shook her head but smiled. "It's a classic movie. The point of watching them is for entertainment." She looked at Candi. "You and I are the only ones who like shower curtains."

"I don't know what it is or why to fear one," Candi admitted. "That's why I didn't raise my hand."

"They are not solid like the doors on the showers in our apartments. They have safety glass so they would be hard to break, even with a knife. What about where you were held?" Halfpint asked as she got up from the floor.

"They had an open stall where I showered. Before that I was at Mercile. I don't remember much from when I lived with my mother." Candi glanced around. "What is a shower curtain?"

"It's a plastic covering that acts like a wall to keep the water from reaching the floor and it provides privacy." Kat walked toward the kitchen. "I think we've had enough learning today. I say we take a break. You guys are not teaching Candi good things."

"Yes, we are." Bluebird unplugged the vacuum and then kicked it. "These things are dangerous. Remember that. Have your mate use it."

"Just offer him sex and he'll do whatever you want." Sunshine grinned. "It works for me. I had a male rearrange all the furniture inside my home last week. I told him it turned me on to watch him lift things."

Kat groaned from the other room. "I heard that. I'm failing as a role model."

"We don't let our males handcuff us," Rusty called out. "Should we start? Maybe you and your mate can show us how it's done. We could hold a class."

Kat returned from the kitchen holding a plate of cookies. "Very funny. I'm sorry I shared that with you guys. I'm never going to live it down."

Sunshine winked at Candi and lowered her voice. "We like to tease her. Her male is very controlling in the bedroom and she allows it. If you want to change things inside your home just tell Hero it makes you wet seeing his muscles tighten up, and you won't be stuck moving the heavy things. Most of these homes are set up so the bed is against two walls. It means there's only one side to climb off or you have to crawl to the end of it. It's much better to move it to the center so you can have three sides to get off."

Rusty nodded. "That's true. Some of us have grown tired of having the same setups in our homes. I put my bed in the living room and turned my bedroom into a library with shelves of books. The couch and coffee table fit in there where the bed used to be."

"Why don't you just use the library down here? It's got a ton of books." Halfpint peered at her curiously.

Rusty hesitated. "I bought a lot of sexy books. Some of them are quite arousing. I don't want all of you knowing when I'm reading them and some," she shot a glare at Bluebird, "tease me when I do. Now I have privacy and can shower afterward." She directed her attention on Candi.

"Expect to be embarrassed sometimes because everyone will know things if you don't shower. They will make jokes."

"I can't smell that." Halfpint smiled. "It's good not having a super-sensitive nose. I don't want to know when you share sex with a male, or when you are aroused. I just wish some of you were quieter when you have males over, or at least have them pull the beds farther away from the wall so they don't slam into them." She pointed at Sunshine. "You're the worst offender."

Sunshine chuckled. "I like a good pounding. What can I say? Less talking if the bed is rocking."

"You remembered me saying that, but not how it's just rude to make guys do stuff for you just because you're sleeping with them?" Kat looked disgusted. "Fantastic. Don't tell anyone you got that quote from me, okay? Just do me that favor. I'd kind of like to keep my job."

"Your job?" Candi was curious.

"I help out however I can and teach some classes. It seems I'm also being a bad influence on the women in the dorm." Kat shoved the plate at her. "Here. Eat the whole thing. I didn't cook them or they'd be burned. That should put a few pounds on you. Darkness always asks how my day went when I get home and I want to tell him I at least got you to chow down on a few dozen double-chip chocolate cookies. Otherwise I'll have to confess that I've apparently made everyone here fear household things." She glanced around. "Those horror movies are supposed to be entertainment and help you understand why assholes commit crimes."

"Your job is safe." Bluebird leaned against Kat. "We like you. I especially enjoy it when you get angry. I've learned all kinds of words."

"Fuck," Kat muttered.

"Motherfucker," Sunshine chanted.

"Cocksucker," Rusty chimed in.

"I love this game." Halfpint grinned. "What a dickhead."

Bluebird frowned. "Cock, dick, or head. I'm coming up blank on what to associate that with."

"Son of a bitch." Sunshine chuckled. "Dick, in that sense, makes me think of a bastard."

"Enough," Kat pleaded. "Come on. I'm going to go upstairs and get Missy. That will make me feel better. I know a lot of you are reading her books. She's teaching you way worse things."

"You aren't going to disturb her. She's working on the next book." Rusty crossed her arms over her chest. "I want to read it and she promised to let me see whatever she writes."

One of the feline females crossed the room and stood next to Rusty. "We're Missy's beta readers. We'll restrain you and call your mate to come collect you if you try to interrupt what she's doing. He'll see you all tied up and want to share sex with you. You'll find yourself over his shoulder and hauled home immediately. Missy thinks she might finish the book at some point today so don't try it."

Candi was stunned. They were threatening to tie up Kat, but the female didn't look alarmed. She just rolled her eyes and shook her head.

"Great. Missy gets a set of guards for writing about sex, but what do I get? Jokes about liking a dominant man. You all suck." She shoved the cookies at Candi again. "Do me a favor. Eat every single one of those. Please."

Candi accepted the plate. "There are a lot of them."

"I'll get you some milk." Kat spun around and stalked back toward the kitchen.

Rusty chuckled. "She's the one who sucks," she announced and pointed down at her groin. "She admitted doing that for her mate."

The females around Candi burst into laughter. She didn't understand what was so funny but they were amused.

"I heard that!" Kat slammed something in the kitchen. "I'm never answering your questions again if they involve sex."

* * * * *

Hero entered Security and discovered Justice, Slade and Fury waiting for him. He followed them into a conference room and everyone took a seat. He wasn't sure why he'd been called away from his post but he didn't see any alarming expressions on the males around the table.

"What is it?" Hero glanced at each of them.

Justice spoke first. "A few FBI members wish to speak to Candi."

"They have questions for her," Slade interjected. "It's her choice whether she agrees to talk to them."

"They can't force us to give them access to your female." Fury paused. "You need to speak to her on the matter. They implied they wouldn't upset her in any way."

"No." Hero shook his head. "I don't want any humans around Candi. Why is the FBI involved? I thought human police were hunting for my mate."

Justice answered. "Darkness's mate worked for the FBI. She informed me that they have better resources to handle something like this and your Candi was effectively kidnapped as a child, held at Mercile, and then transferred across state lines when she was taken to that psychiatric hospital. She fears local law officials from the jurisdiction where Penny Pess died might overlook details that could prevent your female from being charged with murder. I agreed with Kat and asked them to get involved. They took over the investigation."

"Candi only killed so she could survive and reach Homeland. I refuse to allow anyone to upset my mate. She's been through enough."

Fury nodded. "That's what I suspected you'd say, Hero. We still had to ask."

He rose to his feet. "I'll return to duty."

Slade stood. "Go home to your mate. We have someone covering your post for the rest of the day. Tell her what is going on. You need to discuss this with Candi and at least ask her if she wants to talk to them. Trust me on this. Females get pissed otherwise."

Justice nodded. "They sure do. Jessie throws a mean right punch to my gut when I make decisions for her. That's what I get for mating with someone from Tim's team. She's sneaky and waits until my guard is down. One second I'm standing there, and the next I'm doubled over and she begins to yell about how she hopes that hurt, like I hurt her feelings."

Fury laughed. "Ellie just yells at me and slams things around."

"Trisha has threatened to slip sleeping pills into my meals and swears one day I'll wake up with my penis glued to my stomach."

Everyone gaped at the male.

He shrugged. "She said it would be the kind that will melt off if I soak in a warm tub so there is no lasting damage but it's an effective threat. I don't ever want to discover how uncomfortable that would be."

"You have a mean mate," Hero assessed.

He shrugged. "She's a doctor. There are a lot worse things she could threaten. My Trisha has a temper, but she gets over things quickly. She hasn't actually done it."

"Just tell your mate what is going on and ask if she wants to speak to the humans." Fury sighed. "Females like to make decisions and you're newly mated. You have a lot to learn. I'm certain she will agree with you. Humans have never done anything but harm her."

Hero nodded and left Security. He decided to walk, thinking as he made his way to the women's dorm to pick up Candi. He reached the front door and knocked. One of the females let him in and led him to the conference room where a group of females were talking with Candi. They were laughing and seemed to be having a good time. Conversation stopped as he hesitated just inside the open doorway. She spotted him and stood to rush toward him. She looked happy to see him and he didn't detect any stress.

"Hi. Is everything all right? I wasn't expecting you for a few more hours."

He nodded. "How was your day?"

"Great. I've learned a lot."

"We're telling her all about the NSO," Kat stated. "The history of it and what has been accomplished. We'd just reached the part about how Reservation is being expanded."

"And all the rescue animals we accept from all over the country," Bluebird added. "It gives the Wild Zone residents a purpose to help those poor creatures adjust to freedom. They have a lot in common with animals who've been caged and abused by humans."

"Thank you." Hero made eye contact with all the females seated at the table. "I appreciate you taking care of my Candi."

"It gives us something to do." Kat stood. "You're on duty tomorrow, right?"

Hero nodded. "Noon."

"We'll see you then," Kat smiled at Candi. "We'll teach you about the world outside the NSO gates."

Hero took Candi's hand and they strolled outside. He took one of the carts parked for general use and drove her to the men's dorm. They didn't speak until they were closed inside their home. She turned to him, studying him with a frown.

"What is wrong?"

"Tell me about your day first."

"I had fun. Now what is wrong?"

"I was called to Security. The FBI has requested to speak to you. I told the males you aren't interested."

"Why do they want to speak to me? Are they planning to arrest me for killing Penny?"

"I don't know what they want. It doesn't matter. They can't do anything to you. You're Species and they have no jurisdiction on NSO lands. They can request things but that doesn't mean we have to submit to them."

She bit her lip and turned away, walking to the window. She crossed her arms. He clenched his teeth, regretting informing her of what had happened. He shouldn't have listened to the males. She'd endured enough upset. He stalked up behind her and wrapped his arms around her waist.

"There's no reason to worry. You're safe here. Humans can't harm you ever again."

She leaned back against him, allowing him to hold her. He followed her gaze out the window. There wasn't really anything to hold her interest. She took a few deep breaths and finally spoke.

"I want to talk to them."

He stiffened. "What?"

She turned her head to peer up at him. Their gazes locked. "I tried to tell all the staff at the asylum the truth, but they ignored me. They didn't want to hear my words or believe them. Someone is finally ready to listen. I want to talk to the humans."

"No."

She wiggled and faced him completely, gripping his forearms. "Yes. I need to do this."

"They will upset you and possibly make threats."

"I understand that, but they are at least willing to hear me, Hero. I was locked away to keep me silent about what was done to my mother. She deserves justice too. Dr. C killed her. I know he can't pay for what he did now that he's dead, but the truth should be told. She had people who cared about her. I remember some of her friends coming over and she talked to them on the phone. They deserve to learn who took her away from them. I want everyone to know what kind of monster he really was. I also want them to know what Penny did to me. Humans shouldn't think she was a good person."

"You told Breeze everything and allowed her to take videos to give to the humans. That's more than enough."

She rubbed her palms against his skin. "I need to do this. It matters to me to look a human in the eyes and tell them my story. Maybe the staff working at the asylum will learn the truth and possibly listen to a patient in the future if they are locked away because someone is paying to keep them there to hide their crimes. I can't be the only one admitted to a hospital to hide secrets."

"It's not your job to educate humans."

"Who does it fall to then? This was done to both of us. Have you thought about what might have happened if just one of them had listened and believed me when I was taken there? You would have been freed long before you were. We wouldn't have lost so many years."

He was torn, and hated the anguished sound of her voice and the haunted look on her face. "I won't allow them to upset you and humans will. I don't trust them."

"Some humans freed Species and helped establish the NSO. I heard it was a rocky start, but a lot of them cared enough to make this possible. They wanted to do right by Species."

"Not all humans are good."

"I heard about that too. There are protestors outside the gates who think we're not human enough to deserve the same rights they have and if offends them. I learned about some of the churches that believe Species are an affront to their God since other humans engineered Species. These are the same people who believe it's wrong for couples to have medical intervention to get pregnant if they have difficulty, or to even use birth control to limit the number of children they have. I learned a lot today. I heard about the ones who think we're a danger to mankind, because they fear we'll breed with humans and eventually spread beyond NSO walls. That's why we keep our babies secret. Some humans fear change and the mixing of races. I learned—"

"Enough," he rasped. "You know then how bad they can be."

"I also met Trisha and Kat. There are a lot of humans like them too. They don't hate or fear Species. They are good females. They told me about the other mates and some of the humans who work with the NSO. They are great people, Hero. I also heard about the ones who support the NSO. They send letters of love to us, and they buy things off the website set up to sell supportive New Species things like T-shirts and autographed photographs of Fury and Justice. They stand outside the gates in opposition against the protestors just to aggravate them."

He sighed. "I appreciate every one of them, but it's the ones who still hate us that worry me."

"Kat worked for the FBI. Her boss ordered her to come to Homeland in an attempt to free a criminal who was being held here. She refused and instead told Darkness the truth. It almost cost her and her best friend their lives to do the right thing. Do you know what that tells me? Perhaps the FBI will send someone here like Kat. They might sympathize with Species and want to do the right thing. I'm willing to give them a chance. That means I need to speak to the agent they send."

He closed his eyes. It was logical. He couldn't dispute anything she'd said. There were good humans, but Candi was his mate. He'd go insane if she was wrong and it turned bad. He'd want to kill anyone who made her cry or yelled at her.

"My pup? Look at me."

He did.

"I want to do this. It's important to me. Someone is willing to listen finally. I've wanted that for so long."

"I can't be there," he rasped.

She stopped petting his arms. "Why?"

"I'd go crazy if they aren't kind." She remained silent for a long time, just staring up at him. "I understand that you want to do this and why, but I'd hurt someone if they upset you."

"I understand."

"Will you refuse to speak to them if I'm not there?"

She smiled. "Is that what you're hoping for?"

"Yes."

"You're so cute."

He scowled. "Does that mean you still will do this?"

"I need to."

He respected her and her decision, even if he didn't agree with it. His female had always been brave. "I'll stay close, but I can't be inside the room. You speak to them here, nowhere else. I'll attack them if they try to take you away from me. Be warned."

"I don't ever want to leave the safety of the NSO. This is where I belong, with you." She slid her hands upward to his shoulders. "How was your day?"

"Good until we had this talk."

She tried to hide her amusement, but failed. "I know what will make you feel better."

"What?"

She released him and backed away, offering him her hand. "Come here. I learned something I think you'll like today."

He allowed her to lead him to the couch and released his hand. He tried to sit but she shook her head. "Stay just as you are."

She climbed on the couch, on her knees, and gripped his belt. He moved to stand in front of her when she tugged on him. He looked down, watching as she unbuckled his belt.

"What are you doing? Do you want me to change clothes?"

"No. I'm just getting rid of this."

She used his body to brace as she leaned forward and placed the belt and his holstered weapon on the table. She began unfastening his pants. He wondered what she was up to. It seemed she planned to undress him. He opened his mouth to speak, to point out that he needed to remove his boots first but she yanked his pants down to his knees before he got the words out. Her fingers curled into the waist of his boxer briefs, slowly lowering them until his cock was free.

"Candi?"

She looked up at him and licked her lips. "There was a joke told today that I didn't understand." She gripped his vest, used it to pull herself off the couch to stand, and gently pushed. "Sit."

He was confused as to why she'd stripped him from his waist to his knees, but she didn't leave him much choice when she shoved harder. He lost his balance with his pants around his knees and collapsed onto the couch, landing on his bare ass.

She went to her knees and stared at his cock. His body responded to her as she splayed her hands on his thighs, brushing them closer to his sex. He cleared his throat and swallowed hard.

"The lotion is in the bedroom."

"Kat does this for her mate. I had her explain why the females were saying she sucked." She held his gaze. "It's my turn to put my mouth on you. Can I try it?"

He forgot how to form words.

"Are you okay? Your mouth is open and you're staring at me in a strange way."

He cleared his throat. "I've never had this done."

She smiled. "Never?"

He shook his head. His dick hardened even more, almost aching at just the thought of Candi performing oral sex on him. Species females didn't do it, or at least never had with him.

"I could be bad at this, but I'd like to try. Kat gave me detailed instructions. May I?"

He managed to nod and dug his fingernails into the couch to grip the cushions. His heart rate accelerated as she licked her lips again, the sight of her pink tongue exciting him even more. Her gaze lowered and she bent forward, one hand wrapping around his shaft.

He watched with rapt attention as she opened her mouth and timidly ran her tongue over the head of his cock. He locked his body in place to avoid jerking at the sensation. She grew bolder then, actually taking him inside her mouth. It was warm, wet, and she sealed her lips around him too. He had to close his eyes when the pleasure began as she moved, taking a little more of his shaft, and dragged her mouth upward. A growl tore from him.

He was afraid she'd stop, but she didn't, seemingly unconcerned with the sound he'd made. She grew even bolder and took more of him. Her mouth was heaven and hell. His toes curled in his boots.

"Fuck," he rasped.

Candi pulled off him and his eyes snapped open. She looked at him with curiosity. "Am I doing it wrong?"

He shook his head. "No."

She smiled. "Good?"

He nodded. "So good."

"Kat said to expect you to snarl and growl. She didn't say anything about cursing. I was just checking. I am not supposed to swallow. Males come really hard and it can choke me. Tell me before you lose your seed and I'll do what she does."

"What's that?"

"Just grip my shoulder and I'll show you." She lowered her gaze and opened her mouth, taking him back inside.

Pleasure coursed through him as Candi tormented him in the best way possible. He tried to just enjoy it, but watching her turned him on too much. She couldn't take much of him but she used her hand to stroke his shaft as her mouth worked the top few inches of his dick. His balls drew tight and he felt ready to explode. He gently gripped her shoulder, careful not to bruise.

She eased her mouth off his cock but hovered just above it. Her tongue swirled around the head. Her gaze lifted and she stared into his eyes. Her hand slid upward to her mouth, stroking his shaft in tune with her licks. He started to come hard. Candi backed off with her mouth, but used the palm of her other hand to cover the top of his dick as she continued stroking him.

He threw his head back and snarled her name. Candi released him. He caught his breath and opened his eyes, staring at her. She had removed her shirt and used it to wipe her hands. He watched as she stripped out of the rest of her clothes.

"My turn." She grinned, backing up toward the bedroom. "I'll get out the condoms."

He bent forward, tearing at his boots. "Give me one minute."

"Hurry. I want you so much. I missed you today."

"You're trying to distract me from our earlier disagreement."

"How am I doing?"

"Excellent."

Candi laughed and spun, running into the bedroom. "Come see how wet that made me."

He got his boots off and stood. He kicked away his pants and boxer briefs, ripping at his vest to get it off. He just threw it on the floor as he stalked after his mate. She was already on the bed when he entered.

Condoms had been placed next to her. She spread her legs and drew her knees up, exposing her sex. The sight made him forget all about his shirt.

He dropped to his knees and lunged, grabbing her hips and jerked her ass to the edge of the bed. He released them and wrapped his hands over her inner thighs, pushing them farther apart and pinning them in place. He loved the way she scented when she was aroused. He lowered his face, fastening his mouth directly on her clit.

"My pup," she moaned.

He snarled in response. He was hers and she was his. He wanted her so much it hurt. His cock, hard and stiff again, ached to be inside her. He wasted no time playing with her. He knew he shouldn't be so rough with her, but her moans urged him on. Her fingers dug into his hair and curved around his head, holding him in place. He stopped trying to hold back.

Candi bucked her hips, almost getting away from his mouth. He growled and pinned her tighter, not letting up. She cried out his name as she jerked under him, climaxing hard. He panted when he rose, releasing her. He grabbed a condom and used his teeth to tear open the wrapper.

His hands fumbled a little as he rolled it on. Candi panted, but suddenly rolled away. He froze, worried he might have hurt her until she crawled to the center of the bed on her hands and knees. She threw her hair out of the way and grinned at him over her shoulder.

"Take me like this."

He followed her up onto the bed. "I take you facing me so I can be more gentle."

"Mount me. I learned all kinds of things today from the females. This is supposed to feel incredible."

It seemed that Candi planned to kill him, but it was a hell of a way to go. He positioned himself over her and gently entered her from behind. He groaned. She was hot and wet and tight, her body so welcoming. Her answering moan as he sank into her helped reassure him that she was okay with the position. He lowered his body over her back and braced his arms beside her shoulders to keep her secured under him. He rocked his hips slowly at first, allowing her time to adjust to him. Candi turned her head and rested it against his arm.

"You feel so good. I love you."

He loved her, and everything about them being together. "You're my everything, Candi."

"Stop holding back. Give me the canine experience."

He chuckled and stopped moving. "The what?"

"It's what the females call it. Do that thing you canines do. Hold me tight and go really fast."

He lowered his head and nipped her shoulder. He pinned her tighter under him. "Tell me to stop if I hurt you. I worry."

"I promise."

He adjusted his legs on the outside of hers to pin her thighs together and placed his calves just under her feet to keep her from being able to move much. His fangs lightly raked her skin to brush kisses along her shoulder. He closed his eyes, focusing on his mate. It felt amazing to slowly fuck her. He'd found the position that she liked best, judging from her response. It only took a few moments for him to be certain he'd learned how to please her. He paused.

"Ready?"

"Yes."

Hero pounded into her. Fast, hard, merciless. Candi cried out and he froze.

"Am I hurting you?"

"It's intense but not painful."

"That's how it's supposed to be."

"Do it again."

He fucked her hard, deep, and fast. Her vaginal muscles squeezed around him and her broken moans grew louder. One of her hands clawed at his, braced on the bed beside her, but he ignored the slight sting of pain. She wasn't trying to get away from him. He clenched his teeth, wanting to come bad. The tighter her vaginal muscles clamped around him, the more difficult it became for him to hold his seed.

Candi screamed his name and he could feel her climax. He threw his head back and allowed his release to come. The howl that tore from his parted lips was unexpected, but he didn't care if others heard him. She felt that good and he couldn't mute his reaction.

Chapter Twelve

Candi stretched, loving that she woke while lying mostly on top of Hero's warm, naked body. He'd removed his shirt at some point since he no longer wore it. She lifted her head to stare at his face. Her male opened his eyes and his cock twitched against her thigh, which was curved over his.

"How are you feeling?"

"I loved the canine experience."

He chuckled. "Are you sore at all? I was a bit rough."

"I don't have a single complaint." She loved touching him, running her hands across his chest and stomach.

"Stop that, or we'll share sex again. You haven't had dinner."

"The females fed me so much today that I'm still full. It's not even dark yet. We can wait a bit on that unless you're hungry. I don't even remember falling asleep. We were cuddling."

"You passed out on me after I turned us to our sides."

She grinned. "Did it worry you?"

"No. I did put a note on the door to leave dinner in the kitchen and told them we'd be sleeping. Then I climbed into bed with you."

"I forgot that the females were planning to bring us food."

"They did that about twenty minutes ago."

She turned her head, noticing for the first time that the bedroom door was closed. "I didn't hear them."

"You were sleeping soundly. They tried to be quiet."

"Are you hungry?"

"Starving."

She rolled away from him and started to climb off the bed. "I'll get you food."

He lunged up and gripped her ankle. "You stay put. I'll get it."

She laughed, rolling over to sit. "I'm really not hungry yet."

"I'll hurry and eat. There's something I'd like to do tonight with you."

"Give me the canine experience again?"

He chuckled. "Perhaps in a bit. No. We're going out."

"Where?"

"It's a surprise."

"What kind of surprise?"

He got out of bed and strolled into the bathroom, coming out a few seconds later with a towel wrapped around his waist. "A good one. Trust me."

"I do."

"I'll bring you a drink."

She watched him leave and got up to use the bathroom. He was seated on the bed when she came out. He had brought a plate of food and used the top of the bed as a table. The towel remained around his waist. She wished he had removed it. She climbed back on the bed.

He held out a bite to her. "Try this."

"What is it?" She leaned forward, opening her mouth.

"Chicken ravioli in an alfredo sauce."

She chewed and nodded. It was good, but she wasn't tempted to eat more. The females had fed her a big lunch and she'd eaten quite a few cookies. Some of the females had helped her finish the plate when Kat wasn't looking. There had been no way she could eat that many.

She loved to watch her male eat. He finished an entire plate and they shared his soda, not touching the one he'd brought her. "What is the surprise?"

He set the plate on the nightstand and stood, holding out his hand. "Let's get dressed. The females left clothes for you in the living room. You won't have to wear any more of my clothing."

"They said they would. I forgot." She let him help her up and followed him into the bathroom. He turned on the shower. "We did a little online shopping today. You go to a website and pick things, then they ship them to the gates of Homeland. That way we don't have to go outside to shop with humans."

"I'm aware."

"I worried that you might have to pay for the clothing, but Kat said it was going on the NSO account and not to worry about it. Money confuses me."

"The NSO sued Mercile Industries and their employees that were captured. We also make money selling things to humans now. We no longer have to depend on the government to fund us. Don't worry about money. Clothing and food are supplied to us. We all work together to run Homeland and Reservation smoothly."

"It's scary in the out world."

He stepped into the stall and pulled her in, closing the glass door. "I hate thinking about all the bad things that could have happened to you out there."

"They had no idea I wasn't one of them. I looked into the eyes of the ones I dealt with. I got away from the ones who made me nervous and refused to accept rides if they looked at my body more than my face. I also spoke to female waitresses who worked at the truck stops where they would drop me off. They helped me find males who were trustworthy. They said they were regular customers and had families."

He turned her under the water and she relaxed as he placed soapy hands on her body, massaging as he washed her. "I like this."

"I love touching you."

"I'll wash you when you're done."

He laughed. "No, you won't. Otherwise we'll never get out of her. It's almost dusk. I told you. I have a surprise for you."

He washed her hair next and she finally turned around when he was done. She lowered her chin. "You're hard."

"I'm always going to be hard when I touch you and you're naked in front of me. Ignore that. I am."

"I can't."

He laughed again and reached out, pushing open the shower door. "Out. Dry off and go get dressed. They stacked the clothing on the coffee table. Find something comfortable. Perhaps thin, soft pants and a short-sleeved shirt. It is warm outside today."

She protested but he gently maneuvered her out of the stall. He closed the door between them and turned his back to wash his own body.

Candi pouted but grabbed a towel off the wall rack, and followed his instructions. She left him and located the clothing the females had brought. Some of the Gifts had gone through their things to donate a few outfits to her. She chose a light-gray pair of pants and a dark-blue shirt to wear. They'd also left a few pairs of shoes for her to try on. A black pair of canvas slip-ons fit. She carried the other clothes into the bedroom and set them on top of the dresser.

Hero exited the bathroom and stopped rubbing his hair with a towel. He smiled. "You look perfect."

Her gaze traveled down his body. "So do you."

"Stop looking at me like that. We are going out."

"We don't have to."

"We do. I thought about something today and I made arrangements. Now wait in the other room."

"You're so bossy."

"I always have been."

"I know." She left the bedroom and waited.

He came out wearing faded jeans, a gray tank top, and a pair of shoes much like hers. He held out his hand. "Come on."

She was excited. They walked hand in hand out of their apartment and took the elevator to the ground floor. He waved at the males they passed in the living room. She smiled at them. He took her outside. The sun was low in the sky. He bypassed the carts and just walked down the sidewalk.

Hero led her inside one of the buildings. A lot of Species were inside and music was playing. She grinned. "What is this place?"

"The bar." He had to raise his voice. "We hang out here, eat, dance, and socialize."

"Are you going to dance?"

He grinned. "Perhaps, but first we're going to have birthday cake. I called today and made sure they would get a carrot cake just for you. It's for all the birthdays you missed."

She threw her arms around him and hot tears blinded her. It didn't matter, because no one could see her with her face pressed against his shirt. He remembered.

He held her tightly, leaned his head down and put his lips against her ear. "It's not exactly the party you missed out on before you were taken, but it's the best I could do, Candi."

She tried to pull herself together but it was tough to do. Her sixth birthday had been approaching before that horrible night her mother had been killed, and her world had changed forever. She'd told him all about how she'd looked forward to playing with her friends and having carrot cake. It had been her favorite. They never celebrated birthdays at Mercile or at the asylum.

"I love you."

He kissed the top of her head. "I love you too. Come on. You have friends here and there are even presents."

She finally pulled herself together and peered up at him. "The females knew?"

"I got them involved."

"They didn't say a word."

"It was a surprise."

He kept his arm around her and turned them, leading her to a big table at the back. At least ten females and six males waited. They'd even decorated the table for her and there were colorful balloons. She was touched that Jinx and Torrent were there. Kat and the male who had to be her mate had come too. Pretty, wrapped presents were stacked next to a big cake. Hero pulled out her chair and she sat, glancing at all the happy faces around the table.

"Thank you."

"It's was all Hero's idea." Sunshine pointed at him. "He plotted it out with Darkness, and he called Kat, and then she whispered it to us while

444

you were busy. Happy birthday, Candi. More of us would have come but they were on duty this evening."

"It's not really my birthday. At least I don't think it is."

"It doesn't matter." Hero took a seat next to her and scooted closer until they touched. "We're celebrating you being home and us being mated."

"This is wonderful." She reached up and wiped at tears. She glanced around again and saw a few alarmed looks. "I'm happy. Right before my mom was killed, we'd been planning my birthday party. I told Hero all about it when we were young. Sometimes when I'd eat carrots at Mercile, I'd try to describe to him how my favorite cake was made of them." She held his gaze. "You are so wonderful to do this for me."

"We have a lot of time to make up. This is one of the good memories we'll share." He looked away from her to frown at the white cake. "I still don't believe a cake made of carrots will be good."

She laughed. "You never did like them, but cake is sweet."

"Will it be crunchy?" He wrinkled his nose.

"Let's find out!" Sunshine stood and started slicing the cake, putting pieces of it on colorful paper plates. She gave the first one to Candi.

Two males arrived at the table, carrying trays laden with glasses of milk, and passed them out. Candi smiled at them. "Thank you. Are you joining us?"

"We're on duty, but thank you for asking." One of the males winked. "Happy birthday, Hero's mate."

She waited until everyone had cake in front of them and cut a piece with her fork. It looked delicious and smelled even better. It stirred a few childhood memories and a flash of her mother's smiling face filled her mind.

"Candi?"

She focused on Hero and offered him her bite. "Try it."

He lowered his head, but paused. "I just hope it tastes as you remember it. The most important part is that you enjoy it." He opened his mouth and accepted the small bite. He chewed and smiled. "Ummm."

She cut another piece and popped it into her mouth. It tasted as delicious as she remembered. They stared at each other, forgetting the people around them.

Darkness leaned back in his chair and put his arm along the back of Kat's seat. He looked at her and she drew close to whisper to him. "What's up?"

"Did you call your contacts at the FBI?"

"I still have a few friends there. They assigned the case to Mona Garza. She's tough but good. I never worked directly with her, but she has a ball-buster reputation. It's tough being a woman in a man's career field."

"That doesn't bode well."

"No. That's great news."

"A ball buster is good?"

"You bet your ass. She's not out to kiss ass. She won't mind making waves, regardless of how deep she has to dig for information. I also learned she's got two dogs."

"So?"

"She loves animals."

He scowled, narrowing his eyes at her. "Is that supposed to be a joke?"

"It means, if any of those good ole boys don't like Species, she's going to get highly offended if they say anything to her like my boss did to me. He thought women might as well bend over and take it from their dogs if they were willing to fuck a Species. Imagine how well that went over with me. She's going to want to fuck up their day as much as I did Mason's. That means she won't leave any rock unturned to look for evidence that supports everything Candi has said."

He grinned. "You're a feline lover now."

"You got that right."

He sobered. "Any word on how the investigation is going?"

She shook her head, watching Candi and Hero eat their cake and flirt with each other. Her heart went out to the couple. They'd endured a hell of a lot and they deserved pure happiness. "Garza isn't chatty and hasn't shared anything that hit the rumor mill. I know she's been putting in some heavy hours and pissing people off by sending agents out to places they didn't want to go. I'm sure that mental hospital was a riot for the agents."

"Sarcasm?"

"Their security is usually anal and the doctors are pricks in most cases. You're sitting across from their desks while they are sizing you up like you're one of their patients. They hate to be wrong. I had to interview one once who accused me of wanting to be a man. Why, you ask?"

"I didn't. There's nothing male about you. He was an idiot."

"It was a she and I agree. It's because I started playing hardball with her. The bitch cried."

"You sound so proud."

"She was saying my perp was nuts, but he was faking it. I knew and she should have too. She cracked like an egg. He was a good-looking rich boy who flirted with her, and she fell for it hook, line and sinker. I spelled out exactly what he'd done to other women he'd conned with his bullshit charm and showed her pictures of the victims. I told her, if he'd scam a lingerie model, what were her chances of him being serious with her? I have confidence, but come on. That model was as hot as they come. I banked on her thinking the same way. She caved."

"I love how tough you are and I love your body. You have curves."

"Sweet talker. Garza is coming tomorrow morning at ten to give an update to the NSO. I know she requested to speak to Candi. Is she going to agree?"

He shrugged. "Hero was supposed to ask her, but he hasn't told Security either way. He wasn't keen on the idea."

Kat glanced at the couple. "Now isn't the time to bring it up."

"I'll ask him if I get him alone for a moment."

"I'll cancel my class and be there. I'll grill Garza like a salmon to make sure she checked out everything to my satisfaction."

He chuckled. "You can't cook."

"You're not much better in the kitchen. That's why we eat here so much."

"It wasn't a complaint." He reached over and slid his hand between her thighs. "I'm more interested in your other skills."

She grabbed his hand. "Tease. Hold that thought until after Candi opens her presents and we go home."

"Do you miss your job, Kat?"

She shook her head. "No. There was too much bullshit politics. The badge was cool though." She grinned. "It made people sweat when I flashed it. Cops just scare people. FBI terrifies them."

He laughed. "I'll get you a badge."

"It's okay. I've got you. You're way better at giving me a thrill."

Hero watched Candi open another present. The sheer joy on her face assured him he'd done the right thing by having his friends throw her a surprise party. They'd raided some of the online store items for her. She'd been given NSO clothing items, a nice messenger bag to carry her things in, and a few of the adorable stuffed animals wearing NSO shirts that human children enjoyed.

He removed his gift from his pocket, grateful that one of the task force males had gone to a store off Homeland for him. Shane had texted him dozens of photos until he'd found the perfect one. Trisha had helped him by telling him the right size to get when she'd examined Candi earlier that morning before he'd dropped her off at the women's dorm to start his shift.

"Candi?"

She turned to him. "Yes?"

He was nervous, but he'd never believed he'd do something like this. He slid out of his chair and got to his knees. He handed her the gift and turned her chair to face him when she accepted it. She looked at it, then him.

"Why are you there?"

"Open it."

The music died and the bar grew very silent. He expected it, but she didn't. Glancing around, she blushed a little. "Everyone is watching us."

"I know. They are curious. Open it."

Her hands trembled as she tore at the wrapping. The black box almost fell off her lap, but he grabbed it from her and opened it, removing the contents. He held it out.

"Females wear an engagement ring and males ask the females to marry them. You are Species, but I don't want you to give up your heritage by blood. You should have the best of both worlds, Candi. You're my mate, but I'd also like you to become my wife. Will you marry me?"

Tears spilled down her cheeks but she smiled, nodding. He hesitated, forgetting what hand the ring was supposed to go on.

"Her left," Kat whispered just loud enough for his hearing to pick up, but not Candi's. "The one next to her pinky."

He eased the ring onto Candi's small finger. It fit snuggly over her knuckle but easily fit on her finger. He held her gaze. "We'll get married next week. I made arrangements."

She slid off her chair and straddled his lap. He sat back, holding her as she clasped his face with both hands. "I love you so much. Thank you for this."

"Thank you for surviving and coming back to me." He fought his own tears. "I'm never letting you go."

"You couldn't be rid of me."

He chuckled and didn't care if everyone watched as he kissed his mate. Loud cheers and applause sounded around the room. He pulled away and grinned. "Your next party is going to be difficult if I plan to make it better than this one."

She leaned in and put her lips against his ear. "You could try to have a baby with me."

He hugged her tightly, holding her. He nodded. "When it's safe."

He helped her off his lap and stood. Their friends gathered around them, sharing hugs and congratulations. Candi showed the females her ring and moved away from him to talk to Species she hadn't met yet. Darkness stepped next to him.

"Nice job."

Jinx came to stand on his other side. "It was a given that she'd say yes. That female loves you."

Hero nodded. "She's mine. This was just so she knows I accept her. All of her. She's always felt less because of her human blood. She tried so hard growing up to become stronger, as if she were Species."

"I hate to bring this up right now, but is she going to be at the meeting with the FBI in the morning?" Darkness paused. "Kat will be there."

"She wants to speak to the humans and tell her story." He hated to admit that. It would put Candi in the room with FBI agents. "I can't be there, but I'll be close. I'll lose my temper if they upset her."

Darkness nodded. "Kat won't allow them to verbally mistreat her. My mate has a temper and a mouth on her. I'd worry more about the FBI agents leaving in tears."

"I'd want their blood if they act as if Candi is telling them lies," Hero admitted. "She really hopes they believe her. I just don't want her to be disappointed. She's seen far too much of that in her lifetime."

"She's a strong female." Jinx grinned.

"I know it. I just want to protect her."

Darkness nodded. "I understand, Hero. Mates are everything, but you have to let her make her own decisions and just be there when she needs you."

Chapter Thirteen

Candi straightened her shoulders and locked gazes with Breeze. The taller woman didn't look happy. Her next words proved it.

"Are you sure you want to do this? Some of these humans with authority jobs are pure assholes. I've sat in on some meetings between us and the NSO before. They treat us as if we're children. They can be rude, conceited, and act as if we lie."

"I will tell you the same thing I said to Hero. I need to do this. I want to do this. I spent years wishing someone would listen to what I had to say. Take me in there."

"Hero looked angry when he said he was coming with you after all. Why wouldn't you allow him to come?"

"Did you see how stressed he is?" Candi winced. "I was afraid he'd attack someone. I'm not as fragile as he believes."

"He's protective of you. We all are. We want you to heal from what you've endured."

"Then let me in that conference room."

Breeze nodded. "Fine, Candi." She pushed open the door, but then snarled when another female Species already stood in the room, leaning against a wall. "What are you doing here, Kit?"

The feline pushed off the wall and placed her hands on her hips. Her gaze landed on Candi and her eyebrows rose. "She's dainty."

"This isn't the time or place to be rude." Breeze jerked her thumb. "Out. The humans should arrive in a few minutes. They are being brought through Security now to speak to Hero's mate."

"That's why I'm here.

Breeze scowled. "What?"

"Hero is my friend and I don't want anyone to upset his mate. I'm far meaner than the male assigned to help you control this situation. I told him to get lost and took his place. I'm your backup. We'll tag team these human males."

Breeze opened her mouth, then closed it. She chuckled finally. "Work on your sayings. That isn't the right one. You make it sound as if we're going to share sex with them at the same time and then switch sexual partners."

Kit lifted her upper lip in disgust and hissed.

"Yeah. Exactly." Breeze pulled out a chair and indicated Candi should take a seat. "Remember they will probably make threats, but they can't do anything to you. They are just meaningless words to intimidate. It stops the moment you stand up and leave. You can at any time." She pointed at Kit. "I'll let you stay, but behave for once. Don't aggravate the situation. Let me take the lead."

Kit inclined her head. "Thank you."

Candi took a seat and the Species females stood on each side of her, right behind her chair. She felt safe. The door across the room opened and a couple entered. The male wore a suit. The female wore a tailored skirt, jacket and button-down shirt. The male Species who'd escorted them pointed to the chairs across from Candi. The humans took seats, staring at her.

Candi didn't feel fear. She tried to assess which one of the two was their leader. The human female spoke first. She opened a thick file and pulled out a photo, tossing it on the table. Candi looked at it, then lifted her gaze without touching it.

"I'm agent Mona Garza. Do you know this woman?"

"That's Penny Pess." Candi didn't have to look at it again.

"Did you kill her?"

Candi nodded. "She planned to kill me first. She said my father died and wouldn't pay her to keep me locked up anymore. She told the orderlies she was taking me to another hospital, but that was a lie. She pulled far from the road in her car, believing I was still drugged in the backseat. She opened the back door to pull me out of the car to end my life. I took the knife from her. We fought and I won."

The woman picked up the picture and closed the folder. "We were informed by the NSO of what happened when they invited us to have a meeting with them. I looked at the file the police had on the murder investigation once the body was discovered. Two orderlies and the gate guard stated that Dr. Pess planned to take you to another hospital. She implied they'd be waiting to receive you as a patient." She paused. "What the police failed to do was check that out. I had our agents do it. We contacted every hospital within a three-hundred-mile range. Do you know what they discovered?" She didn't wait for an answer. "You weren't expected at any of them."

"That's because the doctor planned to kill our female," Kit growled.

Both agents shifted in their seats, watching Kit. Breeze cleared her throat. "It was self-defense. You would have found our female's body if she hadn't killed the doctor."

Agent Garza looked at Candi. "Why didn't you go to the police after it happened?"

"You're human. I had to kill one of yours. I told the truth for years while I was locked up, but no one would believe me. I wasn't willing to risk it. Humans had refused to help me every time. I knew I needed to reach Homeland."

"I understand. We spoke in depth to the staff where you were kept, pulled your medical records, and even the financials for your care." Garza paused, her gaze examining Candi. "I wanted to personally tell you that I'm sorry for what you must have endured."

Candi hadn't expected that.

"I'm just going to put it out there. We had four consultants go through everything and it reeked to high heaven. Your rights as a patient were violated on a daily bases. Some of the drugs they had you on went directly against the listed medical diagnosis Dr. Pess had put down. Only a hack would do what was done to you. We traced the financials out of the country to an account that belonged to a man who'd died over twenty years ago. It was opened weeks after the first Mercile Industries site was raided. We also located the homicide case from when you were a child. You witnessed the murder of your mother and the next-door neighbor?"

Candi nodded. "Loud blasts woke me. I can't tell you how many, but there were a lot. The hallway was dark and I wanted to go to my mom. I was afraid of loud noises. My mom and Mr. Cooper from next door were naked and bloody on the bed. There was a gun lying beside them. I knew what it was, because my father owned one. They taught me never to touch it. He kept it in his office downstairs. I heard footsteps coming so I hid behind the bedroom door. My father walked in with a knife and started stabbing them. He was taking something out of their bodies and putting it in his jacket pocket. He had brought bottles from the bar from downstairs. He opened them, poured them over the bed, and started a fire. It scared me enough to make me move. I wanted to run, but I froze when he turned and looked at me. He took me to Mercile and left me there. I was moved from there to the hospital when I was sixteen."

"Why?"

Candi glanced at Breeze for help. She didn't want to explain what had happened that day with the feline or Hero's violent reaction.

"Because Mercile were assholes," Kit growled. "They didn't inform us of why they abused us or give us any say in the matter. They shipped us off to various locations at times. What kind of question is that?"

Agent Garza looked up at Kit. "I'm just curious because I don't understand why Christopher Chazel bothered to keep her alive. He had her moved from there and paid for her to be cared for somewhere else. I doubt he had to do that at Mercile. Do you see where I'm going with this?"

The door behind them opened and Kat stalked in. She wore black slacks, a button-down shirt tucked into her pants, and had a badge snapped to her belt buckle. She walked to one of the chairs at the side of the table and took a seat. "I'm Katrina Perkins, former FBI."

Garza frowned. "I remember seeing you around. I know who you are."

Kat unclipped her badge and placed it on the table. She tapped it with her finger. "I'm part of the NSO task force now. I've been monitoring from the next room to get a feel for what you're up to."

Agent Garza glanced up at the camera and then back at Kat. "I'm not up to anything, Perkins."

"You're fishing. How the hell would Candi know what that son of a bitch's motives were? He wasn't father of the year and he didn't have heart-to-heart talks with her. Maybe he drew a line at killing his own flesh and blood. He could have had some guilt over the shitty thing he did when he locked her up at Mercile for all those years. You should be asking him his motives, but he's dead. That's like asking the victim, which she was, why the perp chose her. Move on."

Agent Garza clamped her lips together, but turned her gaze on Candi. "Penny Pess told you Christopher Chazel died, correct?"

"I viewed the tapes given to you." Kat leaned forward. "You know the answer to that. She gave details about what Dr. Pess said to her in her office before attempting to kill her. Should I pull a copy of it for you and replay that part of the tape so you can see and hear it word for word?"

Agent Garza glared at Kat. "You know it's procedure."

"You came in here with sympathy and kind words, but you're looking for something to nail her on. I don't appreciate it. You think I don't know the dance steps?" Kat smirked. "Let's cut the shit, Garza. You're probably getting pressure from some desk jockey who hasn't been in the field since Clinton was in office. They aren't good with change or comfortable with the NSO. The cops had her picture all over the news and put it out there that she was a homicidal killer who had escaped from the loony bin. They had her convicted because they were too lazy to actually investigate beyond surface facts. That means the public panicked. She was spotted in what? Four states?"

"Three."

Kat shrugged. "Three. Then it was leaked that she was here. Some loud-mouthed idiots started tweeting about how the NSO is taking in cold-blooded killers. I have a computer and internet access. I've been keeping tabs. They are stirring up shit. Your boss is having his ass chewed out, which means it's coming down the line tenfold to land right on your desk. Have I said anything that is wrong so far?"

"No."

Kat pointed at Candi. "She's a victim. Period. She was five years old when she realized her father was a piece of shit who'd killed her mother. You said you saw the homicide file. Who vouched for his whereabouts at the time of the murders?"

"His supervisor at Mercile Industries."

"There's your link to how and why he kept her there. You're smart, Garza. You did your research on Mercile Industries as soon as you were assigned this case. We both know they had zero morals because of the fucked-up research they did. You want me to level with you? They wanted to see if a Species kid would kill a human one. She was an experiment. They got their answer. Species don't kill children. She grew up in that hellhole until they had no use for her anymore. Chazel sent her to a new hell and he probably paid for her to stay alive because…who the hell knows? Get a profiler and study him to figure it out. Candi killed Pess so she could keep breathing. You know it. I know it. Hell, your boss would know it too if he stopped playing politician long enough to give a shit about what really went down instead of trying to score points with whoever he's trying to impress."

Kat took a deep breath and blew it out. "I've been where you are. That's why I work for the NSO now. I made a choice to do the right thing over the pressure I got from my boss. Plus, I won't deny that the benefits here are way better. Candi isn't dangerous. She's a survivor. Follow the facts and do the right thing. It won't make you popular, but it will help you sleep better at night."

"We're tracking down the financials at the hospital. It's going to take time, but the account linked to the payments where Candi was held helped us figure out where Christopher Chazel might have been living. We'll make certain that information is correct and if he is in fact deceased." Garza looked at Candi. "If he's not, we're going to move heaven and hell to get him brought back here to stand trial for what he did to you, the victims of Mercile, and for the double homicide he committed." She wrote something on the folder and stared at Candi. "Would you testify against him in a court of law?"

Candi nodded. "I would like to know if Penny lied to me about his death. I want him to pay for what he's done."

Garza looked at Kat. "I'm trying to do the right thing, Perkins. Believe it or not, I wasn't dancing with her. I feel bad. Everything I've learned substantiates what she said." She looked at her partner. "Kether and I both agree on that. I'm just trying to cross all my t's and dot all my i's. Otherwise my boss is going to raise hell and question it."

"He's known for reassigning agents if they don't file reports he likes," the male muttered.

Kat winced. "Jorginson? I thought he was retiring."

The male agent snorted. "He changed his mind. Again."

"Shit. He's an asshole." Kat leaned back and relaxed in her chair. "Let's play ball on the same team. How about it? What can I do to help make this work?"

Garza smiled. "I heard you were a bitch, Perkins. You're not so bad."

Kether glanced at the camera. "Can you delete anything on that and make it disappear?"

Kat nodded and lifted a hand, making a slicing motion. "They stopped recording. Only NSO is watching or has access to it. What do you want to say off the record?"

Garza closed the file and stood. "Demand copies of all the evidence we collected. Justice North can get it done. There's no way anyone can view what we've acquired and still think any charges should be filed for Pess's death, or doubt why the NSO is stating she's one of yours." She looked at Candi. "I am sorry for all you've endured. I wish I could arrest some of the staff at that hospital for stupidity. Unfortunately, it's not a crime to be morons." She looked at Kat. "I'd sue the shit out of them. The NSO has lawyers. Use them to get a little payback for her. She's owed it."

The agents left and Candi looked at Kat. "It's okay now, right?"

She smiled. "It's all good."

Kit growled. "That wasn't eventful."

Breeze snorted. "Where you hoping for a fist fight?"

"Perhaps." Kit spun. "I'm out of here. It's my day off."

Candi stood and glanced at both females. "Thank you."

"Go find your male." Breeze hung back and picked up the badge. "Where did you get this, Kat?"

"Trey Roberts was hanging out in Security. I told him I wanted to borrow it and why." She grinned. "He didn't hesitate."

"I'll return it to him." Breeze pocketed it. "Nice job."

"I hate bullshit posturing. I hoped Garza would feel the same." Kat walked past Candi and reached out, squeezing her arm. "You did great. I'm going to go talk to Justice North about pulling some strings to access everything the FBI has."

Candi walked out of the conference room and headed toward where she'd last seen Hero. She spotted him pacing in front of the double doors leading into the building, not far from where he'd parked the cart. He stopped as soon as he saw her. She smiled and he closed his eyes.

Candi was fine. Hero tried to let go of some of his anxiety. Her gentle hands took his and he looked down at her. "They listened?"

"They did and they believed me."

"How do you feel?"

She seemed to debate a moment. "Good."

"They didn't upset you at all?"

"No. They were mostly nice. Kat and the lead agent had words, but they worked it out. She said it's all good."

"They couldn't have done anything to you."

"I know."

"Doc Trisha called me. The last of your test results came in." He smiled. "You're good. She wants us to go speak to her about your nutrition though. She said I can't feed you unhealthy things to get you to gain weight."

"Do you have time before your shift? Otherwise I could ask someone else to take me."

"I traded shifts. I wasn't prepared to leave you alone if the interview went bad."

"That was so nice of you."

"You're my mate. You are my priority. You always come first."

"In that case, can we go see Doc Trisha later? I'd like for you to take me home."

"You are upset." Anger surged. "Who upset you? What did they say?"

She went up on tiptoe and leaned against him. "I want the canine experience. We should celebrate."

He wrapped his arms around her and his temper faded as fast as it had appeared, changing to amusement. "You're soooo bad."

"I am. I'll let you tickle me if we're naked."

He let her go and clasped her hand. "Let's go."

Her laugher made him happy.

Epilogue

Two months later

Hero entered his apartment and flipped on the light switch. Nothing happened. A giggle sounded from the far corner of the room. He growled low and closed the door behind him.

"What are you doing, Candi?"

"Waiting for you to come home. Do you remember playing hide and seek?"

He gripped his vest straps, tearing at them. "Of course."

"How is your eyesight in this light? It's not as dark as our cell used to be."

He spotted her near the bedroom door. She was just a darker shadow in the room. He removed the vest and dropped it. His belt and weapon came off next. "You want to play?"

"I always want to play with you. We have more space in here than we used to have at Mercile. Can you see me? I tried to cover all the windows but it's still lighter in here than I wanted."

"What do I get if I catch you?" He bent, removing his boots.

"What do you want?"

"You naked."

"That's not fair."

He straightened. "Why not?"

"I'm already without clothes."

He softly growled. He inhaled and picked up the scent of her arousal. It stirred his own. "What have you been doing while I was gone, my Candi?"

"Thinking about you, my pup." She stepped in front of the open bedroom door. "Come get me." She ducked inside the bedroom.

He followed, careful not to slam his knees into the coffee table. He entered the bedroom and glanced around. She'd covered the smaller bedroom window more effectively, leaving him without enough light to see as well as he had in the living room. He sniffed the air, tracking her by scent. She was near the bed.

"Not fair," she whispered.

"Who said I had to be? You're naked." He caught her quickly, chuckled and swung her up into his arms.

"You're not supposed to use your senses against me when I don't have the same. Remember?"

"You used to wear clothes. Things change. I never wanted to catch you this bad before." He sat on the bed with her on his lap. His hands roamed her body and he cupped one of her ass cheeks. He gently squeezed. "I love how you feel."

"You like my curves."

His other hand caressed her soft, warm stomach. "I do."

She turned into him and wrapped her arms around his neck. "Can I throw away the condoms? Trisha said I'm healthy. I'm a few pounds over what she wanted me to gain."

"You want to try for a baby now?"

"Yes." She brushed her mouth over his chin, nibbled up across his jawline, and whispered in his ear. "We're making up for lost time."

"It might not happen right away."

"I know. I heard what Trisha said. She didn't want us to be disappointed if I don't get pregnant on the first attempt."

"I'm going to turn on the light. I want to see you."

She was the one to lean toward the nightstand and switch on the lamp. He blinked to adjust his vision and grinned. He studied his Candi. She projected a healthy glow now and no longer looked as she had when she'd first come to him. She was even more beautiful. "You take my breath away."

"You always say that when I'm naked."

"I say it when you're clothed too."

"You don't take on that husky tone though."

He stared into her eyes. "That's because I want to lick you all over right now and be inside you when you start moaning my name."

She smiled and fumbled for the bottom of his shirt, tugging to get it out of the waistband of his pants. "Let's get you out of these."

He leaned back to help her and she shoved the shirt upward. He lifted his arms and she got it off and tossed it onto the carpet. He fell back on the bed and watched as Candi straddled his thighs, her nimble fingers opening the front of his pants. He loved looking at her, watching her. She glanced up and paused, tilting her head slightly.

"What?"

"I'm just happy."

"You'll be more so if you stop lying there and help me get these pants off you."

He reached out and wrapped his hands around her hips. "I need to tell you something."

"What is it?"

"I once told you that you were my weakness. I was wrong. You are my strength."

She bent over him, bracing her hands on his upper chest. "You don't have to say that."

"I do. I was afraid at the time. I mistook how I felt about you as weakness. You mean everything to me and I only existed after I lost you, but I wasn't really alive until you found me again. Thank you."

"You're going to make me cry." Tears filled her eyes. "But they are happy tears."

"I want you to know how I feel."

"I know every time you look at me and touch me."

He rolled over, pinning her under him. He scooted down her body, kissing her lips, her throat, and teasing her breasts with his mouth. She moaned and spread her thighs. He lifted his hips to get his pants off, and shoved them down as he reached her stomach. Her fingers stabbed into his hair, pushing him lower. He chuckled.

"Someone is impatient. I thought you wanted to play."

"I love sharing sex."

"I'd have to work harder if you didn't." He kicked his pants and boxer briefs away, finally free of all his clothing. He reached her pussy and gripped her thighs to hold them open. She had a habit of trying to close them right before she climaxed. He growled when he caught her scent of need, his cock rock hard and hurting to be inside his female.

He played with her clit. She loved his tongue, but she also enjoyed when he used his lower teeth to gently rake over the soft bud. Her moans filled the room and he released one of her thighs, automatically reaching for the box of condoms on the nightstand that he always kept stocked and ready. His fingers brushed it, but then he remembered they no longer planned to use them.

The idea of nothing between them, and being able to come inside her, drove him a little insane. He lifted up and grabbed her hips, flipping her over. "Crawl to the middle of the bed," he snarled.

She didn't hesitate, getting on her hands and knees for him. He followed her up and put his legs on the outside of hers, using his calves to brace her feet. He was excited and knew she was close to coming. So was he. He'd make it up to her later by taking his time making love to her. They could spend hours touching and kissing.

He reached down and gripped her hip with one hand, using the other to guide the crown of his dick to her opening. He pressed against her, rubbing against the seam of her sex, teasing before he entered. She was wet and ready for him. They both groaned as he pushed forward, taking her.

He released the shaft of his dick and came down over her back, using one arm to support his upper-body and reached around her stomach, sliding his palm lower until his fingers brushed over her clit.

"My pup," Candi moaned.

"My Candi," he growled back.

He moved, taking her fast and hard as he pressed against her clit so every drive of his hips rubbed her sensitive bud. Her broken cries and moans told him how much she enjoyed being claimed by him. He loved being inside her. There was nothing that ever felt as right as she did to him.

Sweat slicked their bodies as passion burned them up until she climaxed, his number on her lips. He didn't care that she sometimes fell into old habits and forgot to use his name. She could call him anything she wanted since he was hers and she was his. He drove into her one last time, her vaginal muscles milking him as his seed erupted and filled her.

He howled and threw them both onto their sides so he didn't crush her smaller body with his own. He curled around her tightly while he came down from the high of making love to his mate.

He lifted his head and put his cheek next to hers. He pulled his fingers away from her oversensitive clit and placed his hand on her stomach. "I might not get you pregnant with the first attempt, but I'm going to really enjoy trying."

She chuckled and her hands gripped his arms where the encircled her. "Me too."

"I won't miss the condoms. It's so much better without them."

"I agree. You feel even better. I didn't think that was possible."

He closed his eyes, just holding her as they caught their breaths. "Anything is possible, my Candi."

"Yes, it is, my pup."

Printed in Great Britain
by Amazon